WICKED PRINCES

WICKED PRINCE OF CURSES

STEPHANIE BWABWA

Wicked Prince of Curses

Stephanie Bwabwa

Learn More: StephanieBwaBwa.com

Cover Illustration by: Melody Knighton

Case Design and Typography: Raven Pages Design

Editing and Proofreading: Kayla Morton

Formatting: Elledelle Entertainment

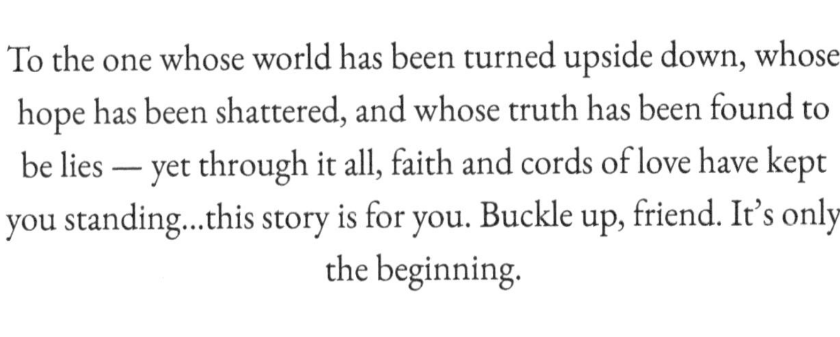

To the one whose world has been turned upside down, whose hope has been shattered, and whose truth has been found to be lies — yet through it all, faith and cords of love have kept you standing...this story is for you. Buckle up, friend. It's only the beginning.

Elledellien,

For your convenience, you'll find a glossary towards the back of this book to help you with pronunciations, definitions, and translations.

Wings high! Welcome to Elledelle.

— Stephanie

Bend, but do not break. Burn, but never bleed.
House of Anathelle Proverb, Fifth Age

PART
ONE

"You have been given much, therefore we must require more. You've been entrusted with much, so what is asked of you is a small gift in return. Ascend, dear Disciple, or enlarge the Hèls."

Accords of the Farasees, Scroll of Lukayi 12:48, Fifth Age

CHAPTER 1

"Nothing in the Temple is given. It is earned."

Farasee Esau Nakumba—one of the priests from the holiest temple in the empyrean—looked over the multitude of Ascendants floating before him. His expression was unimpressed. Almost bored.

"You have until dawn descends into twinight to make it inside Temple Efysis. Fail and you forfeit your Ascension."

Slowly, I tipped my head back and looked up. Then frowned, narrowing my eyes at the sight ahead. It was absurd the distance we were expected to fly before the dawn ended. From where I was floating, I couldn't even see the end of our destination. It went beyond the clouds.

"This is going to be a special kind of Hèls," muttered Ellabeth from my right.

I nodded at my best friend, eyes still glued to the treacherous waterfall we were supposed to fly not up but *through*.

"We can do it. We just need to stick together."

Ellabeth sounded like she was trying to convince herself more than me. I looked at the rushing water, already picturing how I would handle the pressure beating against my wings, as I made my way through it. The water was thick, heavy, and cutting. There was no smoothness to it. It was violent and angry.

This was going to be brutal.

I sighed, lowering my head to look back at Farasee Esau. Wiping dripping sweat from my brow, I scooted closer to Ellabeth. Enough to where our wings—all seven pairs—ended up meshing together. I used the end of one wing to fan myself. It didn't help much. The sweltering island heat was unbearable. But hot air was starting to feel better than no air at all.

I floated above the seafloor with Ellabeth, curling my arm through hers. Sweat formed at the nape of my neck and began slipping down my spine on the inside of my flying gown. I was starting to get annoyed. I didn't do well with the heat, and this dawn was scorching hot.

"You will begin your flight one at a time," Farasee Esau continued. "There will be no hand holding. No assisting one another. Yes, this will be one of the most difficult tasks you will be required to perform. No, we do not care."

The priest glared at us with eyes glowing like molten amber. His sun-kissed skin glowed beneath the sunlight under his ivory robes. Most Farasees had tassels and other ornaments hanging from their robes to show they were a Farasee, and to prove their status among the Order itself. Not this one. He seemed to care less. The hardened planes of his chiseled face was warning enough. He was not the priest to mess with.

"The journey to the temple is simple: fly through the Starfelliel waterfall, then *run*, not fly, across the Goldstone Bridge. Spread your wings, and be prepared to shed your blood. When you finish your run across the bridge you will fly to the temple gates. Make it through the gates and you'll find a clear path to the temple. Make it into the temple and you will have successfully completed the Starfellien Ascent."

He tilted his head, a small smile curling his lips. I shuddered at the sight.

"Then, and *only* then, will we begin to consider you as Ascendants. Once you complete your first trial in the temple, you will become Disciples."

Angelic wings pulsed all around me. The majority of would-be Ascendants began fanning themselves. I relished in the beauty of all the different colors. Red and blue. Yellow and deep green. Every angel here was a Seraphim—the third highest rank of all twelve angelic ranks—and their feathered wings were as colorful as our vibrant island of Ouanaviel.

I looked at the waterfall thinking through my strategy. It was a lot of water to climb without opportunity to get any air. None of us were Merriens—sea bound beings who could survive underwater without needing air to breathe—we'd all been born on land. But the Farasee Order wanted us to fly through a blasted waterfall. Stars. All of it was nonsensical.

"Every generation of Disciples must go through the Starfellien Ascent," Farasee Esau said. "I would assume your parentlings told you this, but in the case they didn't, keep your whining to yourselves. You're not the first to go through it, nor will you be the last. Ascend, or enlarge the Hèls."

I looked around at my fellows who were all seeking the same thing as me. The honor of Ascending as a Disciple who could one dawn join the Farasee Order. To serve our Great Infinite in the holiest temple. To dedicate our lives to the righteous morality of the empyrean.

Selfishly, I also wanted to enter the Order so I could righteously hunt down the Fallen Prince and make him pay in blood for what he did to my Manmi. My mother would be alive this dawn if it wasn't for him. I wouldn't rest until I saw him broken, bleeding, and burning in the Hèls for what he'd done to her.

There was an electric charge in the air, filled with excitement and ambition. Ellabeth and I floated near the back of the gathered would-be Ascendants. The entire class who'd received acceptance scrolls looked to be around seven thousand strong.

That made me nervous. Manmi always said the temple only accepted three thousand Disciples. Which meant she'd been warning me. The competition just to get *in* the temple would be fierce.

It wasn't lost on me that the majority of the Ascendants were all males. Sporadically, spread among them I could make out the heads of those who were females. Almost all of them clung to their male counterparts who seemed to be familiar to them.

I couldn't blame them. Manmi had warned me about that. Male hostility in the temple was a known thing. They'd been indoctrinated with the stupidity that females didn't belong in the Farasee Order.

That never stopped us from trying to Ascend.

But I wasn't stupid. I had to be careful.

I looked at Farasee Esau. I wonder what he thought. Did he hate us, too? Did he think our attempts were futile?

As if he could sense me, those ferocious eyes cut through the multitude of angels and looked directly at me.

Stars.

Exactly what I *didn't* want.

Gradually every head turned to look back at me. I counted down from *three* waiting for them to notice the inevitable.

Sure enough, as the angels looked and saw my eyes, their expressions started changing. In the blink of an eye, I was surrounded by a sea of enemies. I lifted my chin and squared my shoulders.

"Safah Eloise Anathelle, I didn't think you would make it. Good to see you've come to carry the torch of tradition."

Esau curled his lips. It looked more like a sneer than anything else. I said nothing. It was bait. Manmi had warned me about this, too.

Avoid speaking when spoken to, especially if it's a Farasee. Chances are, they don't want a response. They want an excuse to push your limits. And this, my fifi, always ends in blood.

I had too much pride to lower my eyes, but everyone staring was starting to make me itch. Ellabeth squeezed my arm as a cruel voice spoke out over the crowd, dripping with hatred.

"Here we go again. More Anathelle swine trying to pollute the Farasee Order."

CHAPTER 2

I whipped my head around to find the source of the voice. I was ready to beat their wings in and see if they had the talons to say it again.

"Tharic Zamarien, don't be so quick to forget your wings haven't been forged as an Ascendant yet. You will treat Safah, and every angel here, with respect."

Okay, so maybe Farasee Esau wasn't *so* bad. At least I could count on him treating us all equally. I scoured the clustering angels to find Tharic. The egotistical ashrat was towards the front of our numerous group. He floated above the sandy floor as if he were our king.

I scowled. Tharic was tall, broad-shouldered, and muscular. His Papi made sure he'd been trained well. His pale skin looked luminescent under the sunlight. He stared at me with a strong jawline and piercing gold eyes that matched his golden hair and wings. Tharic Zamarien glared at me like I was the sea rot beneath his new sandals. I glared back wanting to peel his skin and let him roast.

Instantly I knew he was cut from the same cloth as the rest of his family. Zamariens were full of pride, wealth, and had the ear of the Empràr. I always wondered how they'd earn the ear and trust of the emperor. They were notorious for demanding the Farasee Order remove all its females since they thought we "tainted" the Order. Females were nothing more than playthings to a Zamarien.

No one was louder on this front then Farasee Kaelthos Zamarien, Tharic's Papi. Manmi taught me, according to him, females were to be seen and not heard. Our place were in our home villas as wingmates, bearing younglings and keeping the villa in order. The thought was so astronomically preposterous I nearly threw up on the spot.

"You don't belong here, Anathelle," Tharic spat. The angels had fallen silent. "You're not *fit*. You're only here because your Manmi is dead. A waste. A bag of bones even the Fallen dogs didn't care to lick up themselves when they finished with her."

I flinched, snapping my head back as if I'd been struck. Stars. That blow hit true. And it *hurt*. As a family, we Anathelles were still mourning Manmi's loss. And this demon of a Zamarien decided to use the loss of her life as a weapon against me.

Well, two could play that game. I was a grown female. Not some suckling child that couldn't defend herself. If he wanted to go low, I would go straight to the Hèls.

"I'm here because I actually have a brain, sunburned ashrat." I crossed my arms. "Or are you so slow you couldn't take two seconds to read that *I* scored the highest marks as both a Spirit Filer *and* an Incense Fuser on my Ascendant exams. It's pretty public knowledge."

I batted my lashes at him, smiling sweetly. Like poison.

"Unlike *you* who needed your Papi to convince the Order to let you in on...let me check my notes again...oh that's right. On *principle*," I said, and pointed to my temple. "Even though you're dumber than a chest of seashells."

Ellabeth wheezed. A male floating close to us, with pretty brown, hawkish eyes, grinned wide, eagerly looking between Tharic and I.

Tharic scowled, his eyes flashing with fire. I watched him. The tightness of his breaths. The veins crawling up his neck. His hands turning into fists. If he was going to attack, I would be ready for him.

Manmi always said Zamariens had short tempers, long mouths, and cruel hearts. I could *never* let myself be caught by a Zamarien, especially alone. Their hatred for Anathelles ran long. Deep. It didn't help I had over seven generations of Matriarchs serving as Farasees in the Temple, outside of Manmi who was killed by a Fallen attack at the Seal Gate—the portal between Hallowed and Fallen angelic realms.

"Enough," Esau cut in, stifling a yawn. He pinched the bridge of his nose as if he was developing a headache just from being in our presence for too long. "There will be no violence in your ascent. Am I clear?"

"As glass, Farasee." I answered Esau, but I kept my eyes on Tharic.

Tharic didn't respond. He didn't need to. His eyes promised all I needed to know.

Violence.

"All eyes on me." Esau didn't have to raise his voice. Every head snapped to attention. Even Tharic.

I linked arms with Ellabeth again, trying to calm my racing hearts. All seven were beating like wild drums. I had to get through my first dawn without fighting. Just this first one.

"I hope he chokes on the way up."

I slid my gaze to her aquamarine ones. "Out for blood?"

"He ticked me off."

I snorted. Same.

"Once complete, your results will be distributed throughout the Farasee Order across all twelve Sorellien Islands. It's important for the temples across the Ouanaviel Empyrean to know about this generation of Ascendants aspiring to be Disciples. Those who excel, will also be noted by High Farasee Manazzra Ahabiah, and the Profèt of our empyrean, Profèt Samael."

Ellabeth and I *gasped.*

High Farasee Manazzra Ahabiah? The male was a Farasee-ical *legend*. He'd been alive since the beginning of the Fifth Age. He'd seen the formation of the Ouanaviel Empyrean from its inception. There would be no Farasee Order if it wasn't for him. Profèt Samael wouldn't even be the leading voice of spirituality for the empyrean, if it wasn't for Manazzra.

If I did well during my first season in the temple, he would know?

Stars.

I'd do whatever it took to make sure the High Farasee learned of me. My Matriarchs had paved the way. Now it was my turn.

"Do us all a favor," Esau said. He crossed his arms. "Don't die."

My eyebrows shot to my hairline.

"I'm sorry," Ellabeth said. "What did he just say?"

"Any questions?" Esau asked with a voice that suggested he didn't actually want to answer any. Hands shot into the air. The Farasee sighed. He folded those battering rams he called arms and picked an angel close to him.

The female had pink hair, tawny brown skin, and a little bounce in her float, her pink wings bouncing, too. I pressed my lips into a thin line. She was too cheery. Too excited.

She was *not* making it in.

"When do the gates close?"

"Why do you care? Make it in before they do. Next?" Farasee Esau snapped.

"I swear, I hope he doesn't become my Presbitari. I wouldn't be able to deal with him as my professor," grumbled the male with the pretty brown eyes. He was wrinkling his nose at Farasee Esau in annoyance.

I laughed. "What if you do?"

The male looked at me. "I'll pluck my own wings out. No lie."

Ellabeth and I laughed.

"Safah," I said, smiling up at him.

"Daelun."

"I'm Ellabeth," Ellabeth said from around my shoulder, keeping her voice low. "Your eyes are really pretty. You could break some hearts with those."

Daelun's grin stretched, his brown eyes glittering. "I'm worse with my mouth."

I grinned wide. I liked him already.

"If we survive this Hèls of a climb, friends?" I asked him.

"Who am I to deny an Anathelle?" he teased, wiggling his eyebrows. "Absolutely *yes*."

Ellabeth and I laughed. He was funny *and* cute. Maybe this wouldn't be so bad after all. We turned back to Esau.

I was ready to Ascend.

I'd been trained my entire life for this moment. Manmi had Ascended all the way into the Order as a Farasee. So did Granmanmi. So did Great-Granmanmi. And my Manmi before her. I would *not* be the first of our bloodline to fail.

"Let us begin. When my apprentice, Apprenti Assefah, calls your name, enter the waterfall. He will only call you once. So pay attention!"

"Taraji Hoksa!" called Assefah, floating by Farasee Esau in his purple Apprenti robes.

I didn't bother looking at who it was. I needed to concentrate. I took deep breaths, regulating my heartbeats. My hands pricked with needles, but I refused to give in to nerves. The time had come. I *would* Ascend.

"Marai Vithoria."

"Anida Melin."

"Kyree Forrest."

"Ellabeth Riventhelle."

Ellabeth squealed quietly. "I love you. I'll see you inside!"

Ellabeth squeezed me, and I squeezed back. "I love you, too. Show them how it's done!"

She beamed, and released me, cutting through the thick crowd with the grace of a dancer. Her light blonde hair shone prettily beneath the sun as her wintry colored wings flapped behind her. Her flight robes were loose around her limbs but still hugged her slender frame in a flattering way.

I watched my best friend—for the entirety of my one thousand cycles—fly forward. Without hesitation, she spread all seven pairs of her wings and dove into the waterfall. Once she was fully submerged, I couldn't see her any longer. I threw up a prayer to the Infinite, praying Ellabeth would be alright and make it successfully to the temple.

More names were called in rapid succession.

"Lavender eyes is all alone now."

"Let's see if she makes it like her weak Manmi."

"Really. She died at the hands of Fallen. How pathetic."

Jeers were hurled my way like bricks but I said nothing, ignoring them all. Manmi always said the biggest key to conquering entry into the temple was focus. Distraction meant death. These idiots would not be given the satisfaction.

"She'll die before she makes it in."

"I hope so. Tired of seeing these Anathelle bloodthorns among the Order."

My cheeks flushed. I didn't give in to the bait. I'd been called a whore before. I wouldn't let it throw me off my game now.

Focus, Safah.

"Safah Anathelle."

Finally.

I flew into the air, above the remaining Ascendants. I reached the waterfall, took one deep, steadying breath, and dove in.

Stars.

The water was *heavy*. At least it was as clear as the Ouanaviel Sea. I could see in front and above me, which was all that mattered. Every few strides there were pockets where I could duck my head in for air before I kept flying.

Bracing myself, I spread my wings and began cutting through the water after the angel above me. While pressing through the heavy peals of water, I heard the call for the next angel to begin the ascent after me. Bone chilling terror spilled into my blood.

"Next. Tharic Zamarien!"

CHAPTER 3

I wasn't going to die. Not this dawn. Not by the hands of a Zamarien no less. I turned my wings into an extension of my arms, using all seven pairs to *scoop* and *push* through the water. Each thrust of my wings allowed me to surge higher, creating distance behind me. I cut through layer after layer of water. I could not let Tharic catch up with me.

I maneuvered through the waterfall with great effort, forcing my way through, pushing against each rushing wave. But the waterfall pushed back. Like a living force, water slammed into me, wave after wave, trying to drag me down.

I found an open pocket, churning with water. Tucking in my wings, I aimed myself like a spear. Pulling on my starfire, I launched through the water. When my body hit the pocket, it shot me higher up the waterfall, like the explosion of a geyser.

Thankful for some momentum, I whipped out my wings,

and began meticulously climbing through this wretched waterfall, pushing higher.

Stars. Ellabeth had been so right.

This was a special kind of Hèls.

My muscles were already straining from the effort. I blinked droplets from my eyes. My chest squeezed. I wanted a break to catch my breath. Looking above, I counted six air pockets. When I made it to the sixth, I would let myself take a break.

Just ahead of me was a brown-skinned male. He was colored like sand, with short-cropped brown hair, and a tall, muscular form. He navigated through the water as if he spent every waking moment swimming around the Ouanaviel Island. The male bent to look down at me. Then he focused on a spot further down, past me.

"Little prey," Tharic called. My hearts seized. "I'm coming for you."

Trying not to panic, I cut through the water harder. Faster. I pushed my wings to their limits. Tharic was both taller and stronger. I was going to have to rely on my nimbleness if I was going to make it out of this waterfall alive.

The male above looked at me and said, "Go. Pass me. I'll distract him."

I blinked. Was he helping me? But we weren't supposed to help each other. He could forfeit Ascension.

"Hey, I know what you're thinking. Don't worry." He nudged his head. "*Go.* I'm not *actually* helping you. I'm just... slowing him down. Which also benefits me."

He winked and moved to the side, waiting for me to swim past him.

"Safah," I called out, finding *thanks* insufficient. "I'm Safah...and thank you. Infinitely."

"Omarion," he called out, using his wings to swim down. "And I know who you are. The Wyliums love the Anathelles."

Omarion winked at me with those light green eyes of his, so light they looked hazel. I kept swimming as he headed for Tharic. The waterfall began to curve, the current flowing down through the columns of the Starfell Mountains. I followed the bend, enjoying the breather with the curve. My hearts pumped less which made reserving my air easier.

Leaning to the side, I used my wings to fly through the water, instead of swim. I gained speed, aiming for the next air pocket. The moment I reached it, I took a deep gulp of air, flooding my internal air reserves, before the pocket launched me upwards.

Sneaking a peek below, I found Omarion already swimming away from Tharic, expertly maneuvering through the water. I searched for Tharic's form, finding him multiple wingspans behind. Whatever Omarion had done had royally ticked him off. His pale cheeks were splotchy with crimson.

After Tharic, a female was swimming through her Ascent. She was pretty with wide silver eyes, deep umber skin, and long, ivory hair.

"Stars, I've waited so long to finally Ascend," she squealed.

Idiot. I wanted to throttle her for opening her mouth.

Tharic heard the female, turned, and rushed down to meet her. Before she could react, Tharic wrapped his wings around her petite frame, snapped her neck, and punctured her chest with one of his talons. He ripped the talon out, and slapped all seven pairs of his wings into her body, sending her hurling through the water until she collided, face first, into the waterfall's side.

I flinched as her body snapped against the rock, her golden blood seeping through the water, turning the waterfall into a grave.

I blinked, conflicted. What about her spirit? Her body couldn't just be *left* here. Her spirit had to be siphoned so it could be filed. Everything inside of me screamed to swim to her lifeless body and collect her abandoned spirit.

"Safah, *go*," Omarion called.

I blinked and realized he'd already reached me, and swam right past, headed for the next peak of the waterfall that would push out to the edge of the Goldstone Bridge. Tharic turned away from the female he'd just killed and looked up at me.

"There's my little prey." He grinned. I felt sick. "You're next."

I whipped around, cutting through the water faster than before. Omarion was swift. One moment, I was pushing through the water after him. The next, he was gone.

Blessed lights.

The bloodshed had already started.

The waterfall curved from the center of the Starfelliel Mountains, and through an ivory cave lit up with chromatic light. I rushed through, taking in bits of the beauty. Ivory rock stacked atop each other, while the water flowed down each step like a rushing river. At the center was a rocky step way that led all the way to the top. At the base of each step, the rock was also lit with chromatic light. In here, the trees were ivory with golden leaves and iridescent colored fruit. It was a magical sight.

I quickly looked away and pushed through the water. The waterfall curved again. Angling my body, I chose to fly. Swimming was too slow. Not with Tharic gaining on my heels.

I took the bend of the upcoming curve, thrusting myself toward the next air pocket. I snapped my wings, the sound like a thunderclap. Loud and jarring, a wave of water rushed down as the motion propelled me upward.

Now it was a straight shot. I'd reached the part of the waterfall that rose into the clouds. Here was where the Ouanaviel Island joined to the the islet above where Temple Efysis was rooted. I repeated the motion, needing to create more distance between me and Tharic.

I navigated through a new rush of water, begging for this infernal stretch of the Ascent to end. With another thrust of my wings through hardened water, I saw the shining edge of the Goldstone Bridge. Propelling myself upward, I raced for the bridge, desperate to be free of this hèllish waterfall. Then:

"Gotcha, little prey."

No.

I whipped around just as Tharic slammed his wings into my spine. I went hurling through and out of the waterfall. I barreled onto the platform of the Goldstone Bridge, rolling over three times before coming to a stop. I screamed, agonizing pain flooding my water-logged body.

Focus, Safah.

I opened my eyes, breathing through my teeth past the stinging heat licking my bones. I'd made it onto the bridge.

MOVE.

I rolled to my stomach, pushed to my feet, and *ran*.

"For Infinite's sake! Just *die*!" Tharic roared, coming up behind me, running after me at full speed.

"How about you piss off, first," I called back, racing across the bridge.

If I wasn't trying to avoid certain death, I would take time to admire the beauty of the Goldstone Bridge. It was long, elongating across a pathway cut straight through the clouds.

On either side, all you could see were the billows. There was no telling just how high we were. There were no rails on the bridge, and each golden brick was three times the size of my head.

I swallowed past the beating drums in my chest. I pushed Tharic to the recesses of my mind. I needed to concentrate. One foot in front of the other. *Run*.

Up ahead were two females. They looked like sisters. As I neared them, I couldn't help but feel sorry. One of them had slipped. The other was trying to pull her up over the side of the bridge.

Both were losing the battle.

Where the one was pulling, it looked like the bricks beneath her sandals were *lifting*. If they pushed up any further, she'd go sliding off the side of the bridge, too. I stormed past, screaming at them breathless.

"Tharic...behind me...hates females. He'll kill you...*RUN!*"

I didn't look back once I passed them. They could do with my warning what they wanted. As for me, I was crossing this bridge *alive*.

I ran until I neared a layer of brick that rose up like steps. I ran up the steps without a thought. Only to find a dead end on the other side. And a wide chasm across to the other side. To cross, I'd have to jump.

Merciful Infinite, help me.

I didn't dare slow down. I raced across at full speed. And jumped.

For a moment, I was weightless. Then my body began hurling towards the bridge floor. When I landed, I rolled twice, pushed to my feet, and kept running. I kept my wings snapped into my spine so I could go faster. Behind me, I heard endless screaming.

Then a *snap*. A *crunch*. Another set of screaming.

Something whizzed past my head, landing several paces ahead. When I ran past the object, I saw it was three talons, ripped from the jointed points of wings.

Burning Tharic Zamarien.

What a barbarian.

I didn't let myself think about the females. About how he'd surely tossed them over like a bag of feathers. All I could do was run or else the next one he'd toss over the side of this bridge would be me.

CHAPTER 4

"You will *not* make it into the temple, little prey."

I ignored him, racing like a pegasus across the bridge.

"You Zamariens don't know when to shut up, do you?"

Tharic's sandals sounded closer. No matter how hard I tried, the distance between us kept narrowing. One moment. I just needed one moment to see how close he was.

I chanced it, whipping my head back. The instant our eyes connected, I regretted my decision. Pure hatred colored his eyes like flaming fire. Tharic snarled, throwing sunbolts at my back.

I whipped around. Drawing on my starfire, I created a shield. It glittered like a million stars. I pounded across the brick needing to catch my breath. I was still tired from the swim. Tharic on the other hand was running like the swim up the waterfall was a warm up.

"Just give in, little prey. I'll keep it short."

"Is that what you tell every female knowing you can't make it longer even if you tried?"

Tharic cursed. I leapt forward, landing hard on a brick just as he whipped out a wing to jab at my spine.

The bridge rumbled. Swayed.

The bricks shifted beneath my feet.

I yelped, tumbling to the ground, rolling with the bridge. To my utter embarrassment, Tharic was still on his two feet bracing himself with his arms spread out. I drew up my knees. Through the cloudy fog, an enormous slide sprang out of the bridge, sliding *down* into the clouds.

I had a choice. Take the slide or let Tharic kill me. I chose the slide.

Without caution, I shot for the edge of the bridge, pushed off the end, and slid.

The slide was carved entirely of gold, looping down into a curl that encircled three times before swirling into a rise that disappeared beyond the clouds. The moment I slid down, my hearts leapt into my throat.

A headiness overwhelmed me. I was utterly mesmerized, and terrified, all at the same time. I couldn't breathe for excitement. For fear. Adrenaline coursed through my veins. Thankfully my flight robes had an under legging component that kept me covered. The further down I slid, the faster I went.

Tharic dove after me.

I silently screamed at his tenacity.

Looking down, I jerked all my wings forward and yanked

on the sides of the slide. An instant rush of speed sent me flying down. I curved with the bend, letting the momentum propel me forward. Tucking in my arms, my body rushed through the loop, soaring overhead as I spun upside down, rushed through the loop and was sent racing down the next leg of the slide.

For a moment, it felt as if it was just me and the clouds. This far out, I couldn't even see the Goldstone Bridge. Couldn't see the other Ascendants running for their lives. I could barely even make out Tharic on the slide through the thickness of the clouds.

I felt weightless. Free. In control.

Then the slide swirled into a zigzagging pattern that sent my body reeling from side to side. I rammed to one side, then I was tossed to the other, before being shot once again into the air.

Except this time, the slide had no end. I blinked.

Stars.

I was going to have to jump.

Hearts thrumming, I squinted through the press of billowy clouds, desperately searching for any inkling of where the bridge was.

I caught a twinkling of gold in the distance.

The momentum of the slide sent me careening into the air. I floated into the clouds, weightless, before my body weight shifted, and began yanking me down. I looked down, only seeing endless clouds. There was no bridge in sight. Panic flittered in my chest.

This could *not* be where I died.

Still tumbling through the air, I jerked. I itched to snap out my wings, but I didn't dare. Bricks of gold rushed into view, crumbling on either side for several long stretches. Ignoring my rising fear, I tucked my knees in. As the bridge rose, and my body descended, I let out my wings just enough to help me tuck and roll.

I collided with the bridge and went sprawling. I'd landed too hard. Too fast. I spun, out of control, unable to stop myself.

"No," I squealed.

I tried clinging to the brick. My hands were as slippery as water. I gripped on to nothing. My body nearly slid off the side of the bridge. Jerking my wings, and gripping the edge, I snapped my body to the side against the momentum and threw myself back to the middle of the bridge.

Finally at a place where I could get control of my balance, I shot to my feet and ran.

And not a moment too soon.

Tharic landed at the center of the bridge. Perfectly. On the balls of his feet, already in a full sprint after me.

My sandals slapped the brick as I raced across the next stretch. It wound into curves and loops. Squinting, I gauged the distance between each gap. As I neared the first set of winding bridge-way, instead of following the loop, I leapt over them altogether.

"At least you're not a complete idiot," Tharic called from behind me.

I turned in time to see him leaping just like I'd just done. I turned back around, breathing opened mouth, gasping for air. My ribs burned. My muscles ached. I needed water so bad.

There were several Ascendants before me running for dear life, all of us trying to beat an invisible clock. The male at the very front leapt off the bridge, tumbling into endless clouds, headed for the temple gates. Then a female followed him. And then another. I envied their progress, forcing my own feet to move faster.

Ahead of me was a male. His gait had slowed. He was limping. He'd been wounded. He had his wings out to help him with balance. That was great and all, but they were taking up all the room on the bridge. Not daring to see how close Tharic got, I rushed ahead and shoved the male out of my way.

"What in the stars—"

"I'm sorry...but...gotta...go," I called over my shoulder, running faster.

"You can't just push angels out of the way like that, Anathelle! You need to—"

Then the angel was screaming.

"All that blasted talking," Tharic snarled. "Burning useless."

I turned my head to the side. The male Tharic had thrown tumbled down, down, *down*.

Then he spread his wings.

No.

I wanted to scream. To tell him to not fight it.

But it was too late.

He opened his wings, starting to fly back to the bridge. Three stareagles surged out of the cloudy heavens. The stareagles rushed him, tearing into his flesh with their talons. They shredded his wings, tore at his skin, and ripped him apart. Then they dragged him away as he screamed.

Focus, Safah.

I started leaping to gain speed and distance. To outmatch Tharic. But the burning asheater still kept gaining on me. Kept taunting me. I thought about Manmi. I thought of all the Matriarchs that made it into the temple before me.

I *had* to make it.

I gained some speed, passing another male. Moments later he was tossed off the bridge by Tharic.

I caught up to, and passed, a female. I heard the snap of her neck, then her wings, before I caught the whoosh of wind as her lifeless body went hurling off the side of the bridge.

So, brutality against females was sport to Zamariens. I made a mental note and cleared more of the bridge.

I ran past three more males, all of whom were tossed off. None got a chance to put up a fight. Nearing the end of the bridge, I threw up a silent prayer of thanks to the Infinite. I ran two more paces.

Then Tharic was on me.

One moment my feet were slapping against brick. The next, I was being body slammed from behind like a bloodhyena into the side of a mountain.

I went hurtling through the air, soaring over the bridge. I

landed on the stones with a definitive crack. I couldn't even tell what was broken. I hurt *everywhere.* I rolled over to get up. But Tharic was on me again. He bashed a wing into my side. Then another. A sandaled foot collided into my face. Then it stomped into my neck. My stomach.

Brutality.

He didn't plan to make this quick. Which meant I had time to get away. Tharic came in for another kick, but I rolled, shot back to my feet, and ran.

"What in the *rot?*" Tharic screamed. "You Anathelles just don't know how to die! Well, except for your *Manmi.*"

Oh, how I wished to turn around and slap the taste out of his mouth. But I had no time. I was close to the end of the bridge. This jungle-raised baboon wasn't going to make me miss it.

I ran with all my might, ignoring the dripping blood. The searing pain. The ache in my body. I had a legacy to uphold. I had a family to make proud. I had an empyrean to defend.

I *would* Ascend.

I ran for the end of the bridge, tasting victory. I slammed my feet into the bricks. Then an explosion erupted beneath the stones. And the bridge beneath us collapsed.

CHAPTER 5

Fear coiled its scaly hide around my throat like a sandviper and squeezed. I had never been afraid of heights—always flying into the clouds where I didn't belong and flying to heights most angels didn't dare. I'd always felt the safest, the calmest, on high ground. Falling didn't easily scare me, either.

But falling while forbidden to fly? *That* was something even Manmi hadn't prepared me for.

My stomach rolled, twisting in knots, as I tumbled weightlessly through layered billows and clouds. Had I passed the bridge? Could I fly now? What if I chanced it and forfeited Ascension?

I tumbled, gaining speed the further I descended. I blinked away tears as my body remained in an awkward tangle while I struggled with what to do. My mind was frazzled. I had to think.

Tuck and roll.

I strained against the wind, twisting the full length of my body so I could bring in my knees. I spread out two pairs of wings, curling them over my form. I spread out another pair so they could be used to push off the ground. The remaining four pairs I kept loose, in case I needed to grip or climb.

Clapping sounds—like shifting rock and thunder—sounded above. I kept my hands out before me, trying to brace for whatever would come. Blinking through the haze of clouds, I saw something shining. It was ivory. Smooth in a few places, but jagged rock in most. There were glittering stars littered all over it. As I squinted, trying to make sense of what I was seeing, the image cleared.

I gasped.

It was the Efysien rock base that upheld the entire islet.

I shifted my weight, preparing for a hard collision. The clouds began to clear. The mountain came into view. And the fast-approaching rocky ground was rushing to meet me.

"Rot," I hissed.

This was going to hurt. Like everything else in this cursed ascent.

I calculated the drop. To the left, the rocky base sloped out into nothing but cloud. I assumed that end led straight to the Ouanaviel Sea far below. Certain death.

To the right was a high slab of white. Very few ridges were on the sides of the mountain. The bridge collapsed before I could make it *on* the platform which meant I still couldn't fly. I'd have to climb the side of this mountain.

I was growing enraged. I was dirty. Hungry. Tired. Wounded. And for stars sake, I now had to *scale* this mountain rock to get into the temple?

Hot tears prickled the back of my eyes. How in the stars would I make it into the temple on time? How was I going to carry on what Manmi died to uphold? Fatigue flooded my body, making my wings droop, and my head hang.

I neared the rocky platform. A sudden gust of wind sent me hurtling into the rock. I jut out my wings, keeping my arms locked around my knees. I hit the rock, hard, my wings taking the brunt. The two pairs kept me rolling over the landing. I found myself skidding to a halt, right at the very edge of the rock. With the other pair of wings, I pushed off, rolling into a run.

The ground beneath me was deceiving. It looked jagged in many places. But it was actually soft.

Too soft.

I slipped, and fell, slamming my shoulder into the ground.

"Burning stars!" I cried. "What kind of torment is this?"

"Ready to give up yet, little prey?"

I wanted to scream.

I'd forgotten all about Tharic.

I shot to my feet, using my wings to walk. I bent low enough so my talons could punch holes into the ground and help propel me forward. I slipped three more times, but kept my footing. Once I reached the rocky side of the mountain base, I looked up. And up. And *up*.

I sighed, my shoulders sagging like weights. Reeling

myself, I took a long gulp of air and began to climb. Smooth as glass, there was almost no hold to cling to. I noticed in random places where small punctures in the rock had been made.

So. *That's* how the angels before me made it up.

Gathering my nerves, I placed hands in the holes and began pulling myself up. It took several minutes of trial and error to figure it out, but I managed. It was painstakingly slow, but I climbed. I heard Tharic through the clouds, slipping and falling, cursing each time he lost the progress he made.

I almost smiled.

Almost.

I wasn't willing to test fate just yet, lest I slip and end up right by him.

The breeze of the clouds carried a soothing chill. Sweat crawled across my brow and slipped down my spine inside my flight robes. Twice my feet slipped. But I kept my hold. A familiar hum of tension in my muscles began to sing. I fell into the rhythm of the climb. Pushing through, I rose higher, until I could start making out the edge of the platform above.

The clouds began thickening the closer I got, making it hard to see the edge clearly. The air smelled light. Like it always did in my home garden at the cool of dawn.

I was getting close to the temple.

Excitement filled my blood. I picked up the pace until I finally made it. I crested the rocky side and pulled up onto a perfect, even marble surface. The golden platform spilled out in every direction. Much like the Goldstone Bridge.

The moment I gained my footing, I spread my wings and took flight. My side throbbed but I couldn't stop to feel it now. I had to make it into the temple. I flew with all my might, beating all seven wing pairs against the rushing wind around me. The harder I flew, the harder the wind pushed against me. But I didn't care, I wasn't going to give up.

Curving through layers of clouds, slicing through the billows, I pulsed my wings. Then the sprawling glory of Temple Efysis came into view.

The obelisk was higher than I could see in full view, even if I craned my neck. It was wider than any building in Ouanaviel.

Twelve angels—one from each rank—hovered above the golden floors by ethèr—innate, supernatural, angelic power—carved out of crystal and glass, sculpted to absolute perfection. Every detail that differentiated their rank could be seen. They each had open mouths, and between each mouth, a ball of iridescent fire burned.

Dripping, curling vines of crystal twisted beautifully around Temple Efysis itself like vines in a garden. Staggering steps led up to the open doors that framed the entrance.

The temple seemed broken up into sections and layers. The higher the levels, the more glass and golden stones could be seen. At the very top was a golden dome with ivory fire surrounding it. A massive sunlion perched on either side, roaring as they watched all of us Ascendants racing for the temple.

That had to be the living quarters of Profět Samael. No one, except for High Farasee Manazzra, could visit with the Profět. I gaped in awe, jaw hanging at the opulence, the grandeur, the absolute resplendence of it all.

I looked at the grand moat around the Temple, with pristine blue waters like the Ouanaviel Sea and swirling, ivory platforms curling through them, covered in an array of large, sculpted, golden bowls. On either side of the long path winding up to the temple, statues of high towering angels stood. Between the angels were the Pagali—Pegasikind, sunlions, and stareagles.

I flew toward the temple in awe. And almost flew straight into the gates...and the creatures guarding them.

I came to a screeching halt, slapping my wings into the golden floor, bringing myself to stop just in time. I had no words for what I saw before me. Stunned, I floated back a few paces.

Without thought, I bowed low, bending my knees, then folding my wings over my body, extending them forward in reverence. The beasts rumbled, pleased at the honor.

They felt familiar to me. I couldn't dishonor them by simply flying by them.

I finally lifted my head and found the seven sunlions with their heads lowered, as they blinked at me. My jaw *dropped*. Each sunlion had the brightest and most beautiful lavender eyes. Just like me. It was like looking into a mirror.

"Wings high," I whispered to them all, looking each in turn in their eyes.

Stars bless me! All of their eyes twinkled, glittering in the dimming sunlight as they looked back.

"Star of the Age. We are waiting for you."

I blinked. "Don't you mean *'We have been waiting'*?"

"No. We still are."

My throat clenched, emotion filling my chest. As one, each sunlion tilted back their head, their ivory fur gleaming beneath the seven suns, and roared. It sounded like a clarion call. Like a summons. Like the ringing of bells to signal someone was home.

The gates behind them *widened.*

I felt a tug, an urge, to fly through.

So I did.

I was mesmerized at this invisible force that called me forward. Pulled me ahead and through the gates. The moment I crossed, they sealed shut. I kept flying, as if in a daze. I flew up the numerous steps to the temple doors. My chest squeezed as I neared the entrance. Then I crossed inside.

The moment my feet crossed the threshold, the sunlions stopped roaring. Then the temple doors slammed shut.

CHAPTER 6

I beamed from ear to ear when my feet landed on plush ivory rugs in a pristinely designed foyer. It was long rather than wide. The foyer spanned endless wingspans, brilliantly lit even though twinight would start rising outside of the temple soon.

My excitement quickly evaporated when I noticed there wasn't a single Ascendant here.

Where was everyone? Why was I alone?

I surveyed the vast hall, unsure of what to do. Every direction I turned was drenched in marble. The floors were carved from ivory slabs with golden patterns intricately woven into them. Overhead had an arched ceiling with different designs, all carved out of ivory stone slabs and gilded tiles.

Wide pillars lined the long foyer on both sides. Each was a uniquely carved angel, sculpted with such detail they seemed to be alive. Golden fire boxes upheld the angelic statues, with iridescent flame burning within. At the top of the pillars were feathered designs that seemed to be welded into the molding above.

Grand floor-to-ceiling windows lined the walls between the pillars, overlooking the outdoors. I squinted, trying to see what lay beyond, but for some reason, nothing came to view. It was like looking through a glass dimly.

"Hello?" I called out.

"Hello, Ascendant Safah."

I yelped, whipping around. Three females stood by the temple doors. They were...smaller. Not like a youngling, but in stature. I wasn't extremely tall for a female, and yet I somehow found myself towering over these three. Each had perfect posture, and kept their shoulders squared, but their eyes remained low. They wouldn't look at me.

Noting the lack of wings, rank markings, and winged ears, it didn't take much guesswork to see all three were goddesses. It helped that I knew enough about the gods, even though in my family home, Manmi and Papi led a different life than most. We had Keepers, but never slaves. I'd heard stories of the gods enslaved by the angels. Bound to serve endlessly, never managing to gain their freedom.

"Good twinight," I said. "Well, at least it will be soon. And you all are?"

The goddesses were unmoving. They didn't budge an inch. They kept their heads bowed. But the goddess in the center responded.

"We're the goddesses of Temple Efysis. We belong to the

temple. To the Farasees of the Order. We're here to guide you to your Sifting chamber, before you can continue your Ascension."

I nodded. That made sense. Manmi had told me about this part ample time. If I made it, I would first be Sifted. I needed to clean up. Physically, spiritually, and emotionally.

The physical part always made sense. Now having survived Tharic Zamarien, the spiritual and emotional parts made sense, too. My spirit had to be cleansed from all I endured this dawn before I dove into any holy temple activities.

"What are your names? If I may ask."

The goddesses looked at each other with their heads still bowed, contemplating how to answer. As they struggled with my request, I carried on.

"Also, would you keep your head up? I would like to look into your eyes when speaking with you."

In tandem, the goddess lifted their heads. At first, they looked past me, unable to meet my gaze head on. The one to the left trembled, terrified. She probably thought this was some test. She probably thought I wanted to hurt her.

"Please," I said gently, raising my hands in a truce. "I don't want to cause you harm. I simply would like to know your name. And what I need to do to get a bath and some rest. I... I'm hurt. And exhausted."

The goddesses blinked at me. Their shoulders relaxed when they realized I meant my words. The one in the middle seemed to be braver than the other two. She gave me a small smile. Her eyes brightened, and she took a step towards me.

"I am Serafina. This is Natalie," she gestured to the goddess who was still shaking. "And this is Caliana."

I smiled back, thankful she was willing to make the effort to talk to me.

"It's good to meet you, Serafina. You too, Natalie and Caliana." I tilted my head, holding my side. My body was beginning to ache badly. "I know you know this, but, I'm Safah. Safah Anathelle. It's such an...incredible honor to *finally* be here."

My words trailed off into a whisper as hot tears prickled my eyes. Holy stars. I'd made it to the temple. I *made it*. I was an Ascendant! All I had to do was survive the first trial, and I would officially be a Disciple of Temple Efysis.

Tears wet my cheeks as I sighed with infinite gratitude. I bounced on my feet. Serafina's eyes sparkled, knowingly.

"You look very much like your Manmi, Amaryss. But something about you is...different than her. We look forward to your Ascension, Ashi—" She bit her lip, cutting herself off. "Ascendant Safah," she quickly amended.

I was too tired to try and puzzle through what she meant. My mind was in shambles. I desperately needed sleep. I yawned, nodding at Serafina.

"Please, follow us."

Serafina, followed by Natalie and Caliana, began walking down the long foyer. I tried as best as I could to take in all the immaculate details.

But *stars*.

I was exhausted. By the time we made it to the other end of the foyer, my wings were dragging on the marble floors. We crossed through an open door. I found myself looking out at an elaborate courtyard, dripping in opulence. Even in my fatigue, I couldn't help but gawk.

"What in the *stars*?"

I didn't know where to look first. The tall, ivory trees. The golden blades of grass. The iridescent birds flying in the air. The endless, billowing clouds that twisted between each of the buildings.

Tall glass towers—interconnected by glass covered walkways—littered the grounds in each direction.

"What am I even looking at?"

Serafina slid her hazel gaze to me, a curious look in her eyes. "This is where you will spend the next twenty-one dawns."

"I'm...sorry. The next...*twenty-one?*"

I whipped my head to the goddess, unsure if I'd heard her right.

She smiled. "Yes, Ascendant. It is the Creed of Sifting. If you don't complete them, you will be considered Unclean. If you're Unclean, you're unworthy of the temple and will be forced to forfeit your Ascension."

I raised a high brow, folding my arms as I balanced on the ivory step outside of the foyer entry.

"So I'm supposed to sit on my backside and sing kumbaya for twenty-one *dawns*?"

Caliana snorted, quickly smothering her laughter with a hand. Natalie's nostrils flared. The goddess bit her lip, holding back her reaction. Serafina's lips twitched, as she met my gaze.

"Yes, Ascendant."

I blinked at Serafina, before looking at the towers.

"What a burning, colossal waste of my time," I grumbled. "I swear dodging Tharic was better than this."

I looked back at Serafina, whose brown cheeks were coloring red as she struggled to stifle her laughter. "You really are...*different*, Ascendant," she managed after a while.

I snorted.

"Please. If you three ran into Ellabeth, you'd realize I'm not *that* different."

"Ellabeth Riventhelle?" Natalie blurted out, her light blue eyes going wide. Her sandy cheeks flushed as she gaped. "You know her?"

"Know her?" I laughed. "Ellie is my best friend in all the realms. We've known each other since before we could talk."

"So much makes sense now," Natalie whispered. "You two have the same...mannerisms."

I grinned wide, showing my teeth.

Serafina chuckled. "Come, Ascendant."

I followed the goddesses as they walked down the steps and made their way to the glass tower. It was only when we'd started crossing the walkway that I noticed all three were barefoot. And they were adorned in pitiful excuses for a gown.

The dress was nothing more than endless chain links looped together to cover most of their bodies. Not that it did anything. Nothing of their curvy frames was left to the imagination. In a temple full of Farasees who were mostly male.

Hot anger ignited my blood.

After going through a series of halls—that looked more like portals into the stars, then walls in a temple—Serafina, Natalie, and Caliana finally brought me to an empty chamber. The door opened on instinct, letting me inside. The first thing I saw was the peek of a washbasin in a small, adjoined chamber. The next thing my eyes found was the bedcloud.

I nearly fainted with relief. I stretched, yawning again. My limbs were on fire. I need to wash, to rest, then I could focus on letting my body self-heal.

"Come Ascendant," Serafina said. Her kind eyes made this new environment feel less awkward. Overwhelming. "We will help you cleanse yourself. Then you can rest."

I let the goddesses lead me into the washbasin. I said nothing as I was stripped bare and led into the tub. Serafina said something to me, but I didn't hear a word.

The moment I slid into the warm water, wings and all, I laid my head on the edge of the tub and fell into a dreamless sleep.

CHAPTER 7

After spending twenty-one dawns locked in the Sifting chamber, I was ready to get out. I'd gotten ample rest, spending most of the dawns sleeping so my body could heal on its own. When I was awake, I recited the passages of the Saccrent all angels said at the start of each dawn. Then I stretched. My limbs, my wings, everywhere I was sore and still feeling the effects of having to outlive Tharic's violence.

I frowned. I wasn't looking forward to enduring anymore of his assaults. He had an unleashed temper and I had a growing suspicion no one was going to put it in check.

"Ascendant Safah? It's time."

I shot out of the bedcloud, grinning. It was a bright and brand new dawn. I was ready to engage in temple activities, *finally*. Serafina stood by the door of the Sifting chamber.

This time she was alone. Natalie and Caliana didn't come. I frowned.

"Where are—"

"The Farasees have requested only I bring you to the auditorium for your inauguration. The goddesses would have come with me if given the permission."

Serafina's eyes were grieved. I looked around. We were alone. I slipped closer, lowering my voice.

"Are you okay? You know you can tell me and I'll keep the truth close to chest. What happened, Serafina?"

She opened her mouth, about to answer. Then something dark flashed across her eyes. She jerked, as if being yanked on an invisible chain. Then she cleared her head, smiling as if nothing happened.

"Ascendant Safah, please. Follow me."

"Serafina, talk to me—"

"Please, Ascendant. Stay close."

Without another word, Serafina led me out of the Sifting towers, and across the temple grounds, until she deposited me at the entrance of a massive cathedral.

"Thank you, Serafina. I—"

"You will not see me again, Ascendant Safah." Her chin wobbled even though her hazel eyes remained bright. "It was a joy being able to attend to you. Please. For all our sakes Ashiris, you must Ascend."

Then she was gone.

I stared after her. Ashiris. Did she mean like the dead star? What in all the realms was that supposed to mean? I didn't call her name knowing it would only trigger punishment for her. I found myself downcast as I turned and entered the auditorium. Chaos was my welcome as I floated inside.

Instantly I felt it. The electric charge of flaring emotion. I could *taste* the tension in the chamber. We'd all come out of twenty-one dawns of Sifting, but it looked like most of the Ascendants were still processing the Starfellien Ascent, and the aftermath, as if it happened yesterdawn.

Ascendants were sprawled everywhere. There were endless columns of seats made of clouds floating in the air. Instead of perching in the cloudchairs, the angels were either floating, pacing restlessly, or sitting on the floors.

I wrinkled my nose. What in the stars was going on?

Not a single Ascendant made it to the Temple unscathed. We'd all managed to heal pretty well, but the evidence of old wounds was prevalent. Every angel had fading bruises and scars.

Several Ascendants looked demoralized. As if the cost of entry to the temple was more than they could afford. One male sat in the corner, huddling by the drapes, head in his hands, sobbing.

"She was killed by that..." The male couldn't even complete his sentence. "She was behind me when he ran up. I was in the middle of turning around...but he grabbed her. Broke her wings. Tossed her off."

I stilled, shuddering. Memories flashed across my eyelids. Memories I thought I'd dealt with the past twenty-one dawns.

Of death. Loss. Violence. Terror. Just how many angelic lives had Tharic robbed?

"Tazuniels, Zamariens, Branais. They're all the same. Violent savages, every last one of them."

I pressed my lips together. I'd been so concerned about steering clear of Tharic, it hadn't even crossed my mind that there were others just like him. I thought he was the worst, I was wrong.

I scanned the crowd, desperate to find Ellabeth, and a sense of security. I caught the flash of several beach-blonde heads, but none of them were her. In my search for Ellabeth, I noticed a frightening new truth. Far less females who'd been accepted into the temple actually Ascended. The auditorium was overrun with males.

I avoided eye contact with the Ascendants. Keeping my head low, I glided to the side, my back to the walls, as I navigated through the angels. The tension in the room was palpable. When I made it further across the chamber, I turned back to the entryway.

Tharic had arrived, flying over the threshold, wings spread wide as if he were a king returning home to his palace. I wanted to rip that smug smile off his face. Crush it like his cold, cruel hearts.

His golden hair was perfectly groomed. His robes were tidy, and in precise order. They fit him well, as if he was a Farasee pretending to be an Ascendant. I hated his confidence. His arrogance. His pride. *Him.*

A chill ran down my spine at the calculating coldness in

his golden eyes. The cunning. The delight in cruelty. The insatiable hunger for blood. For death.

He wasn't done yet. I was on his list—certainly at the top—but I wasn't the only one. I floated by the back wall, hidden by the open wings of angels too focused on themselves to notice, watching Tharic survey the foyer.

I watched as the beast marked every female who Ascended. And every male he thought weak. I shuffled away, pushing through wings and bodies, hunting for Ellabeth in all this mess.

"There you are, little prey."

The Ascendants fell quiet. All eyes turned to me. I froze, mid-shuffle, tossing my head back in annoyance. Stars. When would this come to an end? Before I could take a breath, a bolt of sunfire singed past my head, nearly taking it off. I snarled, whipping around, both hands already thrumming with starfire in them.

"Have you lost every good sense the Infinite gave you?" I yelled at him.

Tharic sneered, eyes blazing with sunfire, hands already raised to blast me again. Ascendants shot out of the way, not wanting to become collateral.

"How stupid are you?" I spat. "We're in the *temple*. Have some respect for holy ground!"

"Respect for holy ground will happen when *you* are wiped from it. Permanently," Tharic snarled. "I *will* kill you, Safah Anathelle."

"Not this dawn you will not."

I came to an abrupt halt at that voice. Tharic snapped his head up. We both stared. When I saw who spoke, I almost started crying.

Stars.

It couldn't be.

I slowly lowered to the ground, forgetting Tharic completely as a wide grin stretched across my face. I looked up into aged—but beautiful and familiar—deep purple eyes. I nearly fell to my knees.

"Granmanmi."

Her eyes twinkled, as her beautiful smile filled every broken piece in my exhausted hearts.

"Hello, granfifi."

CHAPTER 8

I froze, instantly recognizing my error. We were not back home in Port Emprarèl—the capital of the Ouanaviel Island—the epicenter of the Ouanaviel Empyrean.

We were in Temple Efysis. Home to the Profèt, the High Farasee, and the elite of the Farasee Order. She wasn't my Granmanmi here.

"Forgive me, Farasee," I said, composing myself.

I quickly lowered into a respectful bow, curling my wings over my bent form. It was an act of respect to bow to our Farasees. Especially those with a known reputation throughout the empyrean.

"Farasee Asarah," I said, still bowed. "Wings high and good dawn."

The temple auditorium had fallen deathly quiet. You could hear a feather drop. Granmanmi Asarah was no ordinary female of the Order.

She was the only female Farasee who faced a Fallen Shadowlord head on. And won.

Not only had she killed the fallen angel, and took out a quarter of his legion by herself, she also used his decrepit carcass in a ritual that instilled protection of Temple Efysis against Fallen invasion. The empyrean had come to know the ritual as Blood Rites.

To every angel in this room, she was a living legend. And now they were looking at her up close, and would do anything to win her favor.

But to *me*...

She was the one who brushed my hair when I was a youngling, with gentleness and patience, wrangling out stubborn coils with makristi oil. She was the one who taught me how to recite the Davithien hymns. How to cultivate a deep love for the Infinite at such an early age. She fed me mangogos on her knees and snuck me fetafa—slabs of gooey cheese melted and mixed with honey—while Manmi and Papi weren't watching. She was more than a second Manmi to me.

She was home.

"Granfifi."

I lifted my head. Looked into her mauve eyes. There was a weight of love, a world of peace, an overwhelming sense of home I felt in that singular statement. I nearly sobbed.

Granmanmi's eyes filled with pride. With joy.

She threw her arms open wide. Without a word I shot to my feet and threw myself into her arms, squeezing her tight.

"Granfifi," she murmured into my hair. "I am *so proud* of you. Well done, my child."

She embraced me like it was my tenth cycle all over again. For my riseday celebration, she'd made me my favorite cake from scratch. The gooey dessert was stuffed with chocolate, caramel, and toffee in multiple layers. A rare treat since Manmi kept me on a strict diet. But Granmanmi had made me the cake anyway and dared my parentlings to keep me from eating it. Granmanmi wrapped her wings around me now, tucking me close to her chest as she breathed me in.

"I always knew you would Ascend. Only the Infinite knows how long I have awaited this dawn. This season," she cooed, breathing softly in my ear.

I tipped my head into her shoulder, burying my face in her neck, and silently cried. I didn't care if the Ascendants looked on. I hadn't laid eyes on Granmanmi in *cycles*. Holding onto her now was a gift.

"My Safah," she cooed. "How your Papi has tried to keep you from me." She chuckled. "I always told him he couldn't. Now that you are under the covering of this temple, of *me*, no one can come between us."

"Just like old times?" I giggled, looking up at her.

Her eyes twinkled like the stars. It was like staring into the universe and finding your place in the wildness of the realms.

"Just like old times," she whispered, as if she was sharing a secret.

I grinned, clinging to my Granmanmi. It was like listening to a lullaby on a moody twinight while it rained outside. Like when Evanae—my little sister—and I would sit on the veranda and watch the rain droplets kiss the surface of the Ouanaviel Sea as Granmanmi would sit in the rocking chair and hum. She would create light shows for us with her ability to summon the stars.

"My Safah," she breathed again as I struggled to rein in my tears. "Welcome to the beginning of your life."

I shook with tears. Those dawns of Sifting hadn't been enough. The sheer terror and madness of the Starfellien Ascent was catching up to me now that Granmanmi held me. The auditorium watched on. I didn't care. She was *my* Granmanmi. And I had every right.

"Want to know a secret?" She pulled back her head and spoke only for me to hear. "I think that Zamarien fool will reconsider before approaching you again."

I snorted, bursting into laughter. I wasn't so sure about that, but I had to admit, it was good knowing she was aware not only that he came after me, but also that I evaded him and won our not-so-silent war. If Granmanmi knew, then any other Zamarien in the temple would find out, too.

"Amaryss would be so proud," she said, caressing my cheek. My throat instantly swelled again. "Look at you. Carrying the torch." Her eyes shone bright. Pride swelled in my hearts. "We are holy…"

She waited expectantly for me to finish. I lifted my chin, finishing in a strong whisper.

"To whatever end."

"To *whatever* end, my sweet star. Never forget it."

She kissed my forehead, more than once, and tucked me to her chest again in a deep embrace. Then someone started coughing. Loud.

"Safah, *move*. You've been hogging her long enough. It's my turn!"

Laughing out loud I scooted out of the way. I'd barely left Granmanmi Asarah's arms before Ellabeth charged her at full speed in a wide and warm embrace. Granmanmi held Ellabeth like she held me. The same way she had since we were both big enough to fight but still too small to talk.

"My sweet Ellie. Our jewel of the sea."

Ellabeth blushed, squeezing Granmanmi tight. I smiled wide. Ellabeth and I had always been like sisters. Our families were extremely close, as if we'd been one big family for several millennia.

When Ellabeth released Granmanmi, she flew to my side and linked our arms. "Way to show that Zamarien monkey how to fight for his bananas."

I snorted. Loud. Failing to cover my mouth as I burst out laughing.

"We love you, Granmanmi," Ellabeth said to Granmanmi Asarah.

I grinned, nodding in agreement. We flew to either side of her, giving her a massive kiss on both her cheeks in tandem, leaving Granmanmi beaming, her eyes bright and tinged with the kindness of all the Elledelle realms.

"Now," Ellabeth said. "I have a few friends *you* need to meet."

I noticed a fading bruise beneath her eye and the dip in three of her wings.

"One of the males got you during the Ascent, too?"

Her sharp eyes assessed herself then she snorted.

"Some backscratcher named Tavax." Ellabeth shrugged. "Tavax Branai, I think. I got him, too. But he got me worse. I'm fine. Come on."

Ellabeth grabbed my hand, dragging me through the watching Ascendants. They were quiet, looking between me and Granmanmi Asarah. Then they looked between Ellabeth and Granmanmi. Then Ellabeth and me. Too many watched us, calculating if we'd be better as their allies or enemies. I preferred neither.

Floating after Ellabeth, we reached a group clustered to the back of the auditorium on the opposite end of the entrance. Ellabeth beamed, excited to introduce me to the group. Then a voice, clapping like thunder, spoke out in the quiet.

"Tharic, my bibi! There you are. I knew you'd Ascend."

Ellabeth and I shared a look before turning around.

The majority of the room frowned when the new angel surfaced. My stomach churned, twisting with acid as I watched the golden-haired beast—dripping in Farasee ivory—glide to Tharic. Tharic floated like a king—head raised, shoulders back, poised expression.

"Farasee," Tharic bowed his head, "I told you I'd see you again. *In* the temple of course." A pause. "Isn't that right, Papi Kaelthos?"

CHAPTER 9

"So we get the sunfire ashrat *and* his dead-beat Papi," Ellabeth grumbled. "Just wonderful. As if *one* Zamarien wasn't enough."

Farasee Kaelthos looked across the auditorium, finding me instantly. His eyes burned like the suns. Disgust curled his features, as he scowled at me from across the room. His eyes held a vile darkness that made me shiver.

Stars.

Zamarien hatred for Anathelles was unparalleled. I thought Tharic was bad. But his Papi...I looked away from the Farasee, but kept my chin lifted. I would *not* cower to Kaelthos Zamarien.

Farasee Kaelthos placed a strong, approving hand on Tharic's shoulder, turning those fierce eyes from me to his son. He assessed Tharic like a prized pegasus.

"Faring well, my bibi—my son." Kaelthos grinned. "And you thrashed around that bloodthorn Anathelle, too, I hear."

"He thrashed around that *whom*?"

Granmanmi's voice was a silent storm. She didn't raise her voice. But she never had to. The sheer command lacing every word made me shutter. The Ascendants sucked in their breaths. Some angels visibly floated back from the Zamariens. Kaelthos met Granmanmi's gaze but didn't repeat himself. Granmanmi Asarah wasn't satisfied.

"Now Kaelthos," she said, with such poise. Such class. "You're not as much an imbecile as you are the size of a Winterwood bear. Are you?" She tilted her head, batting her lashes. "I'll ask it again. This viper of a bibi thrashed around *whom*? Because I know you're not speaking about *my* granfifi."

Her voice was calm, tranquil even. But the message was clear. She'd bathe this auditorium with his blood if he dishonored the Anathelle name. As if our name didn't hold more weight throughout the empyrean than Zamarien. Kaelthos lifted his nose. His jawline twitched, but he kept quiet. Granmanmi's eyes churned like newborn stars.

"Do not *ever* refer to my granfifi with that filthy, whoring term again. Or I'll remind you why Fallen Shadowlords have good reason to fear my name. Would you like your golden monkey to join in our next Blood Rite?"

Tharic lowered his head at that, his body shuddering. Kaelthos flinched. He first lowered his chin, then he bowed those shining eyes of his.

"Of course not, Farasee Asarah. The temple is...*pleased* to have your granfifi Ascend. You misunderstood my excitement."

"I misunderstand *nothing* that takes place in this temple, Farasee. Dishonor my blood again, and your bibi will be shedding his."

Farasee Kaelthos flexed his hands. A vein pulled taut in his neck, but he pressed his lips together, keeping them shut. Did I smile at Granmanmi putting those Zamarien rotpots in their place? Yes. Yes, I did.

"I know that's right," Ellabeth cheered below her breath.

She and I shimmied closer.

"Well, stars." A male scooted in close. I turned and saw it was Daelun. He was grinning from ear to ear. "I know not to get on her bad side." A wink down at me. "Or yours, either."

"Same here," said someone else from the right of us.

I looked past Daelun and grinned when I saw the familiar light green eyes.

"Omarion," I breathed, relieved to see he made it. Without thinking, I slipped by Ellabeth and wrapped my arms around his waist for a hug. He was so much taller than me. But when he hugged back, I didn't feel small. I felt safe.

Omarion smiled wide, his handsome face glowing without a single scratch. He looked completely refreshed. There wasn't a scratch on him. Sifting clearly did wonders for him at least. Ellabeth looked between Omarion and I, eyebrows wiggling.

"You two know each other?"

I cut a glare her way. I knew that tone. That look.

Blue-eyed gossip.

I shook my head subtly. She pouted in disappointment.

"Not really," I said out loud. "Omarion here saved me from being turned into Starfelliel grave food by his Highness of Blood Tharic."

"Tharic came after you in the waterfall?" Daelun said, eyes widening.

"More than once."

"What in all the stars...How could he focus on anything but breathing and getting through it?" Daelun shook his head. "Burning Zamariens."

"Burning Zamariens," Ellabeth and I chorused.

"Since you're all going to keep talking, I'm just going to jump in and say hi."

I turned my head. Next to Daelun was a stunning female, looking at me with jet black eyes and matching hair swaying in long strands down to her calves. She bat her long lashes, her brow quirking up as she crossed her arms over a plump bosom and jutted out her curvy hip. She was definitely going to turn heads in here.

"Hey," I said, waving with a few starlit sparks at my fingertips. "Safah—"

"Anathelle. Fifi of Amaryss. Granfifi of Asarah. Great-Granfifi of Linora. I know. We all know."

I flinched, crossing my own arms as I pulled away from Omarion.

"Well, since you know so much, who are you?"

The question was more direct than I meant it to be, but I didn't care.

"Isandra," she said, smiling. The curl to her lips made me nervous. "Isandra Marisol."

My jaw dropped, all distrust evaporating.

"*Marisol*?" I gawked.

Isandra flinched back, looking between me and Ellabeth. Ellabeth was grinning wide like she was delivering the best surprise.

"Doesn't your Papi own the Fruitatiya Cafe in the Feather Market?"

Isandra smiled sheepishly, but her black eyes burned with pride. "Yeah, he does."

I shoved her playfully then gripped her arms. "Do you have any idea how *obsessed* my family and I are with your mangogos?" My eyes widened as Isandra busted out laughing. "I could *live* off of them until I died, I swear!"

Isandra laughed prettily, her high cheekbones only amplifying her beauty. "Glad to know we keep you full and happy."

"The Fruitatiya heir?" I beamed at Ellabeth, eyes wide. She was ginning like a fool, too. She'd waited to introduce Isandra as a surprise and it worked.

The Marisols were legends in Port Emprarèl for their delicious fruit and juices. They also did fruit cakes that were simply addicting.

"Well, *my* family isn't as exciting, but hi anyway."

I looked and saw another female. She was shy, her eyes kept low, as she inched closer. She looked younger than us, though she had to be of age. We all were at least one thousand cycles, the age of maturing for angels.

"Oh?" I smiled her way hoping it would make her more comfortable. "And who are you? What family do you hail from?"

She bit her lip, looking around awkwardly.

Bless it. Poor thing was an extreme introvert. She seemed harmless enough. I could see why Ellabeth adopted her. And by the way she was now squeezing my hand, she wanted me to socially adopt the female, too.

"Amayah," she said quietly. "Amayah Kamron."

"You have the most stunning eyes, Amayah."

She looked up at me, blinking her pretty blue eyes. Her cheeks flushed, her warm brown skin coloring, as she shook out her long, coily blonde hair.

"Thanks." She bit her lip looking away, before looking back.

I smiled. I was scared of being too much for her. She looked ready to take flight any moment. I slid my gaze to Ellabeth. Her eyes spoke volumes. We had to keep Amayah close. She was gorgeous but quiet and looked like she scared easily. A prime target for beasts like Tharic.

I nodded. Ellabeth's eyes widened with glee.

I found the last male of the group hanging a bit to the back, eyes disinterested. I quickly took in the shoulder length, wavy black hair, lighter brown skin, honey eyes, and matching wings. He was tall and muscular but still nimble. Like a reed that belonged in the desert. When his eyes slid to mine, I found myself wanting to sit with him alone, to listen to his story for a long time.

"Kazemir," he said, without preamble. "Kazemir Nhanket."

I opened my mouth to speak, but he cut in.

"No family. They were all sent to the Seal Gate many cycles back. They're all dead. I'm only here to taste Fallen blood."

I nodded. "Fair. That's fair."

He nodded back and turned away. I think Kazemir and I would understand each other well. I went to open my mouth when another voice spoke out first.

"Wings high, Ascendants. Glad to see you're the ones who lived."

CHAPTER 10

A Farasee mounted the marbled dais at the front of the large auditorium. I trailed his movement, floored by how good looking he was.

"He's too sexy to be a Farasee," Ellabeth whispered in my ear.

I chortled into my hand. This was why she and I were best friends. Our brains processed the world in the same way.

"I know," I whispered back. "Look at those steel blue eyes."

"And his shock of cropped, ivory hair?" Ellabeth quipped, biting her lip. Her eyes followed the Farasee as he floated to the center of the dais, looking out over the room.

"And his muscles. Burning *stars*." I gave the Farasee a long once-over. His robes were loose, but still fit him in a way that highlighted all his best features. Unlike other male Farasees, instead of sandals, he wore golden boots. He looked more like a Legionnaire then a Farasee.

"I wouldn't mind being held by those," Isandra whispered underneath her breath. I looked her way and found her glaring at the Farasee's muscular arms. I giggled.

"I know, right?"

"You do know there's a name for this," Daelun cut in, sticking his head between us.

"Oh?" Ellabeth quipped. "Enlighten us."

"It's called *objectification*."

We all rolled our eyes.

"He should've thought about that before flying in here like a model," I said, eyes back on the Farasee.

"Congratulations and welcome to Temple Efysis. Please, have a seat."

We all obeyed, filing into the nearest cloudchairs we could find. I sat between Ellabeth and Omarion, crossing my legs underneath me, before looping my arm with Ellabeth's.

"Of the seven thousand of you who began the Ascent, three thousand of you have successfully completed the Starfellien Ascent. Well done. However, don't start celebrating yet. Let me be the first to say, the Ascent was only the beginning."

Grumbling broke out across the Ascendants, as mutuals turned to each other, discomforted by the words. I kept quiet, hanging on to every word spoken. The Farasee continued unfazed.

"I am Farasee Davithius Solman. I'm here to welcome you and give you an overview of what happens next from here."

Farasee Davithius crossed his arms. Ellabeth made a sound in her throat which made me laugh in silence.

"Thus far, you've unexpectedly met Farasee Asarah. A living legend not only among all the temples across the empyrean, but a remarkable Farasee who has worked diligently to establish new protocols that will better equip you should *you* one dawn Ascend as a Farasee. You've also met Farasees Esau and Kaelthos. But these two are not the only ones you will meet in your first season in the temple."

I watched Tharic's back stiffen when Farasee Davithius spoke highly of Granmanmi, but said nothing of consequence for Kaelthos. My lips curled into a smile. I hoped Davithius was *my* Presbitari.

"You're all officially the newest Ascendants of Temple Efysis. Survive the first trial, and you will become Disciples."

He paused to let his words sink in. After a moment, he continued.

"Your first season in the temple will be challenging. That's on purpose. Every moment that pushes you, stretches you, develops you, is by intentional design. We will require much of you, and we will only accept the *best* of you into the Order."

Farasee Davithius overlooked our group, as if searching for something. Those steel blue eyes beamed in the quiet while Granmanmi and Farasee Kaelthos waited for him to continue. Finally Davithius seemed to come to a decision.

"At this time, you will all be brought to our main cathedral for collective studies. You will be divvied up into the four

Efysien Orders. You will also be given your designated Order Presbitaris and..."

He paused. He slid his gaze to Granmanmi. She nodded once, before her eyes came to land on me. I wrinkled my nose wondering what that exchange meant.

"This dawn all of you will be temple-mated."

"We will *what?*" an angel from the front screamed. He shot out of his seat, his eyes bulging. He wasn't the only one disturbed by this.

I surveyed the commotion. I looked at the Ascendants then at Granmanmi. Then Davithius. The Farasees were unmoving. Even Kaelthos looked placid, watching the Ascendants protest. He rolled his eyes as if he was listening to a youngling throw a tantrum. Which...with how old Kaelthos was, he basically *was* listening to younglings throw tantrums.

Granmanmi observed me. She seemed pleased to see I hadn't reacted. I couldn't blame the Ascendants though. Bonding, at any level, was no small thing. Once a bond was sealed, breaking it could lead to potential death for both angels.

"Are you done whining?" Davithius barked. "Want to go back home to your parentlings?" It got quiet. "I didn't think so. Now listen up, all of you will get up, file out in an orderly fashion, and follow the trail of stars until you get to the cathedral. Then you'll wait to be placed in your Orders, and be temple-mated, before you're dismissed. Got it?"

"Awoui, Farasee Davithius!" we said collectively, slapping our wings together once in obeisance.

"Good. Wings high. File out!"

Ellabeth and I let go of each other, floating into the air along with all the other Ascendants. We all shuffled into a neat file, flying through the massive doors that opened to the right.

The ornate walls of the temple were covered in scrolls full of the holy verses. They filled the walls between prayer shawls that hung like enormous curtains, from floor to ceiling. Everything was gold or ivory. Golden floors and walls. Ivory decor and furniture. This hallway was also lined on either side with high standing pillars of gold covered in burning, iridescent flames.

After flying across, we were led through gilded double doors that led to an outdoor courtyard. I gasped at the opulence. I thought where the Sifting towers were located was resplendent.

I was wrong.

The courtyard looked like one built for kings. Marble white floors with golden trim covered every inch of space so far I couldn't see where it ended in the distance. There were a litany of lofty cathedrals, some in a long line of rows, and others tucked away in pockets, all finished at the top with expertly crafted spires. Every cathedral held an open flame above it. All flames were iridescent or ivory.

Spotting the trail of stars, we collectively obeyed Farasee Davithius, flying along the trail as it wound us through the grounds of the temple. As we flew, we reached a fountain that left me in awe. Before I could ogle for too long, we were flying to the largest cathedral just ahead, perched at what had to be the very center of Temple Efysis.

Every Ascendant flew in silence. We were lost in the marvel of the temple. I'd never pictured this when Manmi told me stories about living here when she was Ascending.

Not a flower or shrub wasn't perfectly trimmed. Not a glass window wasn't clean to perfection. Every ethèrlamp was filled with magical light. There were more fountains, angelic statues, and endless billows curling through the differing cathedrals.

"Oh my stars," Ellabeth breathed.

"Mhm." I nodded, at a complete loss for words. "Whew."

Milling throughout the temple grounds were a group of wingless figures covered from head to toe in russet gowns made entirely out of linked chains. They kept their eyes low and stayed out of the way of us angels as we passed. I recognized them immediately. The gods and goddesses.

I thought of Serafina, Natalie, and Caliana. My hearts twinged with sadness. I missed them already. They were slaves to the temple, but they'd started becoming more than just quiet strangers to me.

One female looked up. I caught her hazel eyes. My hearts nearly shattered at the sheer wells of sorrow I found in them.

I wanted to know her name. Her story.

I could just make out her long honey colored hair bound beneath the chains, the headdress wrapped around her head and down the length of her body.

I looked back. The goddess still watched me as I flew by.

Her eyes burned with a fire. A fire I found myself wanting to ignite.

I looked away, following the mass of Ascendants. We flew through the open, gilded doors of the cathedral, past more pillars with endless burning fire, and into a colossal amphitheater chamber that took my breath away.

"Holy burning stars," Daelun breathed. "*Whoa.*"

"Well," Omarion exclaimed, floating close to me. "I never imagined...this."

"I can't believe this is our new home. Where we'll have our classes," Amayah whispered.

Kazemir said nothing, his honey eyes skimming the entire chamber as if he was hunting for all the ways he'd escape if he needed to.

"I for one can get used to this," Isandra said, beaming at the opulence. "If we're going to be bound to this temple until we Ascend as Apprenti, Rabbini, or Farasee, we may as well do it while living well."

I snorted. That was one way to look at it.

I looked around, fighting tears.

Manmi was here. She Ascended *here*.

Ellabeth squeezed my hand. We looked at each other, squealing quietly.

"Feels surreal doesn't it?" Her aquamarine eyes were glowing with excitement.

"This is going to be incredible. I can feel it."

"Ascendants," Davithius called out. "File in."

To where exactly? It's not like we knew where to go. I

scooted close to Ellabeth. Without a word, Daelun, Omarion, and Kazemir formed a half circle around us females. I smiled at the thoughtful gesture, as more of the male Ascendants pressed in around us. Then the doors of the Cathedral closed shut.

The elephantine chamber was jaw-dropping. Ironically, it looked like it could easily hold the seven thousand of us who began the Ascent.

There was a massive, circular platform at the center, of course made of gold, with a beaming pillar of light and fire shining from the floor to the open ceiling above. On either side of the platform were other elevated circular platforms covered in cloudchairs.

More platforms like this filled the chamber. And each had a circumference of light surrounding it. Along every wall, rising level after level, were endless rows of cloudchairs. They hovered off the ground behind desks made of the finest gold, overlaid with a thick crystal glass.

Farasee Davithius, along with Farasee Kaelthos, flew to the center of the dais. I noticed Granmanmi wasn't with them. I tried looking for her but there were listless angels everywhere blocking my view.

"Ascendants, listen up," Davithius said, amplifying his voice with his ethèr so we could all hear him without him shouting. "The Order is divided into the following: Incense Order, Scroll Order, Bond Order, and Manna Order. Now, lift your wings. All of you were tagged for your designated Order. Look around this amphitheater. There are four sections. Manna is the back left. Bond is across it to the back right. Scrolls are to the front left, and Incense is to the front right. You have exactly five wing claps to find your Orders section and sit down, or your entire Order will be relegated to cleaning the stalls of the Pegasi with the gods for the next month."

The very thought made me want to vomit. Pegasi dung was the worst to clean up. Papi made me do it twice, both times out of punishment, and I'd hated the job since.

Quickly I spread my wings and felt a rush of burning flame course through my body. Then I smelled something eerily like... smoke. My wings itched for me to go to the right. A loud clap of wings thundered in the amphitheater.

"One."

I snapped my head to the right, where all the seats for Incense Order were positioned. I began flying in its direction. Another clap of wings.

"Two."

I flew quicker, finding the scent of smoke growing. I was definitely designated to Incense Order. Another clap.

"Three."

I rushed over, hustling into one of the cloudchairs toward the bottom row that put me in better sight of the main platform. I rushed into a seat, my hearts racing. I whipped around looking for Ellabeth, just as she threw herself into the seat next to me. Thank the stars! We'd been designated to the same Order.

Another clap. Louder this time.

"Four!"

More and more Ascendants tossed themselves into cloud-chairs, the billows swaying as the angels tumbled into them, rushing to sit before they were out of time. My grin stretched when I saw Isandra, Amayah, Omarion, Daelun, and Kazemir all file into seats close to Ellabeth and I.

The final clap.

"Five!"

We all turned to see three angels rushing over to Scroll Order. I scanned their section and found Tharic in that Order. My grin split my face in half.

"Looks like Zamarien is wiping Pegasi dung for the next month."

Daelun snorted behind me. All around us, the angels started laughing. As the three angels were about to enter Scroll Order's section, Tharic shot into the air with two other angels. The three of them drew their ethèr, and shot their powers into the angels before they crossed into Scroll Order's section. Within moments the three angels dropped dead.

I covered my mouth, gasping in horror. Without a second thought, Tharic and the two beasts siphoned the spirits of the dead angels from their bodies, pulled them into the air, wrapped the cords of their ethèr around the living spirits, and crushed them into nothing, permanently killing the three angels. My jaw hung.

"What the actual..." Isandra's words trailed off.

I felt ill.

"Holy stars," an angel a few rows behind me choked out.

"Burning Tazuniels, Zamariens, and Branais. Beasts. All of them."

While we all stared, Tharic and the other two angels smugly sat back down. So, these were the angels responsible for there being so few females who Ascended. I marked them, mentally noting my growing list of males to avoid in this temple.

The doors to the cathedral opened. Gods and goddesses filed in. I scanned them quickly. None of them were Serafina, Natalie, or Caliana. I frowned, watching them as they worked. They quickly grabbed the bodies, wrapped them in feathery linens, and dragged them out, shutting the doors behind them.

"Ascendants!"

I snapped my head to the main platform. Farasee Kaelthos floated to the front, beaming with cruel pride.

"Welcome to Temple Efysis. You will learn that nothing in the temple is given. It is earned. Including mercy." He grinned. "Let your Ascension begin."

CHAPTER 11

I blinked at the floor, visualizing the dead. Their spirits would never be filed. They would never have a proper burial. They were snuffed out, just like that. For sport.

The gods took away their bodies but their blood remained. Some of their feathers had also fallen, now stuck to the golden ichor tainting the marble floors. The winged tips of my ears twitched. Farasee Kaelthos allowed the shock to sink in, relishing in our surprise and horror.

"You're all Ascendants seeking to Ascend until you reach the Farasee Order. To do so, you will have to prove you are worthy. And while we demand obedience, we will always expect your sacrifice. Understood?" Farasee Kaelthos bellowed.

As an orchestrated unit, we all clapped our wings once, in uniformity and in accord.

"You all have learned I am Farasee Kaelthos Zamarien. I

come from a long line of Farasees who have served the Order for generations since the end of the Fifth Age. It is with great pride and honor that we serve. Only the best may Ascend. We have yet to see if that will include you. Furthermore, during your first season of Ascension, I will also be one of your Presbitaris. I am the Presbitari over Scroll Order. I will facilitate your classes on *The Principles of Righteous Living and Judgment.*"

"Righteous Judgment? *Him?* No burning way," Daelun muttered.

I snorted at the irony. That class was going to be a joke.

"You now know Farasee Davithius Solman," Kaelthos continued, gesturing to Davithius who was blatantly ignoring Kaelthos. "I'm sure you can tell he looks born and bred for war." At this, Davithius smiled. "It's because he is." Kaelthos's eyes flashed. "While he is a Farasee that does the best he can—" Davithius slid a cutting glare at Kaelthos but said nothing. Kaelthos continued, "He also serves with the empyrean's Legionnaires. Incense Order, meet your Presbitari."

"*Yes,*" I blurted out before I could stop myself. Multiple angels across Incense Order let out their own, tiny outbursts of joy. Davithius looked our way chuckling. I didn't care if he was difficult. At least the difficulty came with a pretty face.

"Definitely looking forward to class," Ellabeth whispered.

"*Never* missing a lesson for sure." I giggled behind a hand.

Davithius snuck a glance at Ellabeth and I as if he could hear us. His posture hadn't changed. He kept a wide stance and folded arms. But his eyes were dancing, and that mouth of his was twitching.

"Here we have Taevia Othru."

Kaelthos gestured to the Farasee—who has perched on the other side of the dais—without even looking at her. I wanted to spit in his eyes for the lack of respect. All because she was a female. And an Anathelle by blood.

I looked at my Tati, impressed with her self-control. She was four hundred cycles older than Manmi, but didn't look a dawn older than me. Tati Taevia ignored him, holding her chin high. Her pin straight black hair hung to her shoulders, not a flyaway in sight, as she blinked her dazzling hazel eyes with traces of deep purple in them. Her dark skin was beautiful under the amphitheater lights beneath her plush, ivory Farasee robes.

"Taevia here—"

"*Farasee* Taevia," Granmanmi hissed from behind Kaelthos. Tati Taevia was her second born and not to be disrespected.

I was thankful Granmanmi was still here. She seemed to be the only one able to keep Kaelthos in check. He was proving to be no better than swine. My distaste for him was growing by the second.

"*Farasee* Taevia," he repeated, mocking Granmanmi. My neck grew hot. "Is the Presbitari for Bond Order."

The males of Bond Order began protesting.

"No burning way. A *female?*"

Tati Taevia didn't take the bait. She kept her chin high

and remained calm. Stars. How long would it take me to master such poise?

"*Farasee* Taevia will also facilitate all of your Spiritscape excursions, should you Ascend past this first season."

"All of our *what*?" Daelun whispered.

Hèls if I knew. That little instruction went right over my head.

"And lastly, we have...*Farasee* Katia."

I looked at my Kouzi—my elder cousin—and smiled to myself. I remember when she was told she'd Ascend. She fought against it. She just wanted to become a wingmate and a Manmi. But Granmanmi made her Ascend. Wed never heard from, or about her, since. I honestly thought something had happened to her. Seeing her now, as a Farasee, filled me with pride.

"*Farasee* Katia is the Presbitari of Manna Order." Kaelthos looked around him. "Presbitaris, join your Order. Farasee Esau, come and take your liberty."

As one, Farasees Kaelthos, Davithius, Taevia, and Katia spread their wings, and flew to the four corners of the amphitheater. They floated to the small platform at the front of their Orders with several cloudchairs and full goblets with gilded platters full of delicious looking treats. Once the Presbitaris joined their Orders, Farasee Esau flew forward. He looked malicious as a Fallen angel, this one.

"He looks like a Fallen," Ellabeth whispered.

"I was *just* thinking the same thing," I exclaimed, looking her way. "It's the scowl isn't it?"

"Definitely the scowl." Ellabeth wrinkled her nose. "He doesn't look like he has a kind bone in his body."

I shook my head. "Not one. It's crazy because he didn't look like that when we were about to Ascend. Now he looks terrifying."

"By now you should know that I am Farasee Esau Nakumba," Farasee Esau announced. He was one of the few Farasees, like Davithius, whose robes looked like fighting ones. His tunic had no sleeves, revealing arms made for wrestling dragons. His jet black hair hung past his shoulders contrasting his sun-kissed skin and glowing amber eyes. They almost looked like two small pools of churning magma. His scowl made me shiver.

"This cathedral is your Sanctuary for your classes. Beyond class, you must endure trials. The Starfellien Ascent was the start. And no. You will *not* be warned about your trials in advance. When it is time to begin, you will receive a scrollport with instructions. That's it." A pause. "Now, look at your desks."

We all obeyed. Beneath the glass, encased in a crystal box, were two emblems, both shaped like smoke. One was a signet ring while the other was a clasp made to attach to our robes. There were other items inside the crystal-encased box. A scrollbook, scrollmap, and a thorn shaped like a diamond.

The scrollbook had our curriculum while the scrollmap showed how to get around the temple and the Citadel—the cloudy city. I'd heard stories about it, but I didn't know too much. Then there was the thorn. I ogled the thing, not even wanting to touch it. What could it possibly mean?

Daelun pulled out his thorn, also in the shape of a diamond, staring at it confused. "This has two letters on it. IV." He looked at us, puzzled.

"Mine have DS on it," Ellabeth said.

"Mine has MS," Amayah chimed in.

"AR," Isandra commented, her face riddled with confusion.

"VM," said Omarion.

"CK." Kazemir waved his thorn like a flag he wanted to break in half. Everyone turned to look at me.

"Well?" Ellabeth prodded.

I looked at my thorn. "QV."

"I swear this is so weird," Isandra, quipped.

"Most of your items—gifts from the Temple for your education and survival—should be self-explanatory. The thorn has another purpose."

"So we're all just going to pretend he didn't just say *survival*?" Ellabeth breathed, her voice rising an octave.

"Oh, we heard," I said.

Kazemir snorted, but said nothing more.

"You're all in your Orders and you have your Presbitaris. Your Presbitari will break you up into your Dominions and Choirs. There are three Dominions and Seven Choirs per Order. Pray you like each other because you will remain together for the entirety of your Ascension." Esau looked at the Orders. "Presbitaris, you may begin."

Davithius flew into the air. "Incense Order, listen up. This is going to be simple. I went through your exams and matched you accordingly. When I call your names, group up and make it quick. I don't want to be here all dawn."

Davithius began calling out names. Angels started shuffling. This was annoying. They couldn't have grouped us *before* we sat down and got comfortable? Or was splitting us up now the whole point?

Without preamble, Davithius flew through the names of First Dominion, and it's first Six Choirs. "Incense Order, First Dominion, Seventh Choir," he called out.

I was about to tune him out.

"Safah Anethelle!"

I snapped my head up. Grabbing my belongings, I quickly threw Ellabeth a look before flying to the front row where seven seats remained for the final angels left in First Dominion.

"Ellabeth Riventhelle!"

"Oh thank the stars!" I cried, spinning around.

Ellabeth bounced with happiness as she grabbed her belongings and flew straight to my side. The seat to my right had the letters QV inscribed on it. But the desk to my left said ER. I got it now. Ellabeth Riventhelle. I eyed the QV to my right once again, my trepidation for whoever would fill the seat growing with each passing second.

"I was about to rage," she said, throwing herself in the cloudchair.

"Seriously, same." I nodded.

"Daelun Shenric. Amayah Kamron. Isandra Marisol. Omarion Wylium. Kazemir Nhanket," Farasee Davithius called in rapid succession. I grinned wide as our newly bonded group found itself close to each other again.

"This entire place was about to be flooded with a devastating whirlwind if we'd been split up," Daelun said.

I laughed as Davithius ran through the names quickly, going through Second Dominion and all its seven Choirs, and then Third Dominion and its seven Choirs. When he was done, he flew back to his seat, crossed his arms, and perched his legs on the banister in front of him.

"And now, for your temple-mates," said Farasee Esau once every Order was seated in their proper Dominions and Choirs.

The auditorium fell deathly quiet. We all sat up, our ears pricked. A bond was no small thing. Whoever these Farasees had bonded me to would have to be an angel I could function with or else it would be absolute Hèls trying to break the bond.

"This season every Order here will partner with a Legion from Azarath Academy."

My jaw dropped, as I shot out of my seat with everyone else. "We are *what?*"

CHAPTER 12

"Have the Farasees gone nuts?"

"The Legions of *Azarath*? Is this a joke?"

"Don't Fallenspawn go to Azarath Academy? Are they coming here, too?"

The Ascendants were vehement. Everything inside of me wanted to erupt. Azarath had Fallenspawn in attendance. They were angels raised since their youngling cycles by the Fallen High King and his Shadowlords. These were the very angels who helped breach the Seal Gate. Because they tempered with a realm gate, my Manmi was dead. I fumed, unable to contain my mounting rage.

"Sit *DOWN*!" Farasee Esau barked.

We did no such thing. Instead, more Ascendants shot out of their seats. "Why in the stars are we partnering with a bunch of pompous Legionnaires from Azarath Academy?" an Ascendant screamed.

“All of you will shut your mouths and sit down *now*.” Farasee Esau slammed his wings into the dais before flooding the Sanctuary chamber with fiery heat so dry I started coughing. As we grew quiet and sat down, he didn’t relent. The heat was insufferable. I started choking, wrapping my hands around my neck.

“Interrupt me again and I will clip your wings and feed them to the stareagles for firstfast!” Esau finally relented, drawing back his ethèr. “As I said, you *will* be partnered with the four Legions of Azarath Academy. Klubari Legion, Hartari Legion, Saixari Legion, and Xadari Legion.”

He looked out over all the Ascendants. Content we were done with the outbursts, he continued. “It is time for you to meet the Azarath Academy Legionnaires.”

As a collective, we snapped our heads to the ceiling. A rumble overhead shook the entirety of the amphitheater. My nostrils flared as a wave of Dragèth began descending onto the roof of the cathedral.

The dragons were enormous. They landed on the roof with brute force. The amphitheater trembled beneath their weight. Their talons made screeching noises that unnerved me. I clamped my hands over my ears, unable to withstand the high-pitched sound. On the back of each dragon was a Legionnaire clad in raven-black leather robes from neck to foot.

“Ascendants,” said Farasee Esau. “Above you will see the Dragèth. Each of these dragons are *parilielthai* of the Azarathien Legionnaires. The same way we Farasees bond to

Pegasi Shifters, the Legionnaires of Azarath bond to Dragèth Shifters. They would rather remain in their dragon forms, so they will not be shifting to descend into the cathedral. At least not this dawn. That doesn't mean they never will."

The Sanctuary was dead quiet. I frowned with displeasure.

Azarath Legionnaires were arrogant, pompous, bloodthirsty warriors. Whether they were Hallowed of Fallenspawn, I had a strong dislike of them all.

Not to mention, they didn't belong here. They had no business being in the holiest temple in the entire empyrean. What were the Farasees thinking?

"Now," Esau continued, unfazed by the quiet. "Meet the Legionnaires."

The angels atop their dragons dismounted and began flying into the cathedral in one fell swoop. They were swift and flew with boldness. Pride. Adorned in leather fighting robes and boots, they soared into the amphitheater like they owned the place.

"Wait a second," Isandra breathed. "They're not all Seraphim, guys."

"What?" Amayah squeaked.

I blinked.

The first Legion flew in. Each had seven pairs of wings with blood-red sigils woven into their leathers. The next Legion also had seven pairs of wings but they had midnight blue sigils in their leathers. The third Azarath Legion flew in, again, every angel having seven pairs of wings. These had emerald green sigils in their leathers.

I was confused. What was Isandra on about? All of these angels were of Seraphim rank. Was she seeing—

The final wave flew in clad in raven black. There was something different about their leathers. Something of a richer quality. Only one of their angels, at the very front, was actually in a ridiculous three-piece suit with emerald embellishments. Of all the Legionnaires, he was the sole angel without fighting robes. I was about to turn away when I counted their wings.

They only had six pairs.

No. No way.

I counted again.

Six wing pairs. Not *seven*.

These angels weren't of Seraphim rank. They were Mortents—one rank beneath Seraphim. And while Seraphim angels were Elementals, Mortents were Benders. Specifically, bodily benders. It was rumoured some Mortents had outlawed abilities like brain bending and bone bending. Even worse, some had the two most horrifying abilities of all: blood and spirit bending.

Azarathien Legionnaires who were Mortents were cataclysmically dangerous. Worse, these angels were also Fallenspawns.

I stilled, my blood turning to ice. Heads started swinging in my direction. It was no secret. My Manmi was dead because of these angels. Their hatred for the Farasee Order, for the

Empràr, for the Empyrean, resulted in the death of an Anathelle. My *favorite* Anathelle. I started trembling as hot, blistering rage ignited my blood.

Ellabeth was seething next to me. "What in all the created realms throughout the Elledelle universe are Fallenspawn doing *here?*"

Several angels screamed at the top of their lungs, shooting out of their seats. Unmitigated rage exploded in across the Sanctuary.

"They're the ones who breached the Seal Gate."

"Clip them all!"

"You're bonding us to *them*? I'd rather burn in the Hèls they came from!"

"Safah?" someone called out.

I barely heard them. I couldn't move. Couldn't breathe. I glared at the Mortent Legionnaires. I glared at their arrogant smiles. The easy confidence in their shoulders. The carelessness of their posture. As if they weren't the scum we were raised to protect our homes, our empyrean, against.

Manmi.

Manmi was commissioned to the Seal Gate because of Fallenspawn.

Manmi had to fight against fallen angels because of Fallenspawn.

Manmi was *dead* because of the Fallenspawn.

I was shaking, unable to catch my breath.

"*Safah.*" Ellabeth held on to my arm, trying to soothe me.

It wasn't working.

I glared at the pieces of filth who thought it okay to sacrifice a Farasee to their Fallen King. I would never hear her laugh again because of them. I would never feel her hands gently brush through my hair or hear her sing as she made our families favorite cakes. I would never see her eyes roll as we did something purposefully dumb just to irritate her.

Manmi was gone.

But these Fallenspawn still lived.

I seethed in the cloudchair. Starfire began bleeding into my palms without me thinking. Before I could stop myself, I was silhouetted in my power, ready to explode. They'd shed my Manmi's blood. And this dawn, I had no problem being the one to shed theirs.

My neck prickled under the weight of someone watching me. Was it Granmanmi? Kaelthos? Esau?

"Ascendant Safah Anathelle, we will not be flaming our temple-mates this dawn."

Every head in the Sanctuary turned to look at me. When the Mortents heard my surname, their jeweled eyes began to glow as profound hatred colored their faces with wrath. Everyone stared at me.

But I was looking at *him*.

It wasn't the shock of perfectly groomed, pitch black hair that got me. Or even his emerald-green eyes that glittered like jewels. It was the *script*. All over his hands. His neck. Down his chest where the button was undone. I wanted to positively *scream*.

Slowly I pushed out of my cloudchair glaring at him. I

bared my teeth practically foaming at the mouth in anger. My nostrils flared as my vision started going black with stars. Starfire thrummed in my hands like whirlpools. I could see nothing past my rage. Only *one* angel—Hallowed or Fallen—had a curse inscribed into them like that.

"Ascendants, listen closely for your pairings," Esau continued when he realized we would no longer remain seated.

Especially me.

"Klubari Legion, noted by their emerald sigils, will be paired with Manna Order. Those with deep blue sigils are of the Saixari Legion and will be with Bond Order."

Curses broke out in the Sanctuary, all consequences be damned. The Ascendants were furious. Esau couldn't care less. He carried on as if none the wiser.

"Those with red sigils are Hartari Legion and they will be paired with Scroll Order."

No. Bleeding. Way.

That meant...

Ellabeth squeezed my arm, holding me steady. The Sanctuary started turning into starlight as my power began seeping into my vision. I was gasping for air, utterly vexed. I held the gaze of the demon with the jade eyes, and he held mine.

We were locked in a battle of will, and *I* would be the one to win. Shadows began seeping into his hands. Pooling at his feet. Wrapping around his neck.

So he was a Shadow Bender. *Great.*

The more shadows he drew on, the more I pulled on starfire.

"And those in all black besides the exception," Esau said. "Are indeed all Fallenspawn who have been conscripted to Azarath Academy, making up the entirety of the Xadari Legion. They will be paired with Incense Order."

"*No*!" I screamed, slamming my palms into my desk so hard I was surprised it didn't shatter. Starfire burst from my hands causing sparks to explode all around me. I saw red as I heaved, unable to breathe. The Sanctuary began to swim in my vision.

All around me, Incense Order was raging. The majority began *fyusing*—the angelic ability of morphing entirely into the elemental power we were born with in our bloodstreams. Screams exploded from our Order as they demanded the Farasees fix this decision.

Presbitari Davithius only shrugged as he looked at Esau.

"If they must, let them fight it out."

Esau grinned, crossing his arms, watching our Order fall apart with unfettered rage. Farasee Esau spoke on as if he relished in this chaos. As if he lived for it.

"Each of you have initials inscribed on the desk and seat next to you. That seat belongs to your individual partner from the Azarath Legion. And yes, this also means they are now your temple-mate."

I grew unnaturally still. Sound seemed far away as I kept staring at the Fallenspawn in the posh suit, who in turn stared at me. His black wings were tucked into his spine, fading at their tips into the deepest shades of emerald that almost matched his bright eyes. He floated in front of Xadari Legion like a statue, entirely frozen.

"Every Legionnaire has a thorn embedded in their palms... except for the Mortents. Theirs are on their bodies from their neck down to their hands." Esau spoke over the cacophony, giving up on quieting us down. "Raise your thorns Ascendants! The angel it calls to is the angel you are temple-mated to for the entirety of your Ascension. Break your bond before then and forfeit your Ascension!"

Not a single Ascendant raised their thorns. The Legionnaires snorted, rolling their eyes. They were a sea of black opposite our sea of gold.

They were a stain.

They did *not* belong here.

To my dismay, our thorns began rising on their own. I watched mine lift itself, spinning around. The stupid thing began making its way through the mayhem. Every Ascendants thorn was now traveling through the Sanctuary, finding its match. My stomach rolled. All around me anger exploded like bombs, then faded to silence, as the angels accepted their fates. The Sanctuary got quieter and quieter until...

"Ascendant Safah Eloise Anathelle."

I glared at the jade-eyed demon refusing to turn to Farasee Esau. My hearts raced. I tried to calm down. But I couldn't. Everything in me screamed for vengeance. For *violence.*

"What kind of living Hèls have we been conned into,"

Ellabeth whispered. "There is no burning way this is actually happening."

"*Rot*," Daelun and Omarion hissed at the same time.

I blinked away starlight from my vision. One moment, the Fallenspawn was floating down below close to the dais. The next, the demon was floating in front of me like an immovable statue, glowering at me with a hatred that made my skin burn. Farasee Esau spoke loud for the entire Sanctuary to hear as starfire erupted in my blood.

"Ascendant Safah, meet your new temple-mate, Quazar Valoryen." A pause. "The Fallen Prince."

CHAPTER 13

I glared at the Fallen Prince. Chiseled jawline. Thick black hair. Full lips. Emerald eyes. A gloriously handsome face that could rival the beauty of a newborn star.

The reason Manmi was dead.

I narrowed my eyes at him.

He glowered at me.

Suspenseful silence charged the air of the Sanctuary.

The Prince blinked. Leaned down. Took a sniff, wrinkling his nose at me, as if he smelled something foul.

"So *you* are the fifi I've had the unfortunate pleasure of hearing so much about."

His eyes were crystal pools of jade thrashing with a shadowy storm. There was an annoyingly satisfying bass that rumbled through my chest at the baritone of his voice.

I slowly sat down and began tapping my nails on the glass of the desk. I took a deep, long breath, giving him a once over, completely disgusted at his sight. I snorted, unimpressed with the Prince of the Hèls.

"Pale-faced demon," I seethed, sucking my teeth. "Just like your ash-rotting Papi." I tilted my head. "You shouldn't be here, Cursed One. A bottomless grave suits you better."

Quazar bared his teeth, thrust out his wings, and shoved them beneath my desk, then beneath my chair. After, he proceeded to lift the desk *and* chair, and flip them over with me in it.

"Safah!" Ellabeth screamed, as gasps broke out among the Ascendants.

As the desk flipped, I *fyused*. In a blink, my powers erupted, turning me into a starry hurricane. I had two swords of starfire in my hands by the time the desk crashed onto the floor.

I lunged for the Prince with lightning speed. The tip of the starry blade caught him in the wing, slicing across his talon. He snarled, flinching back.

"Quazar!" one of the Fallenspawn yelled.

I swung again. The Prince flexed his hands. Shadows pooled from his palms, as his emerald eyes grew brighter still. He looked feral, like a crazed dog. I threw up a star shield around me as Ellabeth screamed something I couldn't hear.

I shielded myself too late.

A large shadow encircled me. It was tall, with slender curves, long hair, and seven sets of wings. I stared at it, finding the shadow eerily familiar.

"Wait a second," I breathed. It took me too long to realize the shadowy silhouette was *me*.

Blessed lights.

I swung my starry sword and found myself tumbling in growing darkness that spread across the entire Sanctuary.

"What in the fresh Hèls is this?" someone cried.

The shadows grew, flooding the Sanctuary as the Prince snuffed out every inch of light. Then he grabbed hold of my shadow. One moment I was flying into the air, making to swing for his head. The next, I was moving involuntarily. My arms bent at awkward angles. My legs wouldn't respond. I jerked my body, but I couldn't move. I screamed when I felt a bone snap. Then another.

Focus, Safah! I chided myself. *Bend, but do not break. Burn, but never bleed.*

I breathed through the pain of my broken bones. Then I tumbled into myself—into my spirit—letting anger consume me. Starfire burned wildly throughout my body. I imagined getting a grip on my shadow, pulling it back to me, and taking control of myself.

Then I erupted. I spun around and slammed my wings, talons first, into the Prince's chest. Like windmills, I whipped my wings in rapid succession, beating him again and again.

While he pulled back to deflect, I jerked, spiraled, and kicked him in the chest, sending him flying across the amphitheater. Without taking a breath, I lunged after him. When I reached him, I punched him in the face. His head snapped back with a satisfying crack.

Manmi was dead because of *him*. Rage boiled my blood. Before he could recover, I swung again. This time, he was ready. A blast of shadows collided into my chest, sending me flying back into the desk. As I rolled, he grabbed hold of my ankle with a strand of shadow and yanked. Hard. I screamed as I was jerked into the air. The Prince grabbed my arm, jerked me around, pinned both arms behind my back between my wings, and slammed me down onto the glass. Face first.

I snapped my head back, head-butting him in his face. I heard the crack at his forehead. Felt the drip of his hot blood onto my neck, but he wouldn't let go. I let my starfire heat my body, turning me into an open flame as I thrashed in his grip.

Shadows began pouring into my ears. My eyes. Darkness filled every crevice. I felt like I was drowning in a sea of black without any surface or pit.

"Get *off*," I screamed.

"*No*," Quazar seethed, his voice—deep, rich, and a little crazed—breathing closer to my ear than I liked. "There's a long list of sins your Matriarchs purchased that *you* will pay for by the time I'm through with you."

Fear. That was unadulterated fear snaking through my chest and growing by the second. He was too big. Too strong. I struggled against him but the Fallen Prince had me beat. And he knew it.

"Enough!"

Quazar and I were ripped apart by fiery tendrils, before we were slapped down into the desk that had been put back in its place. I was forced to *fyuse* back to my Seraphim skin. Before blood could trickle down my temple, I drew on starfire, stitching myself together.

I didn't look at the creature beside me. I wouldn't focus on how he was the spawn of the Hèls but had the face of a god. Or how he fought like a tyrant at war and yet I could tell he was holding back. Being gentle even. Which made no sense.

I didn't want to think about how he smelled like mint and sandalwood, and a hint of ash. I wouldn't give him any time by acknowledging his existence. This temple would crumble into nothing before I stooped so low.

"Now that you all have your temple-mates, your Ascension can truly begin."

The tension in the room was our oxygen. There wasn't an angel—outside of the Farasee Order—who didn't look like they were ready to rip heads and shred feathers.

I glanced at Scroll Order to see who Tharic got paired with. When I found him, I smirked. At least Tharic Zamarien had been given what he deserved. He was temple-mated to some female from Hartari Order who looked like she was a breath away from ripping out his eyes and feeding them to her dragon.

"Before we began our Ascent," I whispered, leaning over to Ellabeth who was glaring past me at the Fallen Prince. "What was it you said? That this would be some special kind of Hèls?"

A snort rang out behind me. "This is a special kind of Hèls alright," Daelun seethed. "The *worst* kind."

"I just knew I should have stayed home," Amayah hissed from somewhere to our right. Isandra was bouncing her leg with an energy that matched the fury coloring her face. Stars. How were we supposed to actually get through the season like this?

Against our will, every Ascendant in this Sanctuary had been temple-mated to a Legionnaire from Azarath Academy. And every last one of us hated it.

I fumed, bouncing my leg like Isandra, wanting *out* of this suffocating cathedral. Next to me, the devil called a prince growled below his breath, equally in a tizzy of rage.

"You each have your scrollmaps," Farasee Esau announced. "Use them. Find your wingtowers. Get acquainted with your new home...and your new *blended* Order."

Snarls and hisses broke out at this. One thing was evident. The holiest place in the empyrean was about to turn us into the most decrepit beings alive. Blood would be shed this dawn. Enough to start a war.

"Dismissed!"

Farasee Esau clapped his wings like thunder. Then he whipped his wings around himself, spun around, and disappeared.

PART TWO

"The Saccrent tells us, "Angels do not live by Manna alone, but by all the written words that come from the Infinite himself." If you choose to live by your stomach, we're given no other choice. We will choose to let you die by it."

Accords of the Farasees, Scroll of Mitari 4:4, Fifth Age

CHAPTER 14

The seven suns beamed high in the sky across the Efysis islet. Beyond the peaks of the Temple, I could see small bits and pieces of the Citadel. I was thankful to be out of Sanctuary and have the rest of the dawn to myself. I needed time to process and heal.

"So we need to head to the front building and then turn, right?" Daelun asked, squinting at his scrollmap.

"No," Isandra said, snatching it from him. "Follow the feathers. See?" She pointed at the center of the map. "The feathers are dancing along this line."

I peered over her shoulder and looked as a golden feather flew through an exact, realistic, replica of the temple grounds.

"Then let's go," Ellabeth said, grumbling. "After that Sanctuary my soul needs a bath."

"That is the truth." I nodded.

Seventh Choir floated into the air and began flying.

"You imbeciles know we're coming, too. Right?"

We all stopped flying and turned around. The female Xadarien who spoke looked eerily like the Fallen Prince, Quazar. She had his same black hair, bright emerald eyes, sun-kissed skin, and six pairs of black wings fading to emerald at their tips.

Then there was her Fallenspawn mark. Thorns crawling up the right side of her neck, down her right arm all the way to her hand. I blinked at her before looking at the rest of Seventh Choir.

Isandra narrowed her eyes. "Coming *where*? Cause it sure as the stars isn't with us."

Kazemir and Omarion crossed their arms, spreading their legs in a wide stance. Ellabeth's hands were beginning to fill with water bolts.

My chest twinged. I could feel it. An itch to fight. The need to go at the Prince's throat again. But what was done, was done. We'd been temple-mated to the Fallenspawn. At worst, we had to tolerate them.

"Guys," I cut in before another fight broke out. "The poison-eyed one is right."

I gingerly touched my face where it had been slammed into the desk. I could feel it swelling up but I tried not to focus on it.

"We're all stuck together until our final Ascension. Pretty sure that includes the same wingtower."

"Stars," Daelun grumbled, eyes burning at the Fallenspawn.

"My name is Ivyana," the female spat, curling her lip.

I rolled my eyes. "I was close enough." I groaned as one of my nerves pinched, sending a rush of pain through my upper body. "Holy *stars*," I huffed, rubbing my neck.

The Fallenspawn watched me with small, victorious grins. I'd gotten my hide handed to me by their Prince and they were proud of it. Omarion was instantly at my side.

"Safah?"

"I'm okay. I..." The rush crawled through my shoulders again. I pressed my lips together trying to hold back my cry. I grunted through the pain doing my best not to whimper.

To my chagrin, Quazar started chuckling. "Beastly creature. This is a good lesson for you." If I had any strength left, I'd tackle him and slap that smug smile from his face. Kazemir and Daelun slipped closer to the Fallenspawn. The Fallenspawn spread their stances, ready to fight if that's what it came down to.

"Hey, I can carry you to the wingtower if you want." Omarion gently laid a hand on my shoulder, rubbing some of the growing stiffness away. Stars. That actually felt wonderful. It relieved enough pain for me to open my eyes. And find the Fallen Prince glaring at Omarion.

"No, it's okay. Worse," I grunted, grinding my teeth together. "I've been through... worse. I...I'll be good. I'll find a Raephim once we settle in."

I desperately needed the mender. I hadn't entirely healed from the damage Tharic had done. And now this scuffle with the Prince had me tweaking.

"Safah, don't be stubborn. I don't mind." Omarion brushed my hair out of my eyes as he shielded me with a wing.

"Forever at my rescue, are we?" I smiled up at him. "It's alright, Omi. I'll make it."

"Sazu, you're sure—"

"Are you deaf? Or were your ears clogged when she answered you the first time?" Quazar cut in. His voice was smooth like velvet. My ears twitched at the sound. I flinched in surprise, looking at Prince Quazar, taken aback.

Omarion blinked at him, his eyes lightening so much they turned hazel. "Excuse me?"

"Omarion, don't let him bait you." I grabbed my friend's hand before he lunged for the Prince. "As for the rest of you," I said to the Fallenspawn. "Since you have no scrollmaps, keep up."

I turned away from the Fallenspawn, levitating into the air. I floated to keep from using my wings and aggravating my wounds worse.

"Come on," I said. "I'm already tired of this insufferable heat."

"Agreed," Ellabeth said, wiping a bead of sweat from her brow. "You'd think with all these clouds it wouldn't be this lambasting hot."

Daelun grunted, spinning away with the rest of us. We followed Isandra letting her take the lead. The temple grounds were beautiful. We passed interconnected gazebos, with golden pillars and glass floors, entirely swarmed by thick billows. Beyond the gazebos, out in the distance, I saw a flock of stareagles flying by with beautiful ivory fur, golden beaks, and golden talons.

"Safah Anathelle?"

I came to an abrupt halt, flying into Daelun's spine.

"Oof." I groaned as my face erupted with fire. One of the Fallenspawn males snorted.

"Stars, Safah. I'm sorry—"

"It's not you," I whimpered, holding the sides of my face. "I wasn't paying attention. And...who called me?"

I looked up into the faces of a group of Farasees. Xadari Legion stopped flying behind us, all scowling. None was more annoyed than Quazar Valoryen. Daelun and Isandra parted so I could be seen clearer. The Farasees looked at me in a way that immediately made my skin crawl.

"Look at those eyes. Lavender as an Ashiris star. Wings high, Safah Anathelle."

I didn't like the way these males were leering at me. Instinctively I pulled back, putting a small bit of distance between us.

"Wings high, Farasees. How...how were you so sure it was me?"

I kept my eyes low. Manmi said in situations like this, avoiding eye contact was optimal. The males of Seventh Choir noticed my discomfort and pressed in, creating a wall between me and the Farasees. Stars. I'd lucked out with getting an amazing Choir.

"We'd be able to tell Amaryss Anathelle's fifi from a star away."

The Farasee who spoke was shorter than the rest, dark skinned with greedy hazel eyes, and a crooked nose. His eyes dragged down the length of my curves, slowly, drinking me in.

"I am Farasee Nathaniel. My, my. You look *so* much like her."

The Farasee floated forward, reaching out as if to touch me. My wings twitched. I jerked back on instinct to pull away. Only to collide into Quazar's chest. *Stars.* I whipped around, facing those jeweled eyes.

"Sorry. I didn't mean to—"

"You never have to apologize to Fallen dogs, dearest Safah."

I turned and found Farasee Nathaniel trying to get closer to me. Omarion and Daelun gave him no room to pass.

"Farasee, if you'll excuse us. We need to be getting on our way..."

"I just want to see if you feel like her—"

The Farasee's shadow lengthened past his natural height becoming monstrous. My eyes widened as the shadow plunged onto the Farasee and began choking him. Then a wave of shadows seeped out of the ground and slapped the Farasee with such brute force, he went flying across the grounds into a distance I couldn't see.

We all turned to look at Quazar.

But Quazar was only looking at me. His nostrils were flared. He looked vehemently angry at having his time wasted.

"Are you ready to go now? Or are we going to stop every

time one of these Hèls-possessed Farasees pisses themselves when they see your eyes?"

I rocked back as if I'd been slapped across the face. Hard. My jaw dropped. I'd used up my storehouse of anger for the dawn. All I was left with was a crushing ache.

I blinked at the Prince for a long time, stunned into silence. Then I turned around and flew away without a word. Disrespectful bastard. I was mentally exhausted and would not deal with him any longer.

A strange emotion formed in my chest, knotting my stomach. I missed Manmi so bad. She taught me so much, yet now that I was facing certain challenges in real time, I just wanted her back. To ask her questions. To just have her give me a hug. I held back tears. I would not let the males of the Farasee Order rattle me.

With the help of Isandra's scrollmap we navigated our way through the grounds. We passed goddesses handling the many gardens littering the grounds, while watching more stareagles fly overhead. We finally made it to a tower with a single level and a winged design carved into the sides.

Above the doors were the smoke insignia of Incense Order. Inscribed above the doors balanced a sign: *First Dominion, Seventh Choir.*

Isandra flew to the doors first, shoving them open without preamble. Sweet incense filled the wingtower. We all floated into a common room that was beautifully decorated and laid out. On either side were hallways leading further into the wingtower. I assumed that's where the bedchambers were accessed.

"I want firsfast," Isandra sighed, her wings drooping.

I nodded in agreement. I pulled off my sandals, then lowered to my feet, opting to walk around. The cold of the marble floors gave me enough of a shock to soothe the burn in my body some. The rest of Seventh Choir removed their sandals. The hall to the left was labeled *Efysiens.* The hall on the right was labeled *Azarathiens.*

I turned in time to see the Legionnaires remove their boots before lowering to their feet. Xadari Legion stood by the entrance glaring at Seventh Choir. And we glared back.

"Quazar?" Ivyana called.

He slid his gaze to her. I watched his face change. He looked...caring. Protective. Gentle.

I wrinkled my nose at the thought. This male was anything but that. His emerald eyes landed on me. The hatred of a thousand generations speared me through. I lifted my chin and crossed my arms. He could try me, if he dared. But he'd be met with a viper that would never relent. We glared at one another. And again, all I could think about was Manmi and her life brought short because of him.

"You," I seethed.

He tilted his head. Slipped his hands into his pockets.

"Me."

Dakairi crossed his arms, as Ivyana followed suit, tilting her head at me.

"Keep your Fallen on your side and we Hallowed will stay on ours."

The Fallenspawns flinched. Quazar looked like he was ready to set me—and the rest of Seventh Choir—on fire. Without another word, he stomped away letting his wings drag across the marble.

"Talons," Quazar barked without looking back.

Xadari Legion followed him as a unit without question. They headed down their hall which was separated by glass walls. The moment they all crossed to their side, Quazar threw up a thick barrier of shadows that coalesced into a black wall writhing from the floor to the ceiling. We couldn't see past it and we couldn't hear a thing either.

One of the front chambers opened and a Raephim flew out.

"Thank the stars," I cried, practically running over to her. "I desperately need mending. I can't even tell you what all is damaged—"

"Ascendant Safah, it's quite alright. Come on in."

"Thank you," I breathed. Then paused. "How'd you know I was—"

"Starry lavender eyes?" she said playfully.

I frowned. These eyes of mine were starting to be a curse.

"And you are..."

"Raephim Zara." She smiled prettily, inviting me into her mending chamber. "Let's get you mended."

I followed her into the chamber thankful to finally be

healed. The moment I sat in the cloudchair, a loud, piercing scream erupted outside of Zara's room.

CHAPTER 15

I shot out of my seat, ready to fly back out. Zara waved her hand, grabbing me with invisible strands before yanking me back down to the cloudchair.

"Ignore it." Zara waved her hand dismissively. "No one's hurt. One of your Choir mates is just getting accustomed to their chambers. They'll be fine."

I narrowed my eyes at the Raephim. She was too calm about the screaming for me. "But how do you know? They sound like they could be hurt."

Zara flicked up her brown eyes at me, her left brow rising to her hairline.

"I have been the Raephim to Incense Order for a full Age, youngling." She smiled sweetly as if dealing with a newborn. "Over one thousand cycles of first reactions to the wingtower. I *know*."

I bit my lip, keeping my mouth shut. I knew when I'd been humbled.

"Now, lay back, close your eyes, and allow me to work."

Obeying her orders, I did exactly as she asked. A fruity scent slipped into my nostrils. Within moments, I'd tumbled into a deep sleep.

It wasn't until I felt a sharp yank on my wings that I jerked awake. Blinking grogginess out of my eyes, I shot into the air, spinning around myself. All my pain was gone. I grinned wide. Zara was floating by her door, holding it open. A dismissal.

"Safah, hurry up! You're not the only one who needs mending."

I chuckled at Daelun's impatience.

"Thank you, Raephim Zara."

"Please," she said, her shimmering skin glittering in the bright light of her chambers. She flapped her four sets of earthen brown wings and smiled in a way that made me feel deeply cared for. "Zara will do. And any time you need a bit of patching, now you know where to find me."

"Yes, Rae...Zara."

I bowed quickly then rushed out of the chamber as Daelun flew in, already topless, exposing old wounds not entirely healed even from Sifting.

Floating to the floor, I relished walking across the marble, barefoot. I looked around, thinking about my home, and how this wingtower would take its place for the foreseeable future. I lived on my own in a villa I purchased many cycles ago, but prior to Ascension, I'd returned to my childhood home so I could be with family before Ascending.

My chest tightened. I already missed Papi and my little sister Evanae. Gabriel, the youngest of us all, had gone to spend the sumyrin season with friends at their family beach villa. His summers were typically spent away from home. I hadn't gotten to see him before Ascension. Not that he cared. He probably assumed he'd have another chance to see me.

I scoffed. I wished to see all of them. My sisters. Brothers. Papi. This temple was already weighing on my soul. Finding my chamber doors—labeled *ANATHELLE*—I walked in. And grinned from ear to ear.

The chamber was lavish like the rest of the Temple. The expansive room had marble, ivory floors. Gilded banisters opened to the cloudy billows of the outdoors beyond the balcony. A short staircase led up a platform where my bedcloud perched. There was an intimate biblarien to the left, with endless scrolls to read. There was a dining corner with an accompanying cafe and cocoa bar, and gilded doors which led to a bathing chamber.

From the feathered drapes, to the crystal chandeliers hanging in multiple spaces, down to the plush rugs and golden tabletops, I couldn't tell if I was still at Temple Efysis, or if I'd transported through a star gate to the palace of the Empràr.

I bounced on my feet, absorbing it all. I padded over to the oversized armoire and threw it open. There were flight robes, temple gowns, twigowns to sleep, and even swimming robes. Every single item inside was bright, shimmering gold. When in the stars would we have time to go swimming?

I raised a brow, pulling out a temple gown. I fished in the drawer for intimates which had all been provided in my exact size and closed the drawer with my foot. Headed for the washroom, I pulled the door open with a wing. The washroom was as opulent as the bedchamber itself.

Really, I could get used to this.

It felt like being home.

Without looking around I waved my hand, drawing all the curtains closed with a flick of the wrist. Without preamble, I stripped bare. Looking at the ostentatious basin of copper gold, I flicked my wrist again, turning the faucet, watching as steamy hot water gushed into the basin. Using the water scents close to the basin, I poured them in, relishing in the light, but sweet aroma.

I stepped into the basin, sank in, and nearly started crying. Stars. My body needed this. I sank into the hot water, still rising, until I was up to my neck. I closed my eyes, just for a moment, breathing in.

I was officially an Ascendant. Soon, whenever the first trial finally happened, I would become a Disciple.

I thought over the events of the dawn. Tharic Zamarien and his bloodthirst. Presbitari Davithius. Presbitari Kaelthos. Farasee Esau. The joy of hugging Granmanmi again. Getting assigned to Incense Order. The dragons. The leering Farasees.

Him.

Quazar Valoryen.

I groaned. I couldn't believe I'd lost my temper like that and attacked him. I was *not* some barbarian like he was. I'd have to watch myself around him. He looked like the type to provoke you on purpose just to have a reason to draw blood.

I snorted, eyes still closed. I wondered if the female who looked like him was his family. Maybe his sister? A younger kouzi? She was physically strong, but looked so young. Why was she enrolled in a war college?

Flicking my wrist, a soft melody slipped into the chamber, soothing my thoughts. I needed to calm my mind. I was thinking too much. Too fast. I needed to mentally rest.

I sunk into the water, soaking my hair completely. I went through the meticulous love ritual of washing my hair. With it being so long, I had to split it into six sections, pinning them each so I could thoroughly wash and condition each section.

I lost track of time as I hummed to the soft melodies while lathering shampoo and conditioner into each strand of hair from my scalp to the very ends of my hair shaft. I gently detangled the strands with my fingers, careful not to let my lengthy nails snag on the ends. I let the conditioner sit in my hair while I scrubbed myself nearly raw, trying to remove the chaos of the dawn from my body. If only it were that easy to scrub my mind, too.

I wouldn't forget the females Tharic tossed off the bridge. The males he killed before they could make it into Scroll Order. I wouldn't soon forget Kaelthos having the audacity to call me a bloodthorn in front of the entire Order. Farasee Esau *enjoying* my being bonded to the Fallen Prince. The Farasees who leered at me like they planned to drag me into their beds. Nor the burning hatred in Quazar Valoryen's emerald eyes.

Enemies. I had many enemies on every side. I had to be careful in this temple. Or I would die quicker than I could dream about becoming a Farasee.

I rinsed my body, my hair, and toweled off, taking my time lathering on lotion and body oil to every inch of skin before dressing in my temple gown. The golden fabric covered the length of my neck, hugged every curve deliciously, while tumbling down the length of my body. I flew to the wall-length mirror in the washroom, taking a good look.

I had to give credit to whoever stocked our chambers. I had an endless supply of hair oils available. I could almost weep. Popping the gilded lid off one, I slathered my hands with oil and began applying it. By the time I was done oiling and twisting my hair so the coils would hang prettily, my arms were burning.

I stalked back into my chamber and found a floating scrollport waiting for me. I ogled the cylindrical object, curious at the message inside. The insignia of Incense Order was branded on it. My stomach growled as I passed a platter of food laid out beautifully for me to dig in. I reached out to take a piece of cheese.

Then paused.

That wasn't there when I entered my washroom.

I blinked at the platter as my stomach growled louder. I looked to the scrollport, at the food, then back at the scroll-port. I opted to open the scrollport first.

The vibrant image of a Babephim—angels of the messenger rank—surfaced. She was beautiful and cheery. I was immediately suspicious of the message she was tasked to deliver. The Babephim floated over the scrollport as if she was actually in my chamber. She looked so real I wanted to poke her shoulder and confirm it for myself. She opened her mouth and began reciting her message.

"Wings high, Ascendant. Angels do not live by Manna alone, but by all the written words that come from the Infinite himself. If you choose to live by your stomach, we're given no other choice. We will choose to let you die by it. Long may you live, and well may you Ascend."

The moment she finished, she wrapped her wings around herself and completely disappeared. The scrollport wrapped itself up on its own and grew dull, no longer shining with a message that needed to be heard. I placed the scrollport on a table and turned back to the platter of food.

If you choose to live by your stomach, we're given no other choice. We will choose to let you die by it.

The food and drink was a test. Starve and pass. Or eat and die.

"What in the stars—"

A piercing scream exploded outside of my chamber doors from the main hall of our Order's tower. I whipped around, running for the door, yanking it open with a wing. When I ran outside, the rest of Seventh Choir was in the hall, equally confused.

"I thought it was one of you!" I yelled.

"So did we!" Isandra said.

Amayah and Kazemir were glaring at our main doors that led to the outside.

"What is it?" Ellabeth snapped, catching them staring.

The scream rang out again. We all looked at each other. Then we ran barefoot, sandals in hand, throwing them onto our feet as we launched into flight. Omarion got to the doors first and threw them open. We poured out after him and froze mid-flight.

Angels spilled out of their wingtowers.

And hundreds of them were being burned alive.

From the inside out.

"What in the stars is going on?" Daelun cried.

"Oh my stars! Look!" Isandra cried.

I could only stare as the eyes of all the burning Seraphim turned from the elements that made up their bodies, into weapons that began choking them out. Every angel struggling to stay alive had fresh food in their mouths. They were decaying from within while they were mid-chew. I covered my mouth with a hand as one female spat out the food, trying to get it off her tongue. But it was too late. Her wings began withering. Shriveling. Decaying. She screamed in agony. Begged for help.

But what in the stars could *we* do?

We will choose to let you die.

"This is a trial," I whispered.

Seventh Choir snapped their heads in my direction.

I kept my gaze on the dying Ascendants.

"*If you choose to live by your stomach, we're given no other choice. We will choose to let you die by it.'* This is a trial..."

"Holy..." Ellabeth ogled the dying, horrified.

"Those who read the scrollport or just took too long to notice are spared," I continued.

"And those who got greedy..." Omarion's words trailed off.

Seraphim began dropping like flies, the feathers of their wing pairs deteriorating. My spirit ached at the waste of their lives. They died simply because they wanted food. Manmi always said only the strong, the vigilant, and the worthy survived to Ascension. Were they not worthy just because they were hungry?

If you choose to live by your stomach.

The words wouldn't stop echoing in my mind. If not food, then what were we suppose to live by?

Angels do not live by Manna alone, but by all the written words that come from the Infinite himself.

My nose wrinkled. Something about all of this felt... wrong. I couldn't fathom the Infinite taking our lives like this. Not so carelessly. But Manmi had said there were things in the Temple I wouldn't understand. I had to simply trust the process and Ascend into the Farasee Order if I ever wished to make a difference on an impactful scale.

With all of Seventh Choir, I slipped back, leaving the dying Ascendants to their fates. It seemed we all came to the same conclusion. We came here to Ascend, not to die in the process. Those who didn't make it, may the Infinite guide their spirits into the Ellelights.

I couldn't help but feel like something in me was rotting away with them. I watched as the angels burned, and rotted, and screamed. Until my ears rang with their cries, and my eyes were stained with their golden blood. Until they died one after another until all that was left was silence and their phantom, desperate pleas to be saved.

CHAPTER 16

There was a reason for all this death. There had to be. I knew it in my bones. Temple Efysis was the epicenter of purity and holiness throughout the empyrean. Manmi had warned me time and again, to become dissuaded by nothing. To be shaken by nothing. Everything wasn't as it seemed, and even if I didn't understand, there was a purpose for it.

I trusted Manmi.

I trusted the Farasee Order.

I trusted the Infinite.

As the bodies of the Seraphim disintegrated into nothing, I made a personal note to be careful. Vigilant. Smart. Even when fatigue bowed my shoulders, I needed to keep watch.

I turned away from the carnage as gods started floating over. They began gathering fallen feathers. Bones that were scattered around. Goddesses came up behind them to scrub out the bloody stains from the pristine, golden stones. One of the goddesses looked up at me through her chainmail gown.

Hatred. Profound hatred swam in her pale eyes as she paid no mind to the sweat dripping down her deep brown arms baking beneath the suns. I masked my face into neutrality.

Looking at the gods and goddesses, I wondered what brought them to the temple. How they were kept here. Maybe it was a treaty they signed with the angels. A pact they made. Either way, this goddess looked ready to pluck my wings and burn them.

I turned away from her.

She had her plight and I had mine.

Floating back into the wingtower, I took a deep breath. My stomach grumbled.

"You sound like you could eat a pegasus." Omarion chuckled. Kazemir snorted.

I leveled a flat stare at them both. "Because I actually *could* right now," I grumbled. "I'm starved. I'd go home just to eat and come back if I could. The only thing is, I'd have to hear Papi. Again."

"I take it Papi Cassandrel fussed at you," Ellabeth cut in, flying to my side as she kicked off her sandals. "Before the Ascent. But why would he be grumpy? I thought he supported you Ascending? Through all of our endless cycles of training together, he never actually said *no*."

I kicked off my sandals and floated down to rest on my feet."Supported me," I snorted. "Please. He *tolerated* my ambitions because of Manmi. Now he swears the temple is unsafe and that I'll end up like Manmi."

Isandra, Amayah, and Daelun all raised their brows.

"I mean," Isandra shrugged, "Its not like he's entirely wrong."

I waved her off. "Listen, Manmi's had me training to be here since before I could talk."

"True," Ellabeth agreed. "I got dragged into those lessons."

"Also true," I confirmed.

I looked at the rest of them.

"She prepared me for what I've been encountering here." I folded my arms. "Yes, it's been wild. But seriously, its *Temple Efysis*. They didn't have us Ascend just to butcher us like cattle. There have been deaths but all things have their purpose, even when we don't understand."

"Agreed," Ellabeth chimed in. "They only want the best of us remaining for a very specific reason."

"That makes sense," Omarion said. "I mean, if you can't even discern through a scrollport, you probably shouldn't be allowed into the Farasee Order."

We all nodded.

"Exactly. Is it cruel for them to prepare us for the true work of the temple? It's a lifelong commitment that must be kept by those who prove themselves worthy of it."

"I don't give a rot about worth. Fallen blood. That's what I'm here for," Kazemir mumbled.

"Well," Ellabeth said, pointing to the other side of the wingtower. "Go get it."

Kazemir's honey eyes flashed, his lips pressing together. "I said Fallen, not *Fallenspawn*. There's a difference."

I glared at him. "Fallenspawn were raised by the fallen angels. What *difference* are you talking about?"

Kazemir leveled a weighty gaze at me. He said nothing for a long time. He stared at me as if he was looking straight into my soul. "Just because you're raised by monsters doesn't mean you are one."

Then he spun away and padded off to his bedchamber, quietly closing the door behind him.

I stood there, dumbfounded.

"I disagree. Wholeheartedly." Daelun rose his chin. "A Fallen's a Fallen's a Fallen."

"Our point exactly. Anyway, I'm going to meander. My room is like a small palace."

"Same," Ellabeth chimed, clapping her hands excitedly.

"Hopefully we *are* allowed to eat at some point this dawn and we can all meet up here and go together?" I asked.

"Good with me," Omarion said, starting to pull off his tunic while padding barefoot into his chamber. The amount of muscle that lined every inch of his back was startling. I found myself gawking, watching him go until he walked inside and closed his door.

"I'm definitely telling him you three were drooling."

Ellabeth, Isandra, and I flinched, blinking away from Omarion's door.

"Shut up," Isandra said, before going to her own chambers.

I didn't bother giving Daelun the satisfaction of a retort. I turned and found Quazar's thick wall of shadows still effectively blocking us all out. I scoffed and went into my bedchamber, shutting the door.

My gaze fell on the platter of food that I couldn't touch. My stomach grumbled. Loud. I tossed my head back, frustrated. How was I supposed to witness and process so much death on an empty stomach.

I spun around, deciding I'd prefer to meander around the tower instead and see what else was present outside of our collective chambers. When I pulled on my knob, the door wouldn't budge. I raised a brow. Tugged on the knob again. Nothing.

I pulled the knob again, yanking it hard. It still wouldn't move.

"What in the stars..."

I grabbed the knob with both hands. It refused to turn and open. I was locked inside.

"Is this some kind of trick? What is actually happening?"

I slapped the handle. No dice. I slammed a wing into it. It remained unmovable. Panic started filling my chest. The aroma of the food platter grew, filling my nostrils, sending my groaning stomach into overdrive. A small headache began pulsing at my temples.

No.

Somehow, this was some kind of trap.

If you choose to live by your stomach, we're given no other choice. We will choose to let you die by it.

"No, no, no," I squeaked.

The food aromas grew. My stomach growled. I banged on the door, slamming my shoulder into it. My foot. My wings again. The burning thing would not budge.

Spinning around, I ran toward the banister open to the outside of the wingtower. I pushed the curtains back relieved to see the space between the archways open and clear. I spread my wings and launched myself, flying out of the chamber. I looked to my right and saw both Ellabeth and Isandra doing the same.

"My door won't open!" I yelled over the distance.

"Neither will mine," Ellabeth cried back.

A gust of wind surged out of the clouds, sweeping through her blonde hair. The gust spun her around, wrapping her in the cloud like a bedroll, then tossed her back over the banister, back into her bedchamber.

"What in the stars—"

Distracted by Ellabeth, I failed to see the same thing happening to me with the moving billows below me. Before I could fight it, I was wrapped entirely by cloud and flung back into my bedchamber.

CHAPTER 17

I rolled across the plush rug, shoulders colliding into a scrollshelf. I was instantly back on my feet, flying over the banister at full speed.

From the corner of my eye, I saw Isandra racing across the clouds. Then a billowy tendril shot out, latched around her ankle, and tossed her back into her bedchamber.

A shift of the clouds below snagged my attention. Cloudy hands started reaching for me. I angled my body and began flying upward. The clouds caught me anyway.

The billowy hand wrapped around my ankles, yanked me down, then flung me back into my bedchamber. I shot to my feet, threw myself over the banister and collided into an invisible wall between the archways so hard I thought I felt something snap.

I threw myself again. I ran into the wall between the archways once more. I couldn't go further. I was trapped in this infernal bedchamber.

I floated back, landing on the rug. There were no windows or doors between rooms, so I couldn't go to Ellabeth to see what all was happening on her side. I thought about the rest of Seventh Choir and how they were faring.

Panic. This was meant to throw me in a panic.

I smelled the food, but I blocked it out. This was a battle of mental will and I would *win*. I wasn't about to throw an entire millennia worth of work down the drain because of food.

I paced across the room, thinking of what to do. It was still high dawn, so going to sleep was out of the question. Especially since whatever Zara gave me had me fully awake. I was starving so I couldn't keep using up energy I didn't really have.

"Special kind of Hèls indeed, Ellie," I whispered to myself.

I shook away the distracting thought. This was Temple Efysis for Infinite's sake. If I couldn't face this, I wasn't worthy of joining Granmanmi and my Matriarchs. Stars.

Granmanmi.

How I wish I could ask her what the point of all of this was. I kept bouncing on my feet, going back and forth, until finally settling for digging into the scrollmap.

Grabbing my belongings from Sanctuary, I planted myself at the gilded desk facing the outside. An outside I was trapped from flying to. Relaxing my wings, I crossed my legs beneath my thighs, opened the map, and let the scenery unfold.

I loved playing around with scrollmaps. Once they were opened, they vividly portrayed what you wanted to see. The fun of it was going *in* to the scrollmap and flying around it as if you were in the location in real time. I drug the scenery around with a finger, moving away from Temple Efysis. I shrunk the view to see what all was around geographically.

From this view, I saw the entire Efysis islet. There was the Temple, at the very center. To the west was the Citadel—an enormous city on the islet built for the Farasees and their families to have enjoyment and a sense of living without having to return to the main islands. To the east there seemed to be nothing but a collection of pools, and further beyond were waterfalls. The islet itself was held up by a large, strong mountain base with caves within all around.

Intrigued, I began digging around, trying to see what I could find. I leaned over the scrollmap and decided to physically go inside of it and explore.

Tucking my wings into my spine, I zoomed in on the Citadel. I flew from my cloudchair and magically entered into the scrollmap. I flew all throughout the islet. There was no telling how much time I spent moving around in the scrollmap.

A resounding *click* sounded from inside my bedchamber. Without waiting, I flew out of the scrollmap and returned to my room, finding the door wide open. I blinked at it, unsure if it was another trick.

"The temple is messing with us," I mumbled to myself.

I flew out of my room, waving my sandals over, slipping

them on. Quazar's shadow barrier was gone. The Talons unit stood wide-legged, arms crossed, glaring at Seventh Choir.

When I flew out of my chamber, they all turned to glower at me. Quazar's eyes snagged on my freshly washed hair. Then onto my body-clinging gown. The feral look in his eyes made me pause. Then his eyes hardened as he erected a wall over his features. I scowled, turning to Seventh Choir.

"How many times did you keep trying?" I asked Daelun.

"I stopped counting after eighty-seven."

Ellabeth and I laughed.

"I quit after the third time. I got slammed into the floor." I laughed.

Omarion's shoulders shook as he laughed along. "I can see it."

"I'm *starved*," Isandra drawled.

"Same." I shook my head. "Burning, same."

"Can't believe Ascendants died for food," Amayah whispered.

I frowned. She was right. I thought of how they died, decayed, and just disintegrated. A horrifying way to go.

And without their spirits being filed, I knew they wouldn't enter the Ellelights. Just like the ones Tharic killed on our way up the Starfellien Ascent.

I looked around, quickly passing over Quazar, who was still watching me in a way that unnerved me. This time he wore loose fighting robes and leather boots like the rest of Xadari Legion, instead of that ridiculous suit he had on. Like the rest of his Legionnaires, he was dressed for war. I almost laughed. Where did they all think we were going?

Then I spotted the star gates.

My eyebrows rose to my hairline. Galactic light spilled out of the gates, as the travel portals swirled. I shared a look with Ellabeth.

"Guess it's time for the real trial to start," Daelun said, looking at the star gates.

My nostrils flared.

"So we just...go through them?" Ellabeth said, eyes glued to the star gates.

"Why are they even open? Did a Babephim come to say anything?" I asked.

"No Babephim." Amayah shook her head. "But I'm pretty sure we are supposed to go through the star gates."

"That's obvious, but for what?" Omarion crossed his arms. "There's no instructions. I'm not ending up like Fifth and Sixth."

"Agreed." I nodded.

"Only one way to find out." Daelun floated towards the first gate. He stepped through. And was promptly spat back out. "What in the stars?"

"Getting rejected by a star gate is wild," I said, my brows rising to my hairline.

"Maybe we need to go in by pairs."

We all turned and looked at Kazemir. He shrugged, eyes on the star gates, a deep frown bowing his face.

"Define *pairs.*" I glared at him, not liking where this was going.

"We have new temple-mates, don't we?" he whispered.

I glanced at Quazar. He was grinning from ear to ear, his eyes wild.

Oh no.

He *wanted* us to go through together. Which meant we'd be alone. And he could hurt me, kill me, without consequence. "I don't think—"

"Daelun is right. We just have to find out." Ellabeth lifted her chin, looking straight at Dakairi. She flew over to him, looking up into his jeweled, royal blue eyes.

"Can you handle testing the theory?"

"If you can handle not being a baboon's rot."

My jaw fell, unhinged. "Ellabeth, I *know* you're not going to let him talk to you like that."

I lifted my wings, already feeling my starfire flood my palms. Ellabeth turned to me smiling.

"Let him." She flipped her hair over her shoulder floating to a star gate. Then she looked at Dakairi, her eyes turning to raging oceans. "Talking is all he can do."

I snorted, slow clapping. "Touché."

Ellabeth stepped into the star gate. Dakairi followed, his eyes burning. Neither of them came back.

Blessed lights.

I turned to Quazar. He was positively beaming, hands swirling with shadows.

"After you, *Starling*."

My hearts raced. I drew on more starfire. Turning to the central star gate, I drew on my courage and flew through. I could sense when Quazar flew in after me. I kept my wings close as the star gate shot me through a pool of endless stars. My stomach plummeted as I felt my insides clench and twist.

A burning sensation raced through me before an icy chill flooded every limb. I couldn't shake off the feeling that something inside of my body, inside of my spirit, was permanently *changing.*

"Please tell me it's not you *in my mind, Spawn of Anathelles."*

Oh! Oh *no.*

The star gate spat us out onto our faces on another islet I was vaguely familiar with. I turned on Quazar, jaw hanging. Did he just talk into my *mind*? Did crossing the star gate together seal our bond as temple-mates? There was absolutely no way—

"There is absolutely every *way."* Quazar's eyes burned like holy fire. *"Your precious Temple has bonded us. But don't worry, it won't be for long."* He nodded toward something behind us. *"I assume you won't survive."*

Survive? Survive *what?*

I spun around. And screamed.

Terror flooded my body with bone-chilling cold as I looked up and stared directly into the Seal Gate.

CHAPTER 18

Gaping at the Seal Gate, I floated in place, paralyzed by my fear. As a youngling I used to harass Papi for stories about the Gates.

Who made them? Why did they exist? Did angels ever cross them? Why did my brothers have to go to them?

The only details Papi would fess up was of how tall the Gates were. The Seal Gate specifically was made entirely of the whitest bone. Long bones, short ones. Bones intact, bones broken in half.

Papi always said the Gates looked like an open mouth, yawning out the cosmos from their throats while connecting realms separated by time and space, bridging them together for crossing. Whoever controlled the Gates, controlled the endless existing realms throughout the Elledelle universe and all the planets within them.

As a youngling, so young and naive, I thought Papi was

just telling me stories. Giving me nightmares early to try and restrain my curiosity.

Until now.

I stared at the Seal Gate and quivered. I was supposed to be at Temple Efysis. Why in the *stars* had I been sent here?

I looked up the length of the Gate, tilting my head all the way back to see the height of the open portal as endless stars swirled at its center. I was at a loss for words. I had no idea what to do. If this was a trial, what was the test?

I looked around and found the islet deserted. Which couldn't make sense. Empyrean reports always said Legionnaires constantly fought at the Gates, especially the Seal Gate. They fought with their lives to keep all of the darkness out. But as I looked around, I found I was entirely alone.

Wait.

I spun around, searching the deserted island for signs of life. Where in the realms did Quazar go?

A cacophonous rumbling came from the center of the Gate. I backed away, looking back at the realm gate while also hunting for that traitorous Prince. We came here together. We obviously had to leave here together. At least, that's what I thought. But like a coward, he'd disappeared.

"Not a coward, Starling. There are infinite ways an angel can die. This option isn't particularly attractive to me."

What was he on about? I spun back to the gate, eyes widening, as a tear started forming at the center. It was loud, making my ears twitch irritably. Then a claw poked out.

"Burning stars." I whipped around, searching for what to do. Where to go. I was stranded. And alone.

"What a shame we didn't get to have more fun together. I enjoyed our first dance. Even if you did sneak in a couple cheap shots. Nonetheless, say hello to your Manmi for me when you're sent to meet her in the Hèls."

"You can rot in the Hèls, Wicked Prince," I spat as loud as I could in my mind. I wasn't sure how the temple used a blasted star gate to bond us, but I'd stop at nothing until I found out how to break it.

"I'll be there, that's certain. Pretty sure your new friends will bring you there, too."

He chuckled darkly, the sound curling around the threads of my mind, filling my every thought. I shook my head clear. I wouldn't fall for his nonsense.

The Gate had attempted breaches, but most were unsuccessful. Manmi was at one of the last recorded breaches. If there were no Legionnaires here, even if it was a realm gate, it had to be because the threat of Fallen breach had been contained.

I began turning away, when the tearing sound happened again. I covered my ears. Looking back at the realm gate, an angelic head pushed through.

I froze. Starfire churned in my stomach, flooding into my bloodstream as I remained perfectly still. More and more of a body surfaced. Winged ears, tall, porcelain skin, and long, bone straight hair. Everything inside of me screamed for me to fly.

But I was too curious.

I stayed, unsure if this was a Hallowed angel coming back home, or a Fallen bursting through.

"It's neither, Starling." Dark laughter curled around my mind. *"You're so optimistic. I need you to think of* worse."

My knees began shaking. Something was wrong. But there was no cover here. Nowhere to hide. There was nothing on this islet except rocks, bones, and scattered twigs. Whatever life had been here once, had been razed to the ground. I was completely exposed.

I scoured my brain to place myself geographically. All around me was nothing but barren, wasted land. And with the Seal Gate being here...My eyes widened. I wasn't on any ordinary islet. This was an *island*. The island of Barrenrock.

Rot.

As one head popped out of the Seal Gate, then another, I was almost relieved. They were Hallowed angels. And from the looks of it, they had to be of Seraphim rank.

The angels pushed through the realm gate with seven wing pairs, their heads bowed low, their bodies wrapped in tattered ivory robes. Then they lifted their heads.

I screamed and screamed until my throat was raw.

Cruel laughter flooded my mind.

"Have fun, Starling."

I floated back in terror as, one...two...four...*seven* filmy eyes blinked at me, the largest at the center of the forehead with the other six balanced evenly on either side. Thank the stars I hadn't eaten. I wanted to puke. The creature sniffed the air, all eyes pinned on me.

"Mmm," it hissed. "*Seraphim.*"

Stars.

I racked my brain for what to do. The creature shot out of the mouth of the gate, landing on all...fours.

Not a Seraphim. Definitely *not* a Seraphim.

Horns the length of my arms began protruding from its head, as it opened up a mouth that stretched from ear to ear revealing rows of jagged teeth. My pulse quickened. Another of the creatures surfaced. Then another.

Dead. I was so burning dead.

"Probably."

"Shut your rotting mouth!"

"That's pretty foul language for a pious, little Faraseespawn like yourself, don't you think?"

I ignored the traitorous asheater and focused on the monsters in front of me. I didn't know what they were, but I knew I would have to fight my way out of this. Where were the Legionnaires? Why was I here alone? Why did the temple send me here?

"Maybe you're a problem and this is a convenient way to get rid of you."

"Shut up!"

"Why? Because you can't handle the truth?"

I didn't dignify that with a response. I wouldn't listen to his lies.

"She smells like the stars."

"She smells like the Elder Age."

"Maybe she'll taste like it, too."

"This one we cannot consume. We must bring her to *him*."

Before I could open my mouth to protest, the three monsters moved as a coordinated unit. They launched themselves forward, closing the distance between them and myself.

I had no chance to block the blow before it landed at the center of my chest. My body jerked, wrenching from the ground.

I was flung across the expanse of dirt, thrown like pebbles. I crashed, spine first, into a massive rock, before crumpling to the ground. I coughed, my vision spinning. When I looked down, there was large tear at the center of my chest. And golden blood spewed.

I drew in ragged breaths, working hard to use my starfire to heal myself. I pushed to my hands and knees as my chest started stitching itself together.

Only to be plucked up by my wings as long claws slashed through my gown and ribs, drawing more blood.

"Well, well. She lives again" the beast holding me said with glee. "We've found her. It is *her*."

CHAPTER 19

"Infinite, *please*," I begged, throwing up a silent prayer. "Please don't let me die. Not like this."

Terror filled my mind. My chest.

I was going to die.

"Pathetic," Quazar's cruel voice rumbled across my mind. *"You can't handle one little blow? Embarrassing."*

Tears burned at the back of my eyes. My death could send Papi to an early grave. He still hadn't recovered from Manmi. If I fell, after he begged me not to Ascend...

And Evanae. My sweet Evanae. We were sisters by birth, but best friends by choice. I couldn't fathom her sorrow. Nor Ellabeth's...

No. I may leave here bruised, but I was *not* dying this dawn.

The creature smacked me into the ground, shoving a sharp item into my back. I screamed, crying against the pain.

Another grabbed my hair, yanking on it, ripping out several strands. I wouldn't last much longer like this. The object in my back started...*draining* me.

Wait. *No.* Draining?

These had to be Spirit Harvesters.

"Bingo."

I fumed.

He knew. He burning *knew* that Spirit Harvesters were here and he *left* me. I screamed. Not from pain. But from rage.

I *fyused*. In the process of transfiguring, the object slipped out of my physical body, releasing me. I kicked out with my feet, swiping under two of the Harvesters. They lost their balance, giving me just enough room to get a better advantage. I blinked back stars, pushing past the shock of my wounds.

Summoning star bolts, I shot one after another at the monsters, aiming for their heads. I took flight into the sky. They flew after me, without hesitation. I shot the biggest one in the head and kept flying across the deserted island.

The blow did nothing.

I summoned a spear and shot it at another of the Harvesters. It caught him square in his chest.

And did nothing.

I tried weapon after weapon, using my starfire to heal what I could internally, while trying to fight off the Spirit Harvesters. But it wasn't working. None of the blows landed fatally. It was almost like they wanted me to strike them because they knew it wouldn't work.

I was in such eternal rot. Flying with all my might, I curved around torn down stumps. I pushed higher into the sky, hunting for a way out of here.

All the way in the distance, I could spot a star gate.

My mouth fell open.

I bet Quazar had flown straight for it, leaving me here to fend for myself.

"Correct. No need to kill you myself when the Harvesters are more efficient." A laugh. *"If you survive, there's fresh sugar cane waiting for you. Assuming I don't eat it all."*

I hated him. With all my hearts and might, I hated him.

A bony hand wrapped around my ankle and yanked me hard. I jerked in the air, my starry wings flinging haphazardly as I was snapped to the right then flung to the ground.

The star gate. I had to get to the star gate.

I could *not* fight this. Not alone.

If you choose to live by your stomach, we're given no other choice. We will choose to let you die by it.

But I didn't have anything! This wasn't remotely fair!

"Fair." A snort was heard down my mind. A brush of shadow pushed against my thoughts. *"She thinks her precious temple is* fair. *How adorable."*

"Shut up!" I screamed out loud as I shot to my feet, taking off again.

"You dance too much, Star of the Age."

"That's not me!" I screamed, racing for the star gate.

I blocked out the sound of the Spirit Harvesters, and somehow, I put a protective shield around my mind against Quazar. I changed my flight pattern, flying in zig zag motions to throw off my pursuers. I begged for another Seraphim, a Legionnaire, *anyone* to show up and help me.

No one did.

I pushed harder, unwilling to just give up. If I could make it to the star gate, I would survive. I felt lightheaded, nausea weakening my flight, as hunger made me sway despite my adrenaline. But I kept flying. If I slowed, I would—

Jagged teeth latched onto a pair of my wings, shredding through the tips, dragging me down. I screamed, tears streaming down my face, as my wings were torn through to the bone, golden blood spewing.

"*Why* can't we feast? She is *delicious.*"

I drew on my starfire, using it to boost me into the air. Then I shot out another burst, that sent me careening with such brunt force over the islet, I nearly missed the star gate. As my vision blackened, I focused on the star gate, while pulling every trace of blood back into my *fyused* body, unwilling to let my leaking blood reveal what hid beneath my skin. Especially not in the presence of these monsters.

I could feel my blood vessels reforming, healing, coming back together, as parts of my body patched itself enough for me to remain intact. The Spirit Harvesters lunged for me again. I reached the star gate, and threw myself into it, racing across. The moment it spat me out, the star gate closed.

I rolled over and over across the marble floor before

landing in a heap. My breaths were ragged, as I covered my body with my torn wings. My vision blurred. I had a splitting headache and everywhere burned.

Hèls. That was absolute *Hèls.*

But I survived. By some burning miracle I survived.

I cried, the stinging tears snaking down my cheeks. I'd nearly lost my life in a miserable way again. Terror filled my chest as I tried clinging to my sanity. I couldn't shake away the nightmare that was the Spirit Harvesters. Maybe if Quazar and I had worked together, maybe I could have ended the life of at least one.

Instead, I got my tail rocked. Bad.

Someone started slow clapping as I wiped my tears, still hiding under my draping wings, hyperventilating. I checked my hands. My arms. They were bare. No exposure of what lay beneath my skin. Embedded in my blood.

Bend, but do not break. Burn, but never bleed.

I was failing miserably at that.

I slowly lifted my head, my cheeks wet with tears, to find Quazar's eyes glowing with triumph. He squatted by me, tilting his head

"Well, well. She survived."

"I hate you," I seethed, baring my teeth at him.

He waved a hand. "I don't really give a rot, Starling." His eyes fell to my hands. I tucked them into the folds of my wings. "You evaded Spirit Harvesters. How?"

"She *what?*"

Several gasps broke out. I glowered at Quazar, who was glaring at me.

"*How*?"

"Piss off, traitorous demon. I almost *died* thanks to you," I snapped.

I rolled away and pushed to my feet. Hobbling, I held my side with an arm and threw the other to my back where I'd been stabbed. I needed Zara, immediately. From my quick scan of everyone, I was the only one who'd been wounded within inches of her life.

"Ellie," I breathed, my vision swimming. Stars. I needed to sit down somewhere.

Daelun flew over, but I floated away.

"Leave me be," I snapped. "Ellabeth, where is she?"

I looked around.

Ellabeth was nowhere to be found.

Then I remembered the anger in Dakairi's eyes as he followed her through their star gate. Slowly, I turned my gaze on him. Something feral churned in my gut. Rage flushed my neck hot.

"Where. Is. Ellabeth?"

Dakairi shrugged, nonchalantly, crossing his arms. Then he grinned, his eyes dancing.

"She was getting tired." He tilted his head.

The Talons grinned, wickedly.

"So I put her to sleep."

Dakairi's blue eyes blazed.

What had he done to my best friend?

Something in me snapped. I didn't think about my pain. Or the fact that I could hardly walk. I didn't think of my shredded wings. Or how I kept putting my body through endless Hèls since the dawn I came to this temple.

Without thinking, I *fyused*. I whipped out my wings and slapped Dakairi across his face so hard, his body snapped, jerked back, flew across the hall, and slammed into one of the wingtower pillars. Hard.

Before the angels could react, I launched myself at Quazar, and slapped him just as hard. His head snapped back, golden blood gushing out of his mouth.

The Xadari Talons snarled. Their jeweled eyes began to glow. They launched themselves at me.

But Seventh Choir got to me first, shielding me. Every last one of them *fyused*. Before I lifted my wings again, Seventh Choir attacked. Then my Choir, and the Talons, tumbled into an all-out brawl.

CHAPTER 20

Electric light exploded into the charged air, setting the tower alight with destructive energy. Quazar snarled at me, rearing back on his legs as he spread all six wing pairs. Then he launched himself forward, tackling me.

I was ready for him, bracing my wings in front of myself as I tried to shield myself against the brunt of his weight. Through slitted eyes, I watched him lick the golden blood trickling from his lips. His eyes were ablaze.

Daelun laughed, darkly. "It was about time things got fun around here."

His skin had shed itself, becoming the very tendrils of wind and air. All that remained were his dark eyes as he tackled Ivyana. His body slammed into hers, throwing her across the great room. As Daelun charged again, Ivyana's emerald eyes glowed. Daelun thrust out his arms. A sky quake began trembling the tower, shaking the edifice. I dodged

Quazar's incoming blow, as Daelun exploded with a strong gust of wind, throwing Ivyana into its loop.

I grinned.

Then Daelun started screaming.

I narrowed my eyes, searching through the thickness of his air affinity. To find Ivyana with her hands out, bending them. Every direction she bent her hands, Daelun's limbs also bent.

Holy stars.

She was a Limb Bender.

A heavy blow to the side of my head sent me reeling. I crashed into a pillar. A bone popped. I wheezed in agony. Head swimming, I blinked and watched my shadow grow. My shadowy limbs stretched, becoming abnormally long. Then they contorted. Every muscle in my body twisted, spasming all at once.

I shrieked. Starfire burst out of me, cutting through the shadow tendrils clinging to my body. But the pain refused to let up. Drawing on starfire, I turned my arms to swords, shooting straight for Quazar's chest. He dodged the first several blows. I huffed, striking again and again, but the shadowed demon kept evading being struck.

Think, Safah. I chided.

So you've been winging it this entire time? Quazar's voice slipped into my head, full of ridicule. *No wonder this feels like dancing with a child.*

Angrily I swung.

And missed.

I fumed, ditching the swords for bolts. I began to throw bolt after bolt. And I hit true each time.

Quazar snarled, ducking as a flash of earthen spikes flew past his head. Omarion met blow for blow against another brown-skinned Mortent with Omarion's same green-hazel eyes, and dreads tied up in a clasp with his head shaved on either side. I couldn't tell the Mortent's Bending abilities, but he was making Omarion and his earthen elements work hard for his victory.

These Talons were extremely skilled in combat. I swallowed nervously as I shot for Quazar again. This time, he left my shadow alone. He flexed his hands and let a dark mass of black shadows pour out, trapping me in a dome of darkness.

"What in the stars is going on?" a voice I wasn't familiar with called out.

"Xadariens...attacked...one of us...so we're striking... back," Daelun said through gritted teeth. "Ella...Beth...is missing."

I threw a star shield around myself, glittering like the galactic stars, refusing to let Quazar strike me again.

"Over-confident temple brat," he spat. "Let's see how well you do in the dark."

"I don't think so," I raged. "Let's see how you handle the light!"

I shot out a canopy of starlight so bright, the sight burned my own eyes as it filled every crevice of the dark dome he'd put around me.

Before I could defend against it, a large form rushed

through the darkness, ancient script writhing along the columns of his bare skin, as he slammed into my shield, nearly disintegrating it.

"If you think I'm afraid of the light, Starling," Quazar whispered, "You underestimate my relentless odyssey to claw my way out of the dark."

I paused, stunned.

A mistake.

Quazar took advantage of it, punching through my starry shield, shoving his chest into mine, pushing against me until my back slammed into a wall. He gripped both my hands, pinning them above my head with one of his wings, while he glowered into my face.

I wriggled in his grasp, fighting to be free. The movement rubbed my shredded wings the wrong way, making me wince with pain.

"Release me."

"No."

I twitched, trying to break free. I drew on starfire, but I was growing weak from fatigue. Tendrils of thick shadow wrapped around my neck. And squeezed.

Tears filled my eyes as Quazar sneered, his full lips curling with hatred. I was consumed by those jade eyes, glittering like jewels.

"Your Granmanmi is the reason I have to suffer like a dog through your temple's hellish Blood Rites." His deep voice curled around my ears. Seeped into my chest, and began choking out my hearts. "Your Manmi is why we die like cattle—"

"If you all weren't murderous Fallen trying to bathe the empyrean in blood—"

"Are you always this stupid?" he snapped. "For starters, we are *not* Fallen—"

"Not Fallen? Yeah?" I cut in. "And I'm a Celestial. Didn't you know?"

"Cut the bullrot," he snarled, pressing me harder into the wall. "Since your Manmi loved seeing our blood shed so much, we'll see how they like it when the golden teardrops that fall are *yours*."

In the back and forth, I hadn't noticed Quazar's talons curling around his wide frame. Hadn't seen them lengthen, sharpen, *curl*. When I did, my eyes widened in horror. I looked back at him, our faces so close our noses could touch.

"No," I breathed.

He grinned, cruelly. The shadows around us pressed in forcing my star shield to wink out. We were in total darkness except for my starry silhouette shimmering beneath Quazar's shadows.

"Say hello to your Manmi from the Hèls for me."

Quazar raised a talon to run me through. I panicked, terrified of the bloody way he'd end my life. Then Quazar stilled. His eyes were glued to my neck. I remained trapped in his grip, breathing heavily.

"Well, you asheating coward," I spat. "Get on with it!"

"How long have you had those?" he said, his voice suddenly husky, barely a whisper.

"Had what, ashrat?"

"These inscriptions?"

Rot.

It was then I realized he'd landed a blow I hadn't felt. And I was bleeding.

Tired and hurting everywhere, I didn't even realize it so I could heal myself before what lay beneath my skin began to surface and expose me.

I looked into Quazar's glittering eyes, my entire being consumed with fear. No one could see this. No one could know. And now, here was the one angel I'd hated for as long as I could remember, who'd already spotted the one thing Manmi warned me to hide with my life.

I didn't answer, working to pull whatever scraps of starfire I could to heal wherever I'd been bleeding. I held Quazar's gaze as I felt my ethèr—the warm, deep, wells of my angelic power—traveling though my body and blood, knitting open wounds that were bleeding, until they stopped. As they did, I could feel the inscriptions seeping back into my skin, disappearing.

Quazar's eyes widened. "How in the rot did you just do that?" he breathed, his wings squeezing my trapped wrists.

He pressed closer, his chest against mine, his lips just a small lean away from mine. The heady scent of sandalwood and mint overwhelmed my senses, flooding me with a strange feeling I refused to entertain. I got a bit lightheaded, lost in those demanding eyes.

"I..." I stammered. "I've just always done it."

What in the stars was I doing answering him? I was an idiot for responding. But I couldn't stop.

"Manmi taught me how to...to keep from bleeding."

Quazar opened his mouth to respond when something behind him collided. Then exploded. He turned his head, searching through the dark. I wasn't sure what in the stars he was looking at. I couldn't see squat.

"Ascendants!"

"Rot," Quazar cursed quietly. He looked back at me, staring at where my inscriptions had been moments ago. "This isn't over, Starling."

Quazar dropped me, floating away as if he didn't want me to contaminate him. Then he dropped the shadows. I immediately drew on my waning starfire, drawing starry daggers.

"What in the Infinite's name is going on here?"

CHAPTER 21

I swung my head to the side turning to look at who'd spoken. And froze.

Stars.

We were all in colossal *rot*.

The wingtower was a *mess*. Sofas had been torn. Gilded pillars had been dented. Tables had been broken. Glass shards had shattered throughout the great room. There was evidence of fire, water, earth, wind, and even metallic damage. Shredded wing feathers covered the floor. Worst of all.

There was golden blood everywhere. And several bodies lay sprawled in contorted fashions that confirmed they were no longer alive.

Among the dead were angels I didn't recognize from Seventh Choir—but their robes had the Incense Order insignia—and Xadari Legionnaires who had the Fallenspawn mark, but weren't from the Talons unit.

I bit my lip at the carnage. Stars. This was my doing. I'd started the fight that ended in this.

I looked up and found Farasee Esau, Davithius, and Kaelthos glaring between all of us. All the Seraphim had remained in their *fyused* forms. Most had arms raised with weapons drawn.

All the Talons were in offensive stances, glares on their faces, with their own ethèr drawn. We looked like we'd been stalled in the middle of a war zone. In all this, Ellabeth was still nowhere to be found. And the Farasees noticed.

"Where is Ellabeth Riventhelle?" Kaelthos asked, eyes searching diligently for her.

"She is resting in the mending chamber."

We all turned to find Raephim Zara floating—head held high in her pristine blue robes—perched by her doors.

"Ellabeth came back from the trial...wounded. So I have been tending to her." She leveled a look at Dakairi.

Hot rage filled my chest. The Farasees turned around themselves, glaring around, mainly at the Xadari Talons.

Farasee Davithius spoke up after assessing just how much damage we had done to the tower and to each other.

"How do you expect to win against the Fallen, when you are so busy destroying each other?"

"I'll rot in the Hèls before I *work with* Fallen," an angel spat. Their smoke insignia was in the shape of a six. They were from First Dominion, Sixth Choir.

"This isn't even your wingtower, Ascendant," Davithius barked. "All of you who aren't in Seventh Choir. Out. *Now.*"

Several angels got up and obeyed, immediately, flying out of our wingtower.

"As for the rest of you, wings down."

No one moved.

I kept an eye on Quazar, while trying to keep the other on Farasee Kaelthos, who oddly, was staring at me. I kept my expression neutral, refusing to give away anything. My gut had been right. That boar of an angel *had* hurt Ellabeth. Or at the very least, endangered her to where she was wounded enough to be laid up with our Raephim. I fumed for my best friend. Finding where Dakairi was floating, he and I made eye contact. I promised vengeance for Ellabeth. Dakairi simply winked at me.

This wasn't over.

"Wings *down*."

Davithius barked the order this time. I *fyused* back into my Seraphim skin, eyes still dancing between Quazar and Kaelthos. I hovered in the air, refusing to stand in the blood bathing the floors.

"This is disappointing and unacceptable," Davithius began.

"Presbitari, they started it," Daelun said easily, dropping to one of the broken couches.

"We just chose to finish it," Omarion said, crossing his arms.

"Mess with one in our Choir," Isandra said, raising her chin.

Amayah's small voice filled the space after her. "And you mess with us all."

Not an angel from Seventh Choir had avoided getting bloody.

"What say you, Anathelle?" Kaelthos asked.

All eyes turned to me. I had a feeling the Farasee was purposefully trying to get a rise out of me.

"Like Daelun said, they started it. Ellabeth is my best friend. As younglings we were *known* for setting mangogo—and kakonut trees from our neighbors villas—on fire when their younglings tried bullying either of us." I squared my shoulders. "I don't care what the consequences are. I never expected anyone to..." I looked at the lifeless bodies. "Die. That notwithstanding, Ellie is my sister. I'd die defending her honor."

Something unreadable flashed in Davithius's eyes. Esau scowled like he'd been given rotten fruit to eat. Kaelthos glared, his fiery eyes churning mercilessly.

"All of you must go through Purification after such senseless death," Davithius said into the quiet, finally.

"What was senseless was that ridiculous trial in the woods," Isandra hissed.

"*Without* instructions, might we add," Amayah whispered.

The...woods?

I blinked, perplexed. Everyone had been sent to the woods while *I* had been sent to the Seal Gate? I looked around and found Kaelthos watching me with a keen eye. I looked away, refusing to give away anything. My mind was reeling.

Just what exactly was going on here? Why had Quazar and I been sent to the Seal Gate? And while it was abandoned, no less.

Fire exploded from the floor, shooting up into the room, drying out all breathable air. We began coughing, Talons included, as Farasee Esau slammed all of his wing pairs together seven separate times. When he was done, my ears were ringing.

"Let this be the last time you question the Farasee Order. If you can't handle a simple trial," he looked around. "*Forfeit*."

I placed a hand over my chest as I tried breathing through the racing beats of my hearts.

"As I said," Davithius jumped back in. "All of you." He looked at the Fallenspawn, nodding at them. "You Talons included, *must* go through Purification. We will be having our first Titombwe service. It has been called by the Empràr, encouraged by Profêt Samael and High Farasee Manazzra, to welcome and celebrate all of our newest *Disciples*."

Stars!

That's *right*.

We all completed our first trial. We were no longer Ascendants. We were Disciples now. I frowned. We became Disciples at great cost.

Davithius's eyes fell to the dead angels. "Those who survived anyway." He looked back up. "Attenting Titombwe without being purified from the death you've just caused is forbidden."

Davithius floated to the center of the great room, taking all of us in individually. His eyes flashed when they landed on me. The senseless deaths were a weight I'd have to carry. But my rage for what Dakairi had put Ellabeth through still superseded any regret I had.

"You will all clean this mess *together.*" Davithius was still looking at me, but I had the feeling he also had an eye on Quazar. "And you will get it done before Titombwe begins at twinight. If any of you are late to Titombwe, or miss it altogether, *all* of you will be tasked with cleaning the Scourgers chambers for a month."

My jaw dropped.

No burning way.

There was a shadowy explosion in my mind. I winced. It felt like shadows were trickling into my thoughts and screaming. I railed against the outburst of emotion, knowing it was Quazar losing his mental temper.

I fought to push the shadows back to his side of the veil. When my starry light shoved his shadowy darkness back to his side, I used starfire to mentally thicken and widen the veil, sealing the Fallenspawn *out* of my mind. I threw a glare at Quazar, whose face was contorted in a snarl in return.

I considered *fyusing* again.

But I was spent.

Davithius cleared his throat. I turned my attention to find him looking between me and Quazar. His steely blue eyes revealed nothing, but the vein in his hardened jawline was tight.

"Clean up this mess, together, *now.*" A look around the room. "Then make your way to the Purification Hall. Time is not on your side. Waste it and you'll find yourself cleaning the Scourgers chambers. Take it from me, the Scourgers always like to practice new tricks on anyone who dares to be present."

With that, Davithius and Esau wrapped their wings around themselves, and winked out. Farasee Kaelthos remained.

"Are you all deaf?" he barked. "This blood isn't going to clean itself!"

CHAPTER 22

I wasn't sure what to start cleaning up first. The blood or the bodies. I remained motionless, looking between the deceased angels and the floor.

"Who started this mess?" Kaelthos asked, eyes scanning the room.

Seventh Choir kept their eyes down and mouths shut. To their credit, Xadari Legion also kept quiet, refusing to answer Farasee Kaelthos. I swallowed and lifted a wing.

"I did, Farasee Kaelthos." I lifted my chin, meeting his golden eyes. "I take full responsibility."

His nostrils flared.

"Your irresponsibility led to the deaths of six Disciples." He looked at me with disgust, hovering above the floor so his robes wouldn't touch any blood. "You should be ashamed."

"Yes, Farasee." I lowered my eyes. "I am responsible for the loss of these six Disciples and three Fallenspawn."

Quazar looked at me when I acknowledged the Fallenspawn. I didn't have the energy to make sense of his confusing expression. Like a mix of hatred and...gratitude? I couldn't be sure.

"Farasee Kaelthos, I have been injured in a way I cannot self-heal. May I please see Raephim Zara—"

"No."

My gaze snagged on the Farasee. Cruelty filled his eyes.

"Since you caused this, you will help your angel-mates clean up this mess. Then the two of you are coming with me to bring these bodies to the wingyard and to file their spirits."

I raised a brow. "*Who* two?"

"You can't be this dense." Kaelthos pointed a wing. "You and the Fallen bastard."

"Quazar Valoyen and his Talon did provoke me..." I started. "But they're *not* responsible for this. I struck his Talon, Dakairi, first. Then the Prince. He doesn't need to be dragged into the wingyard with me. I will go alone."

"He can and he will," Kaelthos said, finality in his tone.

"Farasee Kaelthos—"

"You will not argue with me Anathelle, or I'll have you sent to the Scourgers."

I flinched.

Quazar's shadows pooled at his feet, his eyes piercing through the Farasee's back since Kaelthos wouldn't address him to his face.

There was no reason for me to be defending Quazar or any of his Fallenspawn. But Papi had raised me with integrity.

I'd lost my temper, and my loss of self-control ended in nine lost lives. I'd have to live with the weight of my blind rage.

There were Disciples and Fallenspawn that wouldn't see another dawn because of my anger. It was a weight I would always carry. Now that the adrenaline of the first trial had passed, and I was wounded and exhausted, something became undeniably clear.

Rage was expensive. It was deadly and came at a price I couldn't afford.

"Forgive me, Farasee Kaelthos. I didn't intend to argue."

Stars, I hated having to be polite with this brute. But he was a Farasee. He was one of the leading heads of the Order. An Order I was striving to be a part of. I had to respect him out of reverence for the office he held.

Waving my hands, I summoned a stack of large towels into my hands. I kicked off my sandals, lowered to the floor—wincing as I got down—and kneeled into the blood. The blood drenched my gown to the knees. It was still warm. Still full of life.

Stars. What had I just done?

Ignoring everyone watching me, I began dabbing at the blood on the floor. The first two towels were instantly drenched with how much blood I'd soaked up. My hair spilled over my shoulders into the blood. I didn't care. I kept wiping as much as I could, wiping the floor of my shame.

Amayah flew to my side, summoned her own stack of towels, and began wiping up blood beside me. I took in her warm brown skin, and beach blonde coily hair as it fell, like mine, into the blood on the floor. She didn't push her hair out of the way, either. Then Daelun joined us. Isandra. Kazemir. Omarion.

Quazar had removed his waistcoat, remaining in a fitted black shirt that clung to every shred of muscle he had. The shirt ended at his biceps, exposing his arms and the inscriptions running all along his arms and down to his hands. Eyes focused, he began wiping up the blood of the Fallenspawn. The rest of his Talons followed suit.

Every angel kept their wings tucked into their spines. I kept mine open and hanging. Tucking them in was too painful. The Spirit Harvester had done severe damage, and Kaelthos refused to let me get treated. He floated by the doors of the wingtower like an overlord, watching us all.

I didn't even realize what I was doing until I was moving. I got up, flew over to where the Fallenspawn were soaking up the blood from the floors, and with fresh towels, I began soaking up the blood of the dead Fallenspawn. Every angel in the room froze. Quazar's eyes widened.

"What in the Hèls are you doing?" he whispered.

"What does it look like, Quazar? You tell me since I know you're not blind."

I kissed my teeth, vexed at the stupid question, and went back to soaking up the blood of the Fallenspawn. I wiped until my stack of towels were gone. I summoned a new stack and kept at it. I was growing increasingly tired. My muscles were sore, and all I wanted to do was sleep.

But I caused this. So I would make it right.

The room was so quiet you could hear feathers falling.

Fallenspawn or no. Hatred or no. They were angels, and they'd just died. In their deaths, they deserved to be honored. That's what Papi taught me. All who died needed to be honored and their spirits preserved. It was the Infinite who had the right to make a final call once an angel had gone, no matter who they were or what they had done while they still lived.

I was raised to hate all Fallen and Fallenspawn. But even Papi taught me, all angelic life, once it came to an end, had to be cared for as we allowed the Infinite to do what He willed with their spirits as they crossed from our realm into the realm of the Ellelights.

I wiped up as much blood as I could, then rose to my feet alongside everyone else. I began walking away, then I spun back, stopping in front of Dakairi.

"Did you hurt her?"

His eyes flashed. He was silent a long moment.

"No, Anathelle. I didn't."

That made all this even worse. All of this bloodshed was for nothing. My hearts clenched at the truth of what I'd done.

"I'm..." I frowned, ashamed of myself. Both Seventh Choir and the Talons watched me with curious gazes, but my eyes were on Dakairi. "I'm sorry. I...was...I *am* wrong. And I acted senselessly. It cost you your friends. A debt I will never be able to repay."

I looked up into his shining blue eyes. His jawline was taut. I could tell he was grinding his teeth.

"I'm not asking for your forgiveness, Dakairi. You never have to give to me what you fundamentally believe I don't deserve. But I am giving you my repentance. I was angry with you, with Quazar, but your friends didn't deserve to die for it."

I turned away before he could say anything. Ivyana and Quazar both trailed me, their emerald eyes glittering with an expression I couldn't understand.

Farasee Kaelthos summoned three large baskets made of woven clouds. I dropped the towels in them and wiped my hands on my filthy gown. I looked at the bodies, laid out haphazardly where they'd fallen. Three of the Disciples were very large males. How was I supposed to lift them?

Sighing, I spread my wings. The Disciples of Seventh Choir hissed when they saw my damaged wings.

"Safah, what happened?"

I lifted my eyes. Could I tell them where I'd been sent for my trial? What I'd seen? What I'd survived? I shot a look at Quazar. His face gave away nothing.

"Don't. They're not ready for that truth yet, Starling."

He spoke to me down the bond, his dark shadows brushing against my mind.

"Don't call me that."

I couldn't for the life of me understand why I was taking his advice. I didn't like him one bit. I didn't trust him. And I still blamed him for Manmi's death. But I listened anyway. Something in my gut said I should keep quiet. Especially with Kaelthos listening to every word.

“I…fell. On…rocks. The big ones? Anyway. Got my wings shredded in the process. It hurts a *lot,* but I’ll be fine. Once I can see Raephim Zara,” I hissed, cutting a glance at Kaelthos. Fire flashed in his eyes, literally blazing as if they’d shoot out of his sockets and burn me to a crisp.

“Let me help you,” Omarion said, flying over to help me start lifting bodies with my wings.

“I said,” Kaelthos cut in, barking. “Anathelle and the dog will bring the bodies themselves to the wingyard.”

“His name is Quazar.”

The words were out of my mouth before I could stop them. I cleared my throat, ignoring the angels who were now all gawking at me. The Fallen Prince included.

“I suppose he can also be called Prince. Highness.” I lifted my eyes to Kaelthos, whose neck was turning dark shades of red. “*Dog* is a bit crass for a Farasee so esteemed, I think. Quazar is simplest.”

I shrugged, flicking my sandals over to lace them up. I finished and lifted my head to find Quazar’s gaze burning holes through me with a curious expression. There was a slight curl to his lips. His eyes danced with amusement.

Focus, Safah.

I remembered my family proverb.

Holy. To whatever end.

Even if it meant putting up with Kaelthos. Even if it meant obeying a tyrant. All the females before me did what they had to so they could Ascend. So would I.

I flexed my wings, gently wrapping six wings around the

lifeless angels, one of them being Fallenspawn. How ironic we were all so different, but in death, the Hallowed and the Fallenspawn all felt the same as I held them in my wings. Their bodies weighed me down. At most I'd only ever carried up to four angels as their bodies were brought to Papi for angelic embalming before their spirits were siphoned for filing.

"Don't be ridiculous," Quazar said down the bond.

I turned to him, just to see he'd put the waistcoat back on, picked up the other bodies with his wings, and had taken two Hallowed from my weight. I didn't protest. I already felt so much lighter. Without a word, Farasee Kaelthos slipped out of the doors. Quazar and I followed him while everyone else quietly watched us leave.

CHAPTER 23

The journey from the wingtower to the wingyard was long, more winding than I thought possible on the Efysien Islet, and exhausting. We'd left the temple grounds completely, flying to a stretch of land that was one massive graveyard.

Tomb portals littered the cloudy floor. Most were closed of course since there were no visitors in this wingyard. Cloudy rivers snaked through the wingyard tumbling through cracks in the mountain base that made them fall like a waterfall made completely of iridescent clouds. Bushels of varying flora littered the ground throughout the tomb portals.

"Follow me," Farasee Kaelthos said.

Quazar and I shared an uncomfortable glance. His face was rigid, set into a contortion of rage and something else I couldn't put my finger on. I looked away, taking the lead in following Kaelthos. We flew through the wingyard, navigating to somewhere near the back. I couldn't help but notice how there was still so much land. As if countless more deaths were expected, and more tomb portals would be going up. I frowned at the sight.

"Here are the tomb portals for the deceased angels."

Kaelthos turned to us.

"Release the bodies so their spirits can be siphoned and their bodies burned by holy fire." His golden eyes fell to me. "You're chosen for Incense Order because we know this task is no new thing to you. You will do the spirit siphoning and you will hold onto their spirits until you reach the Spirit Filing Hall."

I nodded. "Yes, Farasee."

"You maybe begin."

I gently laid the angels I'd carried down. Quazar laid those he'd carried down also. We kept the Hallowed together, and the Fallenspawn together. My body screamed for me to get mended, but there was nothing to be done about it now.

I pressed past my pain, my exhaustion, and focused. It was the least I could do. I closed my eyes. A holy hush fell over the wingyard. I thought about the angels, their lives cut short, and how eternally regretful I was that they lost their lives as collateral due to my own anger.

Tears burned the back of my eyes. I *fyused,* letting my starry light fill the graveyard. I could sense both Kaelthos and Quazar staring at me intently, even with my eyes closed. I pushed them both far away, let my ethèr spread out over the nine bodies, as I said the prayer Papi taught me since he began training me in Spirit Filing.

"To the Infinite who is, was, and will always be, I commend these spirits. Both your Hallowed and Fallenspawn. For all things, there is a season, a time for all activities in the realms beyond Pasaille. A time arrives for us to be born, and also a time to die. You, Infinite, have made all things beautiful in their time, and placed the Ellelights in the hearts of your angels."

A light breeze slipped into the quiet of the wingyard as I continued.

"Oh Infinite, let us be wise as the stars, and be taught to number our dawns, to never forget the vapor that is life, and the brevity of our time in the realms. May we remember our dawns are mere sighs, breaths taken in one moment, and the ending gone in the next. All of us angels are shadows, and our coming and goings come to swift endings, though we live for an Age past another Age. Therefore, every wing of hope we contain, lies with you, forever at your feet."

Tears streamed down my face unbidden as I continued the prayer to its finality.

"When we are in our darkest valleys, fear will never move us, because there you are, always beside us. Your scepter and crown protect, comfort, and guide us all. Infinite, we have full confidence your goodness and unfailing love will never stop pursuing us, each and every dawn of our lives, through the Ages. And we will forever be privileged to live in your house, all through the Ellelights, always and forever. Arèmen."

Done with the prayer, I remained *fyused*, flexing my hands over all the bodies. I released my starfire, first over their bodies, then into them, sifting and searching for their spirits. With all gentleness and care, I gently took hold of the hands of each angel's spirit. Each spirit was thrumming and lively even though their physical bodies were dead.

Tenderly, I urged them out of the bodies, siphoning each spirit one by one. Holding onto my starfire, each spirit began siphoning from the bodies, slipping past hearts, souls, and all entrapments of angelic will. With one last gentle tug, I pulled all nine spirits out of their angelic bodies. They were each silhouettes of shining, golden light with ivory, luminescent eyes that blinked out at me.

"Come," I said.

Summoning multiple Spirit Spheres, I opened up nine cylindrical containers made of the purest crystal mined especially for filing. I first coaxed the Hallowed within their respective cylinders, letting them hover into the air. When I began coaxing the Fallenspawn spirits into their cylinders, Kaelthos's nostrils wrinkled in a nasty curl.

"That won't be necessary."

I snapped my gaze at him, my starry body shimmering under the descending suns.

"I'm...*sorry*?"

Before I could process what he was doing, Kaelthos shot out three fiery, smoke tendrils from his palms, latched them onto the spirits of the Fallenspawn, and began choking them out.

"Farasee Kaelthos!" I screamed.

Stars! This was pure *sacrilege.*

"Have you lost your mind? What are you doing? Desecration of spirits is an abomination *and* forbidden before the Infinite!"

I tried reaching for the spirits, but Kaelthos dodged my futile attempts. Before I could stop him, he used his sunfire mixed with some dark majik I didn't recognize, and completely burned out the spirits until they were gone. Without their spirits being filed, the Fallenspawn were dead for good.

I blinked, absolutely horrified as pure rage colored Quazar's face. Then Kaelthos set the Fallenspawn bodies on fire.

Without thinking, I shot out a blast of starfire. But it didn't work. The fire wouldn't light out. I thrust out more starfire, but the flames wouldn't die. Quazar added in his shadows. But the bodies kept burning. And all we could do was watch until they turned to ash. I stumbled back, mouth hanging.

"What have you done?" I whispered, fresh tears stinging my cheeks.

Never in all my life had I ever seen the spirit of the dead treated so carelessly. I thought Tharic was cruel. Kaelthos was a bonefide monster. Tharic learned every bit of his savagery from his Papi.

Quazar blinked over and over as if he was holding back

tears. He clenched his fists, clearly fighting to rein in his rage. Shadows spilled out of him, tumbling all around us.

"Control yourself, Fallen *dog*," Kaelthos sneered.

Then he turned to me.

"As for you, careful with the spirits of the Hallowed. You're dismissed from here. Take them to be filed." He sniffed the air around me. "Then go purify yourself. You smell like the Hèls."

He turned around, waving his hands. The bodies of the Hallowed lifted into the air, as Kaelthos began maneuvering each through a tomb portal, where they would be laid to rest. Where the Fallenspawn were robbed of the honor.

My mind was unraveling. I'd expected many things from the temple, but I never thought I'd witness this. I blinked through my tears. If Papi were here, he'd be so ashamed. Hating Fallenspawn was one thing. Destroying their spirits was something else entirely. I couldn't move from where I was. I glared at where the Fallenspawn were, as Kaelthos disappeared into one of the tomb portals.

Then his voice rang out.

"Fallen will never have a place among the Hallowed. Remember that, Safah Anathelle. Never forget it if you wish to Ascend."

CHAPTER 24

I tilted my head back, looking up at the two elephantine pillars of gold. Wide as a cathedral and taller than I could visibly see, it seemed the entrance to the Spirit Filing Hall had no end. As an Incense Fuser, I'd be spending a good deal of time here with my Order, just like I'd done back home with Papi.

I floated, rolling a stiff shoulder as my wings hung limp. I didn't have it in me to look at Quazar. My mind had remained relatively quiet.

But I'd gone snooping into the tendrils of where we were connected by temple-bond. Where the veil that marked where I ended, and he began, was. No shadows crossed over. No husky voice spoke through. But the veil vibrated with tension. As if it was being barraged on the other side.

We'd flown to the Spirit Filing Hall in silence. Not like I had the energy anyway. How in the stars was I supposed to make it through whatever this Purification ritual was *and* a Titombwe service without first being mended?

"Disciples first."

Quazar's voice gave me chills. I snuck a glance at him and found him glaring at the pillars. They were etched in carvings I'd seen throughout the Pasaille Scrolls when Papi would let me read his copies, but I hadn't a clue what they all meant. I bet if I had been assigned to Scroll Order I'd have to learn them.

"Any dawn now," Quazar grumbled.

Moody rotpot, I thought to myself.

Nodding, I flew through the gilded pillars and into a hall that stunned me into place. I'd only flown a few paces before I had to stop. I gawked, utterly in awe at the wonder of this Spirit Filing Hall.

The one we had at home was a shame compared to this. Alit by ethèrlamps and endless candles, we flew into a cavernous hall brimming with a holy hush that demanded reverence. I flew forward, slowly, drinking in the beauty.

Everything from the ceiling, to the floors, to the endless row of pillars, was carved out of gold. Between each golden column stood an angel. Upon closer inspection, I realized they were all Farasees.

They looked so real, as if they would blink and come to life at any moment. I passed each, bowing my head in respect until I reached the first set of archways leading further into the Spirit Filing Hall.

I turned and watched Quazar. He looked around, chin lifted high and proud. I couldn't help noticing his confident posture as he held a wide stance. Those stunning eyes took in every detail of the hall. His pitch-black hair and obsidian suit stuck out like a stain on a freshly painted canvas. My golden gown made me blend right in. His raven suit made him a blatant anomaly.

After studying every detail, as if satisfied, Quazar didn't fly. He stomped down the center walkway. And as he did so, he lifted and curled his wing in such a way the middle was bent but the edges were lifted. Then with his right hand he lifted his fore and middle fingers, curled them around each other, and flipped off every single carved statue of the Farasees.

My jaw dropped.

When Quazar reached me, he harshly shoved a feather beneath my chin and slammed my mouth shut.

"Unless you want the males around here filling that pretty mouth of yours however they'd like, I suggest you keep it shut."

He stomped past me leaving me stunned.

Then I felt the spirits wrestling in the containers I had them in.

Right, they needed to be filed.

I rushed after Quazar, still walking. Then I walked past him. He had no reverence for holy work. I wouldn't be shackled to some irreverent demon who couldn't be made to see sense.

Navigating through the halls, I found the architecture curious. At home each wall was straight with precise definition. Here, they were curved, bending in all random directions with circular mirrors hidden in pockets glowing with incandescent light.

Each wall was covered in sparkling starlight that made them even brighter. I flew for a while, curving laterally until I had to start flying vertically. I flew up and up, straining my wings. Wincing against the pain, I tried steeling myself with long breaths while also pulling on strands of starfire to help stitch together whatever I could.

I finally reached the filing chamber and smiled. Being here felt like being home.

I breathed in deeply, taking in the scent of freshly fused incense. It smelled both smoky and sweet giving me a heady feeling. Light poured down like rivers. I had to keep blinking to not feel like I was going blind.

I began humming, the same psalms Papi taught me when I was a youngling, and pulled out the Spirit Spheres with the spirits in them. I looked up and found endless shelves, covered with encased spirits.

All of these were still in the Time of Mourning. They couldn't be moved until the time had passed for them to be properly mourned and grieved. Then they'd moved to the Time of Crossing, taken to another chamber where prayers would be made before the spirits of the angels would be released so they could begin their journey to the Ellelights.

I loosened my wings, letting them hang. I *fyused* and began to float. I hovered higher and higher, searching for any open spaces for the new spirits to enter the Time of Mourning.

"We haven't got all dawn, Starling," Quazar said. A stroke of shadow, surprisingly gentle, curled through my mind. It was a complete distraction. The more the shadow touched, the more I couldn't focus. *"Or did you forget what we'll be cleaning for a month if we're late to Titombwe?"*

Stars. He was right. We couldn't be late for the mass ceremony. Especially with it being my first as a Disciple. I looked around, my starry skin mixing with the incandescence of the chamber, as I hunted for a free spot. I finally found a ledge many levels high, open for the encased spirits I had.

"I commend all of your spirits into the hands of the Infinite. May he bless you, guide you, and keep you with perfect peace. Wings high, dear Hallowed."

I placed the spirits on the shelf and floated backwards. Pulling my wings tight into my spine, I let myself free fall. I dropped like a stone, tumbling alongside the river of light as endless angelic spirits moved around in their eternal cases around me. When I reached the floor, I landed on my feet, *fyusing* back to Seraphim skin.

I found Quazar leaning against the archway frame, his arms and legs crossed, those jade eyes watching me with an expression I couldn't discern. He took in every breath, every step, every flutter of my wings, as if he was memorizing each detail.

I almost snorted. He was probably memorizing where I was broken. Weak. So he could try to end my life again. I frowned, bitterly. His gaze hardened when he saw my face change.

"Ready to be Purified, Starling?" he asked aloud.

"Always," I said, tossing my hair, and walking past him.

CHAPTER 25

I wasn't ready at all. I gawked at the gilded doors, barred shut to all on the outside of it. On either side sat two great sunlions watching us as if we were trespassers.

"Wings high." I bowed my head and wings to each. When I rose again, their starry eyes were shining.

"Star of the Age," the largest on the right breathed. "You and the Wings of Namenthys have come to be Purified."

I blinked, whipping my head towards Quazar. He was glowering at the sunlion as if the beast had just revealed some deep secret. Like I understood it. Namenthys was no longer an existing island. It was now Barrenrock. And for good reason. And what did *Wings of Namenthys* even mean? What did Quazar have to do with the island that was so special?

I watched Quazar with a funny look, staring between him and the sunlion. They seemed locked in a silent battle. One that the sunlion clearly just won. Quazar's cheeks and neck burned hot. The inscription on his neck began to glow and move around. The same happened with his hands. I raised a brow, curious.

"Move your paws," Quazar said out loud. "Or you'll be dealing with Kaelthos breathing fire down your necks."

The sunlions growled, baring their large teeth. I floated back, instantly clearing their personal space before my face was clawed off.

"That *Farasee* has no business here," the other sunlion spat.

"But Quazar is right," I cut in, floating forward again. "We need to go through...whatever this Purification is. And in time for Titombwe. Please, may we pass?"

The sunlions blinked at me, at Quazar. Without another word, they rose to their great paws, unfurling beautiful ivory wings from their spines. They tilted their heads back and roared. Fire shot out of their maws like plumes, burning the shut doors. Once their flames touched the doors, sigils etched into the gold began coming alive. When every sigil was glowing with incandescent light, the doors opened on their own.

I remained still, unsure of what to do. Quazar stomped past me and walked through the doors.

"Wait," I called, rushing after him. Once I was through the doors, they closed shut. When I saw what lay before me, I wanted to scream.

"No burning way."

Quazar chuckled without mirth.

"Welcome to the Temple of Hèls. Where *everything* is a test. Should've kept your wings intact. You'll need them."

I bared my teeth, lifting my wings into position to strike him.

"Safah Anathelle," a deep voice rang out through the air. *"You have participated in enough violence this dawn. You will not strike the Prince. Not in our presence."*

What in the Hèls was going on?

I looked around, unable to see who was speaking. Before us sprawled a long golden staircase that stretched out horizontally into the distance. On either side were endless billows of clouds. There wasn't another spirit in sight. Yet the reprimand terrified me.

I lowered my wings, keeping them to myself.

Quazar slid his gaze to mine.

"So that's what it takes to get you to stop being so...wing-stabby? A voice in the clouds?"

"Seriously," I kissed my teeth. "Piss off."

I pushed past him and began walking along the long stairs. Quazar followed, chuckling to himself. We walked the length of it in silence, until we walked out into an open courtyard with a large basin at the center full of...

"Am I losing my mind, or is that water iridescent?"

I ogled the pool, shocked.

"That's weird," Quazar said from behind me. "Where in all the Elledelle realms did this bleeding temple find iridescent water?"

"They didn't."

The female voice spoke out clearly as a figure slipped out. I dropped my eyes instantly. *Lights*. The angels who handled Purification weren't the Farasees. They weren't Seraphim at all. I took a peek, and saw even Quazar had his head lowered. I couldn't believe we were in the presence of an Iris.

"What are the chances this Iris sings a prophecy of death over us and we both just drop dead like stones right here?" Quazar asked in my mind, slipping past the veil.

I snorted, choking back my laughter too late. How did he get through so easily? Especially when I couldn't get through it to get to *him*.

"Why would you think so ill of us, Namenthien?" the Iris female responded.

In our minds.

Great. More voices in my head.

I kept my mouth shut. I really just wanted to get this over with. I needed a Raephim, not an Iris. I didn't dare speak that out loud, though. Even if it seemed she could read our minds.

Iris were the second ranking angels and higher ranks to Seraphim. With galactic skin, unseeing eyes that glowed like white lights, and ivory hair tumbling to their feet, they all contained immeasurable ethèr within them. Their power was endless. Breathtaking. They were Revelators. If they sang it, said it, or even whispered it, it would come to pass. And with far more cataclysm then any angel could ever fathom.

Iris were not to be played with. They were so powerful, they didn't see with their eyes. They saw with their minds.

I felt so exposed, standing here before her. Or them? She had said "us" after all. Stars. I wanted to turn around and fly.

"Raise your heads and look out," she commanded gently into our minds.

We obeyed her. My nostrils flared at all the ceremonial bowls, baskets, plates, vases, and other items I didn't recognize. These had to be for the Purification ritual I assumed. Or maybe they wouldn't be used at all. While the waters in the large ivory basin were iridescent, the surrounding trees, rooted in the clouds, were ivory with golden leaves.

On a dais beyond, stood seven Iris. Each had different colored galactic skin, with their unseeing incandescent eyes. They wore long, lavish robes that fell down their bodies from the neck down in wide silken waterfalls, colored in shades of ivory, sky blue, lavender, and gold. Each one had strong facial features with thick brows, full lips, winged ears, curvaceous bodies, and bone white hair hanging by their ankles. They were gloriously stunning.

"Mortent Quazar and Seraphim Safah, please remove your clothing, down to your bare coverings. Then enter the purification waters."

"Remove...what?" I looked between the Iris and Quazar, my face flushing. I had to...strip? Stars no. I was not doing it. I wouldn't stand here nude with this son of a Fallen King staring at me like the Farasees had earlier in the dawn. Absolutely *not.*

"Seraphim Safah, you will obey by will or by force. Choose now."

The female Iris left no room for debate in her statement. Quazar began unbuttoning his waistcoat, dropping it to the floor as if he was removing shackles from off his shoulders. Then he started unbuttoning the pressed shirt beneath.

"Are you nuts?" I asked him, eyes widening. "You can't just get naked—"

"Listen," he cut in. "*You* may be willing to go toe to toe with an Iris." He removed the shirt, then started for the buttons of his pants. "Me on the other hand? I've been blessed with the wonderful gift of self-awareness. I'm not getting my tail rocked by higher ranks over some exposed skin."

I watched him drop his pants, kick off his boots, then socks. I couldn't help staring. Stars. Those hypnotizing eyes. Those full, very kissable lips. And *lights*. Those biceps. Strong, muscular...touchable.

I wanted to reach out and brush my fingers down their length. And that stomach. Covered in abs, with a slight sheen of sweat from the heat. But beyond his ripped muscles, my eyes were glued to the inscriptions.

Line after line after line was meticulously inscribed into his skin. I looked them over, but they were in a language I couldn't understand. They curled around his neck, and went down his torso, arms, hands, stomach. And lower still.

I took a peek at his feet, and saw they were covered, too. Every inch of him had these inscriptions. And between the lettering were different images embedded throughout his body, like linguistic emphasis for the written word beneath it.

I blinked several times, mesmerized. Then I remembered I was staring and wrenched my eyes away. Quazar lowered his eyes to mine.

"Well?" He raised a brow. "Titombwe starts at the end of dawn." He blinked, looking into the cloudy heavens. "The suns are descending, Starling."

"I told you to stop calling me that."

"Then stop stalling."

I glared at him.

"I am *not* stalling. This is inappropriate. I am not just going strip myself and—"

"You can't be this grown *and* prude. It just isn't possible," Quazar rumbled. "You're jittery over the body of a male? I'm in my rot...*burning* male briefs. Get a grip on yourself. I'm not cleaning the chambers of the Scourgers because you're afraid of skin," he snapped. "Drop your stupid gown so we can get this over with."

He was right. If I didn't listen, we'd be late for Titombwe, or worse, miss it altogether. I wouldn't give Kaelthos the satisfaction of sentencing us to be handled by the Scourgers.

I turned around, giving my back to Quazar. Stars. I'd never had to expose myself like this to another male, or an audience of higher ranks, before.

Holy. To whatever end.

Our family proverb rang out in my mind, anchoring me. To *whatever* end.

I reached for the clasp at my neck, trying to unfasten it so I could remove the gown. It was stuck. I fumbled with the clasp finding it enmeshed with my tangled coils and some of my feathers.

"Stupid gown," I muttered.

I kept messing with the clasp, but I couldn't undo it. Then large palms covered mine, gently pushing my fingers out of the way. My hearts instantly skipped ten beats, racing wild. My neck grew hot as Quazar gingerly lifted the bottom strands of my hair where it was caught in the clasp.

"Stupid, pretty, curls," he muttered, so low he probably thought I hadn't heard him. "And why does it smell so rotting good?"

My stomach twisted in knots. My hands grew clammy.

His fingers brushed my neck as he gently pulled on the strands. After a few tugs, they slipped out of the clasp where they were stuck. I shifted on my feet as I felt him trying to pluck out my loose feathers. Burning wings. They just had to shed. Quazar finally got my clasp free and loose, undoing it in the process. It fell open, leaving my back exposed. Then he pulled away.

The absence of his body from mine felt like a chasm. Strangely, I felt cold. As if I wanted him to draw close again. I shook my head. I was losing it. It had to be the blood loss. He was the Fallen Prince. The Fallen Prince who got my Manmi killed. I wouldn't be so easily moved. I cleared my throat.

"Thank you...for helping me."

Quazar just grunted.

I frowned. Burning animal. I quickly removed my gown, letting it fall to the floor. I undid my sandals and removed my slip dress. I straightened myself, covered only in the sparkling fabric that wrapped and curved around my bust and the matching underskirt that hung just below the curve of my bottom.

Burning stars, I felt as if I was standing there nude. I turned, refusing to look at Quazar, keeping my eyes straight on the seven Iris. They stood on the dais, impeccable in their perfection, and unmovable. There wasn't a trace of emotion in their expressions.

"You will intertwine your wings, clasp hands, and enter the purification waters. Together."

"Oh you have got to be kid—"

I choked on my words as Quazar stepped close and took my hand in his. My hearts raced as he laced our fingers together. His palm was warm, and surprisingly gentle. He lifted one of his wings to mine. Still looking away from him, I raised a wing that hadn't been shredded by the Spirit Harvesters.

Stars. I was hot, dirty from the trial, covered in bruises, dried blood, and with broken wings. I felt utterly inadequate. Unworthy. To be here. To enter the pool. Even standing by the Fallen Prince, he seemed more redeemed than I.

I bit my lip, wrestling with my foolish thoughts. I looked a mess because I had survived Spirit Harvesters.

And you started a full-on brawl that ended the lives of nine angels, I didn't say to myself.

"Ready?"

Without thinking, I lifted my head, turning to meet

Quazar's gaze. I had to tilt a bit to meet them properly. I thought his gaze would be taunting. Mocking, even. After all, he'd just gotten annoyed at me for being prude.

But his eyes weren't that at all.

The eyes of the Fallen Prince were dark. Ravenous.

His eyes trailed the ringlets of my hair, coiling even more from the heat at my temples. They traveled leisurely down my face, the planes of my neck, the length of my curves, until they slowly made their way back up to my eyes. I shuddered as a delicious heat crawled through my body.

Quazar looked *starved*. He looked at me as if I were a meal he'd gladly lay on a platter and devour whole.

Shadows brushed past the veil in my mind, breaking through to my side of our bond, slithering into my thoughts, pressing up against my very will. For a moment, I couldn't breathe. Couldn't think.

"I..." I stuttered. "Yeah...Yes. Yes, I am."

I rushed to shut the veil between us, struggling to get his shadows out of my head. It was like trying to push back a mountain with my bare hands. Impossible.

Quazar Valoryen curled his lips into a smirk, his jeweled eyes glittering. Then he pulled me with him as we entered the purification pool.

CHAPTER 26

I kept my eyes on the shimmering, iridescent water.

The Fallen Prince kept his eyes on me.

"You are both before us to be purified from shed blood and the loss of innocent lives."

"Innocent lives," I thought in my head. *"I didn't see them dragging Tharic to be purified when he killed the Ascendants trying to join Scroll Order."*

"And you never will, Starling."

He was seriously too good at just slipping in whenever he wanted.

"You can't just keep doing that. I didn't give you permission."

"Boundaries aren't really the point of bonds, Starry One."

"I don't remember ever asking to be bonded. Especially to the likes of you."

"And yet, here we are. This will be good for you. Now you'll

be forced to see how gluttonous you've become, gorging on generations of lies."

"Egotistical, pompous—"

"Are you two done being distracted?"

The Iris cut in, breaking off our mental debate. I pressed my lips into a thin line. I noticed a small grin etching onto Quazar's face. I huffed quietly.

Pretty, gloriously sexy, demon.

I wrenched my eyes away from him, annoyed at how beautiful he was. Annoyed at how every inch of him lured me in like moth to flame.

Quazar held my hand possessively, squeezing our palms as he rubbed the back of my hand with his thumb. I shifted on my feet, twitching at the delicious sensation it triggered down my body.

The female Iris who'd been speaking the entire time opened her arms wide, gesturing to us.

"To purify yourselves, you must dip together *seven times. After you've completed dipping in the waters, we will pour sacred oil over you, pray, and give you of the sacred cup to drink."*

"Drink what exactly?" I blurted out.

I covered my mouth with my free hand. Mentally, even though his face hadn't changed, I felt Quazar laughing on his side of the bond. The Iris's eyes flashed.

"So many questions for one Unclean."

I flinched. Ouch.

Quazar tensed at the rebuke. I was probably imagining it,

but it felt like his fingers wrapped around mine just a bit tighter.

"You may begin."

Quazar and I looked at each other, our wings intertwined, hands still clasped. We bounced on our bare feet at the pool's center. I was still tall enough for my head to remain above the water's surface but Quazar's shoulders were above it. Looking at one another in the eyes, we began to fully submerge ourselves in the iridescent pool. Once, twice, all the way to seven.

By the time we finished, the water had affected the density of my hair. My curls had shrunken tightly. Instead of being past waist length, they were now above mid-back. I wanted to cry. It was going to take forever to air them out, and finger detangle them again.

Quazar and I remained where we were. He was so close, his chest almost pressed against mine. He was a breath away. And the way he looked at me...stars.

I imagined the way the Infinite made the stars, the great lights, the heavens, and cradled them in his hands. How he must have looked at them with such pride, such joy, admiring his eternal handiwork.

That's how it felt to trapped in the prepossessing gaze of the Fallen Prince. It felt like time was slowing. Not only could I feel the writhing movements of his thoughts, but I could feel what he felt. Rage. Hunger. Desire. Need.

The constant flow of his emotions flooded my hearts,

overwhelming my senses. And I sensed something else, as he held on to me, tighter by the moment.

Shadows didn't just fill my mind. It was as if shadows, *his* shadows, were in my very blood, coiling through my body. As if Quazar, or at least his essence, had been fused into me. I felt heady. Hot. Flummoxed.

As if in a trance, I leaned into him. And was shocked when his hand lowered to my waist, and instinctively pulled me close, pressing my chest to his.

"Safah, Starling. Don't start any fires if you're going to put them out. I won't be robbed of my fun."

Our proximity finally clicked in my mind. Quazar's arm was locked around my waist, the other lost...in my hair? And my arms were around his neck.

Wait.

When did that happen? The corners of his lips curled as his eyes danced.

I opened my mouth to say something, my hearts still racing wildly, as the water of the pool grew to a still. I turned and saw all eight Iris, bare feet, walking along the surface of the pool. They didn't make a single ripple, as they elegantly walked over to the center where Quazar and I remained entangled.

Each Iris held in their hands an angel lamp, curved at the neck with a wing-shaped handle, full to the brim with oil. When the Iris reached us, I wanted to look up at them. Instead I felt compelled to keep looking up into Quazar's eyes.

This close to him, I could see how rich the emerald was,

much like the stone itself. Deep within, when I looked hard enough, I saw his irises had circlets of gold around them. A strand of black hair fell into his eyes. Without thinking, I brushed it away, lost in the spell of this male I was supposed to hate.

The Iris began chanting prettily, almost as if they were singing a song. I'd heard some of the words before in old songs Papi would sing to me at twinight so I could fall asleep. Most of what he sang came from our Saccrent, the holy verses. What the Iris were praying now sounded older.

A cool breeze seeped into the Purification chamber, rustling the watery surface of the pool. Without thinking, I leaned into Quazar, resting both hands on his chest before letting my eyes flutter closed. His grip on my waist tightened, sending a flood of heat through my body.

Then the oil began to pour. There was so much. Oil lamp after oil lamp was tipped over our heads. I was coated entirely in the holy oil from head to foot as it slipped down my body all the way to my feet beneath the water. When the Iris finished their singing, I opened my eyes.

Quazar was as soaked as I was in oil. He quirked the smallest of smiles. The sight made my hearts jump. For a moment, I forgot about the fact that he was the Fallen Prince, and I was the fifi of the Farasee he'd gotten killed by helping Fallen breach the realm gates.

In this moment, he simply looked like a handsome male with eyes full of mischief. Then Quazar's eyes grew cold. Hateful. Angry.

I froze.

Every ounce of warmth I'd just felt towards him withered. I tried to pull away from him, but he kept his arm locked tight around me like a vise. I was disgusted with myself for being stupid enough to think any good about him.

Without looking up at the Iris, eyes still piercing into me, he asked, "Are we done here?"

Acid slithered in my gut. I felt as if I'd been cut through with a knife. I curled my lips at him, ripping my hands away.

"No. The sacred cup remains. Take. And drink."

I was given the cup first. It was a gilded goblet with a drink that looked much like angel wine. Without questioning it, I downed the entire thing.

The goblet refilled on its own. I shoved it at Quazar, letting it go so he was forced to catch it without being able to touch me. When he finished, the goblet vanished.

"Your Purification has ended. You may leave with our blessing."

Before Quazar could turn away first, I was already rushing out of the pool, and up the steps after snatching my gown and sandals. The moment I was no longer in the pool waters, the oil seeped into my skin, fusing into my blood with a warm hum. I bent over and gasped.

I didn't feel any pain.

I stretched from side to side. Pulled my wings in front of me. Mended. I was completely mended.

My wings were back in perfect shape. My bruises were gone. I'd been made whole in the purification pool. I threw a silent prayer at the Infinite, beyond grateful at my injuries being removed before they could get worse and get infected.

I ignored Quazar completely, flooding the veil between our bond with my starfire, sealing it shut, and kicking him out of my mind entirely. I dressed swiftly, clasping my gown and donning my sandals.

"Thank you—" I whipped around to thank the Iris.

But they were already gone.

Without waiting for Quazar, I spun around, spread my wings, and shot away. Instead of the long walk, I flew over the elongated trail of stairs through the cloudy billows.

My eyes stung with hot tears. I bit them back. I would never shed a tear for that cold, cruel, heartless thing called a Fallen Prince.

I flew with all my might, shooting like a star in gold across the cloudy expanse, until I made it to the doors. They were open again, as if they'd been waiting for our exit.

I flew out, quickly bowed to the sunlions, and raced out of the Purification Hall. I navigated through the large building, flapping my wings to give me speed. I raced with all I had, fighting the tightening knot forming in my chest.

How had I been so stupid? So foolish to believe he'd... What? Changed? Idiot. I was such an idiot.

I rushed out of the Purification Hall and began flying over the ridiculously vast expanse of the temple grounds. The Purification Hall was perched on a hill to the east of the temple. Even by flight, it was some distance to the main cathedrals. I flew hard and fast, cutting through cathedrals, flying over fountains, rushing past the perfect landscape that made up all of Temple Efysis.

When I finally made it to the common areas, I couldn't help but notice the gods and goddesses. This cluster were laughing with themselves, being entertained by something. Their chained gowns clang, making noise as they moved around freely. Until they saw me coming.

Immediately they stopped laughing. Stopped enjoying themselves. I felt awful, as they lowered their heads. Tears flooded my eyes. One of the goddesses lifted her head. She frowned when she saw my forlorn expression.

Before she could say a word, I looked away, flying higher, angling through the twists and turns of the grounds, until I made it to the wingtower of First Dominion, Seventh Choir.

I raced through the doors, yanking off my sandals. I instantly spotted her blonde hair and aquamarine eyes.

"Ellie," I broke, my voice choked off.

Daelun and Omarion looked up at me, concern lacing their faces as they looked between me and Ellabeth. I threw myself into my bestfriends arms, overwhelmed and no longer able to keep everything that had happened inside.

Ellabeth wrapped her arms around me and squeezed. Then she took my hand and flew me to her room. With the door shut, and the both of us sitting cross-winged on her bedcloud, Ellabeth leaned in, her eyes blazing like churning oceans out for blood.

"Tell me everything."

CHAPTER 27

Stepping out of the star gate into the massive amphitheater was jarring. For a brief moment, all that existed was the quiet of the gate as I traveled, feeling like I was being shot across the galaxy through the stars. I was entirely enveloped in starlight with a rush of breezy wind.

As I stepped from the star gate, and planted myself midair, I hovered over a platform that led into Titombwe—the largest amphitheater in all of the Ouanaviel Empyrean. Empràr Zadkias had an obsession with them.

Smaller versions could be found throughout Ouanaviel, and across all the neighboring islands. He enjoyed the thrill of having mass ceremonies performed in them. He also used them for entertainment. Sport. Terror.

One never knew what Titombwe would consist of. Either worship of the Infinite, or a game of angels versus gods where they had to fight to the bloody end.

"Something about this Titombwe feels different."

I looked at Ellabeth as she floated over from her star gate.

"What do you mean?" I asked.

"The air is charged with something..." She looked around, squinting across the darkness. "I can't put my finger on it. But something's...off."

"Mm." I looked around Ouanaviel's colosseum. The trimoons hung overhead, the bright silver stars etched in ivory shining down on us. A light breeze kissed the air of the night promising a soothing chill. "I don't know, Ellie. It seems like any other Titombwe mass we've ever attended. Come on."

I began floating around, hunting for a good seat. Presbitari Davithius had given us free will. Titombwe was a public event, where angels and the other Elledellien races were invited to come watch and participate. Since everyone who chose to come would be here, all Disciples were allowed to split up and be with their friends and family from outside of Temple Efysis.

I searched the dark for silver eyes with purple streaks, purple eyes, thick hair, and swirling starlight. If my family was here, streaks of their starry ethèr would give away their position. I scanned the millions of angels present, as they all filed into the innumerable amount of cloudchairs available.

"You really don't sense it, Sazu?" Ellabeth asked. She was scanning, too. I followed her gaze and fanned out into a close direction. If we could find the blonde headed, water-ethèred Riventhelles, then I'd spot the Anathelles, too. "The air is charged."

"Ellabeth." I flew across rows of cloudchairs, passing gilded upholsteries covered in glass with platters of food, Saccrents, and bowls of incense. "It's Titombwe. There's a gazillion angels here. Not to mention, the Gods, Giants, Shifters...*everyone* is here. Of course there is a 'charge' in the air. But it's not anything sinister."

I flew up several levels, passing row after row, aiming for higher ground to scan the mass of Titombwe better. Stars. Why was the colosseum so stars-forsaken large?

"Whatever." Ellabeth kissed her teeth. "I'm telling you, something's up."

I didn't answer. Flying to an archway, I hovered by the ivory stones, looking over the sea of golden cloudchairs already filling up with angels, and the differing races, from all over Ouanaviel. Down by the lower levels, reserved for nobility, Farasees, Empyrean Legionnaires and Watchers, and angels of Seraphim rank, I spotted a flash of starlight.

Found them.

I spread my wings and shot down from my high perch like lightning. The fresh wind brushed my cheeks as I descended endless rows, flying past all the attendees until I made it down to where most of the Disciples were seated with their loved ones.

Up close, I spotted a head of ivory. When he turned, his silver eyes with purple streaks plastered the widest grin on my face.

"Ezekiel!" I shrieked. His head snapped to my direction. My eldest brother floated to me, arms wide, and scooped me up. I squeezed him tight, fighting tears. "I've missed you! Stars. We haven't seen you since you left for the Seal Gate!"

"Sazu," he said, affectionately. "You did it. You burning did it. You're a Disciple."

"Did you ever doubt me?"

He scoffed, pulling his head back to reveal a wide, white-toothed grin. "You're an Anathelle. I'd never doubt you."

"Stop hogging the little runt!"

I spun and found Hosea already reaching over to scoop me out of Ezekiel's arms and into his tight embrace. I laughed as my brother squeezed me like I was still a youngling.

"Save some for us, too, yeah?"

I opened my eyes and found my other brothers, Uriah and Gabriel, waiting for their embrace. I threw myself into the warm hugs of my brothers, before a throat cleared itself.

When Gabriel, who was younger than me by a few hundred cycles, put me down, I turned to find Jael and Evanae with crossed arms but beaming eyes. They stared at my golden Disciple gown with shining pride.

I grinned as I threw myself into their arms. All three of us squeezed each other for a long time. Stars, I'd missed them so burning much. So much had happened since I'd left. It had only been several weeks since becoming a Disciple, but it felt like I'd already been in the temple for *cycles*.

"Gold looks good on you."

Jael smiled at me, making me flush. My older sister had always been hard to impress. But seeing her mauve eyes glitter with pride made something in my chest swell. Evanae slipped closer, looking like a youngling version of Papi, with bright silver eyes, bone white, braided coils down her spine, and umber skin.

"Do you like it in there?"

Evanae watched me with a curiosity that almost made me laugh. I slipped her hand into mine, lacing our fingers.

"It's been...interesting. To say the least."

"What does interesting mean?" Hosea raised a brow, his purple eyes watching me intently. Like me, he got Manmi's features. Sharp eyes, brown skin, dark brown hair.

"I don't even know how much I can share?" I shrugged. "Manmi prepared me for a lot, but there's still so much I wasn't ready for. The amount of deaths being among them."

"I'm...sorry." Jael butted in. "*Deaths?*" Her eyes widened. "Of whom?"

"Disciples, Jayi," I whispered. "They've been dropping like shadowbats with everything we have to do in there. Surprise trials. Bonding us to the Fallenspawn—"

"The *whom?*" my siblings chorused all at once.

Trumpets began blaring as tanbou drums began to beat all over Titombwe.

"Letters," Hosea said, leaning into my face. "Write them. *Send* them. With details."

I snorted. "As if *you* can read them, *Watcher* Hosea! Deployed Watchers in active combat don't have time for letters."

"Yeah? Well, Incense Fusers *do,*" Jael said, raising a brow.

I opened my mouth to say something else when the trumpets blew a final warning for everyone to take their seats. I sat in the middle of my siblings, with Evanae to my right, still holding my hand. Jael sat at my left. Uriah and Hosea sat on the other side of Jael, while Gabriel and Ezekiel sat on the other side of Evanae. Papi had always instilled in my brothers to shield us Anathelle females at all costs, no matter where we were, regardless of age and distance of time.

I leaned forward, tilting my head to look for Ellabeth. I found her, also nestled at the center of her three older brothers. We smiled at each other, before I leaned back in my cloud-chair and faced forward.

I looked around, marveling at the diversity of life all around Titombwe. The Shifters all sat in one section this twinight, remaining in their dominant form.

The Dragèth sat perched on stone mounds. The dragons clustered together, sitting tall and proud, their large, scaly bodies gleaming beneath the starlight. The Pagali were adjacent to them, as the Pegasi sat on their haunches, their hooves scuffing the ground. I didn't see any Unikai. It seemed the unicorns opted not to show up. But the Ylisks were also here. I stared at the terrifying basilisks as they swung their serpentine heads, looking around as if searching for prey.

Then there were my fellow Angels. All the angels sat mainly with their own ranks. The only ranks that weren't present were the two higher than Seraphim: the Calvaethim and Iris.

Thank the living stars.

Calvaethim lived in a separate realm where the Infinite

himself physically called home. The realm of the Ellelights. Their presence here would mean certain judgment and cataclysmic punishment.

I frowned. I knew there were Iris angels here because eight of them were in the Purification Hall. But none of them found this Titombwe mass important enough to be present.

"Strange," I muttered. "Not only are there no Calvaethim and Iris angels, but I don't see the Giants or the Merriens, either."

Uriah snorted, running a hand through his braided, ivory hair.

"The Giants are definitely not coming. They're protesting."

Ezekiel laughed. "As if the Empràr will actually give a rot."

"And the Merriens?" I asked.

"At war," Hosea chimed in. "They don't have time to come and sit around."

Evanae sighed dreamily. I glanced at her and traced her gaze. The corners of my lips began curling into a sinister smile.

"Not you having the hots for the Faerèth?"

"The fae are just...*whew*."

Her eyes were glued to a Faerèth male with deep brown skin, pointed ears, light green eyes, and dark hair down his back clasped by gemstones. He was dressed like a royal, and had the posture of one.

"Angels don't mate fae, Vava," I nudged her.

She snapped her head toward me. "And why the stars not?"

"Are you nuts up here?" I tapped her temple. "We rarely even mate outside of our own rank. You think it's simple to mate outside of our race?" I pointed at the male. "You're an angel, Vava. A Seraphim no less. He'd *never* be able to handle you."

"She's right," Uriah said, piercing eyes on the Fae male. "He'd also die quicker. You forget one cycle for us is one *thousand* for them. We age much slower than the Faerèth. Then *all* of the other races. Wanting a male that isn't an angel is literally begging for heartbreak."

"Granmanmi's up," Hosea butt in.

I squeezed Evanae's hand in support as she sighed sadly, finally turning away from the fae male. We sat back into our cloudchairs, our wings hanging over the back. Granmanmi Asarah floated out of a chamber. It took me a moment to realize it was the imperial box of the Empràr.

"Wings high, Elledelliens of Ouanaviel!"

"Wings high," we all chorused. Every angel leaned forward, slapping their wings together twice, before leaning back.

Immediate silence fell over Titombwe. Granmanmi was in her pristine, ivory Farasee robes, her hair adorned beautifully as her purple eyes gleamed in the starlight.

I noticed she was scanning the mass of Titombwe, looking for something. When she spotted us, her grand-younglings, she beamed. Alongside my siblings, I bowed my head, acknowledging her with reverence. Satisfied, Granmanmi kept speaking.

"On behalf of Empràr Zadkias Claudevin and the entire imperial family, the Farasee Order, and Ouanaviel at large, I want to welcome all of you to our first Timtobwe..." A pause. "With our newly Ascended Disciples."

A raucous shout exploded across the colossal amphitheater as Angels, Shifters, Faerèth, and Gods all cheered.

"Would every Disciple from Temple Efysis please stand."

Hearts swelling with pride, I pushed out of my seat and floated into the air. Each of us Disciples, spread out across the amphitheater, received an ovation. Even from where I sat, I could tell who belonged to which Order. I kept my chin high as Granmanmi watched me, a proud smile on her face as her eyes danced.

"Each of these Disciples you see have all flown and survived the first Starfellien Ascent in over one thousand cycles."

Wait. What? What did Granmanmi mean the first one in a millennia? That couldn't be true. Farasee Esau and Davithius said—

"*What*?" Jael cried, tilting her head up at me. My brothers did the same. The look in their eyes made me question the joy that was flooding through my veins. They all looked...angry. But why?

"*That's* what she meant by bodies dropping," Hosea grumbled. "No one makes it through that Ascent without shedding their blood." His eyes burned. "Let me guess. Started with seven thousand and ended up with three?"

I pressed my lips together, my joy withering. My chest tightened. He wasn't wrong. He was spot on. And the anger flashing in his purple eyes told me he knew more about the Ascent than even I did.

"I cannot believe you were thrown into a rotting culling," Ezekiel spat. He turned his head to Granmanmi, the veins in his neck growing taut.

I lowered back into my seat with all the other Disciples as Granmanmi began a long, elaborate but eloquent speech about her love for the Infinite, Temple Efysis, and being a willing servant to the Saccrent.

I squirmed in my seat as Ezekiel consistently snuck glances at me, his eyes fuming. He was *not* happy to hear I'd had to fly the Starfellien Ascent. I bit my lower lip, trying to stay focused on Granmanmi's words.

"We want to acknowledge all of our other guests present. The Shifters, Gods, and Faerèth. Thank you to all of you for joining this momentous occasion. Unfortunately, the Merriens were attacked once more by the Serène and couldn't make it. We pray the Infinite will give them a sure victory over the sirens."

"Arèmen!" We all chorused together.

"Now." Granmanmi gestured to the large audience. "This cycle is also special, because the Infinite saw fit to challenge the Farasee Order in a new way. As a means to continue strengthening our defenses against Fallen attack, and breach of the Seal Gate, we launched a new initiative. The pairing of our Hallowed Disciples..." Granmanmi paused, letting her words hang in the air. Then. "With the Legionnaires of Azarath Academy."

"No *rotting* way," Uriah seethed. "Are they nuts?"

Ezekiel slowly swung his head my way. His eyes had lost all color, the hue becoming raven black. My spine began tingling. Stars. What was my brother trying to piece together?

Granmanmi was undeterred, speaking through all the hushed whispers that broke out.

"We have brought a small subset of the Azarath Legions into Temple Efysis."

She took a moment to let it sink in. I knew the bomb she was about to drop before she did it.

"Including the Xadari Legion, which is made up entirely of Fallenspawn."

A roar broke out, mainly over the angels, as bellows exploded at the mention of the Fallenspawn. Granmanmi spoke without shouting, using ethèr to amplify her voice over the millions of shouting angels. Ezekiel's gaze burned into my skin as Granmanmi kept speaking.

"And yes, the Xadari Legion is led by none other than Quazar Valoryen. Fallen Prince—and heir—to the cursed, exiled, and Fallen angel, Zemshaza Beliah, High King of the Souls Court and ruler of the six, abominable, Hèls."

CHAPTER 28

I sucked in a sharp breath at the revelation.

"You're the WHAT?" I shouted down the bond at Quazar.

It went nowhere. He'd sealed the veil between us tight. No matter how hard I mentally slammed myself against it, the burning veil didn't move.

I sank into my seat, wings twitching as Granmanmi continued. A sinister gleam filled her eyes as she spoke again, quieting the uproar.

"I'm sure you all remember the attack on the Seal Gate three hundred cycles ago, when the hèlborn—demons of the Fallen—crossed through the gate. They came as a coordinated hoard, destroying so many of our precious, Hallowed lives. But one of those lives broke me above all others."

She grew quiet here, her eyes turning to me. To my siblings. Stars. She wasn't about to bring that up here, was she? We all tensed. Jael and Evanae scooted closer to me. My brothers sat ramrod straight, eyes glued to the dais.

"What many may or may not know, is we had several Farasees commissioned to the Seal Gate to assist with that warfront. Among the Farasees was my precious fifi, Amaryss Anathelle."

A pause. Granmanmi turned her gaze elsewhere. When I tracked where she was looking, I found her glaring at the long row of Fallenspawn sitting at the very front. And in front of them all, was Quazar, in that accursed, finely pressed suit, while all the other Fallenspawn were in black, fighting robes.

"That warm, bloody dawn, my fifi was slaughtered when a small group of fallen angels broke through the gate and killed her, among many others. Because, well." Her eyes flashed. She smiled, sweet as poison, at Quazar. "They had help from a certain *Prince*."

My eyes fluttered shut. I tuned out the noise of the angels erupting with rage. Evanae and I squeezed hands, holding onto each other for support.

My little sister still grieved deeply every cycle when it got close to Manmi's birthdawn. I could feel her trembling, fighting not to break down with tears. Jael and my brothers sat stiff as boards. We were all power kegs waiting to explode.

"But! Death should always inspire ways to prolong life."

I opened my eyes to look at Granmanmi. Something in her tone pricked my hearts. Her small smile seemed to curl, cruelly.

"So thanks to the Fallen Prince, I took it upon myself to

create something that would make sure the Fallenspawn could prove their loyalty to the empyrean."

I sat up in my seat. What was she on about?

Granmanmi looked up and around. She spread out her arms, letting a wave of starlight twirl around her.

"My Elledelliens. We all know the Creed! We all clap our wings to the law! Blood for blood!"

"Blood for blood!" the angels chorused.

"What in the six Hèls is she talking about?"

I looked at my siblings. My older siblings remained quiet, eyes glues to the dais. Evanae shrugged, confused. Gabriel looked between us and Granmanmi but said nothing.

"Blood for blood!" Granmanmi called out again.

"Blood for blood!" the angels chorused.

A deliciously dark hum slipped into my mind from the other side of the veil. A small trickle of shadows danced into my mind.

"Ready to witness the sins of your Matriarchs, spawn of Anathelles?"

Before I could respond, the shadows receded, disappearing altogether before the veil in our minds slammed shut. My throat felt dry like the sands of the Ouanaviel seashore.

"After seeking audience with the Infinite in our great, and holy, temple, searching for a way to turn the tragedy of my fifi into progress, the brightest idea came to me."

I leaned forward. It felt like everyone had. From Angels, to Faerèth, to Gods, to Shifters.

"Alas, thanks to our dear Prince—with the blessing of High Profèt Samael and the wise guidance of our merciful, and righteous, High Farasee, Manazzra Ahabiah—I thought of, and began to implement, what we call Blood Rites."

"What in the stars-forsaken Hèls are Blood Rites?" I called down the bond, shoving the question at the veil, hoping it would break through.

It didn't.

Since the Purification Hall, our bond had gone quiet. Not dark, but quiet. Which ticked me off, because now I needed answers only he could give the way I needed to hear them.

"Rather than explain to you about the necessity and power of these Blood Rites, this twinight we will demonstrate the ritual instead."

Granmanmi gestured to the Fallenspawn. "Now, the Blood Rites were created for *all* Fallenspawn to participate. For them all to share in the burden of proving fealty to the empyrean. Instead, their Prince, Quazar Valoryen, negotiated, really he begged the Farasee Order, to let him take the full share of the burden unto himself. And in our generosity, we obliged."

My nostrils flared. I found myself holding my breath. Clinging to the sides of my gown, fisting my hands in the fabric. When I released her hand, Evanae latched onto my arm, clinging to me with terror. My hearts began racing.

"Quazar?" I called out. *"Quazar!"*

Nothing.

"Before we begin the Blood Rites and continue on with our Titombwe mass, I would like us to stand and take a moment of silence for a great loss to the empyrean. The loss of Farasee Amaryss Anathelle who laid her life down for the protection of her empyrean and Empràr."

My siblings and I shot to our feet, alongside every one else. I took deep breaths through my mouth, trying not to hyperventilate.

Then my siblings and I floated further into the air, hovering above the rest. Eyes across Titombwe looked up at us. Including the Fallenspawn.

Together, we bent to our knees, then bowed over in the air. Lifting our wings, we bent them forward in a bow while covering our heads with a pair of wings. A sign of honor, reverence, and mourning.

"These are the younglings Amaryss left behind, thanks to Quazar Valoryen, Zemshaza's heir," Granmanmi said with a clear, but saddened voice. She was intentionally making a point with her choice of words, and it was working. "Legionnaire Ezekiel, Incense Fuser Jael, Watcher Hosea, Cadetti Uriah, Disciple Safah, and younglings Gabriel and Evanae."

Titombwe remained silent. As one, every angel rose, lowered their heads and folded their wings in quiet mourning. After a long while had passed, Granmanmi cleared her throat.

"Thank you for taking a moment for our beloved Amaryss. Now," She pointed at Quazar. "Fallen Prince, please join me on the dais."

I sank back into my seat, a mess of all kinds of emotions.

Rage. Anger. Brokenness. Longing for my Manmi. Grief. Vengeance for the head of the handsome Fallenspawn now making his way to the dais.

I found it odd how all of the Legionnaires from Azarath Academy wore their loose fighting robes with leather attachments, but he didn't. He was constantly in that ridiculous looking suit.

"Dressed like the Prince you are." Granmanmi Asarah chuckled, gesturing for him to fly to the center of the dais. "You know what to do *Prince* Quazar."

I raised a brow, my eyes glued to the charades. Quazar kept his back straight. His chin lifted. There wasn't a thing out of place on him. His hair, clothes.

He had no weapons, but none of us were fools. *He* was the weapon all by himself. He floated to land on his feet at the end of the dais, sauntering over to the center where Granmanmi pointed.

"What's Granmanmi doing?" Hosea whispered.

Ezekiel grunted, tossing and catching a dagger he'd slipped out from his waist. He continued the motion while his eyes remained below. I watched my siblings. We all bore the same tension in our taut shoulders, and angled jawlines. Each one's winged ears were twitching, as if they were on high alert.

I looked back to the dais. And found Quazar standing barefoot, half naked, with his chin lifted high. Even from where I sat, I could see his emerald eyes blazing, the golden trails around them glowing.

He looked like a god. A conqueror. Like the whisper of death from an open invitation. One that I was dumb enough to consider accepting.

He wore nothing but obsidian leggings that clung to him like liquid. I couldn't help but drink in that chiseled body, those hypnotizing eyes, and the pride that squared his wide shoulders. He kept his wings loose behind his back, as if he was being examined by a Raephim on just another random dawn.

"He's pretty to look at," mumbled Evanae wistfully.

"I wonder who this wicked prince is actually bonded to since Safah said the Disciples were made to temple-bond to them," Uriah said, eyes looking at Quazar with an unreadable expression, masked heavily in the twinight.

I kept my mouth shut.

My older siblings, Jael and Hosea, would know immediately from my tone if I was hiding something. And right now, I was not about to tell them *I* was the one bonded to the Fallen Prince.

"What in all the realms is on his body? It's everywhere."

My brothers nodded at Jael's observation.

The inscriptions.

I thought they'd just been on his body from his neck to his stomach and down his arms and hands. Instead, they covered his entire body from neck to foot.

I swallowed. What in the stars did it mean? He had other images and symbols engraved into his skin colorfully, but for the most part, it was the inscriptions.

"Maybe he's cursed," Evanae whispered, reaching for my hand and taking it into hers. "A wicked prince of curses."

I snorted.

That was a generous way of putting it.

"May the Rites begin!" Granmanmi called.

Silence reigned across Titombwe.

I stilled. I tried to breathe. I couldn't.

I looked at Quazar.

Somehow, despite the innumerable number of angels, dragons, fae, and all of the different races present, somehow the Fallen Prince still found a way to find *me*.

Those jade eyes snapped to mine, glittering with profound hatred. He breathed in a deep breath, hands clenching into fists, his eyes promising nothing but absolutely Hèls for me.

As if *I* was the one parading him before the entire empire like some unicorn for auction. I was tempted to pull my eyes away from him, but I didn't. I *wouldn't*.

The Fallen Prince glared at me.

And I glared back.

Crimson red ethereal cords shot out through the glass top platform, latching onto Quazar from all ends. Several Fallenspawn shot to their feet, crying out. They were yanked down by their fellow Fallenspawn by their wings, keeping them quiet and in place.

I studied the cords. I'd never seen them before.

"Those are bloodletters," Jael said barely above a whisper, almost in shock. "The Farasees have access to *bloodletters*?"

"Holy stars," Hosea breathed.

I watched as what Jael called bloodletters latched onto Quazar like leeches. There were so many of them.

My seven hearts began racing. I tried anticipating what was about to happen, but I'd never been exposed to Blood Rites before.

As I looked at Quazar, it seemed like the world fell away. As if in this moment, whatever was about to happen, while it was in front of the world, it was almost like it was happening just between him and I. I checked the veil of our bond. It was still there, stronger than ever.

Yet, I couldn't help the sensation as if I could still *feel* Quazar. In my blood. My bones. My soul.

I felt his hatred and how it grew for me with every passing moment. I wish to the stars I could make him feel mine. After all, he was on that dais now because of what he'd done to my Manmi.

"Blood for blood," Granmanmi said softly, but every ear in Titombwe heard her loud and clear. "For the Infinite, for the empyrean, for Farasee Amaryss. Blood for *blood*."

The last word was spoken like a curse.

Then Quazar began to roar.

The bloodletters pierced into his body with spikes jutting out from their ends. I shot forward in my cloudchair, slamming my hands over my mouth. A cacophony of excitable screaming exploded across the arena. Lust for blood tainted the air as angels screamed for more.

The inscriptions on Quazar's body came to life, glowing

bright and golden across his skin. Whispers filled the air, reading the text aloud for us to hear. But it was an old tongue. A dead language. No one knew what it meant.

Poised like nobility, Granmanmi Asarah floated close by, watching Quazar as he was bled out, intently. Quazar strained against the bloodletters with all his might, but there was nothing to do for it.

As Quazar screamed, the bloodletters drained his blood. Every last tendril began filling with the golden ichor, as it began seeping down the tendrils, into the glassy foundation, and beyond to who knew where. I hyperventilated as the beast of an angel, tall as a mountain, and probably strong like one, too, was brought to his knees. His limbs began contorting from an unseen force. Black veins began crawling up his bronze-kissed arms, his neck, his face. As if he was being drained of life. Being drained of his very spirit. His soul.

My stomach twisted, forming a knot that made me ill. I thought I would turn over and vomit with how nauseous I felt.

Quazar roared in agony. The angels roared back, demanding he give more of his blood. The more he bled, the more his inscriptions came to life, evidence of his curse.

My Safah. My precious fifi. Bend, but do not break. Burn, but never bleed. Never, ever *let them see you bleed, Safah. Promise me.* Manmi would say.

Who, Manmi? I'd asked.

Everyone, she responded gravelly. *No one can see you bleed, my Star.*

I ground my teeth together unable to wrench my eyes away from the curse crippling Quazar. From the blood being drained from him. *Stars*. There was so much blood. My hearts galloped at a speed I wasn't sure I'd survive. My hands shook. I struggled to breathe.

"*You* are the one bonded to him, aren't you, Safah?"

I didn't look at Ezekiel.

But now all my siblings were looking at me.

I only had eyes for the Prince who'd now fallen to his knees and was writhing in agony from the torture. My nostrils flared as tears pricked my eyes.

This was what I wanted, wasn't it? I wanted him to pay. I wanted him to suffer.

I wanted him to *break*.

But now that he was, now that he was being ripped apart, not just in front of me, but in front of the entire empyrean, why wasn't I happy about it? Why did I feel sick to my stomach?

He'd earned this when he'd set my Manmi up to be slaughtered. And yet, his pain, his anguish, didn't satisfy me. Every last one of my seven hearts were breaking instead.

"Safah," Ezekiel pushed. "Is the Fallen Prince your temple-mate?"

Hèls. After what we'd experienced through Purification earlier, he was probably more than that now.

"Yes," I whispered.

Quazar let out a scream so wrangled with pain, I bowed over, gripping my chest over my hearts. Still, I didn't look away. I felt like I *had* to keep watching. Like I owed it to myself. To Manmi.

It was sick and twisted, but I made myself watch as blood seeped down his arms. His legs. Bathed the floor where he'd fallen, rolling in his own death.

Now, the Blood Rites were created for all Fallenspawn to participate. For them all to share in the burden of proving fealty to the empyrean. Instead, their Prince, Quazar Valoryen, negotiated, really he begged the Farasee Order, to let him take the full share of the burden unto himself. And in our generosity, we obliged.

Stars.

They would bleed him out for every Fallenspawn. I looked over to where they'd been sanctioned to sit. Every last Fallenspawn was on their feet, necks tense, hands clenched in fists, jawlines hardened as they watched their Prince get tortured like an animal for sport.

Then they all started to turn and look up at me. My brothers scooted in, spreading their wings around my sisters and I. I closed my eyes.

I didn't know what to do. How to feel. The bloodletting went on and on. My mind filled with the symphony of Quazar screaming. But never, not once, did he beg for it to end. Did he ask for them to stop. He took it. He let them bleed him. Because if he didn't bleed, the Fallenspawn would.

Unbidden, tears began streaming down my face. I felt torn. By truths I'd worn like armor only to find there were chinks in the mail. This was what I wanted but it felt so *wrong*. It didn't satisfy me. Instead, it tore me apart.

"Sazu," Hosea whispered, wrapping a wing around me, as Evanae leaned in, clinging on to me.

"Sissy," she whispered. "I'm sorry."

I let the tears flow. I sobbed uncontrollably, clinging to my gown at my chest. I felt his anguish. Felt his pain. Felt his tears. His sorrows. I let my mind rail. Let my hearts break. For Manmi. Myself.

For *him*.

Finally satisfied, Granmanmi Asarah called out once again. "Blood for blood!"

"Blood for blood!" the arena screamed out, as if on a high.

The bloodletting tendrils disappeared. And by some outrageous miracle, Quazar rolled himself over with his bloodied wings, pushed to his feet, and began hobbling off the dais. I watched him take every agonizing step, until he finally reached Dakairi, who immediately took him into his arms. Then Quazar collapsed into his best friend.

I bowed over, dropping my head in my lap. Soothing hands brushed my back. I didn't know who it was. I didn't care.

"Let Titombwe commence!"

I didn't recognize the voice. It wasn't Granmanmi.

Stars. *Granmanmi*. How many times had she done this?

The amphitheater exploded with raucous joy and applause as music began playing. I figured the Cherubim had come out to sing and celebrate.

I couldn't move. My head remained low and in my lap. I felt disgusting. Entirely ill. I couldn't stop these rotting tears from flowing.

The soothing hand on my back never stopped. As Titombwe continued, I never stood up to join in the celebrations. And as time went on, I realized that none in my family had either.

CHAPTER 29

I stared at the door of my bedchamber, frozen in place. I didn't want to go out there. Since Titombwe, I'd locked myself inside. Seven dawns had gone by and I still couldn't go an hour without crying fresh tears over what I'd witnessed.

Papi always said vengeance bore a weight most angels could never carry. Ellabeth tried to see me, but I wouldn't let her in.

Raephim Zara forced herself in twice. She wanted to make sure I was eating. Getting out of bed. Functioning.

"The temple will drain your soul if you let it," Zara said during a visit. "Don't."

A blaring ring sounded throughout the wingtower once again, signaling it was time for Sanctuary. Stars. I wanted to be anywhere but there. All I could see was golden blood on glass floors as the crescendo of agony crashed into it like cymbals. I wanted to stay here. Hide. But it was time to face reality. And determine where I would stand in it all.

I pushed open my door with a wing, walking out barefoot with my head hanging low. I was met with melancholy silence. I took a deep breath, anchoring myself as the chill of the floor seeped into my feet.

Deep breaths. In, out.

For Infinite's sake. I felt so heavy. So burdened. Like an elephant was sitting on my chest, cutting off my ability to rightly breathe. Tears prickled the back of my eyes. Flashes of Titombwe seared my memory.

Granmanmi's speech. The moment of silence for Manmi. The bloodletters. Quazar.

What made it worse, my siblings seemed to know something I didn't. Including my young, sweet Evanae.

When the angels danced and celebrated. When the Faerèth joined in. While the Gods remained in their place and the Shifters seemed outraged, not one of my siblings participated in the Titombwe celebrations. Not one took joy in the brutalization of Quazar.

That made matters much more complicated. I had to know more about the dawn Manmi died. Papi said Temple Efysis refused to allow him access to the records about her passing. So be it. *I* would find them. And stars willing, I would find the truth.

Eyes still closed, I flexed my hands and summoned my sandals. Burning stars. Everything ached. Doing the simplest of tasks required a world of energy.

"Come on, Safah," I muttered to myself in the quiet. "Get your wings together."

I took a deep breath, trying to steady myself as a fresh wave of tears threatened to spill over. I could not let myself break down again. Especially not when I had to face the likes of Tharic in Sanctuary.

"Bend, but do not break." I opened my eyes, and stared at my hands, my voice breaking. "Burn, but never bleed." I swallowed, feeling the tears fill my eyes anyway. My chin shook as I forced myself to push ahead. "Holy. Safah, you will remain holy, to *whatever* end."

The tears streamed down my cheeks.

I felt sick. Ashamed.

First, my temper cost nine angelic lives.

Then, when my hunger for blood came to reality, it not only horrified me, it left me feeling disgusting and physically ill.

I cleared my throat, batting a hand at my tears. I lifted my head to find Ellabeth's beautiful aquamarine eyes shining with tears of her own that she held back.

"Ellie," I flinched. "I...I didn't realize you were floating there." I quickly wiped my face, holding back a new wave of tears.

"Hey," I said.

"Hey," she whispered. "Missed you the last few dawns."

I nodded. Looked around.

All of Seventh Choir was there, watching me, eyes

weighed down with concern. My throat bobbed as I tried straightening my shoulders. Forced a smile on my face.

"Wings high."

"Wings high, Sazu," Daelun said, using the pet name for the first time. I kind of liked it. "You alright? Since Titom... Your Granmanmi is something else, huh?"

"What the Hèls, you moron!" Isandra hissed, slapping him upside his head with a wing.

"Good job, genius." Omarion crossed his arms glaring at Daelun.

Daelun flushed, his cheeks turning red. "Uhm, yeah." He cleared his throat. "So, like Ellabeth said. Missed you."

I tried to smile. Really I did.

I failed.

"Safah." Omarion floated over and wrapped me in a large, warm embrace. I held onto him, thankful for his kindness. But truthfully, while I desperately wanted a hug, he wasn't the one I wanted it from.

Omarion gently petted my hair, squeezing me tight enough to bring a smile to my face. If Ezekiel were here, he'd have given me the same kind of hug.

"You okay, Sazu?"

"I'm...I'm alright." I took a breath. Blinked away my blurring vision. "Really. I'm fine...I'm totally fine. Promise."

"Liar."

I stilled.

It was then I noticed the intoxicating scent of mint and sandalwood curling through my nostrils. Fire immediately ignited my blood. I blinked, shoving the sensation down, and out of my mind. Ignoring the voice in my head, I pulled away from Omarion, and slipped on my sandals.

"Titombwe was...nothing." My tongue felt like it was coated in ash. "I just needed to...process it all. That's it." I cleared my throat. "I'm good."

"Really, Starling. You are an awful liar. I'm glad to know that about you."

I whipped around and flinched.

All of Xadari Legion stood in a wide stance, their arms crossed, covered all in black. A contrast to us Disciples dripping in golden robes. They glared at me.

The small one especially with the same eyes as Quazar. She watched me with a curious expression.

They all seemed like dogs on a leash, waiting to be given the command to attack. On a good dawn, I would've rushed away. Against all of them, I was beat. Especially with them all being hardened warriors, and I was just a Disciple.

This dawn though, I just remained there. I was so mentally exhausted. It was Quazar who'd been drained, but somehow, because of our bond, it felt like I'd been siphoned of my life source, too.

I turned my gaze to Quazar. And stars burn it all if all I could see was him on that dais being broken, contorted, and drained of his blood and life. My stomach knotted so tightly I wanted to bend over and scream.

"You don't look so good, Starling. What's got you so sad?"

This fool had just been within the threshold of death only

dawns ago, and he was standing here now like nothing happened? He was cracking jokes?

Blood for blood!

All I could hear was the roar of vengeance from an arena of multi-millions. All I could see was golden ichor staining polished glass.

My nostrils flared. I lifted my shoulders. Dropped them. My wings hung limp. I looked into those emerald eyes. I saw twisted limbs. Broken bones. Raven black tendrils crawling up his skin. Glowing inscriptions burning to life.

Tears stung my eyes. I commanded them not to fall.

They disobeyed me anyway.

I took a shuttering breath, looked at Quazar through blurrying vision, and turned away. The sight of Granmanmi stained my eyes. The anger of my brothers, my sisters, raced by right after. My mind and my hearts were in utter turmoil. I had a splitting headache and I didn't know how to make any of it go away.

I covered my face with my hands unable to stop wave after wave of tears. I grieved my Manmi, but it was only now I came to realize I didn't have it in me to carry the weight of vengeance that came along with that grief. Bitterness was a root easily planted, but too great a challenge to maintain.

The wingtower was quiet. So quiet.

Ellabeth looked torn. I knew she wanted to hold me. Help me feel better. But we had a lifelong rule. We always gave one another space until the other asked for entry. And I wasn't ready. Not to be held. To be comforted.

I swear it felt like the Infinite was punishing me. Breaking my mind for being so hungry for blood. Feeding me a feast of it and making me choke until I felt like I'd been bathing with swine.

I wiped away at my eyes, giving up on my tears. Stars. This was going to be a hèllishly long dawn. If Tharic saw me like this, I'd be finished.

I made to start flying away, headed for the front doors of the wingtower, but a shadowy hand stopped me. I looked down and found a ring of shadows gently wrapped around my waist, holding me in place. I looked back over my shoulder. I was such a mess of tears, Quazar seemed to have three heads.

"Tears for me, Starling?" Quazar said out loud. Seventh Choir whipped their heads toward him. I looked at him, saying nothing. "I didn't know you could be so kind."

Ellabeth narrowed her eyes, looking between us.

What in the...I blinked at him. His statement caught me so off guard, my tears ceased instantly. I wrinkled my nose at him, suddenly...annoyed.

"Stars, Valoryen," I frowned. I felt a flash of red-hot fire lick my bones and flood my veins. Something dormant ignited in my blood. I lifted my chin, crossing my arms. "Honestly, you're insufferable."

Quazar's lips did a slow curl upwards. Then he smiled.

He actually *smiled*. Teeth and all.

And.

Was that a dimple?

"There you are," he purred. His deep voice slipped into my chest, curled around my seven hearts, and squeezed. "I was nervous. Thought I'd lost you there, for a second."

Now it was Dakairi's turn to look between us, his expression colored in immense confusion.

"Ill," I said, wrinkling my nose at Quazar. "You're ill."

I whipped around, waited for no one and rushed out of the wingtower. A dark chuckle followed me out the door and across the temple grounds, all the way until I reached the main cathedral for Sanctuary.

CHAPTER 30

Flying through the cathedral doors, I flew through Disciples, navigating around them until I made it to my seat. A moment later, Quazar plopped himself into the seat beside me, crossing his legs over the desk.

"Care to have *some* kind of decorum?" I grumbled.

He turned his head to me, lowering his eyes to mine.

"Oh, so I have to dress like a Prince *and* act like one, too?" He raised a brow. "That's a lot of rotting demands, don't you think?"

A lot? He wasn't serious.

I looked into his face.

He *was*.

I ignored him. I didn't have capacity to be riled up by him again, lest some poor fool from Manna Order pay the price.

"Wings high, Disciples."

We all shot to our feet and clapped our wings twice.

"Wings high!" we all called out at Presbitari Davithius.

Well. We all as in all of the Disciples.

Not a single Legionnaire rose to their feet, let alone acknowledged Presbitari Davithius.

"You could at least show a little respect," I hissed quietly, only for Quazar to hear.

"At *least*?" he questioned. Loudly. "And what would you have me do at most, Starling?"

Davithius's eyes found Quazar and lingered, before he let that steely gaze find me, full of curiosity. I ignored Quazar, keeping my mouth shut. He would not get the chance to draw everyone's attention to me.

"Take your seats Disciples," Davithius said when he realized the Legionnaires weren't budging.

When we all sat down, he raised his hands, summoning a projection so vivid it looked real enough to touch. I pulled out my scroll and feather pen, prepared to take notes.

"Welcome to Sanctuary. This dawn, you will begin learning about the Realm Gates."

"I'm sorry," an angel called out from Bond Order.

She was a female.

Every male around her turned around and sneered. Stars. Thank the lights I hadn't been sent to Bond Order. "What do you mean Gates, as in plural? I thought there was only the Seal Gate?"

"Maybe if you'd shut up and let him teach, you'd learn there are *four* Gates, imbecile."

The male who spoke up was from Scroll Order.

Of course.

I refused to look over there. I ground my teeth, keeping my mouth shut. I would mind my business this dawn. *I would mind. My business. This dawn.*

"There's no need to reprimand a fellow Disciple like that," Davithius called out, frowning. "It was an innocent question."

"Every male knows these preliminary details. Four Gates accessible by the Four Fallen Kings. *Everyone* knows that," Tharic said.

He was so smug. So full of pride. So full of *rot*.

I was incensed for the female Disciple. The words left my mouth before I could stop them.

"You know Tharic, I'm not saying you're the dumbest angel in all the realms, but you'd better pray for your sake that the dumbest angel doesn't die."

My voice carried out over the entire cathedral. Every head turned to me. Except for Quazar. He was too busy memorizing the stitching on his boots. But I caught the twitch of his lips, and the shake of his shoulders, as he played with a writhing ball of shadows in his palm.

"What was that, Anathelle?" Tharic snapped.

I turned and found him glaring, his eyes already alit with fire. Stars. I thought I had a temper.

"You might want to speak up if you want to sound like anything besides a bloodthorning goddess."

My eyes widened. Ellabeth began pushing up out of her

seat. I gripped her arm, pulling her back down. I gestured at Tharic, unimpressed by his attempt to intimidate me.

"See what I mean? Still dumb as a chest of seashells." I bat my long lashes at him. "*I said,* you half-shaven baboon." I tilted my head as Quazar snorted to my right. "There aren't four Realm Gates." I paused letting the words hang in the air a moment. "There are *three*. Three Realm Gates. Each Realm Gate contains two portals within. And each of these portals leads to one of the six Hèls. Each of these Hèls have an overseeing Shadowlord. And these six Shadowlords all bow their knees to *one* High King." I slid my gaze to Quazar who'd stilled beside me. "Fallen High King Zemshaza Beliah."

The cathedral was silent.

Then.

The majority of the males tilted their heads back and began cackling at the top of their lungs, their shoulders shaking. My cheeks heated. I almost thought I was wrong. But then I noticed not a single Fallenspawn was laughing.

Tharic grinned wide like the pompous rotpot that he was. "What a load of absolute bullrot—"

"She's right."

"She's *what*?"

Davithius's baritone voice cut through the laughter, instantly silencing the angels. Everyone looked at Davithius, slowly turned to me, then back to Davithius. It was so quiet you could hear a feather drop.

"Disciple Safah is correct," Davithius said again, crossing those big arms over that chiseled body beneath his fitted robes. "There are *three* Gates, not four. And there are six Shadowlords but only one Fallen High King."

I sat straighter, tucking my wings close. I lifted my chin like a shield against the subtle glares aimed my way from around the cathedral. Even from the females.

"You know how to keep a target on your back, don't you?"

"Piss off."

A slip of shadow curled into my mind, tickling my thoughts as a low chuckle danced around my head flooding my body with heat.

"Now, who knows where the three Gates are located?"

Wings shot into the air waiting to be called on.

Davithius called on a male from Bond Order, Second Dominion, Third Choir.

"The Seal Gate is here in Ouanaviel on an abandoned island only Legionnaires have access to."

Only Legionnaires my rotting backside. I snorted low, remembering the Hèls that was my first trial in the Temple.

"Didn't like your playdate with the Spirit Harvesters?"

"Stay out of my head."

"No," Quazar responded down the bond. *"It's too much fun."*

"Burning, pale-faced demon."

"Pale? Yes. Beautifully chiseled by a Pasaillien Celestial? Also yes."

I looked over at him slowly. Did he seriously just say his face had been carved by the Celestial beings who crafted the entire kingdom of the Infinite with their own hands?

"So not just a bastard," I said. *"We're a* cocky *bastard."*

"Only the best kind."

Quazar grinned wide. It was only now I saw the slightest sharpened tips of his teeth. Like they were made for biting. My gaze lingered. His grin stretched.

I looked away, focusing back on the lesson. I slammed the veil in our minds down, effectively blocking him out from our bond. Quazar huffed below his breath.

"So *all* Anathelles are no fun," he whispered. "Got it."

I took a deep breath, fighting my rising fury.

"Which island?" Davithius called out.

No one answered.

Ellabeth leaned over to me.

"So you're not going to answer when you know where it is? Or?" She raised her brows, prodding me with that fierce gaze of hers. I sighed, lifting a wing.

"Disciple Safah."

All heads turned to me.

"The island of Namenthys, though we now call it Barrenrock. It was...purged after it was discovered that the Hallowed who lived there were fraternizing with the Fallen, eventually giving them access to the empyrean by letting them breach the Seal Gate."

"Correct again," Davithius said. He gave me a weird smile. As if there was more truth to what I'd said and he was disappointed I hadn't realized it already.

"Is that what you were told? That the Hallowed of Namenthys were responsible for their demise?"

Quazar's question caught me by surprise. Obviously that's what happened. The worst slaughter of Hallowed angels, of all ranks, in the history of the last Six Ages, happened when the Namenthiens let the Fallen in. Every scrollbook known to angelkind was full of the detailed history. Surely he knew this. I looked over at him. His jade eyes pierced into me.

"And you believe it?" he pressed.

I nodded. *"Why wouldn't I? It's literally a fact. Crack open any scrollbook and every account aligns."*

Quazar stared at me a long time without a word before simply turning away. I frowned. Why did I feel like I'd just flunked an exam? He went back to playing with his shadows, as Davithius prowled on.

"The Seal Gate is indeed in Barrenrock, formerly known as Namenthys."

Davithius put his hands into the projection and spread them out as if he was tearing a long strand of feathers. The more he pulled his hands apart, the more the projection zoomed in. We went from overlooking the barren island, to narrowing on the spot I'd been in just weeks ago.

I narrowed my eyes, glaring at the Seal Gate. Even in this projection, it seemed massive. Davithius snapped his hand back, and the projection filled the entire cathedral. I sat up, my back ramrod straight. It felt like I was on Barrenrock all over again. I began breathing fast, my hands growing clammy.

"This was the first Gate created. It was made by Shadowlord Abbadani. We don't pay much mind to the other two: the Trumpet Gate and the Vial Gate. Why is that?"

"That's easy," Ellabeth called out. "The Fallen from those realms don't care about the empyrean or trying to invade. They've left us alone, so we leave them alone."

"That's right," Davithius said, looking across the cathedral. "They stay on their side of the Gates, and we stay on ours. However, the Seal Gate is growing to be an increasing problem."

I raised a brow.

"Define *problem,* Presbitari," a male called out. I didn't bother looking to see which Order they belonged to.

"An invasion one," Davithius said with finality. "Fallen are not breaching the Gates, but their hèlborns are."

"What?" another male called out. "Demons can't cross without being given access from *our* side. That's not possible Presbitari."

Davithius leveled a gaze at him. The male was sitting to the very back of Manna Order.

"You're saying I'm an uneducated liar?"

I lowered my gaze. Davithius's tone took the same one Papi did when he told us to *keep going*, which effectively meant we'd better stop pushing him or our wings would suffer the consequences. My ears twitched. I hated second-hand embarrassment.

"No, Presbitari, of course not—"

"Shut up and let him teach!" Tharic barked.

Silence fell. I rolled me eyes, but I kept quiet.

"As I said, the hèlborns are coming through, and they aren't coming through alone. They're bringing fiendish creatures with them that would spit out your bones and feast on your souls."

"He's talking about Spirit Harvesters, isn't he? I asked down the bond before stopping myself.

"Are we back to talking again? I hadn't realized."

"For Infinite's sake. You know what—"

"It's called a joke, Starling. Breathe. Yes, he's talking about Spirit Harvesters. But they're not the only problem."

"This is why the Legions of Azarath Academy have been brought into Temple Efysis this Ascension cycle. More than ever, Disciples and Legionnaires must work together. Your ability to bond and defend against what is crossing the gate will determine if the empyrean stands or falls. If you can't work together for the good of the empyrean, the Fallen will breach the gate and conquer us all."

Ellabeth and I shared a look.

Manmi had taught me about perfecting my skills as an Incense Fuser. About the Starfellien Ascent. About standing my ground against males in the Order. About needing to maintain the spiritual morality of the empyrean. About hating evil and doing everything I could to Ascend and make a difference in the empyrean by serving the Temple for the rest of my life. She *never* said anything about me being trained to defend in war.

"You have all been assigned to your Order's based on your ethèr and your lifelong abilities. All in Bond Order are fully equipped to help on the communal front of the war effort. The morale of Legions can make or break a war. Manna Order, you're all equipped with sustaining the Legions. Tell me how many starving legions win wars?"

Silence.

"Exactly." He turned to the side of Scroll and Incense Order.

"Scroll Order, you have the most powerful weapon to exist: The Holy Saccrent. You're able to extrapolate the verses of its divine laws and morph them into weapons for the battlefront."

Then those steely eyes landed on Incense Order.

"And Incense Order. You are Spirit Filers. Incense Fusers. Taking the prayers of the Hallowed, fusing them into incense, and sending them directly to the Infinite or collecting them as incense powder for weapons. This is one of the greatest gifts you can give to this empyrean."

He used his wings, gesturing to our bonded warriors.

"Each of these Legions will rely on you *collectively* should a war take place with the Fallen kingdoms. They need all of you, and you all need each other. Is that clear?"

"Awoui, Presbitari Davithius," we cried, giving him a resounding *yes* in the common angelic tongue.

"Good." His eyes chilled like ice, dancing with excitement. "Now open your scrollbooks. There's much to dissect about the Seal Gate."

CHAPTER 31

"I'm so hungry I could eat a bloodhyena."

All of Seventh Choir wrinkled their noses at Daelun as we flew toward the food hall.

"A bloodhyena?" I asked, raising a brow. "Gross. Not even if they were the last living thing in the entire Elledelle universe."

"They're fat and full of meat. I'm definitely feasting," Daelun said, angling his body to fly as if sliding through the air on his side.

"Bloodhyenas eat anything," Omarion said. "You can't be serious."

Kazemir leveled a look at Daelun, his face wrinkled. He nodded in agreement with Omarion.

"So what I'm hearing is, none of you have what it takes to survive?" Daelun lifted his chin.

"Yeah, okay." Ellabeth rolled her eyes. "Anyway, are we not going to address the fact that we just spent our entire high dawn learning about defensive *warfare*?"

"Ellie's got a point," I called over my shoulder. I flew in twirls, spinning myself like a slow torpedo as I weaved through the cathedrals. We flew into the main tower of Temple Efysis and began our flight down the corridors to the food hall.

"Seriously. I came to be an Apprenti and to learn Incense Fusion. Not to go fight in Empràr Zadkias's war."

We looked at Amayah. Her quiet words rang true. I hadn't come here for lessons on war, either.

"I mean, it's not like *we* are fighting," Isandra pointed out.

"Yes we are," Ellabeth said. "That's the whole point of forcing our bonds to the Fall...to *them*." She tossed a look at the Fallenspawn who were flying leisurely behind us, pretending not to listen to our conversation. Their pricked ears told another story. "If they get deployed, so do we. *We* create their weapons."

"So we don't," Daelun said.

"Good job, genius," Ellabeth snapped. "We don't use our Order's abilities to make weapons, they have nothing to defend with. If they can't defend the empyrean, invasion is inevitable. If we are invaded, we're as good as dead. Is that what you want?"

"Okay when you put it like that..." Daelun said wistfully.

I rolled my eyes and kept flying. When we reached the

food hall, a delicious aroma collided with my senses. I breathed in deeply, licking my lips.

Stars, I was ready to eat. The hall was packed. Disciples from each Order spilled out across the hall, sitting at long, gilded tables covered in endless platters of food.

I noticed most Orders stayed amongst themselves. The angels didn't commingle with Disciples from other Orders.

I flew in quietly with Seventh Choir, nestled between Ellabeth and Isandra. That didn't stop several hundred heads from turning to gawk.

I fought the urge to cut tail and fly away. Most glared at me, starting with my lavender eyes, before lowering their gaze to my deep and dark purple wings that blended into gold at the tips. I found too many males ogling, staring at my breasts, then my hips, and the length of my body. It felt gross and made me want to bathe all over again.

"Ignore them," Ellabeth said.

I looked at her as she lifted her chin. I wondered if she'd said that for my sake or hers. I looked again and found the males gawking at all four of us. They danced from me, to Ellabeth, then Isandra, before their eyes landed on Amayah, who was subtly trying to remain hidden behind our wings.

Chin up, I flew down the length of an empty table and sat down. Seventh Choir joined me. To our right, the other six Choirs and two Dominions filled out the remaining table except for Fifth Choir who was sitting elsewhere since they'd arrived earlier than us.

I picked up a plate, pulled a cover off one of the platters, and salivated. No amount of hate would ruin my happiness at seeing the gilded platter of honey greased bacon with herbs sprinkled on top. I started filling my plate with bacon, then reached over to tackle the stack of fried plantains.

Suddenly the food hall fell silent as a grave. I looked up, mid-reach with my fork on a plantain, when snarls began breaking out across the hall. I turned and saw the reason for the rising tension.

The Fallenspawn had arrived. All of Xadari Legion flew in brazenly, as if they owned the temple itself. Chins high, muscled arms exposed through their fighting robes, they floated over to Incense Order's table. Each began filing in to the empty tables on our left until only one seat remained. The seat by me.

Blessed lights.

Ellabeth and I locked eyes over the platter of fried plantain as I heard the *click, click, click* of freshly polished boots. But of course. While everyone else flew in, he had to make a scene.

I turned and watched Quazar strut into the food hall on foot. He strolled leisurely through the tables, looking around, seeming unimpressed at what he found.

He was so tall, so fit, so *regal*. There was an air of pride to him. He had the posture of a High King and the face of a Luminari—the Celestials who lived with the Infinite in the heavenly realm of Pasaille, the angelic paradise. He took his time, as if it bent to his will. Then he stopped and scanned the food hall as if looking for something.

"Someone," he teased down our bond.

I snapped my head down, burning holes into my half full plate. I didn't need to look up to see that heavy gaze had fallen on me. And so did everyone else's.

My wings felt like they were on fire.

The *click, click* of his boots began making their way to our table. To my side of it. Until he stopped at the empty cloud-chair beside me.

"Hello, Safah Starling."

I slowly lifted my head, looking up into his eyes as he slipped into the seat with deliberate leisure, a smile stitching wide across his perfect face.

My neck burned hot. Prickles of shadow slipped into my mind and caressed my thoughts. I gasped at the mental touch. Quazar's eyes widened. Immediately the shadowy touch receded and the veil between our bond was sealed tight. Stars. Had he done that by accident? Because he wasn't paying attention?

"Wings high, Princeling."

I gave him a small nod before I began adding some fruit to my plate. Ignoring everyone staring, from the Disciples to the Fallenspawn ogling their Prince oddly, I began tearing into my bacon.

The first bite sent me straight into orbit. I thought I'd died and gone to Pasaille. The gooey honey glaze married with the juices of the thick bacon slice coated my tongue and made me hum. Without realizing it, I did a little shimmy and dance as I ate.

"That good, huh?"

I didn't answer him. I was going to enjoy my bacon in peace. I tore into another bite. When I reached for my third piece, some kind of spell broke. Everyone else began digging into their plates, too.

"These are the best plantains I've had in a long time," Ellabeth said, her aquamarine eyes nearly rolling to the back of her head with pleasure. "Holy stars! And when you add the pikliz? The spicy pickled cabbage is everything, Sazu. *Everything*."

I laughed around my full mouth, also eating my plantain with pikliz.

"I could live off of this," Daelun said, shoving some fried pork with pikliz sprinkled on top into his mouth. "A rotting shame those Disciples died in the first trial before having some."

"Daelun!" I cried along with the other females of Seventh Choir.

"No truly," I said. "What is actually wrong with you? Something isn't quite functioning upstairs."

"Piss off." Daelun waved me off, scarfing down more pork. "I'm not wrong. You're just too pious to say it."

"Don't you think the Infinite wouldn't be too pleased at us speaking about the dead so lightly? Their spirits haven't even crossed to the Ellelights yet."

Quazar snorted at my left. I whipped around, staring at

him. He gave me a closed smile since his mouth was full. He wriggled his eyebrows at me, his eyes blazing. I choked on my food, my eyes starting to water.

I didn't understand him. One moment he looked like he'd set me on fire with his bare hands. The next, he looked like he wanted to be...friends or something. It was strange behavior and I didn't like it. Papi always said clarity was the best policy.

Daelun patted my back until my coughing fit stopped. I turned to him, nuzzling my nose into his shoulder in thanks. He smiled big, brushing a tendril of hair out of my face, locking it behind my ear. Swallowing my food, I turned to Quazar to ask him something.

Only to find Quazar glaring at Daelun's hand.

"Have you been deployed to the Seal Gate yet?" I asked him, trying to distract him from severing Daelun's hand from his body. Quazar glared at the hand a long time, then at Daelun in the face for a moment longer, before turning to me, his expression softening.

"Of course I have. Myself, and every Fallenspawn who has graduated and successfully made it through the Empràr's Pass."

I noticed the Talons had their heads down while they ate, but somehow they were still completely tuned into everything he was saying to me.

"The Empràr's Pass?" I asked.

Quazar leveled a gaze at me.

"You are Amaryss Anathelle's fifi and you know nothing about the Empràr's Pass?"

I shook my head.

"It's not like Manmi told me everything. What do you think she did? Gave me the secrets of the universe? No. I was taught enough. What to study. How to fight. Which books in the Saccrent mattered most. What the Farasees would be looking for. That type of thing. She also taught me everything I needed to know to survive. Nothing with that includes this *Empràr's Pass* though. What is it? Some kind of exam or something? And what's it got to do with Manmi?"

"I, too, would love to know what this has to do with my Tati."

I nodded as Ellabeth leaned forward, her eyes pools of swirling oceans as she popped a piece of dragonfruit into her mouth.

Quazar kept his eyes on me. He stared, searching my face, as if looking for something he swore he'd find. He narrowed his eyes when he seemingly came up short.

"You really don't know," he breathed.

"Don't know *what?*"

I blinked as the winged tips of my ears twitched. Quazar blinked those hypnotizing emerald eyes and tilted his head like a confused lord unsure of how to proceed.

"Before Azarath Academy fourthlings graduate, we have to cross through what is called the Empràr's Pass. An endless stretch of rocky terrain in the far northern plains of the Ouanaviel island. It's one of several ways to access Barrenrock and reach the Seal Gate. But the Pass is guarded."

"By?" I asked, raising a brow.

His eyes glittered. The corners of his lips twitched.

"Bats."

My brows shot to my hairline.

He was lying. He had to be.

"Ouanaviel has bats?"

Those lips quirked up even higher. "So sorry. We have *ashbats*."

"Ashbats," I repeated. "Well, then."

I started turning away.

"Ashbats are the size of a small cloud, with teeth sharper than that of a viper, membranous, hideous wings, and a ferocious appetite for blood. Hallowed blood to be exact."

I snorted, going back to my plate. "Guess you can make the crossing just fine then."

"Pray tell, Starling." Quazar leaned in close to me, his lips near my ear. I swallowed the knot in my throat. "When your Granmanmi nearly bled me dry. What color blood did you see? Was any trace of it obsidian?"

I stilled.

I'd tried hard since Sanctuary to avoid thinking about Titombwe. About the blood. About his breaking bones and body. Sanctuary had helped me forget. But now the events were at the front of my mind again.

I thought of his blood. So much of it. Every last drop had been gold. I met Quazar's piercing glare.

"Obsidian or gold, my beautiful Starling?"

Omarion's head snapped up at the endearment, his nostrils wrinkling. Something dark flashed across his eyes, but he said nothing. I swallowed my nerves, trying to ignore my galloping heartbeats.

"Gold," I whispered. "Every drop was gold."

I looked down, fighting the threat of new tears. A visible strand of shadow caressed my chin, lifting it gently so I looked Quazar in the eyes.

"Gold." The gilded rim of his jade eyes seemed to burn. "Yet you call me Fallenspawn. Is it easier to think of me as Fallen than Hallowed? Does it make wanting to see me bleed again easier?"

"No!" I flinched back, snapping my chin from him. "That's not...that's not what I want. I—"

"Mm." He seemed tickled at my reaction. "Ask me why the Empràr's Pass is a special kind of Hèls for us? Ask me which Legionnaires cross it and which don't?"

The food hall had fallen silent, but Quazar had my full attention. Appetite lost, I refused to back down. Back away.

"Okay, Fallen Prince." I leaned into his space, crossing my arms. "Who flies through the Pass? What happens? How do they kill the ashbats? What's the survival rate? Who is even responsible for the exam anyway?"

Quazar smiled. The sight pierced through my chest, cutting me open. He showed just the tip of his teeth. Enough to send my mind reeling as I struggled against the intoxicating scent of sandalwood.

"The Empràr's Pass is typically crossed by around one thousand angels, annually. Usually, only three hundred survive. Once you cross it, you don't ever have to again.

You've officially proven yourself ready for war. The ashbats can't be killed. Trust me." He grinned. There was no joy in it. "I've tried. *Many* times."

He…what? Was he insinuating he'd gone back?

"Oh that's right. You asked *who* flies through." He chuckled darkly. "*We* do. Of course. The Hallowed don't have to go to through such lengths to prove their loyalty to the empyrean. As long as they bond to their Dragèth *parilielthai* from Dragonkind, they can graduate and head to Watcher Hold. But for us," he looked back, looking over the Fallenspawn, all glaring at me with their pretty, jewel-like eyes, and the massive print of swirling thorns all over their neck and arms, "well, we have to prove we are Hallowed, even if our blood runs gold like you."

His eyes blazed as they fell back to me.

"If we refuse to cross the Pass, we die. If we try to run, we die. The majority of us who have gone through, have died. We fly into the Pass. Most of us never return."

I felt that sickening feeling overwhelm me again. I covered my mouth in horror, letting my eyes fall shut. That was absolute *madness*. It was *sick*. Who would come up with that? Who could be so…evil? It couldn't have been the Profêts idea. Stars!

Was it High Farasee Manazzra Ahabiah?

I opened my eyes to Quazar.

"Who created that…that sham of an exam? That's just…*cruel*. It's…it's wicked."

Quazar grinned wide.

My hearts shriveled in my chest.

"Who?" He chuckled. My chest squeezed tight. "What a good question, my Starling. The Farasee responsible for making every one of my angels prove their loyalty to the empyrean by going on a suicide mission through the Empràr's Pass was none other than *your* Manmi, Amaryss Anathelle."

CHAPTER 32

I froze in place, unable to hear a thing beyond the galloping hooves of my hearts. My ears rung like bells. Everything I'd just eaten threatened to come back up.

"Bullrot," Ellabeth spat, shooting out of her seat. "No!"

She pulled at my chin, turning my face to hers.

"He's lying. Tati would never. She would never! He's *lying*. It's his way of getting even. Don't fall for it."

"She seems pretty convinced. But tell me, Starling," Quazar said down our bond. *"Am I lying?"*

I thought back to Titombwe. I wouldn't have believed Granmanmi would bleed out an angel as an act from the Farasee Order in front of the empyrean. Yet she had. And she'd done so until he was just within an inch of completely losing his life.

What about Manmi?

I'd asked her many questions she wouldn't answer. What did she know?

Better yet.

What had she *done*?

"Safah." Ellabeth snapped her fingers before my eyes. "You're not going to believe him. *Him*. Over Tati Amaryss's honor?"

I took a deep breath. Once again I found myself in a place where all of the angels were staring at me and seeing what I would do.

I thought about Granmanmi. I thought about Manmi. I thought long and hard of how celebrated all the females in my family were. The list of accolades for all they'd done for the empyrean was a long one.

Would they receive all the praise if it had nothing to do with crushing the Fallenspawn? It was no secret the Fallenspawn were the bane of the empyrean, but they couldn't simply be killed off or else the Fallen High King would invade with his Shadowlords and raise Hèls.

Azarath Academy was a way of culling the Fallenspawn. Papi made it clear, Azarath was a blood factory. Many angels went in, few came out. The majority were Fallenspawn. I didn't put it past the Order to do what they could to slowly wipe the Fallenspawn out. I didn't put it past the females of my lineage, either.

What was the *real* reason only Anathelle females were accepted into the Order?

I leaned back in my seat, taking a deep breath.

"Safah?" Ellabeth questioned, her eyes narrowing.

"Enough," I snapped.

She flinched back, those eyes turning to thin slits.

"I...I need to think."

I rose from my seat. Seventh Choir watched me intensely. I looked at Quazar, ignoring his table of Talons who continued studying me. How could I blame them, considering it was my Granmanmi that publicly drained their Prince like some rabid animal.

"I'm forced to be your temple-mate. Your bonded."

I watched his face for any trace of lies. Of mockery. I had to see if he was playing with my mind. Or if I really had been lied to all my cycles of growing up, preparing to join this stars-forsaken temple.

"I must work with you, Prince Quazar." I tilted my head. His eyes flashed. "But can I trust you? Trust your word?"

Shadows immediately slipped into my mind. Quazar shoved open the door to his side of the bond, bearing his shadows, his soul, to me. No one could see it, or feel it. But I did.

His gentle caress caused me to visibly sigh with relief. Somehow, I knew in my heart of hearts. Quazar was telling the truth.

Dakairi flicked a look at Quazar, as if trying to piece together what had just transpired between us. Dakairi wasn't the only one who'd caught the shift. Ellabeth had, too. And so had Ivyana, who was now watching Quazar with fascinating curiosity, plainly written all over her face.

"Starling," Quazar purred. The pet name dripped from his tongue like honey, making my toes curl in my sandals. "I'll always tell you a joke. But I won't ever waste my breath telling you a lie."

I took a shuttering breath. Checked my hearts, my gut, once again to make sure what I felt was true. Was real.

Something deep inside me, something that refused to be lied to just *knew*. Quazar really *was* telling the truth. I couldn't say how I knew, but there was something in his eyes. And something deep within myself. And the vulnerability of our bond.

Quazar Valoryen had not lied to me.

Which meant Manmi had.

Manmi was behind the birth of the Empràr's Pass for the Fallenspawn to do annual crossings. Just like Granmanmi was behind the creation of the Blood Rites.

"Ellie, he isn't lying," I whispered.

It was hard to stand. The closest tables to us heard my words, and gasped. Others scoffed, as if they didn't care. As if it was a *good* thing for the Fallenspawn to go through an annual culling they were more than guaranteed to not survive.

"Sazu—"

I looked at her, my eyes blazing with fury.

"He. Is. *Not*. Lying," I bit out. "You can lie to a face but you can *never* lie to a bond. Manmi...she...she's the one who did it."

We are Anathelle's Safah, Manmi told me often, dawn in and dawn out, as I trained for the inevitable dawn I would Ascend. *We are holy, to whatever end.*

To *whatever* end.

How far did that end go?

My mind was reeling. I placed my hand at my temple. A splitting headache exploded at the front of my head. I forced a breath through my lungs as my thoughts clouded until they were thick walls I couldn't pierce through. My mind suffocated on slow unraveling truths I wasn't sure I was ready to face.

"Your Granmanmi gave us Blood Rites," Quazar said in the quiet. The angels around our table leaned in, hanging to every word. "Your Manmi gave us the Empràr's Pass and made it mandatory, or else we'd die. And don't get me started on what your *Great*-Granmanmi did."

Quazar tilted his head, studying me. "What will *you* create, spawn of Anathelles?"

I refused to answer. Refused to look at him. To look at anyone. A thought occurred to me. I met Quazar's gaze.

"If you graduated but are still at Azarath, do you have to keep going back to the Pass?"

"She *is* brilliant," Quazar mused. "*If* this is going where I think it is."

He smiled at me. Seventh Choir leaned in, trying to piece out what I wasn't saying. Ellabeth most of all.

"Yes, my Starling. If we stay at Azarath, we must continue going through the Pass."

“Why would you stay at Azarath?” I asked.

“If Dakairi and I leave, who would train Ivyana? Who would protect her? Who would defend my angels? I, *we*, stay so we can help those after us. Permission we’ve attained because it’s been told the...*Hallowed* get nervous when I am loose.”

He grinned wide this time. He didn’t have one dimple. The gorgeous Prince had two.

Rot, rot, *rot me*.

That smile would unravel me thread by thread. I tried looking away, but there wasn’t a chance in the Hèls I could. He smiled as if he’d sat at my kitchen table and heard Papi warn again and again about the Fallen Prince running loose and causing Hèls across the empyrean.

“Do you ever go to the Seal Gate?”

Quazar blinked at me. He watched me a long time. Ellabeth visibly leaned forward. I had a feeling she caught on to where my thoughts were going.

“I do. Usually with the Legionnaires when they’re on defense. Always during the wintrien season. The gate is messed with often when it’s cold and most islanders are bogged down in their homes.”

There’s no way.

There was absolutely *no way*.

I couldn’t have been lied to.

Not to this magnitude.

“During...wintrien,” I repeated.

He nodded.

Quazar's Talons looked between him and me. They hadn't caught on to where I was going with my questioning. But Quazar had. And so had Dakairi and Ellabeth.

"Blessed lights," Ellabeth hissed.

Dakairi's jeweled, royal blue eyes were dancing.

"When does the Empràr's Pass take place?"

Quazar tilted his head, pretending as if he was thinking about it. My hearts raced at lightning speed, tightening with every second that ticked by.

"Hmm, end of springtari as we enter the sumyrin season. And in fallari we learn, train, and rest."

The gate had been attacked during sumyrin. At the same time Quazar would have been at the Empràr's Pass. Not at the Seal Gate. When Manmi died, Quazar wasn't there. He wasn't anywhere close.

The Farasee Order of Temple Efysis had lied.

Which meant Granmanmi... *Granmanmi*!

My knees buckled, and I fell back into my seat. The revelation was too much. I blinked at nothing, unable to face the hard truth that had been dancing in my face all along.

"What in the Six Hèls just happened?" Daelun asked, head swinging between the shocked expressions on mine and Ellabeth faces, and the sympathetic ones on Quazar and Dakairi's.

"Looks like your princess is starting to wake up." Dakairi winked at Daelun.

Seventh Choir stared at me wide-eyed, waiting for me to

say something. If Quazar wasn't responsible for Manmi's death, then who *was*? Who else had any motive to kill...

No. Kaelthos Zamarien would never stoop so low to betray his own. Would he?

For the first time since Ascending, I looked around the temple walls and felt anything but safe. I'd spent cycles hating Quazar. Hating the Fallenspawn. I idolized the temple, believing I would come here and make a difference for the empyrean and get revenge for Manmi. I'd been taught to hate the one angel who had nothing to do with the source of my greatest pain.

And the temple...

I lifted my eyes to Ellabeth who'd also sat back down. Her sun-kissed cheeks were red. Her eyes churned like a tempest. I knew that bright-eyed, wild look she had. Rage. Ellabeth was furious.

"Sazu," she whispered, reaching for my hand.

I let her take it. Because what else could I do right now? Everything I thought was true was a burning pile of rot.

But I had no clue how to make sense of anything else. I had to speak to someone. But who? Could I write a letter to Papi that wouldn't be meddled with? My head throbbed. I needed to know more. I needed to know the truth.

I shoved away from the table, pushing back my cloud-chair. "I'm going to the biblarien. For research purposes."

If anywhere in this temple had the truth, it would be the library.

"Don't follow me," I said, as Seventh Choir started gathering their belongings. Everyone stopped and looked at me. "I'm going alone."

I yanked up my belongings, discarding my half-eaten plate, spread my wings, and rushed out of the food hall headed straight for the biblarien. As I raced out of the doors, a familiar trail of shadow followed me all the way to the library and never left my side.

PART THREE

"Fear of terror at twinight—nor arrows at dawn—should ever befall you. Whether a thousand fall at your side, even if you witness ten thousand die around you, evil will lay no finger on you. Keep your wings and become the pride of the Order. Lose them and be their ridicule."

Accords of the Farasees, Scroll of Davithius 91:7, Fifth Age

CHAPTER 33

"Nothing in the Temple is given. It is what?"

"Earned!" chorused the Disciples of the four Farasee Orders.

I scribbled in my scrollbook taking notes as Farasee Kaelthos barreled on. There was a wild glint in his eyes this Sanctuary. I didn't like it. I noticed this dawn that the Farasee Order wasn't present. Including the other Presbitaris. Whatever Kaelthos was thinking, I hoped to avoid it at all costs.

"Including mercy," Kaelthos said. "Welcome to *The Principles of Righteous Judgment,* where you will learn how the Farasees maintain order across all Ouanaviel temples, and the empyrean at large."

Kaelthos looked across the cathedral, lifting his pointed nose at us.

"In Temple Efysis, every Disciple has a responsibility to

learn how the Farasee Order maintains the Creed—our political laws upheld with the approval of the Empràr—and the spiritual morality of the empire."

I watched the Farasee turn as he spoke, making sure he faced every Order, until he came to a stop.

Facing Incense Order.

I immediately brought my eyes to my scrollpapers.

"Much of these principles are aligned with dealing out judgment in the form of punishment. Specifically, the physical kind."

"I don't like the sound of that," Ellabeth whispered just so I could hear.

I tilted my head her way, a nod that I agreed with her.

Why were we, Temple Farasees and Disciples, punishing anyone? Especially physically? Had I missed a chapter when studying the Farasee Accords?

"It could be for small offenses," Kaelthos continued, those fiery golden eyes still locked onto Incense Order. "Such as a stolen cinderwolf from a Cherubim farm. A pilfered piece of dragonfruit from a chariot-stand at the Feather Market." He lifted a finger. "Then there are the greater offenses. An attempt on a Legionnaire's life. Wanting to usurp the Empràr's throne. Helping fallen angels and hèlborns breach the Seal Gate."

Farasee Kaelthos floated into the air and hovered above the gilded dais. I twitched in my seat, observing him from behind low lashes. Something was odd about Sanctuary this dawn. There was a charge in the air. My ethèr stirred inside of me nervously.

I slipped low into my seat, lifting my wings a touch, rounding them out so they shielded my body. Quazar threw me a glance from the corner of his eyes, one of his eyebrows raised. I said nothing, keeping my eyes between my scrollpapers and the Farasee.

"What in the stars are you doing?" Quazar asked down our bond.

Since my trip to the biblarien a few dawns ago, I'd learned nothing new about Manmi's death. But it was emphatically clear. Quazar, nor his angels, had anything to do with her unexpected death. And since then, he and I had become... cordial? Friends? If this odd connection between us could ever be called friendship.

"Trying not to be noticed by the fire-breathing demon who'd toss me to the Scourgers for sport if he ever got the chance. Has it ever occurred to you that the only *angel he hates more than me is* you?"

Quazar snorted. *"Like I give a rot."*

"Yeah, well. You're not a Disciple, almighty Legionnaire. *I am. To a degree, I have to care, or he'll find a way to make me forfeit Ascension."*

Quazar remained still in his seat, tracking Kaelthos's every move. But down our bond, he chuckled until the sound reverberated into my chest and bounced around my mind.

"The Farasee Order consistently strives to be one of

mercy. We create margins for error the angels may find themselves in."

I scoffed under my breath.

An Order of mercy. Yeah, sure.

I kept my head down while I noted the bullrot coming out of Kaelthos's mouth. The veil mentally separating Quazar and I warmed. I slipped into my mind, edging closer to the veil between us. Quazar was laughing...no. Positively *cackling* on the other side.

I shook my head. Stars. How I wish I could possess such levity. I sealed the veil shut and sank further in my seat. My recent actions surfaced all over again.

I'd blamed him for a death he did not cause. Loudly. I'd lost my temper, going off on him, causing nine angels to die. All over misplaced rage. Over truth that was a farce. I'd stewed for the last several dawns in guilt, in shame. The Fallenspawn...

They weren't even Fallen. They were Hallowed, just like us. The only difference were their engraved, thorny marks on their left arms curling up to their necks.

"Sink any further and he'll call you out for it. You're dealing with enough. Don't give Kaelthos a ramp with enough room to fly."

Ellabeth had barely moved her lips, but I heard her loud and clear. She was right. Kaelthos would use any reason to call me out. I sat up, lifting my head.

"This dawn, take note of this principle."

The fire in those golden eyes seemed to blaze afresh as they landed squarely on me. Quazar shifted in his seat. I blinked, perplexed. He...he just scooted *closer* to me. Very close. And I liked it. I fought the twinge at the corners of my lips as I kept my eyes on Kaelthos.

"Sacrifice is better than obedience."

Kaelthos Zamarien crossed his strong arms, as the fire in his eyes grew, turning gold to living, breathing flame.

"These are the principles you must live by if you plan to Ascend. How you fare will determine if you remain as Apprenti, rise to Rabbini, or join the Farasee Order itself."

He tilted his head at me, as if sending a personal message.

"And on the *rare* occasion you Ascend from Disciple to Farasee, it will be because these truths of the Age burn bright within you. Enough for our Profèt to deem you worthy of the Order."

"Such a grandiose speech to say a whole lot of bullrot," Daelun whispered, his mouth full of peanut brittle. I chuckled under my breath. Of course he found a way to sneak in snacks.

Farasee Kaelthos gestured around the cathedral.

"As a Disciple with the intention of one dawn becoming a Farasee, to you much is given, so in return much will be required. It is with this weight you will have to carry out judgment. Whether it is of Angels or Gods. Shifters or Giants. Faerèth, Merriens, or the Edennite mortals. At some point you will judge and give out sentences. It is part of your duty on behalf of His Majesty, Empràr Zadkias Claudevin. Do you all follow?"

"Awoui, Farasee Kaelthos."

As one, every Disciple clapped their wings together twice. Not a single Legionnaire, Hallowed or Marked, participated. Not that they needed to. They weren't Disciples.

Still.

Kaelthos took note of the lack of respect from our Azarath companions. His cheeks grew hot. Irritation thickened his neck.

"Now, it's easy to *speak* on righteous judgment. And like all Presbitaris, I love a good presentation myself. But I have always believed demonstration was better."

There was a lift in Kaelthos's tone that made my spine tingle. I cut a glance at Ellabeth. She looked back, her eyes widening with concern.

"Eyes down," I whispered.

Ellabeth nodded. We both fixed our eyes on our scrolls. Quazar scooted even closer, letting his shadows loose around my hips and ankles. Whatever Kaelthos was up to, even the Fallen Prince was concerned.

"If our Scourgers would please present themselves."

My head snapped up.

Ellabeth shot out a hand, gripping my arm, her eyes wide.

Three Scourgers stepped forward from a burst of obsidian light. Their raven black wings hung heavily to the floor of the dais, as they landed on their unseen feet shrouded beneath the skirts of their long, dark robes. Their faces were mangled. Like they'd been beaten badly and never went to see a Raephim for mending.

"Why in the stars are there Scourgers here?" Omarion hissed, kissing his teeth.

"This can't be good," Kazemir grunted.

My hearts began pounding. What was Kaelthos up to?

Bend, but do not break. Burn, but never bleed.

The Anathelle proverb sang in my mind. Quazar had removed his feet from our shared desk and sat up. He was unnaturally still, eyes glaring into the three Scourgers below. He slipped a hand to my knee, gripping it tightly. I found myself placing a hand on top of his to help him calm his nerves. He'd clearly had encounters with the Scourgers before and was triggered by them now.

"Farasee Kaelthos," called out a Disciple from Bond Order. "What are Scourgers doing here in Sanctuary?"

"We are here to teach a lesson child," the tall Scourger in the middle said. His breath was like a dying whisper. Airy, strained, yet dripping with ancient cruelty. "And we have names. You will address me as Scourger Jeroah. These are my fellows, Refayim and Lilithine."

"Scourger Jeroah, thank you for taking the time to be with us," Kaelthos said, too excited for my liking. "Please choose the Disciple you deem best for this illustration."

Without hesitation, all three Scourgers turned their crimson blood eyes to Incense Order.

And they pinned them on me.

Scourger Jeroah raised a crooked, umber finger, pointing it in my direction.

"We choose Disciple Safah Anathelle. It is tradition for this illustration to be performed by one with Nebulae blood. Like her Manmis before her, she is our choice this dawn."

"But Scourger Jeroah," I blurted out, trying to reason with the harbinger of punishment. "Disciple Tharic is a Zamarien. Surely *he* is the better choice." I gestured over at Tharic whose face turned from pearl to scarlet. "He has Nebulae blood, too!" My hearts hammered in my chest. Fear prickled my palms as I begged for the Infinite to make me disappear.

"You are correct, young one. But we have no need of sunfire this dawn," Jeroah wore a small, conniving smile. "We need the fire of the stars."

"Rot," Omarion cursed from behind me.

"Hèls-infested temple," Isandra whispered. "I don't like this."

I wanted to scream. Everyone was staring at me now. Waiting to see what I'd do.

Quazar was frozen in his seat as he watched me with unreadable eyes. He retracted his shadows, and his hand from my knee, as his face hardened. When I poked around our tethered bond, I found the veil sealed tight.

Great. There went the bit of progress we'd made.

I stood up.

"Do you accept to demonstrate, Disciple Safah?"

Like I had a burning choice. I nodded, bowing low.

"Yes, Scourger Jeroah. I accept."

"Come, child."

My wings twitched nervously as I floated to the ramp separating the isles and began walking down. I could have flown, but I wanted some time to think. I searched my brain recklessly, trying to see if this had anything to do with something Manmi had taught me and I'd forgotten. But no matter how hard I searched, I couldn't think of a single lesson where she mentioned I'd be summoned by the Scourgers.

What did they mean this was an Anathelle tradition?

And where in the stars was Granmanmi?

When I reached the floor, I floated to a hover in front of Incense Order. The moment I looked at the Scourgers, a table surfaced. I looked down to find three Dragontail whips. Each was meant for shredding through bones, wings, and skin.

"I like where this is going," Tharic commented loudly. "We should do illustrated lessons more often."

I sniffed a trap and knew I was in the center of it. My hearts slammed inside my chest, beating like drums. Without thinking, I reached down the bond with my starfire, brushing against the veiled door separating Quazar and I. Without hesitation Quazar dropped the veil and let me in. My starlit tendrils seeped into his pool of shadows. It felt like being hugged. Like being held. It felt safe.

"Remember Disciples *and* Legionnaires"—Kaelthos glared at Quazar—"sacrifice is better than obedience. You cannot interrupt or intervene. Any angel who does, forfeits their Ascension. Their Legion." A beat. "And their life."

Gasps broke out across the cathedral.

"You cannot assist Disciple Safah. Nor can you assist those being judged."

I looked at Kaelthos. The resounding hatred and triumph glittering in his eyes terrified me.

"What do you mean '*those being judged*'?"

Kaelthos beamed. "Turn around, Disciple."

I did.

At first, I just looked back at Incense Order. A sea of pearl, brown, and umber skinned angels all clad in Disciple gold or Legionnaire black, stared back at me. Most were confused, unsure of what in the stars was going on. I looked into Quazar's eyes. They were glowing. Wild. A growing rage seeped to their surface.

Then ten Marked came into view. Their hands, feet, and wings were shackled. They'd been bloodied and beaten, bodies already littered with visible bruises beneath their tattered clothing. When they looked at me, looked into my eyes, terror colored their faces grey.

"She's an Anathelle," one female whimpered. "We are so dead."

"Please," cried a male. "We haven't done anything. *Please*."

I looked at Quazar. He watched me behind that mask of neutrality. I couldn't get a solid read on him. I poked into our bond. He'd let me stay in his shadows. He hadn't shut me out. I couldn't place why, but that was probably the most comforting thing I could hold on to in this moment. I took deeper steps into that well of shadows, sinking further, desperate for this moment to pass. I squared my shoulders, still facing Incense Order with my chin raised.

"Farasee Kaelthos, I fail to understand what is going on here. This lesson is about righteous judgment. What are the Marked doing here? They're not part of Xadari Legion."

"Good observation, Disciple Safah." Kaelthos's voice dripped with sarcasm. "These *Fallenspawn* abominations have been caught in the Shaele, trafficking hèlborns into the Ouanaviel island."

"It's not true!" the first Marked cried. "We've done no such thing."

"Silence!" Kaelthos snapped.

It was dead quiet in the Sanctuary. Many of the Disciples looked on, horrified. I'd always known Kaelthos was unhinged. But this was too far.

"Disciple Safah, your job is simple. These Fallenspawn have been accused and brought to *me* for sentencing. As part of the Farasee Order, I judge them guilty of treason. Their sentence is death."

My ears were ringing. Death? Just how many lives was this stars-forsaken temple going to take?

I began slipping to a place far away in my mind. Shadows curled around my starfire silhouette and held me tight. The gesture was sweet. But it wasn't going to be enough. I looked back at the table. At the three Dragontails.

We need the fire of the stars.

I pressed my lips together, letting my eyes fall shut as

Farasee Kaelthos gave me the rest of my instructions with a sickening bounce in his voice.

"Disciple Safah, you will siphon the spirits of these ten Fallenspawn. You will use your starfire to drain them. You will then crush the spirits into nothing. When you're done, you must set their carcasses on fire until every last one of them have completed their sentence. Death."

CHAPTER 34

I squeezed my eyes shut, shaking my head. A blazing heat crawled through my limbs as I wrestled with what I'd just been told.

I couldn't have heard him right. Kaelthos Zamarien, a Farasee, did *not* just ask me to commit murder. In the holiest temple of the Ouanaviel Empyrean. I was not being asked to shed the blood of innocents.

"Farasee Kaelthos," I began, pinching the bridge of my nose. "I...You can't...You're not..." I stuttered, trying, and failing, to get my words out. I couldn't open my eyes as disgust began swallowing me whole. "You can't *possibly* expect me to... expect me to *murder* innocent angels—"

"*Judge* them, Safah Anathelle. The word you are looking for is righteously *judge*."

Kaelthos was a monster. Truly. I didn't bother dignifying his point with a response.

"And furthermore," I continued, "If I am to siphon the spirits of these Marked, why are these here?" I gestured to the Dragontail whips. My stomach churned.

A dragon had to die for this. For their scales to be used as the leather for the whips. For their spikes to be woven in intervals meant for sticking into flesh and ripping it apart. For their talons to be turned into the tips of the whips.

Not to mention, if they were bonded to an angel, it also meant the angel had also died. Because the loss of a bond between dragon and angel was equally devastating as a wingmate bond between angelic mates.

A tendril of shadow gingerly brushed the edges of my mind. I found myself like a starving youngling, throwing myself into the touch. Desperate for its comfort. Its strength.

"Ah yes. The Dragontails."

Kaelthos chuckled darkly, as if something funny had been said. I shuddered at the sound. Shuddered at the gleam that lit up the eyes of all three Scourgers.

"Disciple Safah, they are here in case you'd like to be the first female of your family to break tradition. Now remember, this lesson is about sacrifice being *better* than obedience."

I spun to face Kaelthos. The smile stitched on his face made all seven of my hearts shrivel.

"Either you obey and kill the Fallenspawn. Or," he lifted a finger, "you sacrifice *yourself* and take a beating in their place."

I flinched, stumbling back. I had no words. He couldn't be serious. I had to...I looked back at the Dragontails. The whips weren't for the Marked.

They were for *me*.

"She has to *WHAT?*" Ellabeth screamed, her voice bouncing off the walls in the Sanctuary.

"There's no burning way—"

"Silence!" Kaelthos cut off Daelun's outburst.

"Disciple Safah, you will kill the Fallenspawn or receive one hundred lashes in their place. If you don't keep your feet, and your wings, to receive every lash, they die. If you try to escape, they die. If you try to foil their fate and rescue them yourself, they die. If you die before receiving *all* the lashes... you guessed it, the abominations will die."

I swayed in place. I rose a hand to my temple, rocked with a wave of nausea and shock. This couldn't be happening. Manmi *never* said anything like this would come my way. What in the stars was I supposed to do?

"You accepted to demonstrate, therefore you will. Or they will *die*. And to be clear, Disciple. *No* angel has survived passed the thirty ninth lash of *one* Scourger. Let alone three."

I looked at Scourgers Jeroah, Refayim, and Lilithine.

They looked back at me. And all three of them smiled.

Merciful Infinite, help me.

I looked at the Marked, completely lost for what to do. I could save myself, but I'd have to kill them. I could save them, but then I'd probably die in the process...which would *still* get them killed.

Bend, but do not break. Burn, but never bleed.

I closed my eyes, picturing Manmi. She floated behind me

while I sat in a cloudchair as she did my hair, swathing my curls with makristi oil, gently detangling each strand.

"We're Anathelles fifi. Holy, to whatever end."

Obedience or sacrifice. The choice rang loud in my mind like the bells at high dawn. I pinched my eyes as they welled up with tears.

This would be a dawn that would stain me forever. A dawn that would mark my spirit black and change me in a way I never dreamed Temple Efysis would. Tears streamed down my cheeks. Guilt, shame, humiliation, bowed my shoulders, sagging my wings.

I raised both of my palms.

Aimed them at the Marked.

Obedience or sacrifice.

"I'm so sorry I failed you, Manmi," I whispered to no one. "I'm so sorry I didn't Ascend like you trained me to."

I summoned my starfire into my palms. They morphed into spears, the bristling lavender and ivory light cascading all around the cathedral with their brilliance. In rapid succession, I launched a volley of the starfire spears directly at each of the ten angels. I hit each target square on. The spears collided into the chains of the Marked, disintegrating them. I lowered my hands and took a long, deep breath steeling myself. Preparing to pay the cost of setting the Marked free.

"So," Kaelthos said, disgust flooding his tone. "Sacrifice it will be then."

Gasps broke out across the Sanctuary.

"She didn't do it," the Disciples whispered among themselves. "But she's an Anathelle. Why didn't she do it? They're just Fallenspawn."

I paid them no mind. I found Ellabeth. Tears stained her cheeks crimson. I tapped on my breastbone over my hearts three times, holding her gaze.

"My sister," I whispered up to her, even though my voice carried for everyone else to hear. "My dearest partner in bringing Papi and Manmi constant grief." I gave her a weak smile. "My best friend."

Ellabeth's shoulders began to shake as her tears turned to outright sobs. I caught when Dakairi slipped his wings around her shoulders, wrapping them around her slender frame tightly. I knew she would be inconsolable. But there was never truly an option. Kaelthos wanted me butchered, and he'd found a way to do it.

It wasn't lost on me how the Xadari Legionnaires of Azarath were now all sitting straight. Now all watching me with newfound respect. Their faces were bowed in deep frowns. They knew this wasn't fair. It had always been a trap. One I was too slow to spot. Too naive to believe would ever be set up for me. I was an Anathelle after all. Things like this didn't happen to us.

I almost laughed at the irony.

I looked away from Ellabeth, from Incense Order, and from the Xadari Legionnaries.

I turned my gaze to Quazar Valoryen, the Fallen Prince whose name alone bowed the shoulders of even Farasees with fear. His nostrils were flared. His lips were curled with such profound hatred the sight made me shiver. His emerald eyes blazed with holy wrath as he glared fiercely at the Scourgers. Slowly, I watched the emerald morph into raven black as the muscles in his neck strained with his anger. He began pushing out of his seat.

"*Anyone* who intervenes in the fate Disciple Safah has chosen, will be responsible for the deaths of the Fallenspawn *and* Anathelle herself."

Kaelthos's voice cut through the silence in the cathedral like a sharpened blade. No one spoke. Breathed. You could hear a feather drop in the place.

All the well. Soon it would be my bones on these marbled floors. Maybe the gods would mop up my blood and be tasked with dragging me out.

I heard the Scourgers move behind me. I took a deep breath. Squared my shoulders. Lifted my chin. I met the eyes of Incense Order and Xadari Legion. The eyes of the Fallen Prince.

I proudly accepted my fate.

Quazar remained standing, fury visibly radiating through his body. Something heavy and metallic slammed into my spine and locked onto my wings, clipping all seven pairs of my wings together.

I cried out.

I blinked back tears, lifting my eyes to the ceiling. It was only then I saw a long line of Dragèth perched atop the pointed dome over the cathedral. I found the eyes of a black dragon, so massive I couldn't believe the glass could hold his weight. His bright silver eyes burned into mine, holding my gaze until I looked away.

"One hundred lashes," Kaelthos stated.

The angel was soulless.

I looked at Quazar. Held his gaze.

Then the first lash landed.

I would find no sympathy here. Not from where it mattered. I had to move. *Now*. Or the Marked were dead.

Tears streamed down my cheeks, mingling with blood as I pushed to my knees. Stars. My limbs, my bones, everything was on fire. Arms trembling, I pushed back, rocking on my heels. Then ever so slowly, I pushed to rise until I stood again on my feet.

"No way," someone whispered. "She's still standing."

Breathing ragged, I raised my blood drenched face and lifted my chin facing the Disciples.

Every angel in Incense Order was on their feet. So was every Legionnaire of Xadari Legion. A wave of black and gold met me in solidarity.

The Disciples had all *fyused*, shedding their Seraphim skin for their ethèr ones. The Legionnaires looked down at me with their jeweled, glowing, Mortent eyes, the only hint that they had drawn their powers, and would strike when released to.

I looked between them and found that Quazar wasn't among them. My hearts crumpled. Somehow, through this chaos, this darkness, he'd ended up being the one angel I wanted to see. *Needed* to see to get through this.

Why had he left? Where had he gone? I searched the rows looking for the Fallen Prince. But he wasn't there.

Quazar Valoryen was gone.

CHAPTER 36

"Dramatic, little gangster. I'm down here."*

I looked down to the marbled platform.

There he was.

In front of the Marked. Just a wings length away. The Fallen Prince, clad in obsidian finery, his shadows swirling around him, had come to be near me. As close as he could get without Kaelthos calling it an interference and deeming my life forfeit. His eyes blazed like jade stones. That alone was enough for me to lift my head higher. For me to take a few more breaths. For me to withstand the pain a bit longer.

"There you are," he purred. *"I'm not letting you cross into the Ellelights yet."*

If I had the strength, I would have laughed. But then another lash came.

"Forty."

"Forty-one."

"Forty-two."

I held on to Quazar's gaze. It was all I could do to keep from breaking. If I didn't endure, the Marked would die. And stars. I was tired of lives being wasted in this temple.

Shadows slipped into my mind, caressing me. They seeped further, curling into my spirit. Shadow danced with starfire as Quazar traipsed all along our bond, determined to distract me by any means necessary. The feel of him along that tethered, ethereal bond between us warmed me. Reassured me. Strengthened me. I sighed, leaning into his touch.

"Fifty-three."

I could no longer stop the tears. I tried.

I failed.

They fell freely now, burning my eyes, triggering a throbbing headache. By the seventieth lash, I could no longer stop screaming. I swayed, finding the cathedral spinning around me.

To whatever end.

The whispers of my Manmi's vow curled into my thoughts. I held on to them like oxygen.

"Seventy-seven."

One moment the ceiling was above me. The next, it was under my feet. By some odd miracle, I got up again before staying down got too comfortable. I was shivering uncontrollably.

I could feel death rushing for me, demanding I take its hand and enter eternal darkness. I shoved back the temptation to quit. To give in. I endured the lashes as they fell. Screamed through the agony as more pieces of my body, my soul, were violently ripped from me.

My spine felt raw.

My hearts were weakening. Pumping slower.

Life drained out of my body like undulating ocean waves. Crawling black seeped into the corners of my vision coaxing me towards a bright light. The hands of the Ellelights reached for me.

And stars.

I reached back.

"No."

Quazar snarled down our bond. His voice was so loud. Ferocious. Commanding. I jolted alert, flinching at how aggressive it was. I blinked through the haze, finding his eyes piercing into me.

"Safah, do not yield! You will not *enter the Ellelights, do you hear me? I recognize the soft surrender in your eyes. The bow to your wings. The admonition of defeat. To the bottomless pits of the Hèls with the Ellelights. Eternity will not claim you this dawn. I am* not *letting you go."*

"Eighty-seven."

Lash.

"Ninety-two."

Lash.

My knees buckled. My body grew numb. I tried using more starfire to stave off the excess blood flow. But I was getting so tired. So weak. My only consolation was that these wretched inscriptions hadn't surfaced. I'd begged for them to stay hidden. And for once, they listened.

"If you do not rise, Safah Anathelle, not only will you be an embarrassment to your bloodline, but the lives of these Fallen abominations will end with yours. You chose sacrifice. Now get up and prove you are worth it."

Who just said that? The voice was cold. Cruel. Merciless. Was it Kaelthos? One of the Scourgers? I couldn't tell. But it was probably Kaelthos. Dung eating ashbat.

"I'd advise you shut the Hèls up or I'll drown you in shadows and remind you that darkness does not simply bend to me. It bows."

That was Quazar. *Definitely* Quazar.

No one else would have the spine to speak like that to a Farasee? A Scourger? Who in the stars was he talking to? Everyone, everything, seemed so far away. I couldn't hear. Couldn't think. All the sounds were growing muffled. Distant.

"Starling, I have been on my best behavior. Shackling myself to these stupid temple rules. But if you don't get up, that asheater of a Farasee will not only kill my angels, he will kill you. *And I swear to the Infinite, if that fire breather lays even a finger on you, I will lose control. This entire realms-forsaken temple will drown in tormenting, never-ending darkness and burn to ash until there is nothing left. Get up, my Safah, or I will* rage."

I tried to move. I really did, but I had nothing left. My tank was empty. Shadows erupted along the tether of our bond, pouring into my body, giving me a strength I didn't have. I twitched, turning my head to the side.

The Marked were looking at me with wide eyes. I couldn't tell if their terror was for me or themselves. I was laid out on the floor, entirely drenched in my own blood. It was hot and sticky and had a foul odor. I smelled like decay. Like death.

"Kill the Fallenspawn," I heard Kaelthos say from a faraway place.

Something inside of me *snapped*. I'd have every feather of my wings plucked before Kaelthos would get the liberty to kill for sport.

"NO!"

Starfire ripped out of my chest. My open palms. The power poured out of my mouth. I launched myself from the floor, newly charged with a primal instinct to protect these innocents.

"Do not touch them!" I roared. My breathing was ragged. My voice a broken, feral thing. My voice bounced off the walls of the cathedral in tremors. The Disciples across the Orders gasped. Some slid down in their seats, lifting their wings to shield themselves. Others were taken with the ferocity that had overcome me and leaned forward as if I was a creature they had never seen before.

"If you want to get to them, you're going to have to get through *me*."

I threw myself in front of Quazar and the Marked. Starfire bled out of my hands forming a starry shield around the Mortent angels, blocking them from attack.

"Holy stars," someone whispered. "How is she... *Whoa*."

"I think the real question is *who* is she," another angel whispered. I didn't hear the rest. Stars. This was taking so much out of me.

"Just know, this dawn changes everything. For us." A beat. Then. *"Between us."*

Despite the Hèls I was presently enduring, my lips curled into a smile.

"Should I survive, oh Wicked Prince of Curses, I would enjoy no longer trying to kill you."

He snorted down the bond though his facial expression never changed.

"Don't flatter yourself, my Starling. You could never."

"Is that a bet?"

Another lash.

"Ninety-four."

I ground my teeth. Planted my feet. Conversation forgotten, I heaved trying to breathe beyond the foul stench of my insides spilling all over these perfect floors.

"Ninety-six."

I dropped the shield. My shoulders bowed, my wings hanging limp to the floor. Four more. Just four more...

I swayed, nearly stumbling to the marble.

Quazar took a step toward me.

"If you help—"

"I haven't!" Quazar thundered. "Keep pushing me Zamarien," he challenged, his voice dangerously quiet.

Farasee Kaelthos kept quiet.

“Ninety-nine,” Lilithine cried.

I fell to my knees. It felt like I’d shattered my kneecaps.

Face first, I fell into the pool of blood.

“Starling...”

“Don’t. I...I’ve got this. I must *do this. On my own.”*

By some miracle, before Kaelthos’s bloodthirst could win, I pushed to my knees. Then my palms. Then onto my ankles, and slowly, stars, so slowly, I stretched up to stand. Through the tears. The blood. The pain. With my shattered mind and my broken hearts.

“Do. Not. Yield. Starling.”

Quazar’s words stunned me.

They anchored me.

“One hundred.”

A fierce, final, *fatal* strike ripped into my spine. One of the Dragontails wrapped around my waist. It ripped the fabric open as sharp scales tore through my skin over my ribs. Blood gushed from my rib cage, pooling down my gown.

That was the blow that finished me.

As if slipping through water, my body tumbled backwards. My eyes rolled into my head, my arms flung in different directions carrying the momentum of my body with them. The whips *cracked*, and *snapped*, jerking me into a spiral, releasing me into the air.

Several reptilian roars erupted from above outside the cathedral. Then the roof overhead shattered as the Dragèth—bonded to the Xadari Legionnaires—dove into the cathedral.

“Dragons!” the Disciples screamed.

Some Disciples took off flying. The moment they were airborne, the black dragon with the silver eyes flamed them, burning them to a crisp until there was nothing left. Not any skin, bones, or even their spirit.

Endless screaming filled the building. A bright light settled like a film over my eyes, as I felt myself drifting far away. Like I was leaving my body. Like I was leaving this life.

I heard the sound of bodies *fyusing*.

Of Ellabeth swearing vengeance.

When gravity began to yank me down, strong arms, corded with muscle, grabbed hold of me before I fell to the floor. The gentleness with which they held me brought fresh tears to my eyes. Shadows covered all my open wounds and helped to hold my head.

"Safah Eloise Anathelle, don't you dare yield. Not even to the Ellelights."

Quazar's voice was shrill. Filled with panic.

Choking.

Like he was fighting tears.

Like he was racing against time.

His delicious scent of mint and sandalwood filled my nostrils. I hung limp in his arms. I felt light. Weightless. As if I was being flown to somewhere else. Somewhere away from this blood chamber the Farasees had the nerve to call a Sanctuary.

"Starling, please. Please."

Such sweet, comforting words.

But I was tired. So tired.

And the Marked, they would live.

The Marked angels were free. I could sleep now. I smiled, closing my eyes. Then I tumbled into an endless light. I let go, free falling into that welcoming abyss of ivory. But as I fell, a voice bellowed again and again.

"Safah, do not enter the Ellelights. SAFAH, DO NOT ENTER THE ELLELIGHTS."

CHAPTER 37

I drifted on a cloud of ivory, flowing through the tears between Time and the ethereal beyond. It was tranquil here. Peace enveloped me, welcoming me home. I lifted a hand, reached for that portal leading to a realm where Time was no more...

But it closed. Sent me back.

"No," said a voice. It was deep, authoritative, yet comforting. It sounded like Papi would, if he were several hundred thousand millennia old. "Not yet, Star of the Age."

I gasped, stirring from the dream.

With effort, I forced my eyes to open, slowly meeting the bright sunlight illuminating every corner of the chamber I was in. It took me blinking for several moments to realize I was in my bedchamber. In my bedcloud.

I breathed deeply trying to make sense of the fuzziness in my head.

I lifted my fingers. It was about all I could do without triggering a wave of nauseating pain. Every limb was stiff. Every muscle sore. The entire length of my back burned like the Hèls.

Stars.

What happened to me?

I groaned, twitching with anguish. I wanted to move but I couldn't. My head throbbed. Something large, warm, and inviting brushed my cheek, then caressed the side of my face. I leaned into it, still working to blink away the sleep and deep mental fog.

I tried remembering why I felt like I'd been run through by the talons of stareagles. I felt discombobulated. I shook my head which caused my neck to ache and my body to tremble.

Then I nuzzled back into the warm hold. After a moment I realized what was caressing me was a hand. A large one. I blinked, looking at it. It was pale. With inscriptions embedded into every inch of available skin.

I angled my head. Looked up.

Two glittering, emerald pools, rimmed in gold, met my gaze.

"There you are, Safah Starling."

"Quazar," I whispered. I was shocked at the sound of my voice. Why in the world did I sound like that? Like I'd been screaming until my throat was raw and my voice hadn't returned? "What..."

"Shh," Quazar cooed. "You're still recovering. You have a little ways to go."

"Re...recovering?"

I stuttered, my mind already growing tired. I'd said little more than three words and I was already exhausted.

"From what?" I whispered as my eyes fell shut. As the world grew dark once more.

"Shh, my Starling. Sleep."

Sleep? Sleep.

I could do that.

"Quazar?"

I nestled deeper into the sheets. Deeper into a warmth that could only be *him*.

Stars.

Was I in his lap or something?

I was too tired to be bashful. To care.

"Stay with me."

"Always, my Starling."

He finished saying the rest down our bond while brushing his fingers through my hair.

"Even when the stars fall, and the realms fade. When the twinight is no more, and eternal light is our home. You have my word and my hearts. I will always choose to stay."

CHAPTER 38

The delicious scent of melted butter and sugar mixed into rich cocoa wafted beneath my nostrils. My eyes snapped open as I sniffed around for the source. I looked around for the door of my bedchamber. I fully expected to see Manmi and Evanae float in with a bowl bigger than my head full of my favorite cookies. But when I looked out, I was disappointed. I wasn't back home. Manmi and Evanae weren't here.

I sighed and dropped back into my pillows.

Blessed lights! When had my pillows gotten so hard?

I grumbled, shifting to sit up, stretching out my limbs. I arched my back, popping my spine, elongating for an even deeper stretch. While still arched, I opened my eyes.

And found Quazar grinning down at me like a fiend.

"Good dawn, Starling."

I gasped, and jerked, slamming into the bedcloud while

unwinding my limbs. Blushing, I rolled over, looking up at Quazar. His eyes churned with mischief.

"So she does *have a sweet tooth. Good to see our starry princess is finally awake,"* he said down the bond. *"If I'd known smelling a bowl of sugar was all it took to wake you up, I'd have you drowning in my scent weeks ago."*

"You're insufferable, Valoryen."

Quazar smirked. His eyes glowed like jewels. Heat pooled in my belly. I stared at his full lips. I wanted to taste them. To tease them between my teeth as I drowned in his scent. Black ink, in beautiful script, curled around his neck, pulsing with every breath he took. The sight of it made my stomach clench.

"Careful, Starling. I warned you once. Start nothing you won't finish."

"Cause you won't be robbed of your fun, right?" I finished for him, eyes still glued to those full lips just begging to be devoured. *"Quazar, what are you doing in my bed?"*

I trailed the inscriptions down his neck to his bare torso, revealed through the open neckline of his loose tunic. For once he wasn't in that rotting suit. Thank the stars. My fingers itched to touch his chest. To feel those hardened muscles beneath the planes of my palms.

"Being on my best behavior. This is a new record for me."

"What in the stars is that supposed to mean?"

"It means I'm keeping my hands, and my mouth, to myself."

Quazar leaned forward. He gently readjusted the strap of

my twigown. I looked down. It was thin, short, and sensually revealing, hugging me in all the right places.

I froze. *Who* had put me in this?

I lifted my eyes to him.

"Unfortunately, I am not responsible. But I've already given Ellabeth my thanks for her lovely taste."

I swatted at his chest, then crossed my arms. I rolled my eyes but couldn't help the smile filling my face.

"How long have you been here?"

"Every dawn since Dung Eater Kaelthos turned your body into a butcher shop."

My eyes widened. All the memories came flooding back at once. The lack of Presbitari and Farasee presence. Our lesson on *The Principles of Righteous Judgment*. The Scourgers. The accusation against the Marked.

"Stars! The Marked!"

Quazar looked at me for a fleeting moment. He was sitting cross-legged, observing me. Then he leaned forward, gripped my thighs and pulled me to him, resting my knees between his legs. He wrapped a pair of his obsidian wings around my waist. The emerald tips brushed my hips. Quazar brushed my hair away from my eyes.

"They're safe *and* alive." His throat bobbed. "Thanks to you."

My shoulders sagged with relief. Thank the burning stars. I snorted, looking down at our tangled legs.

"Obedience or sacrifice. What a twisted..."

My words trailed off. Kaelthos's lesson burned into my

mind. I reached a hand to my neck, remembering the beating. The torture. The humiliation. The *breaking*.

I was covered in scars now. A lifelong reminder of what it truly cost to be a Disciple in this Hèls-infested temple.

"Manmi never said it would be like this."

I rubbed the scars. If my neck was like this, what was my back like? And why had Zara left me like this? Her mending could remove any scar.

"I assume she was given strict orders not to say a word."

I lifted my eyes to meet his. They were soft. Gentle. This was a side to him I didn't see often. Not around the others. It was a side he kept hidden from everyone except for me.

"How long have I been recovering, Quazar?"

"Six weeks."

"SIX?"

"Six. It would've been shorter, but thanks to Kaelthos you weren't allowed treatment from a Raephim. Zara tried to sneak in twice and mend you. She was caught each time and removed from the wingtower until you mended on your own."

"Golden-eyed monster," I whispered down our bond.

I knew the Zamariens hated us Anathelles.

I didn't realize how deep that hatred ran.

"I can't believe he's a Farasee."

I stopped short. That was rich coming from me. Because what the Zamariens had done to me, the Anathelles had done to the Marked.

And worse.

For Ages.

I bit my lip. It was time I took responsibility for my actions. The actions of my Matriarchs.

"Quazar, I owe you an apology. It's not enough, but I will give it nonetheless."

He stilled, his eyes burning like a bright green flame. I looked him head on, swallowed my pride, and confessed.

"You never hurt my Manmi. You weren't anywhere near her. Near the Seal Gate. You were probably still at Azarath at the time. The empyrean likes to blame you. The Marked. You're the scapegoats of the islands. We automatically blamed you. Blamed your angels. We called you Fallen. We said you were cursed. I was raised to hate you. I was wrong."

I paused, swallowing my nerves. Holding his shimmering gaze, I pressed on.

"I'm sorry. For misjudging you. For believing a lie. For acting on that lie. I won't ever know how many Marked have died because of Manmi. How much blood has been shed because of Granmanmi. I'm profoundly sorry for the absolute Hèls my family has put you through. The Anathelles are why you suffer. I don't know how to fix it. And I'm so ashamed. But most of all, I am so rotting sorry. For all of it."

I bowed my head in shame, wrapping my arms around myself. I thought of the angels who died because of me. The angels who lost their lives annually due to Manmi's cruel idea for a graduation exam. It was nothing more than a culling to decrease their numbers. Then there was Granmanmi's public humiliation of Quazar.

How long had all of this gone on? Why hadn't I seen the truth before? And why had Papi not said anything?

I brushed my hands along my scars. This was all so wrong. I hadn't signed up for this. Trained my whole life for this.

Where was the Infinite? Where was His judgment? Surely our sins in this temple would catch up to us. And if the temple was like this, what was really going on across the empyrean?

"I forgive you, Starling."

I snapped my head up, my eyes instantly welling with tears.

"It doesn't make any of what happened okay, but I no longer blame you for the sins of your Manmis. At the end of the dawn, it's not you. It's the system that made you. Made me. Let's be honest, I'm no Saint either."

I looked at him. Quazar brushed a strand of hair behind my ear, then brought his hand to my chin, keeping our gazes level.

"You've been here every dawn, haven't you?"

"Every last one. Ellabeth, too. She washes you up. Makes sure your hair isn't a tangled mess. Which is hèllishly annoying. If you only knew what your hair—coily, unbrushed, loose, and free—does to me. But I stayed, each dawn and twinight. I made you a promise, Starling. Even in death, I won't break it."

My throat bobbed at the raw honesty. At the truth hanging on every word. We were supposed to be enemies. Supposed to hate and kill each other.

And now, we weren't just friends. That was too vague a

term for this unspoken thing between us. Quazar turned to the small table by my bedcloud, leaned over, and grabbed a glass bowl.

"Word got out about what Kaelthos did to you. Your brother, Ezekiel, came to visit but you weren't awake yet. After raging against the Order, your family got permission to send you some love items from home. Your little sister, Evanae, sent several bowls of these."

I took the bowl from him. So I hadn't been losing my mind. I *did* smell my favorite cookies. I sniffed the bowl, fighting fresh tears.

"These *have* to be her Toffeedoodle cookies! It has toffee pieces, cookie dough chunks, is filled with caramel, and is soaked in rich condensed milk, finished off with salt and cinnamon sprinkled on top."

Snatching the lid off, I breathed in the scent of Pasaille. I squealed, leaning back as I kicked my feet while beaming at the full bowl. Baking this much would have taken Evanae dawns to make. What I wouldn't give to hold her now and squeeze her tight.

"My sweet, sweet, Vava. I miss you so much," I whispered, staring at the cookies. "Thank you, my heart."

I bit into one of the chunky cookies, relishing in all the sweet, salty, and gooey flavor. I rolled my eyes in pleasure, tipping back and falling to the sheets as I savored each bite.

"Mmm," I moaned. I was definitely gorging on these the rest of the dawn. I sat back up and found Quazar watching me. His eyes were ravenous with hunger, darkening to a shade that made my chest tight. My stomach clenched as he leaned in.

"If it's that good, I want a taste," he whispered, watching me from beneath his long, dark lashes.

I tried breathing around the thick knot in my throat. He leaned down, gripping my thighs. I fed him the cookie I'd just bitten from. He placed his mouth around my fingers, tugging on the cookie, then sucking on my fingertips, licking both. I hissed with pleasure. With need.

Stars. I wanted him.

When he swallowed, he didn't pull away.

"That was rotting delicious." Quazar's eyes burned. *"The cookie wasn't too bad either."*

Rot. I let out a short gasp, arching into him.

His eyes fell to my mouth.

Mine rose to his.

Then he slowly leaned down, working to close the gap between our lips.

CHAPTER 39

A resounding *thump* pounded against my bedchamber door.

"Quazar!" Ellabeth yelled. "She's *my* best friend. You can't just put shadow locks on her door so no one can get in but you. That's not fair!"

I blinked up at him without pulling away, relishing in our proximity.

"You *what?*"

He shrugged, trailing my bottom lip with a thumb.

"I put shadow locks on your door. The Zamarien youngling tried getting in here once. I taught him his lesson, then I made sure it would never happen again." He tilted his head. "Does that upset you?"

It didn't at all.

"No."

"Good," he said, down our bond. He drew me closer, back

to closing the gap between our mouths. He squeezed my thighs again. I arched into him on instinct, opening my mouth for him. *"Now where were we?"*

"VALORYEN." Ellabeth pounded on the door. "Open this burning door *now.*"

Quazar sighed.

"But *of course* your best friend is as demanding as you."

I grinned wide, pulling away from him.

"I'm coming, Ellie," I called, shoving my feet into slippers and rushing down the gilded steps before hopping to the door of the bedchamber.

"You're awake?" she cried. "*Valoryen.*"

"You know, I prefer hearing my name that many times on your tongue."

I snorted into my palm. *"How in the stars do I unlock a shadow lock?"*

"Easy. Just get close. It'll detect your ethèr, and automatically respond to your starfire, opening on instinct."

"Wait. I'm not the only one with starfire. Granmanmi—"

"She could never." His gruff voice cut in. *"I made this shadow lock, Starling. It only reacts to* you."

Well, it was time to test that theory. I padded to the door. Before I could even lift a hand, the shadow lock *clicked*. Ellabeth immediately shoved the door open and threw her arms around me. We held each other tight.

"Thank you for taking care of me," I whispered into her hair.

"I thought I'd lost you. I...stars."

I brushed her hair as she wept. I could feel the weights falling off of her. Relief. Worry. Fear.

"Kazemir paces every dawn, completely *fyused*. Daelun, Isandra, and Omarion have gone after Tharic. *Twice*. I keep catching Amayah reading about undetectable poisons... Everyone is just angry. This temple..."

"Isn't what we were told it would be?" I finished for her. I pulled back and gave her a small smile.

She nodded, swiping at her tears. "At all."

"You'll have to catch me up on everything I missed. Burning Zamarien won't let me live it down if I fall behind."

"Trust me. We know."

I bit my lip. "Does...does Granmanmi know?"

Ellabeth looked at me. Then her gaze fell on something behind me, as if she was searching for the right answer.

"I think so," she finally said.

"Has she been to see me?"

Ellabeth's face tightened. I knew that look. I already knew what she'd say before she said it.

"No, she hasn't."

I nodded, turning away. Stars. That stung. A familiar tendril of shadow snaked its way to me, rising to rest beneath my chin before lifting it.

"I don't like seeing this pout on your face, Starling. Get rid of your bestie so I can thoroughly rid you of it."

Despite myself, my lips twitched into a smile. I looked at Quazar, who'd taken the liberty to sprawl out over my bed. He winked before popping a cookie into his mouth.

"Mm, these really are burning good. But not as delicious as you. And that was just your fingers. Imagine when I finally get my tongue in your—"

I cleared my throat, fighting with all my might to keep my composure. My face burned as I blinked through the haze that was quickly consuming me.

Quazar grinned, those pointed tips of his teeth turning my mind into an unraveled mess. I trailed my gaze down his exposed torso, and those muscles begging to be touched. Down the length of the tunic, until I reached the hem of his pants. And lower. What I saw made my knees weak.

"Forcing me to settle for these rotting cookies when I'm clearly meant to have you *is entirely selfish, if you ask me."*

I coughed, trying to keep my face from turning the deepest shades of crimson.

"My...my hair." I spun around, breathing in short, quick spurts. "Will you help me with my hair, it's...Well. You see it."

Ellabeth looked at me a long time, studying my expression. Then she looked over at Quazar, who was downing my cookies one at a time, eyes glued to me. She looked at me again. Then at Quazar. Then back at me one last time.

"Hair," she said slowly.

"Yup. Hair."

She raised a brow.

I said nothing.

Quazar chuckled darkly down our bond.

She snuck another curious look at him, narrowing her eyes, before looking back at me.

“Sure,” she drawled. “I’ll do your hair.” A beat. “But only if Valoryen takes his leave.”

I opened my mouth to answer.

“No.” Quazar answered before I could, with such ferocity my hearts skipped three beats.

Ellabeth glared at him.

“We’re going to be doing hair and having *female* talk. Why would you want to stay?”

“Maybe I’d like to know how to do Starling’s hair.” He grinned, chomping on his fourth cookie. “Maybe one dawn *I’ll* need to do it...you know, because she’ll be too sore to do it herself.”

My jaw dropped.

Ellabeth’s eyes widened almost to the size of her head.

I swung my head at Quazar. He snuggled deeper into my pillows, wriggling his eyebrows. He wasn’t going anywhere.

“Just leave him. Come on.”

I grabbed Ellabeth’s hand, dragging her up the stairs to the platform my bedcloud was perched on. Quazar wouldn’t move, so I shoved his legs out of the way, plopping into the middle of the bed while Ellabeth settled on the other side. I waved a hand summoning hair gel, oil, mousse, a wide-toothed comb, bristle brush, spray bottle with water in it, and hair clips.

“Well, well,” Ellabeth grumbled, reaching for the spray bottle after parting my dry, tangled hair into six large sections. “I guess we can thank crack-kisser Kaelthos for turning us into one big happy family.”

I snorted loud, wheezing as I cackled. Quazar laughed with his mouth full of more cookies while Ellabeth began wrestling with my hair.

CHAPTER 40

"So hear me out," Daelun said, shoving another cinnamon roll into his mouth. He waved his gooey fingers, his eyes dancing. "We're in some kind of simulation and we're all trapped. Us, the gods, the shifters. Everyone."

I stopped mid-chew, my mouth half full of bacon, while I held two pieces of fried plantain. My eyebrows rose to my hairline.

"I promise he gets dumber," Isandra said, rolling her eyes. She flipped her long, black hair over her shoulder while digging into her plate of spaghetti mixed with sausage links.

"And more ridiculous," Amayah chimed in quietly, sipping on her mangogo cider. "The conspiracies keep growing with this one."

"Your friends are idiots," Quazar said down our bond

while he continued piling meat onto his plate. His mouth was full of eggs and bacon, and he used one wing to grab a platter of fruit, while using another to refill his goblet with more mangogo cider. *"The astronomical kind."*

"Piss off," was my only answer. He chuckled down the bond while stuffing his mouth with more food.

Seventh Choir and the Xadari Talons had taken to eating all meals together since the dawn Kaelthos nearly had me killed by the Scourgers.

A wall had broken between us from that moment on. It felt nice no longer being separated by Quazar's wall of shadows. Or glaring at one another every second of each dawn. Now we were all in the mess hall of our wingtower, scarfing down firstfast before it was time to go to Sanctuary.

"Daelun," I started slowly after swallowing the food in my mouth. "We are...*not* in some kind of simulation. This is very, very real."

"I don't believe it." He shook his head, determined. "Because we are in a *temple,* Safah. A temple! All of this bloodshed. All of this death. All of this torture. In a temple?" He looked around, looking for support. "Come on. I can't be the only who thinks this is a simulation. This can't be entirely real. This is not a Spiritscape."

Dakairi snorted, filling his plate as full as Quazar's. Ellabeth watched him. Her face was wrinkled with an interesting expression. She had a twinkle in her eyes.

Ellabeth watched Dakairi scarf down his eggs and bacon.

Then he took a sip of his cider. Some of the juice slid down the planes of his handsome chin. Ellabeth trailed that drip of juice all the way down until it fell onto his plate. Dakairi licked his lips. Ellabeth's cheeks flushed.

"What the heck happened between those two that I missed?" I asked Quazar.

He slid his gaze to me, the emerald of his eyes twinkling.

"That's not our business you know."

"They are our best friends. Everything *about them is our business. Spill!"*

Quazar smirked, turning back to his plate.

"This conversation isn't addressing anything important," he said out loud. Every head at the table turned to him. "What I want to know is, why in the Hèls have they not fed us any rice and beans yet?"

"Now *that* is worthy of discussion," Ivyana chimed in. She lifted a piece of bacon off her plate, chowing down. I noticed her plate was as full as all of the Talons. Stars. How much did these Legionnaires need to eat? "I want rice. Beans. Pikliz. Plantains. Fried pork. Yuka."

"Same, little sister. Same." Quazar nodded.

So, she *was* his little sister.

A million questions popped into my head. Chiefly, how in the *stars* did she get conscripted into enrolling at Azarath Academy when she was clearly so much younger than the rest of the Talons? Had she been raised by the Fallen King, too?

"I don't think there's anything serious between them." Quazar snuck his tendrils of shadow across our bond, letting

them slip into my hearts. Into my spirit. *"Pretty sure they get on each other's nerves."*

"I know Ellie better than I know myself. It's not her expression to look at. It's her eyes."

Quazar slid his gaze to Ellabeth who was seated across Dakairi. Her eyes were swirling aquamarine, growing darker with hunger. With need.

"Mm, she wants him."

"Bad," I added.

"Good thing is he's been wanting to taste her, too. Now, has he? Don't know, don't care. That's his business."

I scoffed out loud. Ellabeth's gaze snapped to mine. I tore into my plantains playing off the outburst.

"And us, Princeling. What is happening here?"

Quazar lifted his gaze to mine, bringing his goblet to his lips. When his pearls of emerald met mine of lavender, his eyes darkened.

"Not nearly enough for my liking," he rumbled down the bond.

I clenched my legs as knots twisted in my stomach.

"We hated each other basically two dawns ago."

"We're grown, Starling. That's behind us. We've dealt with it. Now I'm focused on what's in front of us. Well..." He tilted his head. Licked those full lips I wanted to taste, to explore, so badly. *"Until we can focus on what's* inside *of us."*

I'd started sipping on my mangogo cider and choked, coughing on the sweet drink. The entire table turned to look at me. Omarion patted my back with a wing until my coughing fit passed.

"You okay?" he asked.

I nodded, not trusting myself to answer. Ellabeth looked between me and Quazar, her eyes slanting. Dakairi kept his eyes on his plate but he chuckled to himself longer than I appreciated. I opened my mouth to speak when a scrollport surfaced at the center of our table.

"Burning Hèls," Daelun grumbled.

I stiffened. What was this about?

We all put our forks and goblets down, waiting for the burning thing to unfold. The scrollport unfurled until a Babephim surfaced in its center. The messenger ranking angel was beautiful with wide eyes and a sweet demeanor.

"Hello Disciples, it's time for your next trial. Fear of terror at twinight—nor arrows at dawn—should ever befall you. Whether a thousand fall at your side, even if you witness ten thousand die around you, evil will lay no finger on you. Keep your wings and become the pride of the Order. Lose them and be their ridicule. I wish you the Infinite's Blessing. On behalf of Profèt Samael and High Farasee Manazzra Ahabiah, wings high. Ascend, or enlarge the Hèls."

"I'm sick of this temple," Daelun muttered.

"Truly." Isandra sighed.

I waved my hand, summoning my sandals. I slipped them on, lacing the straps up my calves.

I snuck a peek at Quazar. Neither him, nor any of the Talons, moved to get dressed. They continued eating like nothing happened. He was in his loose robes again, opened over his chest. He looked relaxed like this. In his element.

"You're staring, Starling."

"I have a good view."

He smirked, sliding his eyes to mine. A tendril of shadow slipped out from him, curling around my waist, squeezing. I bit my lip at the sensual touch, instantly hungering for more. A second tendril of shadow curled around my thigh. It slipped higher, making my breath hitch.

"That little breathy sound might just be my undoing."

The shadow squeezed my thigh again. And rot if I didn't skip another breath. Quazar brought his goblet to his mouth. My eyes fluttered shut as my breaths became labored.

"Safah."

Quazar's shadows crawled up the length of my curves like sin until they settled beneath my chin.

"Eyes here."

He brushed a lock of my hair behind the winged tip of my ear, as he studied the side profile of my face.

"You are a glorious distraction," he breathed down the bond, sending shivers down my spine. *"One I want to lose myself in and see what I find."*

"You two good?" one of the Talons asked.

Vashari I'd heard Ivyana call him once. I looked into his light green eyes, so light they looked hazel, and flushed.

"Yeah," I bit my lip, grabbing my goblet. I cleared my throat. Twice. "Why...why wouldn't we be?"

Stars, I was hot. Seriously, I needed a breeze or something

to cool down. How suspicious would Daelun get if I asked for a bit of wind? Better yet. Could I trust him to keep his mouth shut? Quazar chuckled down the bond, clearly amused at my visible distress.

"Don't know," piped in another Talon.

Chen.

He was as big as Dakairi, with short black hair, tattoos from the neck down, including his mark of thorns, and with the same hawkish eyes like Daelun. The sheer size and height of him was...astounding. Between him, Dakairi, and Vashari, Quazar had a group of titans in his Legion.

"You two look like you need some privacy," Chen continued, smirking. "It's getting a little steamy in here. Should we clear the table?"

"You can find the nearest cliff and jump off of it instead," I said sweetly, batting my lashes at him.

Ellabeth, Isandra, and the Talon called Ariella, snorted into their plates. Ivyana nodded with a full mouth, pleased, snapping her fingers twice. Even Amayah chuckled behind a palm, covering her mouth.

"Spicy," Chen and Vashari said at the same time, their eyebrows wriggling.

"Just the way he likes 'em." Dakairi grinned.

"But my *friends are the idiots,"* I threw down the bond.

Quazar laughed out loud, throwing back his goblet before refilling it for the fifth time. Just as he slipped a pair of wings around my shoulders, bright light exploded behind our table illuminating the hall. Seven star gates surfaced.

"Blessed lights, "Daelun hissed.

"Playtimes over younglings," I grumbled, pushing off my cloudchair and away from the table. I looked at Quazar.

"No matter what it is you face out there, do. not. yield."

I swallowed the growing lump in my throat. I nodded.

And for some stupid reason, without thinking, I leaned down and kissed him sweetly at his temple, letting my lips linger on his skin.

I was keenly aware of how deathly quiet the chamber had become. I held Quazar's gaze, ignoring the rest.

"I won't."

Quazar smiled. Raised a wing and intertwined it with mine.

"You come back to me unharmed, or I will rage," he promised out loud. His deep voice slipped between my hearts, making me feel stupid, reckless things.

I rose to my full height, standing tall. I turned to the star gates. They were each labelled with our surnames. When I saw mine, I frowned.

"Well, then." I faced Seventh Choir and the Xadari Talons. "Wings high."

The Talons instinctively clapped their wings once, all at the same time. Seventh Choir nodded their heads while looking at their own star gates.

"See you when we get back," I said to my friends.

"In one rotting piece, Safah," Daelun barked.

I looked at him, seeing the anguish on his face. Seeing the

memories of watching me be beaten and tortured in front of the entire Disciple Order while he could do nothing.

"I'll do my best." I took and squeezed his hand. He squeezed back before letting my hand go.

Then I summoned my starfire. With my powers present, and my chin lifted, I floated through the portal as a tendril of shadow brushed my spine and remained until I entered the next trial.

CHAPTER 41

The star gate spat me out onto a cold, marble floor. I yelped, landing hard on my side. My wings bent awkwardly, pinned beneath my body. I pushed to my knees and looked around. I found myself in an empty chamber, surrounded by glass, with no doors.

Refusing to panic, I waited. I paced around. Recited verses. Recounted everything that had happened and changed between Quazar and I. After what seemed like an eternity, out of the blue, a voice from behind me cried out.

"Help! Is there someone there? Help. *Please.*"

I spun around, finding three angels bound. Hand, foot, and wings. I frowned. What kind of Hèls was this...

The first angel was old. He wore the fine robes of a Farasee, his linens woven of the purest ivory with tassels hanging from the tunic that hung low over loose matching trousers.

Like the other two angels, his eyes were covered with a thick cloth tied around his head. When I looked closer, I saw the fabric had been sealed by ethèr.

"Is someone there?" the Farasee questioned. "Remove me from these shackles at once."

"Help me, please," came the whimper of the young female beside him.

When she jerked on her chains, her galactic skin—of varying shades of blue and white—shimmered under the bright light of the glass dome. Her five, feathered wing pairs tried breaking free of the wing manacles, but she couldn't.

"I don't understand what is going on. I've done nothing against the empyrean. *Please.*"

From her skin to her wing pairs, I could see she was from the Chronophim rank. But what was a Preserver doing here? She should be in the Hall of Accords with the classified records of the empyrean. Not used as bait for some temple trial.

A snort from her left made me notice the last angel.

I was so shocked at his condition I stumbled back on my feet, nearly tripping. He was so badly beaten I couldn't tell who I was looking at.

It was obvious he had skin like pearl and beautiful, raven black hair. But there was so much blood dripping from his face, neck, hands. He hung his head low. Limp. As if it required too much energy to do anything else.

He had to be from Azarath. Was he from Xadari Legion? Or maybe Klubari?

I couldn't tell. Not from this angle. And not with all these lights. I was about to reach for the bond and ask Quazar about him when horrifying snarls broke out across the chamber. I whipped around and froze with terror.

A hideous horde of demonic creatures were making their way forward. Most had their eyes on the angels behind me. All of them had somehow gotten inside of the glass chamber.

"Rot," I hissed.

"Who dares use such foul language in our holy temple?" cried the Farasee.

The Legionnaire snorted, as if he'd heard something funny. I couldn't help seeing all of his golden blood and thinking back to when I'd been rolling in my own the dawn Kaelthos let the Scourgers have their way with me. I summoned more of my starfire.

Whether a thousand fall at your side, even if you witness ten thousand die around you, evil will lay no finger on you.

The horde sauntered forward as a coordinated unit. I realized my task instantly. Keep the angels bound alive, until I could set them free. Well, that was going to be a huge challenge. I was completely outnumbered and I had no help. It was me and my starfire against this army of hèlborns.

They had decaying skin colored like ash, with soulless eyes—some obsidian, others lavender like mine—with teeth made for tearing. Their membranous wings had sharpened talons that concerned me. Clad in fitted black linens like skin, they marched forward, gazes hungry. I floated back, planting myself in front of the Hallowed. I kept my eyes on the demons.

No matter what it is you face out there, do not yield.

The first lines of the hèlborn screamed, then charged. In the same breath, I slammed my wings into the ground, pouring my power into the clap. I drew up a large shield of starfire, surrounding the bound angels.

The moment they were sealed, the hèlborn began colliding into the shield. As the hèlborns mindlessly screamed, frothing at the mouth, trying to satiate their thirst for blood, I shot into the air. A line of hèlborn followed after me. Mid-flight, I *fyused*. The moment I took on my starry skin, I let my starfire explode in a rampage.

"We were promised the blood of the Hallowed," a hèlborn screamed. "And we *will* receive our due. We've done what your bleeding Farasees said. Now give us our blood!"

A hèlborn launched at me. Angling my body like a battering ram, I barreled into the hèlborn, and the three that were close behind, flattening my wings so they could sharpen and slice across all the hèlborn at the same time. Wasting no time on the ones dying before me, I scanned the horde.

There was an innumerable amount of demons here. I would have to kill them in droves, or else I'd get tired and make a mistake which could lead to death. One never knew how far this temple would go to prove a point. I had to kill the demons en masse.

"I don't care what you were promised," I spat. "The

blood of Hallowed are not up for exchange. Especially to hèlborns."

I began spinning like a spiral. I gained speed until the chamber around me was a complete blur. When I couldn't go faster, I focused on the brimming well of starfire within myself that fueled every inch of my body. I took a breath. Continued spinning. Plunged into my inner wells of power.

Then I erupted with a numberless count of sharp-tipped spears made of starfire. Like a volley of arrows, the spears launched out from me as I threw my arms wide, and flexed my hands. In moments, hundreds of hèlborns were tumbling to their feet, screaming. My starfire burned them until there was nothing left but ash.

Wasting no time, still spinning, I jerked my body and plunged *down*. I pulsed my wings, hard, gaining speed the further down I went.

"Cursed Hallowed," one of the hèlborn spat. "We'll take our time with you. We'll make you pay."

"You'll have to catch me first!"

I kept flying, focused on my target. As I neared the horde beneath me, I grunted at the barrage of hèlborns trying to break through the shield surrounding the Hallowed. There were so many. And I alone was here to defend them all. Fear began gripping my hearts.

Do. not. yield.

Refusing to give in to the fear, I leaned into Quazar's words. It was the only encouragement I could muster and it would have to do. I erected a barricade around my hearts and mind. I would not fear. I would not relent.

Facing the hideous horde head on, I reinforced the shield around the Hallowed. They would not die. Not this dawn.

I forced more speed into my descending spin. Then at the last moment, when I got close to the hèlborn, I jerked to the side and flew parallel to the top of their heads. A large number of the hèlborn turned from the shield and began racing after me. Demons were land bound. They couldn't fly which worked to my advantage.

Balls of black fire flew past my head as the hèlborns began unleashing their power. I dodged attack after attack, weaving in the air as I charged for the far end where glass met marble floors. If I could get their eyes off of the Hallowed...

I screamed as a ball of fire plowed into my shoulder. I stumbled, losing momentum. I nearly dropped from the air. Another bolt struck me. Then another. I wouldn't outlive this barrage.

Golden, hot blood trickled down my body. Pressing beyond the stinging pain, I kept weaving. I put energy again into spinning as fast as I could. Before the hèlborns could strike again, I shot for the marbled floor. When I got close, I pulled up short, jerked my body, and slammed my wings into the ground with ferocity.

Fissures of starfire snaked through the marble, seeping beneath the stone. As the hèlborns rushed me from all sides, I grunted and screamed, grabbing the air in a yanking motion, pulling on my power, ripping it up from beneath the marble.

The starfire I released exploded from the ground like galactic tentacles. Starfire sliced through an endless amount of hèlborns, cutting the demons through.

I pulled the same maneuver again and again, yanking hard as I thrust my powers into the demons. It was exhausting, straining every muscle I had. But the horde began dropping left and right, until only a small handful were left. I rushed over to the remaining hèlborns who were trying to break through my shield.

"Enough!" I screamed out, filled with holy rage.

I threw my hands out, shooting starfire bolts at the hèlborn. They screamed, disintegrating under the fire. The rest turned from the shield, deciding to fight me instead. As they charged, I released more starfire. I spun around myself, whipping my wings like swords, cutting and piercing. One by one the last of the hèlborns dropped lifeless, until there was none left.

"Good, burning, stars."

I dropped to my feet on untouched marble. The cold of the stone was a nice reprieve to the heat draining me of all energy from the struggle with the hèlborns. I huffed and puffed, bending over my knees, trying to catch my breath.

"At what point will you do what makes the most sense here and release me!" the Farasee shouted.

I snapped my head up, narrowing my eyes at him. Rotting dung eater. This brute seemed to be as bad as Farasee Kaelthos.

"Farasee, I will do my best—"

"You will rid me of these shackles now," he snapped.

Impatient, pompous—

"I am almost certain Farasee Nathaniel is responsible for this. Liberate me so I can address this matter at once."

"You're as demanding as a female in heat, *holy one*."

That voice. That attitude. I looked at the Legionnaire again. I tipped-toed to him so the Farasee couldn't hear me.

Using my starfire, I jerked on the Legionnaire's blindfold, half singeing the stupid thing to break through the ethèr that kept it bound. I used the shredded blindfold to wipe away blood from the Mortent angel's neck.

Oh, Infinite.

I rushed around, falling to my knees in front of him.

"Quazar?"

CHAPTER 42

"Quazar?"

I reached up starry fingers to his blood-stained cheeks. He blinked blood out of his eyes, looking down at me. Even in this condition, the defiant Prince managed to smirk.

"She *does* care about me."

"Of *course* I—" I took in his wounds. "Who did this to you?"

A primal desire to protect him came over me. I was ready to throttle whoever had put their hands on him.

"Bleeding the Fallen Prince is the Orders favorite sport. Didn't you know?"

"Was it..."

I didn't want to say out loud. But I also had to know. He knew who I meant without me finishing.

"No my Starling. It wasn't your Granmanmi."

I released a tight breath. This grievance wasn't our fault. Not this time. It felt like an invisible weight had slipped from my shoulders.

Since his blindfold was soaked in blood, I lifted the bottom of my gown to my knees and began wiping away the blood from his face. My nails brushed the heat of his skin, tapping over the endless inscriptions on his neck. I trailed them down in the neckline of his loose tunic. Even bloodied, he was the most handsome male I'd ever seen. My hearts raced as I brushed his hair back from his eyes.

"You're a vision," he breathed. "All I have been greedy to want and everything I know I'm too cursed to have."

My hearts pounded in my chest.

What was he saying?

What was I supposed to do with that?

"Disciple!" the Farasee snapped. "Whatever it is you are doing, stop at once and rid me of these cursed shackles."

I flinched at his shouting. Quazar snarled, the sound escaping his lips, feral and raw.

"She's not your slave, *swine*. Stop whining like a little—"

I brushed my thumb over Quazar's bottom lip. He instantly forgot what he was saying. His eyes snapped to mine. They darkened, and I knew, in this moment, I could get him to do whatever I wanted.

I was lost in his eyes, entirely mesmerized. The trial slipped from my mind as I found myself leaning into him. Lifting a leg over his thigh. Reaching my hands to the nape of his neck, tugging on his hair.

"You're so rotting lucky I'm in these chains," he said, his voice husky, all breath. "If I could get my hands on you—"

A heavy slam against the glass of the dome caught my attention.

"Oh my stars," I gasped. "What *are* those?"

"Starling, promise me you won't freak out."

"I won't freak out." I slid my gaze to him. "Why would I freak out?"

Quazar's eyes remained on the seven monsters outside of the glass chamber.

"Because." A beat. "Those are Stareaters."

"They're *what?*"

"You said you wouldn't freak out."

Quazar was calm. *Too* calm if you asked me.

Stareaters were nightmares. Figments of the imagination. Fiction. *Myth.*

Papi told us stories about Stareaters to scare us at twinight. To get us to shape up when we were misbehaving. They weren't supposed to be true. They weren't supposed to be real. Dread sank in my stomach like stones. This trial was far from over.

"Help them first," Quazar commanded, seeing my expression. I nodded and dove for the youngling Chronophim.

"Please," she shrieked. "Get me out of here, Disciple. Please."

"I will little one, don't you worry," I promised her.

"You will attend to me *first,*" the Farasee raged. "I am a Farasee of the Order. We are taken care of first!"

I ignored him. Honestly, I wanted to shoot him in the face with a starbolt just so he could shut up. The Stareaters banged on the glass, slamming it with their unholy powers as I wrestled with the Chronophim's blindfold, then her shackles. The blindfold came off relatively easy. The shackles on the other hand were putting up a strong fight.

"Burning..." I grumbled, murmuring beneath my breath as I struggled with her manacles.

"Starling..."

"I'm working on it!"

I turned my hand into a starry hammer. I banged against her shackles until the lock finally *popped*. The Chronophim quickly shook it off, her bright galactic eyes swimming with stars. When she looked at my eyes she gasped.

"You're Safah Anathelle. Thank you, Disciple Safah. *Thank you*," she cried.

She squeezed my hands and turned. I looked up and found an open door on the back wall of the glass chamber, wide open.

"Go." I shoved her forward. "Get through the door and fly free little one. *Go*."

"I'm not trying to rush you or anything," Quazar drawled.

I turned to find his eyes on one of the Stareaters. When I turned, I saw the creature had managed to chip the glass, creating fissures that now spread along the rest of the glass.

Rot.

I raced for the Farasee, using the same hammer maneuver. I refused to remove the blindfold from his eyes first. I wouldn't look the parasite in the eyes while he was being vile. It took some work, but I popped his lock. Without a word, I flew behind him, jerked on the blindfold, and loosed him. The Farasee instantly floated up with an air of superiority as he glared at me.

"I told you numerous times to free me first, Disciple," he seethed. "You females are as stupid as you are useless. The Order will hear about this. Mark my words. You'll learn what happens to those who put anyone above the Order."

I flinched. He couldn't make me forfeit my Ascension. Could he? I'd worked so hard, survived too much, for some greedy, careless Farasee to ruin all of my efforts.

"Such a shame," he said, his eyes dragging down my body lewdly. "You *are* a pretty one. Even prettier than Amaryss. And she was a vision to behold. You're not smart like her though. You don't have her cunning. Her sharp mind. You do not *obey*. But maybe you can be taught, yet."

The Farasee whipped around without another word and flew out of the open door. I turned to Quazar, unable to process everything the Farasee had just said.

"And then there were two."

Quazar's eyes were dancing. How could he make light of something as terrifying as this? I set my efforts on Quazar. I reached for his shackles and hissed jumping back. His shackles had a thin, black flame around them. When I looked closely, I saw his skin had been burned raw.

"Quazar," I screeched. I looked up at him. He was still smirking. But his eyes told the truth. He was in great pain.

The Stareaters began cracking through the glass. Through the narrow gap, they shot bolts of black fire our way. I dodged the first three, yanking Quazar out of the way. The fourth slammed right into my wings. And burned. I cried out.

"*Safah*!" Quazar yelled.

Tears instantly welled in my eyes. This was the same pain I felt when the Spirit Harvesters had come after me and were tearing me apart. If the Stareaters were the same in ferocity as the Spirit Harvesters, I wouldn't be able to fend them off. Especially not seven of them.

"I'm okay," I grit through my teeth.

I forced myself to focus on Quazar's shackles before I started circling him, desperately trying to think of a way around these manacles.

A table had surfaced beside him. And on top of it was a dagger with a crimson blade and a gilded hilt. Inscribed on the side was the proverb of Temple Efysis:

Ascend, or enlarge the Hèls.

I went to pick it up—

"Starling, don't!" Quazar snapped, his eyes full of panic. "It's poisonous. Crimson blades, like obsidian blades, are laced with dark majik. If your skin comes into contact with it you're dead."

"But why is it here?"

I looked up. That's when I noticed the door that was open earlier was also gone.

"Wait...They want me to...to *end* your life?"

Quazar smiled at me, but there was no joy in it.

"You didn't expect anything different, did you?"

"This is *wrong*," I seethed.

"You think your little bloodthirsty temple cares?" Quazar chuckled. "Besides, I'm a *Fallenspawn*, remember? I'm their beloved Prince. And *you* are the sweetheart of the temple. Of course they'd use you to get rid of me."

"Sweetheart of the temple is rich considering they let one of the Order nearly wrench me out of this life," I scoffed.

Think. I needed to think.

An idea clicked in my mind.

"Stay behind my wings," I ordered.

I floated in front of him, turning to face the Stareaters who'd broken enough of the glass to shove an arm through. I channeled the depths of my power. I threw an arm in the air and flooded the chamber with starfire, mixed with lavender and iridescent starlight. The power flowed out of my hand like a vortex as my wings flapped. My body thrummed with the energy, creating a strong shield.

As the shield sealed around us, the Stareaters cracked through the glass of the chamber. Burning like a lavender star with an iridescent glow, I turned to face Quazar. He looked up into my eyes, as if staring at a Celestial.

"Beautiful." He blinked at me in awe. "So rotting beautiful."

I smiled sweetly. Picking up the blindfold that had been around the Chronophim's eyes, I gingerly picked up the poisoned dagger. I looked at Quazar's shackles and decided to trust my gut. He said nothing as he watched me bend down, putting the dagger to his shackles. For a moment, it was just the shield of light, Quazar, and me.

I *fyused* back, letting my Seraphim skin return. I pressed close to Quazar, my leg perched over his thigh. He scooted forward. The world fell quiet as we drew close. I tipped my head down. He angled his own, mouth open, drawing me in like a serpent to sin.

I slipped my bent leg further, angling myself over his lap, straddling him. A growl filled the back of his throat. He was completely disarmed, his eyes burning with liquid desire.

I brought the dagger to his shackles and listened as the poison burned through the manacles. We remained like that, the two of us locked in a quiet battle. All I had to do was tip my head and I'd close the gap between our lips.

The lock on his shackles *popped*.

In one swoop, I tossed the dagger as Quazar swung his arms forward and reached up to grip my waist. Like a reflex, I *fyused* again, becoming entirely my starry self. Quazar leaned forward, ready to press our lips together.

A Stareater shoved his sword through my shield. It felt like he'd pierced straight into my spine. I arched, contorting in pain in Quazar's arms, screaming loud.

"Safah!" Quazar roared.

He laid me down gently on the marble, then he was out of my vision. All I could hear was his grunting as I wrestled with a fresh wave of pain burning down my spine. I began choking on acid as tears welled in my eyes. My bones suddenly felt brittle. The sword. It had to be poisoned if it could affect my power like that.

Quazar was already wounded to the point of needing a Raephim. Pain or not, if he was going to fight back, then so was I. Wasn't that the point of all this? For Disciples and Legionnaires to work together? For them to *fight* together?

With tears wetting my cheeks, I rolled over and pushed up to the balls of my feet. I looked out and saw Quazar had already impaled two Stareaters and was working on two more. Good heavens. He was a machine of war.

I watched him move. He was undoubtedly a highly skilled warrior. There was an elegance to his movement. He was ferocious, deadly, and graceful. There was a beauty, an art, to how he killed. How he unarmed his foe and defeated them. He used his shadows like whips, slinging them around, lassoing the Stareaters, before turning the shadows to swords, and impaling them on it.

It was in this moment I realized, every time Quazar and I had gotten into a fight, he'd gone extremely easy on me. I was almost embarrassed at the thought. I was so lost in watching him, I almost missed the Stareater sneaking up behind him.

"Quazar!" I yelled, racing forward.

The Stareater lifted his sword and swung.

But I was faster.

With a blast of starfire, I shoved Quazar out of the way, while simultaneously stabbing the Stareater directly in the chest with my sword. He instantly began to burn, his bone white skin charring away while his horrid, starry face turned to ash.

Reaching Quazar, we launched into the fray against the remaining Stareaters. I lashed out with my starfire, while Quazar used his shadows. I kicked out at a Stareater, snapping the bone in his leg while bending to shove the talon of my wing straight into his chest. I jerked upward and wrenched my talon through his flesh.

Quazar clapped all of his wings together with such force my body vibrated with it. The Stareater I fought against fell face down, falling lifeless. When I turned, Quazar had ended the lives of the other two. All the Stareaters were dead.

I floated before him, a silhouette of lavender galactic fire. Like a burning star. He lifted his head to me, already creating a perimeter of shadow around us, over my starlight. Then he reached up, gripped my waist, and pulled me to himself. We were wounded and hurting, but in this moment, in his embrace, I felt *alive*.

"Come here," he whispered.

I pressed in, placing my hands on his chest. He leaned down, ready to claim my mouth. Then a star gate appeared, dragged us through, and spat us back into the great room of the wingtower.

CHAPTER 43

Sprawled over the cold floor, I looked for Quazar. I found him several wingspans away, laid out on his side, his body contorted at an awkward angle.

"Quazar," I cried.

I pushed to my feet, grunting through the pain of my fresh wounds. I rushed to his side and fell beside him, rolling him to his back. In the light of the wingtower, he looked significantly worse than he did in the glass chambers of the trial. Dakairi and Ivyana rushed to his other side, bending to be by him. Dakairi reached forward, ready to scoop up his best friend.

"I've got him," I told Dakairi, already reaching beneath Quazar's shoulders with my wings to prop him up against me. I brought a hand to his cheek, brushing my thumb over his velvet skin. He groaned, leaning into the touch.

Dakairi and Ivyana watched me in silence. I caressed Quazar's cheek before leaning in to place a kiss on his forehead.

"Come on," I breathed into his hair. "Let's get you cleaned up and to bed. Okay?"

He gingerly opened his eyes. I would always be struck by the beauty of them. Quazar pressed into my bosom, angling his head so I could cling to him better.

"Are you okay if I bring you? Or do you want Dakairi—"

"You," he breathed heavily. "Always you."

I kissed his forehead once more, letting my lips linger at his temple. When I pulled back, I brushed the wayward strands of his raven hair back.

"Come on then. Lean on me. I've got you."

I propped him up, bearing the brunt of his weight with my shoulder. Dakairi and Ivyana continued watching, their eyes shining like jade and sapphire gemstones. I met their gazes, offering a brief smile.

"I'll take care of him. Promise."

To my surprise, both returned the smile, their eyes shining with a knowing. Especially Ivyana. Her eyes were practically glowing.

I got to work, using my wings to propel me to my feet with Quazar hanging onto me. I swung his arm around my shoulders, wrapped my arm around his waist, and held him up with my wings so he could walk without having to use his own strength. One step at a time, I began walking with him.

"How are you..." Vashari's voice broke off from somewhere behind me.

"Brothers," I ground through my teeth. "I... have...brothers."

It took longer than I thought, but I managed to walk him out of the great room, down the halls, and to the side of the wingtower where the Talons stayed. I looked up and found two doors marked *VALORYEN*.

"Which one..."

"Right. Ivy wanted the left. Has a pretty view of the clouds."

"Aww, look at you being a sweet, big brother."

He snorted. "Sweet my backside. If I didn't, she would never shut up about it. I value my peace."

"Yeah, sure you do." I giggled.

He sounded just like Ezekiel, Hosea, and Uriah. They pretended not to care, but they always gave up their preferences for Jael, Evanae, and I. Gabriel was still learning to do that. He was still too young to care.

I trudged him over to his door. Before I could ask how to open it, the shadow lock pulsed in lavender—sensing my starfire—and immediately opened. I stared wide eyed.

"You...you shadow locked your door with *my* ethèr infused?"

"Of course I did. Since the dawn we came back from the first trial and you survived the Harvesters, I knew I'd bring you here one dawn for my own selfish reasons. So I made sure you could access my chambers, access *me*, at any time."

I sucked in a sharp breath. This whole time he'd expected for us to be more than just enemies? More than just temple-mates?

I didn't know what to do with that knowledge. I bit my lip, bringing him into his room. The moment we were inside, the door shut on its own and locked.

I looked around, shocked at how much *smaller* his room was compared to Ellabeth's and mine. As if the Disciples had been given a small palace to live in and the Legionnaires were given...barracks.

"Not as fancy as yours." He chuckled. "I know. Now you see why I like staying in yours so much?"

"Oh, so *that's* the real reason."

He snorted. "Make no mistake. *You* are always the reason I find any excuse to be near you."

His shadows caressed my hips, groping my sides gingerly. My hearts skipped several beats leaving me speechless. I found an empty couch and brought him to it, gently sitting him down. Quazar laid his head back, groaning.

"Safah," he whispered.

I bent down to him, eyes wide. He never referred to me by name in front of anyone else. He only did so in private, when we were alone. When he felt safe enough to let his guard down.

"Yes, my Princeling."

He smirked at that before his face contorted with agony.

"We're not allowed to use the help of Raephim."

"*What?*" My eyebrows shot to my hairline. "But your injuries—"

"I'll have to heal on my own."

"No." I raised my hands to his cheeks. He looked at me beneath those pretty, long lashes, causing my hearts to stutter. "I'll do what I can. It won't be the best, but it should be enough."

"Why'd you bring me to the couch and not the bed?" His eyes danced. "I have so many ideas for what we could do between my sheets, you and I."

Before I could stop myself, I burst out giggling, feeling my face flush. I covered my mouth as I laughed, not wanting to look like an out-of-control bloodhyena.

Quazar pulled my hand away, his eyes blazing.

"No," he said, gruffly. "Never hide the most beautiful sound I get to hear. Your laughter is my favorite symphony."

I blushed.

"In all seriousness, you have too much blood everywhere. I don't want you getting it on your sheets."

Quazar looked down, as if he'd forgotten about being bled out before the trial. I lifted his chin so his eyes would meet mine.

"Do I...do I want to know?"

He looked at me from beneath his lashes again. Shook his head. I swallowed the guilt swelling in my throat. Stars. Who had done this to him? He said Granmanmi wasn't involved. But I had a feeling that wasn't entirely true. I frowned.

Quazar caught my chin between his fingers. Tipped my face close to his. I breathed in the scent of him. Dried blood mixed with sandalwood and that subtle smell of mint. Even in such a gruesome state, I wanted to straddle him and have him take me to places I'd never cared for a male to bring me before.

"Don't worry about me," he whispered.

"It's a little too late for that."

"Safah," he drawled. "I chose this. I'd rather it be me then—"

"I know. But it doesn't mean I have to like it. It's wrong. The weight of all the Marked on *you*? That's insane! One angel bearing the sins of what, hundreds? Thousands? How could you agree to that?"

"Trust me. It was the best deal given. You don't want to know what your precious Order wanted to do, especially with my female angels, if I'd said no."

I stilled. I remembered the males who'd leered at me endlessly in my short time as an Ascendant. Remembered the old Farasee from the trial.

"I think I have an idea or two," I mumbled, lowering my head.

Quazar brushed his fingers over my hair, letting a few get caught in my tangled strands.

"Now amplify it. That would have been the bare minimum. I could never let that happen. And then Ivy...being my little sister..."

"Yeah. Hèls. She'd be living in Hèls."

Quazar nodded.

I sighed, pushing away.

"Can you sit up?"

He nodded, pushing himself with effort to sit straight.

"Let me take care of you, okay?"

I quickly shoved all my hair up into a messy bun, so I could work on Quazar without my hair spilling into my eyes. I rolled back my sleeves and got to work.

First, I unbuttoned his tunic. To my surprise, and great pleasure, my fingers didn't fumble over the buttons. Didn't fumble when I peeled the tunic away, revealing his chiseled chest entirely covered in blood, sweat, open wounds, and those endless inscriptions. I fought the temptation to just run my hands all over him.

Quazar didn't remove his eyes from me once as I started on his boots. I unlaced them, pulled them off, and walked them over to the side of his armoire. I let my wings drag with the cape of my gown, as I padded around his room barefoot. Quazar watched every move, as if memorizing all the little details. As if they were precious and should never be forgotten.

Back at his side, I moved to stand in front of him and tugged at his trousers. Without a thought, he lifted his hips and let me pull them off. Fire sang through my body, from my face down, as he sat in the single couch eyes glued to my moving form, dressed in only his briefs. I took his sullied clothes and found his launder basket, dropping them in.

We stayed in peaceful quiet, as I thought of what to do

next. I could bring him to his washroom to clean him up, but he had so many open wounds. It would be too painful for him, no matter what he said.

As I contemplated what to do, Quazar's body spasmed. Then he tossed his head back and began choking on a rising scream.

CHAPTER 44

"Quazar?"

Forget washing him up. I needed to mend his wounds as best as I could, immediately.

My hearts squeezed as he wrestled against the agony coursing through his body. Instead of combing through the chamber for supplies, I waved my hands and summoned an emergency menders kit to his table.

In a temple dripping in marble and gold, his table was made of wood and stone. I pressed my lips into a thin line, my agitation with the temple only escalating.

Taking out what I needed, I summoned a chair and sat in it. I got to work on all the open wounds on his neck, then his torso. When I looked down, I tried not to stare between his legs, combing his thighs and calves for wounds. Beneath the insurmountable amount of inscriptions carved into his skin, he had wounds everywhere.

"What did those wretched monsters do to you?" I breathed, pulling out a fresh cloth to wipe away the blood, before applying ointment. *"Accursed barbarians."*

"Considering what they did put me at your mercy and care? I'd say it was worth it."

Still bent over, tending to his calves, I flicked my eyes up at him, wrinkling my nose.

"You have issues."

"And yet, here you are," he purred.

I rolled my eyes, my cheeks heating.

"Scoot. I need to see what they did to your back."

Obeying, Quazar moved up without hesitation, bending over. I wanted to scream when I saw the endless lines criss-crossing his back. He'd been whipped, like I had been. But worse.

"Bleeding, rotting, Hèls-damned—"

"Such colorful language for one so pious." He chuckled.

I shoved my knee into his.

"Shut it."

He laughed, still bent over. I tended to the wounds on his back as best as I could. He needed a real Mender. I moved to sit in the chair in front of him.

"Look, I'm no Raephim," I started *fyusing*. *"But I'll do what I can to help seal the majority of these. They'll probably still hurt, but at least they won't get infected."*

He nodded, his gaze lost in my starry figure.

"Why don't you stay fyused *all the time?"* he breathed, running his fingers over my galactic skin.

I shrugged, blushing.

"It draws a lot of attention." I bit my lip. *"Too much."*

I lifted my hands to his face.

"Hold still."

Quazar listened, letting me inch closer as I rested my hands on him. I closed my eyes, seeking out the pool of starfire inside of myself. It was thrumming with the endless galactic power. I began drawing from it, pulling out wave after wave. I forced the starfire into my hands and into Quazar's skin.

He instantly tilted his head back, hissing with pleasure. As I poured my starfire into him, I could visibly see the lavender trails going throughout his body, knitting each open wound it found. Quazar's body shuddered beneath my touch. His pulse raced. His skin turned molten. He fell back into the couch, pulling me with him. I stumbled into his lap, my hands still pressed into his skin.

"Burning stars," he hissed down the bond. *"This feels* incredible.*"*

He rolled his hips beneath me, taking me into the motion with him. I let out a small gasp, straddling him further, pouring out more starfire. He rolled his hips again. And again.

I followed his rhythm, his pace. I leaned my face into his neck, dragging my fingers along his scorching skin. His hands slid down my waist, my hips, until they reached my thighs. I whimpered into his neck as he pushed up the fabric of my gown, inching it higher along my thighs. Then his heated hands were pressing into my skin.

"My Safah," he moaned down our bond.

I couldn't help myself. I pressed my lips into his neck and bit down, sucking on his skin. Quazar snarled like a hungry beast. He gripped my thighs, yanking me closer.

"Do that again, and I'm flipping you over this couch. I will bury myself inside you and mark you. Every Disciple, Farasee, and Legionnaire throughout this Hèls-infested temple will know that you are mine.*"*

Well stars if I didn't like the sound of that. I was flushed all over. I felt like I was going through Purification with him all over again. I brushed a thumb over where he'd just had a wound. The gash was completely gone.

Shocked, I pulled back. Quazar had let his eyes fall shut. Stars. When he was like this—eyes closed, mouth slightly open, expression relaxed—everything inside me melted, demanding to devour him.

"Hey you," I teased. *"Look who is all better. Guess you don't need a Raephim after all."*

He opened his eyes and looked down. I couldn't explain how, but I'd not only stitched up his open wounds, but I'd mended them completely.

"Starling, how?"

"I don't know. But good thing, right?"

He watched me with curious, twinkling eyes.

"'Bend, but do not break'," he said suddenly. *"'Burn, but never bleed.' You're always saying this. Why?"*

"It's a proverb Manmi taught me. I think Granmanmi taught it to her. It's been engrained in me since I was a naive, youngling. It was meant to help me mentally endure the temple."

Quazar nodded, still taking in his brand new skin with those curious looks he kept sneaking my way.

"You know, the temple forced us to bond as temple-mates. Now I'm starting to see the mistake they've made."

"Mistake?" I asked, wrinkling my nose. I brushed his hair with my fingers. *"How so?"*

Quazar laced our fingers together, kissing my knuckles.

"The connection isn't as strong as it would be if we were bonded wingmates, but it's still a pretty powerful one. Especially with you being a Starfire Seraphim and me being a Shadow Bending Mortent. I'm of a lower rank than you, but our powers are of the few contrasting ones that become significantly dangerous when put together. This shouldn't be possible. But because we are bonded, look at what you were able to do."

"But if the Farasees knew that, they'd keep us apart, not forcefully drive us closer."

"Or"—he worried his bottom lip—*"They did it on purpose. They mated us, turning me into a trigger for you. Turning you into bait for me."*

"A trigger for me," I repeated, my mind racing.

I looked out of his window which had a humble view of the clouds. Twinight was starting to rise outside. I was surprised so much time had already passed. I looked back at Quazar, *fyusing* back to Seraphim skin.

"I don't follow. Why in the stars would the Order want you to be my trigger?"

Quazar brushed a lock of my hair behind my ear, not answering right away.

"Quazar?"

"Do you know why they really brought us here?" He looked back at me, his eyes searching mine.

"To prepare for war?"

He snorted. *"Please. When have you ever seen a Farasee at war? We're not here to learn how to work together before we go on the battlefield, Safah. We're here to hunt."*

I raised my brows in shock. *"I'm...*sorry?"

"You heard me. The Legionnaires are here to sift through the Disciples and hunt. The Farasees are looking for an angel, Safah. An angel that carries an old power that has recently been detected to have resurrected. A power linked to the Ashiris star. A power that can call out the lavender dragons from exile."

I blinked at Quazar, not comprehending. I didn't understand a shred of what he was saying. Conversations about some Ashiris star, dragons, ancient power, were ones that never took place in our home. We kept our noses out of such affairs. Papi made sure of it.

I tucked in my knees, leaning my weight on his bare thighs.

"We were brought here as hunting dogs, love. Think really hard about why they mated me, of all angels, to you."

"So...you're supposed to...hunt me? And prove I am this angel...or not?"

He smiled. I nearly lost my balance with how beautiful he was.

"Hunt you. How adorable. I'm supposed to kill *you, Starling."* He leaned in, tilting his head. *"Too bad I fell for you instead."* His grin stretched, showing not one, but both of his dimples. *"Oops."*

I opened my mouth to ask him more questions. Instead, I let out a major yawn. My eyes drooped. I was exhausted.

"Too much. This is all too much. I'm beat," I said, half yawning again. *"Stay with me,"* I whispered. *"Spend the twinight with me."*

He brushed strands of hair from my forehead. His throat bobbed as his eyes colored with desire.

"Are you sure that's what you want?"

"I know it's what I want."

Quazar leaned forward, kissing me on the neck. Once. Twice. He wrapped his wings around our bodies. One moment we were on his couch. The next we were in my chambers.

"Then I surrender. Yes, Starling. I'll stay with you this twinight."

CHAPTER 45

Stretching like a feline, I popped multiple bones in my body before relaxing into the ball I'd woken up in. Yawning, I wriggled around in my sheets. Two iron rod barricades were on either side of my body, keeping me in place.

What in the stars was happening?

I snapped my eyes open, panic threatening to settle in. I turned around. And found myself locked in Quazar's embrace. Those beautiful jeweled eyes watched me, amused. He looked at my head, then back into my eyes, chuckling.

"What's so funny?" I mumbled.

"Your head scarf is so cute."

Quazar's voice was a deep baritone, rumbling over my skin under my twigown.

"Thank you. It's either a cute head scarf or not-so-cute bedhead that will take too long to wrangle when I wake up."

He laughed again. The sound made my hearts sing.

"Thank you," I whispered.

He shifted his head, tilting it down at me. His hair was an absolute mess, the raven strands falling into his eyes. Stars, he looked like the Celestials. So perfect. So handsome.

"For what?" He nudged me with his nose. I cuddled deeper into his embrace.

"For staying. You didn't have to but—"

"I wanted to, Safah. Stars. I *always* want to."

The way he said my name, like he was uttering a prayer, made my skin ignite.

"That was the best twinight I've had in a long time." He nudged me with his nose again. "If you let me in again, I'm coming back. Every time."

"Good. Now, we should probably get ready. We don't have Sanctuary this dawn, but there's always something."

He snorted. "Always something in this stars-forsaken temple," he grumbled. "I don't want to." He threw his weight on top of me, dragging me closer, tucking me into his chest. "Just a little longer."

I nuzzled into him, having no will to argue. I brushed my fingers over his biceps, studying the inscriptions. They were in an ancient, beautiful script. I looked at the swirls, the swoops, the flourished ends. What could they mean?

"Safah."

"Mm?"

"Can I kiss you?"

My hearts fluttered.

"Not with your breath smelling so rank."

Quazar guffawed, laughing so hard into my pillows the bedcloud shook beneath our bodies.

"Safah Eloise, there's no one in this empyrean with a sharper tongue, I swear. Ivyana and Ellabeth are distant seconds."

"Ellie is actually worse than me."

"I can assure you she's not."

He kept laughing while his fingers scratched my head through my head scarf.

"Can I take this off?"

"No."

"What about this piece of string you call a twigown?"

I smacked his shoulder.

"No."

"Your pretty underthings?"

"No."

Quazar scoffed.

"It's so rotting strict around here."

I laughed out loud, wiggling out from beneath him.

"Come on, we need to wash up. We should be dressed and ready for whatever this bloody temple wants to throw at us this dawn."

"Fine."

He yawned, stretching his limbs, before rolling to sit up. The sheer muscles in his body, in his wings, was dizzying. I found myself staring. Damned near drooling.

"So you'll ogle me but you won't let me devour you?" He raised a brow at me. "Selfish."

"Oh, shut up."

I pushed off from the bed, letting my wings hang limp as I floated to my washroom.

"I'll be back, my greedy Highness."

"Please take a long time so I have a reason to break down the door and join you."

I laughed, heading into the washroom, closing the door. I washed up quickly, getting dressed in the bathing chamber before surfacing. Quazar noticed my unclasped gown and licked his lips.

"Soon, Safah," he promised in a husky breath. "Soon, all this fabric won't be in my way."

My eyes fell shut as I strangled my growing need for him. Quazar floated into the washroom leaving the door propped open.

"Quazar!"

"Just in case," he taunted. "I'm always in want of your company, Starling. Fabric-free preferred."

I knew the temple might break me. I could've never guessed that Quazar Valoryen would be my undoing. I shut the door after him before I got tempted.

Quazar took his lambasting time in the washroom. I tapped a foot and hummed while massaging makristi oil into my hair, getting my curls to shine again. My ringlets were perfect, the tight coils hanging down to my calves in lengthy vines.

My wings still had a buzz of pain from the trial where the Stareaters had shot their majik into me. I didn't even bother going to see Zara. I had a feeling she'd been ordered by Kaelthos to never mend me again.

Burning Kaelthos.

I needed to talk with someone from my family to understand why the Zamariens hated us so much. It couldn't be just because we were the only females who'd been admitted to the Order. That was too ridiculous a reason for them to be so hateful. It had to go deeper than that. When I was finally able to see Papi again, I'd have to ask him.

"Rotting Celestials, this *hair*."

I jumped, looking up in the mirror to find Quazar floating behind me. Wearing only a towel around his waist.

"You're not dressed."

My eyes widened as I stared at his chest. His stomach.

Lower.

Holy *stars*.

I wrenched my eyes upward, my cheeks burning hot.

"And you're hungry." Quazar smirked devilishly.

"Of course I'm hungry. We haven't had firstfast yet."

He leaned over my shoulder, pulling one of my curls, twirling it around his finger.

"You know rotting well I didn't mean food, Starling."

I looked away from him, my cheeks flaming.

"Clothes. You need clothes."

"And you need to relax."

He slipped his hands into my hair, pulling me into his

hardened chest. My eyes fell shut as I leaned into him. I sighed, drowning in his delicious scent of mint and sandalwood. He wrapped his arms around me, tucking his head into the crook of my neck.

"I love that we don't hate each other anymore."

"Me, too, Princeling."

Quazar's eyes flashed with gold, his lips curling into a smirk. His arms tightened around my chest. He littered my neck with kisses, nibbling at my skin.

"Hearts-stealing thief."

I angled my head to look at him, giggling.

"It's only fair that we're even."

He looked at me, his eyes glittering like polished gemstones.

"I've lived through an angelic Age, battling against those who brought me war. Finally I've found a safe place to land. To be at peace. You're no ordinary angel, Safah. Your fire, your passion, your seven beating hearts, all of you has become my home."

I twisted in his arms, turning so that our chests faced each other. He wrapped his arms around my waist, pressing me into him. Fire for fire. Skin to skin. I wrapped my arm around his neck, pushing up on my toes, as he angled his head to lean down, about to close the gap between our lips. As his lips brushed mine, sending me into a frenzy, someone started pounding on my door.

I jerked, gasping at the aggressive sound, whipping around to look at the door.

"For Infinite's sake," Quazar snarled out loud, in a quiet, menacing tone.

Before I could move to go open the door, Quazar had already teleported himself there. He yanked it open, his other hand gripping his towel. It was then I saw he was still dripping wet.

"What?" he barked at whoever it was.

"Where in the stars is Safah?"

Ellabeth's voice was high pitched. A mixture of curiosity and mischief. The kind of tone she got before she went on a gossiping spree.

"I'm right here."

I propped up behind Quazar, peeking my head over his broad shoulder.

"What's up, Ellie?"

"Why is he—"

"*What's up,* Ellie?"

She blinked at me, raising a brow. She looked between Quazar and I, raised her hands in surrender, and shook her head.

"Didn't you get a scrollport? We've been told to evacuate the wingtower. The entire temple grounds itself. Stareaters were here. They fed on over half of Manna Order."

"They *what?*"

I nudged Quazar, trying to squeeze forward to stand by his side. Without turning, he wrapped an arm around my waist, pushing me backwards behind him.

"What does Manna Order being offered up to Stareaters have to do with *us* exactly?"

"Quazar!" I swatted at his arm.

"Pretend to be offended all you want to, Starling. I still don't see how the affairs of Manna Order is any of our business. Let them figure it out themselves."

I looked at Ellabeth whose eyes had widened at Quazar.

"He doesn't mean that."

"Yes, the Hèls, I do."

"We'll be ready in five minutes, Ellie."

I closed the door before Quazar could say something else to horrify her.

"You do realize for whatever this is to work," I said, pointing my finger back and forth between us. "Ellabeth has to approve of you. Right? She's my *best friend*. You don't just get me. You get her, too."

Quazar leaned his head back, sighing so deep it sounded like a snarl trying to escape from the back of his throat.

"Fine," he finally spat. "I'll try to be on my best behavior for the little blonde-headed, ocean bender."

"*Quazar!*"

"*What*? I said would try. That should be enough."

I pinched between my eyes. We didn't have time to argue.

"It's going to take you forever. Get *dressed*."

Quazar tilted his head at me, snapped his fingers, and was instantly dressed in his obsidian finery. His hair was perfectly done, not a stray hair in sight, and his sharp, black boots were gleaming.

I narrowed my eyes.

I'd seen him wear this attire. So pompous, even if he was a prince. And I knew deep down, he hated wearing it, too. He did it because the Farasee Order made him. Because the Empràr made him, so they could parade him around like some foolish puppet.

"No. Take this off."

"I'm going out in public, Safah." His eyes were sad. "This is part of my...agreement."

"I don't give a star about any burning agreement. Take this *off*."

I lifted my chin. We'd somehow gotten a moment of reprieve from the temple. He would *not* spend it in apparel that reminded him of the unseen shackles he always wore.

"Starling..."

"Take it off." I took a step towards him. "Or I will."

Those full lips curved into a seductive smile, stretching wide until his dimples showed.

"Tempting." His eyes danced. "I'd let you." His gaze slid to the door. "If I wasn't positive that best friend of yours wasn't going to break down this door before I could have my way with you."

"That's right!" Ellabeth cried from the other side. "Get dressed, your Highness!"

"Ellabeth, stop eavesdropping!" I yelled at the door.

"I'll stop eavesdropping when you stop flirting and hurry the stars up!"

"So rotting demanding," Quazar grumbled down the bond.

With another snap of his fingers, he was dressed in his raven black, loose robes again with the tunic unbuttoned over his chest. He'd changed his boots, too. They were more fitting for a warrior on his dawn off, then a Prince expected at court. The oversized robes fit him in a way that made him a complete heartthrob. I bit my lower lip, devouring every inch of him.

"Mm, you do that to me, too."

I looked up at him.

He looked at me.

I took a step towards him.

Then Ellabeth started banging on the door.

"Let's rotting *go*. We have one dawn to lose our minds in the Citadel and I will force you to take it if I have to."

I laughed.

"We're coming, Ellie."

"She's running out of interruption strikes."

My shoulders shook as I laughed, opening my door. Ellabeth snatched my hand, flying with me from our wingtower, across the Temple Efysis grounds, all the way until we made it to the infamous Citadel.

CHAPTER 46

The first thing that struck me about the Citadel was how overwhelming it all was.

"Why in the stars are there so many angels here?"

I looked around in every direction, unsure of what to focus on. It was so much, all at once. The angels, the colors, the activities, the food smells, the sounds, the chariots...My head started throbbing. I wouldn't be able to stay here long. Not in the middle of all of this.

"Well, there are several thousand Farasees in the Order. Their families have to live and thrive somewhere," Ellabeth said.

"But I thought they lived back on the main island of Ouanaviel?" Amayah said, her voice shaking. "I agree with Safah. There's just so...*many* of them. And not just Seraphim. It seems at least ten out of the twelve angelic ranks are here."

I frowned, trailing a slew of Seraphim flying past us. Many of the elemental angels chose to fly around in their *fyused* skin instead of their Seraphim ones. I watched as bodies of fire, water, ice, earth, metals, shadows, lightning, and other elements I didn't have a chance to process, flew by. None of them were starry like myself, which was odd.

Then I ogled the Mortents, with their jeweled eyes and glossy skin. Unlike Quazar and his Marked in Xadari Legion, these were *unmarked*. I narrowed my eyes at them, wondering how so many Mortents became Marked, yet somehow, these angels had escaped the same fate.

A slew of Lawrents and Goverents flew by. They were so similar. Both angelic ranks had colorful, galactic skin that shimmered like the stars, and five pairs of feathered wings. One would think they were the same rank until you looked into their eyes.

Lawrents had stunning, multi-colored eyes. Many of these had one eye of gold, and another jeweled like color. But the Goverents had brightly lit, incandescent eyes. As if a lightning bolt had ignited behind their irises and never burned out.

Prodding shadows gingerly trailed my arms and hips as my anxious twitching grew more evident. I wasn't liking this at all. I hadn't expected the Citadel to be so overstimulating, and my friends weren't helping.

"We should find the food stalls," Isandra was saying. "I want a drumstick."

"A drum *what*?" Vashari asked, crinkling his nose, and curling his lip at her.

Isandra didn't skip a beat. She tossed her hair, lifting her chin at him.

"Clearly you need a proper education on culinary culture. Come on."

She grabbed Vashari's elbow, starting to fly away.

"I'm not understanding why we would go get food when we just ate!" Ellabeth huffed. "How are we not agreeing to go see the museums first?"

"No one wants to go get lost in some stuffy house of artifacts, Ellie," Daelun grumbled.

"I know what you need." Dakairi chuckled darkly, wrapping a wing around Ellabeth's waist, beginning to tug her away. She swatted at him, which only made him laugh more as he pulled her tighter.

"Screw the museums. I want more shadowbolts," Chen said, crossing his arms.

Ivyana rolled her eyes.

"Why is it *always* weapons with you? This is a happy time. You're supposed to enjoy what makes you happy, Chen."

"Having enough weapons to clear out a legion of carcasses *is* my happy place."

"Are we seriously..."

The words trailed off as I tuned my friends out.

Gentle tendrils of shadow brushed down my spine, before lingering at my hips, squeezing my waist. I slid my gaze to Quazar. When our eyes met, he nudged his head to the side, putting a finger to his lips. I slipped my hand into his. He interlaced our fingers as he pulled us away while our friends kept arguing about what to do first.

"It's like herding goats," I said.

Quazar laughed.

"Where do you want to go?" I asked, thankful to be pulled away from the mayhem of our friends. The Citadel was organized chaos enough. Quazar looked at me, his eyes wistful.

"Nowhere in particular, my Starling. I just wanted to get you away before they made you combust. You have one dawn in the Citadel, I want it to be a good one."

I smiled at him before turning my sights to the bustling city in the clouds. In every direction were interconnected towers joined by glass bridges with gilded side rails. Billowing plumes of cloud buoyed throughout the city, filling up pockets between buildings, fountains, parks, and endless city avenues.

I breathed in deeply, then exhaled in a long sigh, taking it all in. I put away the thoughts of Spirit Harvesters, Stareaters, the temple trials, the Blood Rites. Burning Kaelthos and Tharic Zamarien. This was a sliver of a chance to breathe, and I was going to take it.

The delicious scent of fried plantains, roasting meats, and gooey sweets filled my nostrils, flooding my senses. It made me think of times outside of temple life. It made me feel at home.

Manmi loved taking us to market. We'd buy food, shop until our wings burned and refused to fly us further, and our hearts were content. Tears welled in my eyes as I thought about Manmi and all my beautiful memories of her. Memories that seemed to exclude many truths of what she'd kept hidden from us all. Hidden from *me* as she prepared me to follow in her footsteps.

Chronophim and Raephim angels raced past us. They were intermingled, bonding in friendship though they were of different angelic ranks. They laughed, as they flew throughout the towers rushing from one place to another. My throat bobbed.

"What's wrong, Starling?"

"They look so...happy. So carefree."

"Hmm," Quazar said, pulling me to face him. He kept a hand at my waist, while pushing my hair out of my eyes with the other. A soft breeze twirled around us, chilling my shoulders in a soothing way.

"I hear what you're saying, but I'm not hearing your hearts." He poked at my chest, where the largest three of my seven hearts were beating. *"What really ails you?"*

"I envy their freedom. Their...life."

I looked around. These angels weren't in the Farasee Order. They were just the families and friends. They didn't have to think about trials. About Disciples dying all around them. About having to shed their blood so the lives of innocents could be spared. My chin wobbled as I fought tears.

"Since my youngling cycles, I was trained for this. Every dawn had a new lesson. Every twinight had even more. I couldn't eat certain things. Go certain places. Do certain things. It's like the Farasees say, 'You've been given much. So more will be required of you.' But no one burning talks about when that

more *is beyond what you have to give. When that more breaks you. Robs you of your reasons to smile. Delays your desire to wake up and see a new dawn. When that more threatens to break you. And when you* are *broken, it continues to break you still. Because submission is not enough. Total surrender is just the beginning."*

Tears streamed down my cheeks.

"I was raised to hate the Fallenspawn and to adore the temple. I was taught to believe the Farasees and to spare no mercy for traitorous Fallen. I was taught to live piously and do all I could to be righteous. Because the temple was true. The temple was right. The temple is our stairwell to the Infinite. But it's all turned out to be a rotting sack of lies. The image of the temple is a fantasy." I lifted my palms to Quazar's chest, tears streaming down my cheeks. *"You have proven to be my only reality, Quazar Valoryen. Outside of you, I just don't know what is actually true."*

Quazar pulled me in close, pressing his forehead to mine.

"Your love for your Manmi, your Papi, your siblings, Evanae...that is true*."* He breathed huskily down our bond. *"Your feather-tight bond to Ellabeth is* true. *Your love, adoration, and pure worship of the Infinite is* true. *Your willingness to look beyond what is in front of you, is* true. *Your love for your friends, and your desire to do what's right, no matter what it will cost you, is* true. *You know what's true, Starling. You live it out every dawn. And I'll burn in the Hèls before I let this temple break you. Before I let it make you forget that you're a burning star that*

shines bright enough to light an entire realm. That you're the storm that will shatter their glass walls. The storm they never saw coming. The shooting star that will crash into their pious halls of lies, set them on fire, and watch them burn into endless ash."

I wrapped my arms, then my wings, around Quazar and wept against his chest. I felt heavy weights that had been stacking on top of my chest for months begin to fall off. He held me tight, wrapping his wings on top of mine. We floated in the air, not caring which angels passed us. Noticed us. Made comments. We held each other as if there was nothing else in the world that mattered. Because really, nothing else did.

"Alright, no more tears," he said, pulling away after a while. He wiped my tears away with a wing, grinning wide. *"I'm about to stuff you with Ouanaviel akra, patties, and donuts."*

"I am *a sucker for donuts."*

"You're my Starling. Of course you love donuts. Come on."

Fingers interlaced, we flew across the Citadel. I laughed watching younglings rush into fountains, only for the flow of water to overwhelm their small wings, tossing them straight into the bottom of the basin.

"Poor things." I giggled.

Tendrils of shadow wrapped around my waist, brushing my sides lovingly.

"I can see you doing exactly that at their age. Even if you were told no."

"Goodness, don't you know me so well." I laughed. *"Usually Ezekiel or Hosea had to come and drag me out."*

Quazar scoffed.

"Stars. Little sisters are all the same."

I turned my head to him.

"You had to drag Ivyana out of fountains?"

He rolled his eyes.

"First it was fountains." He paused, grumbling, his eyes darkening. *"Then it was male's beds."*

I tossed my head back, bursting out laughing. Quazar didn't think it was funny. Which only made me laugh even more. We flew across a glass bridge, curving along with the flow of angelic traffic.

There were many gods here. I frowned when I saw none of them were free. The gods wore shackles, as they were dragged around by the angels in front of them, their arms full of items that must have belonged to their angelic masters.

One goddess caught my eyes. Stars she looked so familiar. Her beautiful eyes were the lightest hazel. Her warm tawny skin nearly matched her brown robes made of chain links. The chains had gaps in them, enough to show her curvaceous figure beneath them.

Parts of her body was exposed in a way I was sure she didn't like. She looked at me with profound pain in her eyes. I tilted my head trying to remember why she seemed so familiar. Then the goddess gave me a small, broken, but defiant smile. And it all clicked.

"Serafina?" I gasped.

Quazar stilled beside me. I wanted to fly to Serafina. I had so many questions. I hadn't seen her since the dawn she dropped me off for inauguration. Now she was here. Since I'd last seen her she seemed...broken somehow. And it made me want to rage.

I nudged forward, but Quazar gripped my hand and squeezed it tight.

"Trust me. You don't want to do that. Not here."

"Ashiris, you're a Disciple. You're still alive! Thank the Infinite," she whispered, as she floated by—though she had no wings of her own—following after the Seraphim she was shackled to. "I beg of you. You must Ascend," she said so low, I thought I was hearing things.

Several of the gods beside her whipped their heads around when they heard what she'd said. They looked at me. When they saw my eyes, one of them said, "It is her. It is the Ashiris!"

Then they were pulled away by their angelic overseers and were gone.

CHAPTER 47

I fumed, blinking at the backs of the gods as they were pulled away like shackled dogs. They continued sneaking glances back at me, until they curved around a tower and were gone from sight.

Serafina never looked back. Not once. But I saw her shoulders strengthen. Her chin lift. As she was pulled away a fresh spark crept into her eyes. A spark of hope. A spark of faith. A creeping chill skittered up my spine making me shiver.

How many of the gods were enslaved? Why was their slavery okay? Surely the empyrean could thrive without their forced labor. Who instituted—

Quazar squeezed my hand, trying to get my attention. I turned my head to him, trying to focus on what he was saying to me.

"One dawn," Quazar said. *"One dawn is all I ask. Look*

away from the truth. The darkness. This mirage of piety. Just for this one dawn."

I sighed, nodding. I pushed the thought of the gods to the back of my mind. But I wouldn't forget them. I wouldn't forget what the angels were doing to them in the holy city.

I would never forget the goddess with the hazel eyes.

I would never forget Serafina.

Ashiris, she had said. The only thing Papi let slip once upon a time was that it was an ancient star that had shot across the realms, collided into a planet, and burned nearly everything else around it to its twinkling death. Which to me was entirely preposterous. There was no data or evidence such an event had ever taken place historically.

Quazar flew me through the bustling crowd of angels until we pulled short in front of an ivory chariot stand with gilded wheels. There were platters of food already made, and even more being fried in the compartment behind the angels taking orders. Quazar and I waited in the long line. I was salivating by the time we could fly up to order next.

"Two bowls of akra, patties, and the caramel-filled, powder-dusted donuts please."

I licked my lips as Quazar also ordered us drinks and dropped the pieces of *goud*—Ouanaviel coins worth more than silver or gold—into the angels hand. The greedy fiend grinned wide at the jeweled coins.

"A generous payment," he said to Quazar.

"I'm in a good mood."

The merchant tilted his head at me. He leered, his eyes

going from my neck and down the curves of my body. His eyes danced darkly. I squeezed Quazar's hands, scooting closer to him as my feet floated in the clouds beneath them.

"I can see why," the male said.

I gasped in the same breath Quazar whipped out two wing pairs, slamming the male against the length of his chariot. Golden blood trickled from his temple, as Quazar pointed one of his sharp talons at the male's throat.

"Should I rip out your eyes and show you how to properly use them instead?"

Several angels nearby turned, looking at the scene. Gossip began spreading like wildfire.

"Quazar..."

"What? You'd prefer I rip off his balls instead?"

I shook my head. There was no getting through to him.

"Can we get the food and go please?"

"Whatever you desire, my Starling."

Quazar didn't release the male until I collected the bag with our food and drinks.

"Be thankful she's as sweet as your donuts," Quazar snarled. He slammed the angel one more time, purposefully making sure his head rammed into the sharp overhang, before letting him go. Still holding my hand, he tugged me away through the staring crowd.

"If my wingmate isn't a savage like that, I don't want it," I heard a female say as we passed. I snorted, shaking my head. Angels were nothing if not nosy gossips.

We weaved through the heart of the city passing flower

shops, art stalls with colorful tapestries, and endless fruit stands. We also passed several scrollbook stores.

I shrieked.

"Can we go in? *Please?*"

I'd beg if I had to. I wanted to go in one and get lost for the rest of the dawn. Quazar's eyes twinkled.

"Another dawn, Starling," he answered out loud.

I pouted. He squeezed my hand.

"I *promise* where I'm taking you is worth it. Valoryen's honor. Trust me."

I sighed loudly. On purpose.

"Fine," I grumbled clinging to our bag of food.

Quazar laughed to himself. "Little gangster you are. Killing the rot out of Stareaters one dawn, and pouting cause you can't fly around and smell scrollbooks for hours another dawn."

I looked at him and stuck out my tongue. "Piss off."

He tossed his head back and roared with laughter.

I noticed we began flying away from the city center. Our wings carried us over the clouds to a starry area with endless greenhouses encased in glass and perched on a bed of starlight and clouds. The closer we flew, the wider my eyes grew. I'd never seen a sight so beautiful. And Ouanaviel Island was full of jaw-dropping scenery.

Quazar rubbed his thumb over the back of my hand as he brought me closer to what had to be a park in this city in the clouds. Towards the very end was a garden so mesmerizing I found myself tearing up.

The flowers were ginormous, standing tall and towering higher than some of the city's towers. There were endless rows of the colorful flowers. Some of them had petals made of crystal. Others of glass. A few were covered in jewels. The rest either had gilded petals, ivory, or iridescent.

Quazar brought me to the garden encased in glass so clear I'd probably fly straight into it if not for him. He flew us down to our feet. I instantly kicked off my sandals. There was no better feeling than the brush of clouds against the bottom of your feet.

Quazar bent over, scooped up my sandals into his hands, before removing his boots and socks so he could walk barefoot, too. Holding our shoes in one hand, he tugged me along with the other, again squeezing my hand.

I realized that was his way of communicating his presence, his excitement, his fluctuating emotions. It was all through touch. I smiled at the thought. At the vulnerability. It was so simple yet so pure. And the connection was entirely ours.

We walked along the cloudy floor. I breathed in the refreshing, airy scent of the garden. I shook out my hair, loving how the breeze flowed through my strands. Upbeat music played throughout the garden. I couldn't help but move my hips and shake my shoulders in rhythm to it. I tossed my hair, swaying along, completely forgetting the bag of food in my hand.

By the time I took a break, I lifted my head and found we'd made it to the other end of the garden that seemed to balance entirely on top of the clouds.

On this end, the glass enclosure was open. A great breeze flew into the garden and clouds blew in and out. Quazar sat on a starry bench, his foot crossed over a knee, his arm laid out over the back of the bench, the food and our shoes perched beside him as he watched me.

"You look at..." I couldn't think of the word I was looking for.

"Peace. Peace is the word you're looking for, you magical, prepossessing creature."

I smiled, biting my bottom lip.

Then one of my favorite tunes kicked up over the garden. I laughed, twirling and dancing along.

Quazar left me be, lost to the throes of the music. The spell of the song. I circled my hips, threw my arms into the air, and let my hair swing as I danced and danced. It felt like shackles were falling off with every swing of my hips. Every step of my feet. My wings flapped in rhythm as I twirled in the clouds and laughed to the joyous rhythm of the music. After three more songs I'd worked up a strong appetite.

"Mm, she's ready to eat now," Quazar rumbled down our bond.

"She is," I laughed.

Without thinking, I burst into a run and threw myself on top of him at full speed. He caught me like he'd been expecting it, twisting me in his arms, gripping me tight.

I tossed my head back, the air filling with my laughter. I shook out my hair as I tossed my arms around Quazar's neck. Stars. I hadn't realized how much I'd needed this dawn.

How much I'd needed *him*.

I sat up in his lap, my thighs on either side of his hips, my hands lost in the soft, full tresses of his hair.

"You are so handsome," I whispered down our bond. *"And so deliciously tempting."*

Quazar licked his lips.

"This is not the twinight to toy with my emotions, Starling."

I laughed like a drunken fool who'd lost her senses. I was high on joy. And I was ready to take everything that came with it. Including his mouth on mine.

"Princeling, I want to taste your darkness. To dance with your shadows and be consumed by your twinight."

Quazar tugged me closer and gripped me tight. His eyes had turned to blackened pools burning with insatiable hunger and desire.

"Safah," he grunted, his breaths getting heavier. *"You're dancing in a raging fire."*

"I am made of fire, Quazar." I batted my lashes at him, leaning in to nibble the edge of his winged ear. *"I was born with a hunger to* burn*."*

"*Hèls*," was all Quazar snarled.

Then he crushed his lips against mine.

Holy stars, *yes*.

I pressed into him, flattening my hands against his chest as he wholly devoured my mouth. His lips tasted like smoky flame. Like taunting sin. I wrestled with his mouth, pressing my scorching lips to his again and again as my hands danced from his chest, to his neck, to his hair.

"Stars, you're as intoxicating as I imagined you'd be," Quazar groaned down our bond. A growing pool of heat made my stomach clench as I came unglued in his arms.

I gripped those luscious strands as I spread my thighs over him, sinking my hips onto his lap. Quazar growled, angling his head, taking my mouth deeper. He sucked on my bottom lip, then sank the sharpened points of his teeth into the soft skin.

Heat exploded in the pit of my stomach as I blazed in heat for him. Everywhere he touched me, he left a brand. I was feral for this cursed prince who'd stormed into my world, and made off with all seven of my hearts.

We were fire and passion. We were *lost*. In each other. In desire. In mind shattering need.

I gasped into his mouth, letting out breathy sounds that escaped me as pleasure rolled over me in waves. Quazar slipped his hands beneath my gown, pressing his fingers into my heating skin. He squeezed my thighs, moaning into the back of my mouth. His tongue slipped inside, demanding. Conquering.

I relaxed my body into his arms, melting into him. His shadows erupted from his body—groping my neck, bosom, hips, and thighs—while they simultaneously barreled across our bond, pouring into my mind. My hearts. My burning soul.

Stars.

I loved this male. And his passion. All of his dark edges and every way he was unrefined.

I loved the way he loved his angels.

I loved the way he loved *me*.

"Princeling," I said breathily down our bond. His pet name on my tongue made him groan as he gripped me harder. *"They call you wicked. They call you cursed. But Quazar Valoryen, don't you ever for a second doubt. Don't you ever forget. I call you* mine.*"*

He snarled down our bond, flooding me, lovingly, with a barrage of shadows that made my hearts swell.

"I love you, Safah Eloise Anathelle. Star of my life. Heart of my world. You're the hope I was too scared to believe. The love I never deserved. The dream I never thought would become real. You are the axis on which I spin, and the answer to every one of my blasphemous prayers. I am yours, and you're mine. No matter the realm, across every Age, and throughout every lifetime, you. It will always, infinitely, be you."

I kissed him until I felt my hearts exploding. Until I could no longer tell where I ended and he began.

When we pulled away, we were breathless, gripping one another as if we'd fall apart if we let each other go. A spattering of stars danced overhead, shooting across the skies. I rested on Quazar, nuzzling into him entirely as he wrapped his arms around me, bubbling with a joy I hadn't felt since entering the temple.

After we watched the starlights pass, I looked at him. My Princeling. My love. My Quazar.

"Assuming they're still warm, we should probably eat our food now, huh?"

Quazar laughed, stealing several more kisses, before pulling away. He dug into the bag, pulling out one of the food containers. After he popped it open, he pulled out a sizzling hot fritter, fried to perfection. Quazar's grin stretched from ear to ear, his dimples standing out in his perfectly carved face.

"Okay, you've *got* to try the akra first."

PART FOUR

Can light coexist with darkness? But you choose to let your goodness ensnare itself with what is wicked. Such sins will not stand. Not in the Temple. Never in this realm.

Accords of the Farasees, Second Scroll of Paelithis 6:14, Korinti Isles, Fifth Age

CHAPTER 48

I woke up to a soft knock on my door. I rolled over, smiling through my sleepiness, only to frown when I saw Quazar wasn't still in my bed. I sat up and found a note perched on the twinight stand. I snatched it up, reading it over seven times to make sure I wasn't hallucinating.

> *My Starling, part of the agreement was to stay away from a certain Granfifi when she inevitably Ascended. Looks like our little slice of paradise was caught by a few tattle-telling Farasees. Don't look for me, love. I promise nothing good will come of it. And for what it's worth, not only I regret nothing, but mark my words. I will do it again. A taste of you is insufficient. I will devour you for a lifetime, and I still won't be satiated. I love you infinitely, my Safah. —Q*

My breaths came in short spurts. I was hyperventilating.

My hands trembled as I stumbled to my door, pulling it open. I was already crying when Ellabeth surfaced on the other side.

"Sazu, what's wrong?"

Her bright, aquamarine eyes were flooded with panic. I shoved the note at her chest, slipping to my knees. My tears turned to sobs, then flat out wailing. Stars, what would they do to him?

"*Stars*," Ellabeth hissed, falling to her knees beside me. She held me at the threshold of my door.

"What happened?" Isandra's voice was sharp with concern. There was a moment of quiet. The rustle of Quazar's note. Then.

"This accursed temple!" she seethed. "This can't be the good."

Hands that didn't belong to Ellabeth brushed my hair.

"Safah, I am *so* sorry. I swear if there was anything we could do—"

"There isn't," I whispered. "I don't know where they've taken him. I've checked the bond. It's gone dark. It does every time they have him."

"Stars," Isandra whispered.

"Ellie, why were you at my door?"

Ellabeth was quiet.

I snapped my head up, barely able to see her through my tears.

"Ellie..."

"Titombwe," she whispered. "But the Talons are gone."

My eyes fell shut. My hearts pounded in my chest with terror. In warning. I took a shuddering breath.

"I'll get dressed."

I pushed to my feet in a zombified stupor, unable to clear my vision due to my endless tears. A tremor shook my bones as I wordlessly turned from my friends, entered my room, and closed the door.

As if in a daze, I washed myself, got dressed, and grabbed my sandals without bothering to check my appearance in the mirror.

In the hall of the wingtower, I met up with the rest of Seventh Choir. All of them wore long frowns. Kazemir and Daelun's eyes were blazing.

"They did this on purpose," Kazemir seethed.

I flinched, so unused to him having any kind of verbal response.

"Sending us to enjoy ourselves in the Citadel only to bring us together and publicly crush us the next dawn. The Farasees are sick."

Seven star gates surfaced in the hall as if on cue. I felt ill.

"See you on the other side," I said to no one in particular. Then I flew through the star gate, until it spat me out into the massive arena, already filled with millions.

I searched up and down for my family, trying to find where they were sitting so I could be with them. I squinted, hunting for any sign of starry ethèr bleeding out as a sign of the Anathelles. I could find none.

An eery, sinking feeling settled in. As I flew to my seat

among Seventh Choir, I realized the difference. The last Titombwe, the angels had been lively. Exuberant. They'd been talking, laughing, dancing.

Not this dawn. As I settled between Ellabeth and Isandra, the stark difference hit me like stones falling in my gut. The angels were as silent as open graves.

Scores of angels filled the arena to the brim. Some even hovered in place because there were no seats left. I noticed the Shifters weren't present. None of the Dragèth or Pagali were present. There were no Faerèth either. No Neriphim or Taetàn Giants. Come to think of it, there weren't even Gods. There were only angels in the arena, mainly of Seraphim rank.

My mouth turned to sandpaper.

I sat quietly between my friends, waiting out the start of Titombwe. My nerves were shot as I glared at the dais, waiting for someone, anyone, to get this started.

Granmanmi Asarah finally surfaced, floating to the center of the glass-laden dais, her eyes a churning pool of dark purple storms.

"I know that look."

Seventh Choir, and several from the other Choirs in Incense Order, turned to look me, eyes widening.

"Mhm," Ellabeth hummed, studying Granmanmi. "She's pissed."

"And is about to make someone pay," I finished.

I had a feeling I knew who her target was. I stepped into my mind, poking around the veil between Quazar and I. The veil was sealed tight, our connection cut off. I could still sense his shadows, but that's as far as he'd let me go.

Whatever he was dealing with, he'd pushed me completely out so he could deal with it alone. I worried my bottom lip. Began bouncing my knee, unable to sit entirely still.

"Wings high, angels of Ouanaviel."

"Wings high!" the angels chorused.

I didn't join in. Neither did Seventh Choir.

I studied Granmanmi. She looked perfectly serene. Her ivory robes had been pressed to perfection. Her hair was beautifully done. She even wore a small, pleasant smile.

But I knew my Granmanmi.

She was an Anathelle.

Anathelles told truths with their eyes. And hers looked ready to burn half this empyrean to the ground.

I sat straight, keeping my wings ram rod tight, tucked into my spine. My starfire churned, ready to be drawn on. As if this dawn, blood would be shed and power would be the only way to survive.

Granmanmi immediately spotted me. Her lips bowed into a frown when she caught my lack of response. She tilted her head. Even with the distance between us, she did a once over of my body, searching, scanning, as if she was standing directly in front of me. So often I'd felt nothing but warmth and safety in her presence.

Now I felt violated. Trapped.

And I hated it.

She paused a long while, her eyes piercing into me. She

was quiet so long, the angels began murmuring, until heads began turning my way when they noticed where she was looking.

Fire blazed a trail up my neck as ice chilled my spine. An entire arena of several million angels turned to stare at me. Because of her.

Everyone turned except for Ellabeth, Isandra, and the rest of Seventh Choir. Like me, they only had eyes for one angel. Granmanmi Asarah.

"To our dear angels of the Ouanaviel Empyrean. You've made the sacrifice of being present for such a needed Titombwe, where we need to make an egregious wrong, right. And as you can see, the recent events of what occurred at Temple Efysis has even sorely affected my Granfifi, Safah Anathelle. A name I know this empyrean won't soon forget. It will be burned into the sands of every island of this empyrean as she rises to carry the torch of mending endless wrongs done by our greatest enemies, the Fallen and their Fallenspawn."

"No rotting way," Ellabeth hissed below her breath. "She did not just..."

"Yes. Yes, she just did," I said.

My fury now matched the rolling storms in Granmanmi's eyes. She spoke out over Titombwe, but this dawn, I knew. She had an audience of one. This Titombwe mass was to send a message. And it was directed to one angel. *Me.*

CHAPTER 49

"For those of you who didn't receive the urgent scrollports shared across the empyrean, may I inform you of some unfortunate news. You'll remember last Titombwe I made you aware, that prior to the Ascension of these Ascendants, we, the Farasee Order, decided for the future of the empyrean, it would be wise to bond our Disciples as temple-mates to the Legionnaires of Azarath Academy. This would solidify us in unity and make us stronger on the warfront against the Fallen. This cycle, a delegation from every Azarath Legion was brought to Temple Efysis for this very reason."

"Bullrot," I whispered. Seventh Choir snuck glances at me.

Quazar's words blazed across my mind. How they were all sent to *hunt* us. To hunt a certain angel that the Farasees apparently couldn't find themselves.

"Things were going as expected...until two twinights ago."

I narrowed my eyes at Granmanmi.

Asarah Anathelle smiled at me. There wasn't a drop of the Granmanmi I knew in that smile. I shuddered, holding her gaze. I would not cower down. Not when she'd made me a target to not just the Disciples of the Temple, but the angels of the entire lambasting empyrean.

"The Order goes to great lengths to secure the safety of our Disciples as they go through their seasons of Ascension until the faithful few finally make it into the Farasee Order."

Daelun snorted laughing, not bothering to hide himself. Multiple angels glared at him. "What exactly is your Granmanmi's definition of *safety*, Safah?"

My lips curled into a smile. More and more I was thankful for the friends I'd made in this Infinite-forsaken temple.

Ignoring Daelun's outburst, Granmanmi continued. She had the attention of every angel. They sat up straight, most with their eyes piercing into me, watching my reactions to her fables. I kept still, with eyes only for my Granmanmi. A line had been drawn, and we'd somehow found ourselves on opposite sides of it.

"Temple Efysis has been attacked." Granmanmi's eyes flashed. "What was meant to be a bond of temple-mates for the greater good of the empyrean, turned into a betrayal that we cannot allow to stand. We've already made Empràr Zadkias aware and every Legionnaire at the Seal Gate has been notified. Temple Efysis was invaded by Stareaters."

Cries broke out across the angels. Titombwe descended into chaos. Shouts rang out over the massive arena as angels grappled with the thought of not only the reality of Stareaters, but their holiest temple being attacked, *invaded*, by them.

Granmanmi knew how to rile up a crowd. The angels were enraged. Their fury on behalf of the temple and the Farasee Order rose into a bloodcurdling cry for vengeance against the culprits. I didn't move.

I kept my eyes on Granmanmi.

And she kept hers on me.

She'd lit a match and watched to see how much I would burn before I would break.

Do not yield.

I could hear Quazar's commanding voice in my mind now, breaking down my walls of fear. Barreling across every thought that would make me shrink back. That would make me back down. He would never stand for me cowering, especially to my Granmanmi. So I wouldn't.

I leaned forward, resting my elbows on my knees, refusing to break eye contact. Ellabeth stiffened next to me. Then she scooted closer. An act of solidarity. Granmanmi managed to catch the movement, and make note of it, without ever removing her eyes from me.

"My dear angels," Granmanmi took up again. "Worry not. The Infinite remains on the side of the Farasee Order. On the side of his faithful servants who uphold the truths of the

Temple and have dedicated their lives to making sure what has been established will *never* be undone."

My hearts began freezing over. A tremor pulsed in my hand as the glass dais cracked open.

"The Infinite heard our prayers and quickly exposed our enemies who'd been hiding among us all along."

Ellabeth began trembling next to me. I placed my hand on her knee.

"Do not yield," I whispered to her, eyes still on Granmanmi.

I'd completely tuned out the whole of Titombwe. Since I was a youngling, Granmanmi spoke in riddles. She said it was an act of intelligence if we could decipher what she was saying without her ever making it plain.

Ellabeth took a few moments to relax, but she stopped trembling and sat straighter. She also leaned forward, trying to figure out Granmanmi's game. But I had it figured out.

"They sent us into deadly trials with the Talons," I began, my voice carrying loud enough for Seventh Choir to hear me. "We were supposed to end their lives. More than once. Each time, we spared them." I could feel my rage mounting within me. "Then we grew closer to our bonded. Some of us became friends. Some of us became more."

Isandra cleared her throat, as if she'd been caught in Vashari's bed red-handed. I was in no place to judge. It took Quazar sharing my bed once, for us to sleep together every twinight since. He made me feel safe. Protected. Any chance I had to keep him close, I selfishly took it.

"Then we were given a...dawn *off*." I poured my sarcasm into the last word, realizing it wasn't a moment of reprieve after all. It was a test. Another trial. We just didn't need to cross a star gate to enter it.

And we all failed.

"And while we were busy refreshing ourselves and having a grand time, the Order was watching us. Since we stopped playing along, they changed the game. Stareaters never attacked the temple. They were just a way to get us *out* of the temple. And the perfect rage bait for Titombwe."

Ellabeth grew unnaturally still beside me. From her perch at the center of the dais, as if she'd heard every word clear as a new dawn, Granmanmi smiled in a way that made my hearts shrivel.

"Holy *stars,*" Amayah whispered.

"Hèls-infested temple," Kazemir hissed.

"This is a setup," Daelun breathed. "And if we're not the ones paying the price, then..."

Granmanmi grinned brilliantly, her stunning smile blinding even to me. She was as beautiful as she was cruel, I was beginning to learn.

"But Manna Order," Isandra began, desperately trying to find a loophole in the truth.

"Look around you, Isa," I said. "They're all here. Manna Order was never attacked. The only Order that evacuated the temple, the only Order and the only Choir *told* to evacuate, was Incense Order." A beat. "And Seventh Choir. The temple-mates of Quazar Valoryen and his Talons."

"*Rot*," Omarion spat behind me, brewing with rage.

"Dear angels," Granmanmi announced, already taking her victory lap. "We in the Order have told you many times before, the Infinite will always expose wickedness, and he will always provide a means for us to squash it into nothing so it can never oppose us again. Behold the traitors of your Holy Temple. Behold the traitors of the Ouanaviel Empyrean!"

Granmanmi thrust her open palms at the glass of the dais, pouring out starlight lined with an explosive energy throughout its blast. The dais split open, revealing a rising platform made of stone.

Life left my knees as I stumbled forward, falling off my cloudchair to land on the marbled floor of the arena. My eyes prickled with hot tears as I looked at the platform. At the center were the Talons of Xadari Legion shackled like animals, all half-dressed and chained to the stone. Their wings, hands, feet, and neck had been bound. They all stood proud, their chins lifted, fire burning in their jeweled eyes.

And at the center of his Talons was Quazar Valoryen. Bent over the stone, barely able to keep himself standing. He was bloodied, battered, and beaten within an inch of his life.

"*No*," I breathed, my voice breaking.

"Angels of Ouanaviel!" Granmanmi cried. "What do we do with traitors?"

"Blood for blood!" the angels cried, all of them shooting out of their seats, demanding vengeance. "Blood for blood! Blood for blood! *Blood for blood!*"

CHAPTER 50

My ears rang with the death cries of the angels. The holiest temple in the empyrean had turned her angels into blood-thirsting monsters.

Granmanmi Asarah hadn't removed her gaze from me once. I struggled to gather my bearings looking at Quazar in this condition. His wings had been torn. All six pairs. His skin was littered with bruises and open gashes. He could hardly lift his head.

My Quazar. My heart of hearts. My bonded.

How could she do this to him?

I struggled to breathe. Seventh Choir was paralyzed as we all stared out at our bonded, chained and beaten in some fashion, stripped to such a humiliating degree it almost felt wrong to look down at them.

"Princeling," I whimpered down the bond.

"Don't cry for me, love. I've endured worse."

His breathing was labored, even down the bond. Then the veil fell between us, sealing us on opposite sides. I screamed in my mind, barreling into the veil, slamming at it over and over, until it gave way and released its hold.

The moment the veil moved, I slipped down Quazar's mental pathways, filled to the brim with his restless shadows, and dove in with my starry light. A trail of starfire followed me as I slipped into his mind, his thoughts, and nestled deep, refusing to let go.

While I kept my eyes on Granmanmi, I began leaking starfire into Quazar. At first, he remained limp on top of the stone he was shackled to. But after a few moments, he could move. First one leg. Then the other.

With great effort, he forced himself to his feet. Then he stood tall. As broken as he was, he forced his chin up, lifting his head high. When his eyes found mine, he smiled wide until I could see not just one dimple, but both of them. And stars if I didn't love him even more for it.

I pushed to my feet, sitting back on my cloudchair.

Granmanmi looked at me, then Quazar.

Her eyes darkened. Not with purple. But with a black film. Her fingers twitched, the only visible sign of her sweltering anger.

"The Fallen Prince still stands," angels began crying.

"This isn't punishment enough!"

"Break his pride!"

"What would the Hallowed have us in the Farasee Order

do?" Granmanmi questioned the masses, but her eyes were on me.

"Scourge them!" the angels cried with a loud voice.

"Rot," Quazar cursed down the bond. *"It's always a scourging with these blood-obsessed angels. Why can't the option ever be* 'pray for them'*?"*

My nostrils flared.

I almost laughed at the dark humor.

Almost.

"She won't touch you."

"You may underestimate your Granmanmi's ability to turn this assembly into a blood hungry pack of hyenas, but I don't."

"She will not. You have my word."

"As you all wish!" Granmanmi cried.

An explosion of obsidian starlight burst over the dais.

Then seven Scourgers surfaced.

"You've got to be..." Ellabeth seethed.

I could feel a holy rage burning through my blood.

"The traitors will be scourged! Then they will be placed in the dungeons until they have thoroughly paid the price of betraying Temple Efysis."

She threw an arm into the air and cried, "Blood for blood!"

"Blood for blood!" the angels responded.

Something powerful, and otherworldly—something I'd never felt before—churned in the pit of my stomach. My vision filled with starry spots. I tried blinking them away, but couldn't. A galactic film slid over my eyes, painting the world like the stars.

Down our bond, I felt Quazar's fear. On the outside, he still wore the grin that was pissing off Granmanmi. But inside, he couldn't lie. He was terrified. Not for himself, but for his friends, his Talon family. For his beloved little sister.

"No matter what happens, promise you will stay with me, Quazar. Promise."

"Even in the Ellelights remember? You have my word, my Safah. I will always stay."

My hearts swelled just as Granmanmi turned to the Scourgers. "You may begin."

She was so smug. I wondered if I'd ever known her at all. The Scourgers floated forward, each gripping tightly to a Dragontail. They lifted their arms ready to strike.

I was moving before I could stop myself.

I rushed the dais, *fyusing* mid-flight. I landed with a loud *boom* on the glass, the starfire inside of me churning like a dormant volcano ready to erupt.

"Do *not* touch them," I screamed so loud my voice rang out over the entire arena.

A hush fell over Titombwe as I slammed my wings into the glass, throwing out a shield of starfire around the Talons, effectively blocking out the Scourgers.

Scourger Jeroah and Lilithine were among them. Their glittering crimson eyes took me in, trailing my starry skin as if I was some fascinating creature they wanted to experiment on.

"Well," Scourger Jeroah said. "This is...unexpected."

His airy voice made my skin crawl as if I was covered in spiders. Lilithine said nothing, but she had a vile look in her eyes.

"If you're going to bleed them out," I seethed, turning from the Scourgers to glare at Granmanmi. "You're going to have to get through me."

"You've lost your rotting mind." Quazar boomed down the bond. *"You are so rotting stubborn. Safah, do* not *do this. You've tasted the leather of a Dragontail before. Please. I can't stand seeing that happen to you again. Don't!"*

"I love you, Princeling," was my only response.

I threw up the veil between us, blocking him out. I stood tall. Looking over myself I was stunned to see, this time, even my gown *fyused*. Not an inch of skin or cloth was left unchanged. That *thing* inside me churned again. It was restless. It was angry.

It was hungry.

I looked at Granmanmi Asarah, tilting my head.

"Granfifi Safah. Pride and joy of all Anathelles," she said, her tone like a steel blade. Sharp. Cutting. Merciless.

"Your bravery is commendable but these traitorous demons will be dealt with. I am only disappointed that they managed to deceive you before revealing who they truly are."

"Cut the bullrot, Granmanmi."

I folded my arms. She flinched as if she'd been visibly slapped. An audible gasp rang out across Titombwe.

"You and I both know you've just fed all these angels a

load of crap for them to choke on so you could justify bleeding out the Talons for no reason. They've done nothing wrong."

"You will watch your tone," she hissed, slipping forward.

"And you will set fire to the lies dropping off your tongue like poison."

"As I said, no sharper tongue in this entire empyrean outside of yours."

"Piss off," I said, unsure of how he slipped past the veil I'd erected.

"I rest my case."

"Honestly, Quazar. Now is not *the time, yeah?"*

"Life is short, my Safah. It is always *time."*

Tendrils of shadow tap danced into my mind, warming me through my chest and down to my toes. He was such a distraction. Even now, my hearts warmed up to the sound of his voice. I kept my smile off my face, refusing the urge to turn to him.

"I'm giving you one last chance to step aside, Granfifi."

"No."

Granmanmi Asarah scowled.

"You're as stubborn as that mule of a Papi who raised you. I always told Amaryss, Cassandrel was unfit to be her wing-mate. To raise the next generation who carry our torch in the temple. Look at you. What you are becoming." She sneered at me. "But you're still young. I *will* mold you yet."

Granmanmi *fyused.*

With lightning speed she raised her arms, morphed her hands into swords, then launched herself at me, swinging to cut my chest open, all in the same fluid movement.

CHAPTER 51

I grit my teeth, throwing my arms into a cross—one atop the other—blocking Granmanmi's blow. I checked my shield, careful to make sure the Talons were still protected.

The Farasee Order made a big mistake when they put me in a trial against Hèlborns and Stareaters. It only proved I could hold my shields and stay alive even with the worst odds.

Satisfied the shield was secure, I danced backwards, summoned starbolts, and began blasting them at Granmanmi.

I threw ten. Four landed true. Two jutted out of one of her wings. The third was stuck out of her chest. The fourth had caught her in the thigh.

Unfazed, Granmanmi spiraled. Turned the length of her arms into whips. Then she snapped them my way.

I dodged, flipping into the air.

I flew in zig zags around the dais, avoiding getting

whipped, while throwing bolt after bolt. The angels in the arena watched Granmanmi and I go at it with rapt silence. I noticed even the Talons followed our bloody flight patterns, watching to see who'd be the last one flying.

Twisting my body, I lunged at Granmanmi, launching into a forward assault. Her eyes flashed as she charged, speeding to collide with me head on. At the last moment, I jerked, twisting beneath. I grabbed on to a pair of her wings with my own, twisting us together in a whirlwind spiral.

Granmanmi shrieked as I spun us both uncontrollably. Then I wrenched her wings, yanking them from their sockets, before thrusting us both into the glass. I slapped her body into the dais with full force while bracing my fall with my wings as a cushion.

Blood trickled onto the glass. I couldn't tell if it was hers or mine. It didn't matter right now. I flew up from the dais. And she didn't. I floated back to the Talons, pouring more starfire into their shield while waiting for Granmanmi to counter.

While I kept my eyes on her, I didn't see her inching her ethèr—starlit cords lined with galactic fire—beneath me.

"Safah, look out!" Ivyana screamed.

I looked down.

It was too late.

Granmanmi's cords snagged around my ankles and yanked. Before I could fight back, I was jerked across the dais like a sack of bones, as she slammed me into the glass, face first. Then she slammed me again. And again.

The sharp pain in my nose, my shoulder, and rib cage told me exactly what she'd broken. Blood gushed out. I had no time to think about it. Granmanmi yanked me into the air and slapped me down. Hard.

The splintered glass shattered.

Shards exploded into my face, cutting across my skin.

"STARLING!" Quazar screamed out loud.

Golden blood trickled into my eyes. Down my lips. My head throbbed with a pulsing ache. In the haze, I turned to look out at the crowd. Many of the angels had flown to their feet, watching on, horrified. They assumed this would come to an end. They were naive and sorely mistaken.

Pain searing through my body, I shot to my feet, flying like a rod into the air. I spiraled, grabbing hold of Granmanmi's whip mid-spin, and yanked on it with all my might.

Granmanmi jerked, her bleeding wing leaking a trail of blood behind her. As she raised her hand for another strike, I swiped my wings ramming them into her chest.

I thought of the many times Manmi dragged me into our training chamber and attacked me from all directions, relentlessly, forcing me to defend myself against a barrage. I channeled that training now.

Granmanmi was several millennia old, but she still fought as if she hadn't seen her first five hundred cycles. I whipped out my wings again. Granmanmi dodged, kicking out. Her foot caught the back of my knee, popping the joint.

"You will obey the Order," she seethed. "Safah Eloise, you

will stop this now. You're my Granfifi. I will not continue this with you."

"No," I snarled, rushing her, head first.

I threw all the strength I could into the collision, pushing her body back with my head, throwing her across the long dais. Before Granmanmi regained her footing, I jerked, shoving a wing talon straight into her ribs, cutting her clean open.

Granmanmi screamed.

I wasn't done.

I whipped around, shot into the air, then jerked down, my foot colliding into her sternum, cracking it. Blood poured out. I wanted to care. I couldn't. She'd shed enough innocent blood for my tastes. It was her turn to bleed in the name of Temple Efysis.

I whipped my arms around myself, swung my legs, and spun, a lyrical move that placed me in a position to completely blast my Granmanmi with a barrage of starfire.

"Enough."

The hardened voice did nothing to make me relent. I wouldn't stop until *they* did. I pulled on the now thrashing pool of starfire bubbling up inside of me, demanding I erupt with the power. With vengeance.

"I said, *enough.*"

Granmanmi didn't *fyuse* back.

Neither did I.

She rolled to her feet, glaring at me. Shock and anger colored her mauve eyes as she made a silent vow to repay me for this dawn. We were two starry elementals ready to set this entire colosseum on fire with our wrath.

"As your Empràr, I said *enough*. You will stop this. Now."

I didn't bother turning to Empràr Zadkias. He was a pompous, babbling idiot who took all his orders from the Farasee Order.

I wasn't backing down until every Talon was removed from their shackles and set free, cleared of these bogus accusations being used to end their lives. The Empràr could do nothing of consequence to me. Not an Anathelle.

But the Farasee Order? They could ruin me. I would stand my ground to the very end.

"Your rebellion is so rotting sexy," Quazar purred.

I blinked, unable to hide the flush coloring my cheeks.

Granmanmi caught the change. Her eyes narrowed at me before they slid to Quazar, then slid back to me.

"Disgusting," she whispered.

"What?" I whispered back. "Trust? Friendship? Love? You tell me which of these unsettles you so much Granmanmi, since I can't tell."

"Mark my words, Granfifi"—her eyes blazed—"I will undo the damage Cassandrel did to your mind."

"Papi taught me to be an angel who loved the Infinite. Who loved truth. And who would sacrifice herself for it. I'd say he did a rotting good job, with Manmi, raising me."

"You sound pathetic."

"You sound defeated," I shot back. "Call off the Scourgers."

Granmanmi smiled at me.

"No."

Then I found myself surrounded by the Scourgers.

Rot.

She'd distracted me while the Scourgers drew near without me noticing. Before I could react, the Scourgers body-slammed me with a dark power that sent me sprawling across the dais, leaving me breathless. My ears rang like bells. I blinked back stars, instantly dumbstruck.

Catching me off guard, my shield around the Talons wavered. As a reflex, I pulled on my starfire, reassuring their shield again. The Scourgers may be able to get to me, but I would enter the Ellelights before they touched the Talons.

I screamed as Scourger Lilithine and two others launched their Dragontails at my body. I'd never been beaten like this while *fyused*. The sensation was infinitely worse.

"SAFAH!" Quazar screamed.

His voice was a broken, feral thing.

I could see confusion coloring the faces of many angels as they watched the Fallen Prince thrashing in his chains, trying to break free so he could get to me.

I tried drawing a shield around myself.

I failed.

"Drop the shield around the Fallen, Granfifi, and the Scourgers will yield."

"No. Remember Granmanmi, you taught us to be holy, to *whatever end*."

I whimpered. Blood spewed out of my mouth as the

Scourgers tore into my body violently. Tears trickled from my eyes, but when I looked at the stone platform, the Talons were still shielded. They wouldn't be touched. That was assurance enough. That's all that mattered to me.

My wounds grew as my body looked like a gushing river of golden stars. Only the river was my blood and the stars were my fading spirit. Screams of rage broke out over the angels.

"Stop this!"

"She is the Anathelle fifi."

"This is sacrilege!"

"Make them stop! She's dying!"

A cacophony of wrath exploded. Then there were roars.

They sounded like dragons.

Very *angry* dragons.

My vision faded as the Scourgers mercilessly beat me, refusing to stop until commanded by Granmanmi to do so. She hovered over me, open wounds making her golden blood stain her ivory robes. Even with her bruises she looked regal. Undefeated. Triumphant.

"Do not yield, Starling. Not even in the darkness. Not even when the Ellelights tempt you to come home."

"I love you, Princeling. Even if it was only for a few twinights, it was enough," I whispered to Quazar as I faded out of consciousness and entered a bottomless dark.

CHAPTER 52

A gentle brush of feathers over my cheek pulled me from unconsciousness. I fluttered my eyes, blinking away sleep until the room around me became clear. Brilliant light filled every inch of space, overwhelming my senses. I groaned, pushing to sit up. Leaning back into the pillows supporting me, I took another good look around. Aquamarine eyes, wet with fresh tears, found me first.

"Good dawn, Ellie."

My voice was a ragged, broken thing. Like I hadn't had anything to drink in a long time. I reached out to hold her hand. The tears slipped down her cheeks as she took a deep breath.

"I didn't know if you'd...I wasn't sure...at some point you stopped breathing and..."

She closed her eyes, holding my hand tight. She wept, hanging her head low. Daelun reached over with a wing, wrapping it around Ellabeth's frame. His eyes were wet, too. All of Seventh Choir was present. Not one had a dry eye. Not even Kazemir.

"The Scourgers," Daelun began, stumbling over his words. "They...even when you'd fallen. Even when...you stopped fighting back. Even when you went unconscious... they didn't stop. She...she never told them to stop."

He didn't have to say her name for me to know who the *she* was. Granmanmi Asarah.

"Quazar...he...well. Hèls. Never heard a grown male scream like that before. Your...Granmanmi. She...dragged your body so it was...it was directly in his sight." Daelun paused for air. I shuddered at the visual. "You would've thought his wingmate bond was being broken. Stars. He screamed. Tried so hard to break free to get to you. But his shackles..."

I nodded.

Granmanmi had mastered cruelty. She knew what she was doing. I was the fool for taking so long to recognize it. She'd allow for the Scourgers to butcher me, publicly, as a *lesson*. Stars. If she was willing to do that to me, what had she done to Manmi? To my Tatis? My Kouzis? I wondered if Jael had been exposed to this version of her. Hosea? Ezekiel?

"What made the Scourgers stop?"

My voice was no more than gravel. I tried clearing my throat, but it didn't help.

"The dragons," Amayah whispered. She sat at the edge of my bed with her knees tucked beneath her, her wings hanging off the edge of the bedcloud. "The *parilielthai* of our templemates came. They rushed to the Talons, but Quazar demanded that his *parilielthai* save you from the Scourgers. His dragon ripped the Scourgers apart. Well, Jeroah and Lilithine escaped unscathed. Anyway, by then, their damage to you had already been done. We thought you..."

Were dead is what she didn't say.

"Well, the angels got the bloodbath they wanted," I whispered, dropping my head back to my pillow. Stars. I was exhausted. However long I'd been asleep, it wasn't enough.

"No, they didn't." Omarion's lips twitched into a smile. "They wanted the Fallen Prince to bleed. Not you, the fifi of their beloved Amaryss. And by the hand of your Granmanmi no less! Chaos descended."

I raised a brow.

"Chaos?"

"The angels were begging her to stop. To make the Scourgers stop," Omarion said, leaning close to brush a stray hair out of my eyes. He sat on the other side of me, his entire body a hardened wall of protection.

"She didn't. Some tried jumping in on your behalf," he shrugged. "But they were arrested."

"Some in the Farasee Order had surfaced, ready to shut down the uprising with brutality," Daelun chimed in, excitedly. "So we jumped in, too. Felt good ripping out that big ones tongue. Remember when we first got here and he wouldn't stop staring at you?"

I thought back. I did remember. I'd felt so small. So vile.

"You ripped out his tongue?" I chuckled.

"And his eyes. His rib cage. You know, the necessities."

I shot up into a sitting position.

"You killed a *Farasee*?" I breathed.

"We all did."

I turned to Amayah, shocked at the vengeance in her voice. The bristling rage in her eyes.

"They were going to kill you. So we got to them first. All's fair in Hèls and war. They touched our Choir, we touched their Order."

"Amayah," was all I could say. I was completely stunned.

"You're my friend, Safah," Amayah said. "A burning good one, too. Your Granmanmi isn't taking your life. Not without a fight."

"Burning right," Daelun and Isandra said at the same time. I was touched by the actions of my friends. I sat back, speechless for a moment.

"And..." I steeled myself, braving for my next question. "Quazar? The Talons?"

"Thanks to you"—Ellabeth's eyes shone bright—"Alive. Your shield kept them from being hurt. The Scourgers tried to punish them. They couldn't."

I pressed my hand over my hearts, sighing with relief. He was alive. *They* were alive. And I kept my word. They hadn't been touched.

I checked our bond. The veil was gone. There was an open door on the other end. Quazar was distant, a bit far for me to reach him freely, but for the first time, he'd left the door wide open. The gesture was significant. If I needed him, whenever I needed him, I could access him. My eyes prickled with fresh tears, my hearts swelling. Ellabeth squeezed my hands.

"He's okay," she whispered. "All he cared about was you. His dragon, Rhaevion, stood over you and fought off any angel who dared try to hurt you more."

Rhaevion.

I'd have to find Quazar's shifter and thank him personally.

I wiped the tears from my eyes, sitting up again. My entire body hurt. There was a lingering, pulsing sensation in my elbows, my ribs, and my ankles. My bones were brittle, my nerves shot.

"Has Zara been to see me?"

"She has. But even with her mending...the Scourgers had done a lot of damage, Sazu."

I nodded at Ellabeth's words. So, I'd been on the brink of death. *Again*.

I brushed my fingers through my hair, finding the strands newly moisturized and detangled. My hand came away with makristi oil and a sweet-smelling leave-in conditioner.

"Ellie," I cried, my throat bobbing. She'd taken the time to deal with my mess of hair. I threw myself into her arms. We clung to each other like we often did. It felt good to hold my best friend and know no matter what happened, she was there.

And though it had only been several months, so much had happened in the short period of time. So much abuse. So much pain. So much death. We clung to each other, letting our hug say what our words couldn't.

Then a thought occurred to me.

"Quazar's been shadow locking my room for a while now. How did any of you get in?"

"His Majesty, the King of Shadows, made sure Ellabeth could get in before he and his Talons were deployed to the Seal Gate," Isandra offered.

"To *where*?" I shrieked.

"The Farasee Order said they would remain alive as a means of mercy. But they would have to work double to prove their commitment to seeing a better empyrean for all angels. That meant sending their unit to the frontlines. It's not even the entire Xadari Legion," Isandra said. "Just the Talons."

"Granmanmi," I hissed.

"Granmanmi." Ellabeth nodded.

"On the bright side, they still live here. For now. They just spend way more time at the gate than they do here now. No more classes for them. No more trials with them. From now on, they will remain at the gate. When our complete Ascension ends, if they're still alive, they will be released back to Azarath Academy, and from there, they will be sent to deal with the Fallen conflict on a regular basis."

"Anyway, it's about time you're up. I know you want to sleep more, but you can't. Our Choir has been summoned by the Order's Council. They refused to see us separately. So we've been waiting for you to recover," Omarion cut in.

I frowned.

"It's been—"

"Fourteen dawns. Two weeks. I really don't know how you pulled through," Omarion said.

"Two weeks?" I gasped. "Stars. Alright, you can all leave me now. I'll meet you in the great hall in a little bit."

CHAPTER 53

Floating at the center of Seventh Choir, I looked up into Granmanmi's unforgiving, mauve eyes. We floated in silence as the Farasee Council looked down at us. Granmanmi Asarah was joined by Presbitari Davithius, Farasee Esau, and three Iris. There were other Farasees I didn't recognize except for the final male whose name I didn't know. The Farasee from my trial. I knew he was glaring at me, but I only had eyes for Granmanmi.

"Nothing in this temple is given. It is earned," Granmanmi began. "Incense Order, First Dominion, Seventh Choir has proven themselves to be an embarrassment to the Farasee Order."

"Because we—"

I snatched Ellabeth's arm, squeezing her hard before she said anything else. Granmanmi knew us as if she'd given birth to us herself. I knew the look I saw in my Granmanmi's eyes now. She was using flowery language to bait us. I wouldn't fall for it. I wouldn't let Ellabeth get trapped either.

"You'll have to forgive Disciple Ellabeth, Farasee Asarah," I said, giving a mock bow, bending low, and tilting my head. When I straightened, I smiled at Granmanmi. Her eyes flashed, but she said nothing.

"She has spent endless dawns and twinights attending to my near fatal wounds since the dawn you allowed me to be butchered like an animal for sport in front of the empyrean."

Granmanmi flinched.

My smile stretched.

"You can understand that she is a bit tired, which caused her to speak out of turn. Please, continue."

The males of Seventh Choir grinned, crossing their arms, lifting their chins. The females politely clasped their hands together, but I saw the subtle shifts. Every angel of Seventh Choir had straightened their spines. Lifted their chins. Whatever our punishment would be, we'd receive it with our pride intact.

Granmanmi remained silent a long time. So long I wondered if she'd skip all the pleasantries and just kill me outright. I was surprised she hadn't dragged Farasee Kaelthos into this little show. He'd have loved to be here now, gloating about the failure of the Anathelle line. About how he'd been right this whole time. That females were unfit to be in the Order.

"This Choir has shamed our Order," Granmanmi continued, her eyes storms of fury. "Shamed this holy temple.

Shamed even the Empràr! But no matter." She blinked her eyes at me, then looked at each of us in turn. "We are not charitable with leniency but we are merciful. All of you will remain Disciples of Temple Efysis. Your Ascension will not be forfeit."

My knees buckled. I almost stumbled with my relief. Ellabeth's shoulders visibly sagged. So had Omarion and Kazemir's. We'd been ready to be expelled, but it didn't mean we weren't grateful that we weren't. Thank the living stars.

"You are all still our top students, even if you are the most stubborn," Farasee Esau chimed in. "Despite your streaks of rebellion, Farasee Davithius gained the strongest Choir with you seven in his Order."

Presbitari Davithius's lips curled upwards, his only sign of approval. When I slid my gaze to his, there was a message there for me. But I couldn't tell what the Presbitari was trying to tell me. It felt like he wanted to warn me about something, but I couldn't tell what.

"We will not lose some of our best Disciples simply because you haven't been broken into submission yet. But we have already spoken with Farasee Davithius," Granmanmi continued. "All of you will learn."

I looked at our Presbitari again. He was still smiling, but his eyes told a different tale. A steel storm churned in his eyes, his stark white hair framing his hardened face. If someone needed to be at the Seal Gate, it was *him*.

"Because we will not allow you to simply receive a slap on the hand and restore you to your Order, all of you will be sent into a final trial. It is a test of your loyalty. We will see, and determine, where your allegiance lies. It should be to the Empràr. To the Farasee Order. To the Infinite himself. But this trial will prove if there is hope for you yet."

"And our temple-mates?" I blurted out. All heads turned to me. "What about them?"

"Concerned about the Fallen Prince are we?" Farasee Esau asked. There was a cruel underlining to his tone that made me shudder.

"*You* all are the ones who bonded us. I have a right to be concerned about the well-being and presence of my temple-mate," I snapped.

"Agreed," Omarion said, folding his arms. "If we are to be restored, they must be, too. If you break our bonds now, how do you expect us to survive and carry on through Ascension? It is impossibly rare for an angel to survive a broken bond, even a simple one such as the temple bond."

"Your temple-mates have not been removed from Temple Efysis, nor will they be," Granmanmi Asarah assured us. I wasn't so quick to believe her. "They have their own loyalty to prove, but you all will remain temple-mates until you Ascend into the Farasee Order. Should you make it so far."

She snapped her wrists, thrusting out her palms facing skyward. Her starfire burst free over our heads. I flinched, instantly shielding myself with my wings. Above us, the gilded ceiling covered in intricate, and elaborate art of the angels through Ages past, began splintering open.

"Can light coexist with darkness?" Granmanmi began

reciting. "But you choose to let your goodness ensnare itself with what is wicked. Such sins will not stand. Not in the Temple. Never in this realm. Accords of the Farasees, Second Scroll of Paelithis 6:14, Korinti Isles, Fifth Age."

She looked over us all from the gilded throne she was perched in. Like the other angels, her wings hung over the back of the cloudchair. Overhead, the ceiling opened up to a whirlpool of starry light. Galactic space illuminated above us. I watched as stars and planets orbited past, their cosmic light overwhelming my senses.

"Traitors have been found among our temple. Dissenters who would try to tear apart everything that has been established for the sanctity of the empyrean. You must search diligently, and find the dissenters amongst us, and bring them back with you. Once you've done so, your trial will end, and you can return to your duties as Disciples."

Granmanmi watched me, knowingly.

"Wings high, Disciples," she said, eyes glued to me. I tried not to fidget. "We'll see you upon your return. Do not fail us again," she hissed, eyes flashing.

Then Granmanmi Asarah waved her hands, snapped her wrists, and jerked us from where we were standing. For a moment we all levitated before the Council, unable to move our limbs. Then she thrust us through the open portal above, throwing us into the light of the cosmos.

CHAPTER 54

Feet landing on familiar cobblestones, I stepped forward looking up at my home villa. I covered my mouth with a hand as an instant flood of emotions rummaged through my body. I couldn't stop my tears from flowing as I stood in our driveway looking around. Manmi's chariot was still parked out front—like it had been since the dawn she left...and never returned. Papi's chariot wasn't here. Nor was Evanae's. Mine was parked next to Manmi's, in-between hers and Jael's.

The villa grounds were quiet. I looked around. I didn't see any of our villa keepers flying around. There was usually two outside tending the garden up front and collecting the fruit off the trees.

I'd completely forgotten I was supposed to be in a trial. By whatever luck, I'd been sent home, instead of some stars-forsaken trauma chamber instead. I could only thank the Infinite for His kindness. Floating here now, I missed my Papi, my family, badly. I floated over the golden cobblestones, past the lush greenery of our villas entry, and made it to the door. I lifted my hand to the door knob.

I froze.

The door had been left ajar. And the door knob was hanging off its hinges. My nostrils flared. Panic seeped into my chest. Stars. What had happened?

I looked to the side, noting the stillness encompassing our family home. The waters of our multiple fountains were calm. As if they hadn't been disturbed in some time. The grass was gold, but with closer inspection, I could see the blades were longer than usual. Our villa had endless walls of clear glass upheld by golden pillars and even those seemed like they hadn't been shined in a while. I gently pressed on the front door, pushing it back.

"Hello? Papi?"

The foyer was empty. Dark. Cold.

That was never the feel of our home. No matter the season, our foyer was always bright, filled with music, pleasant aromas, with a warm breeze in the air. Now, it seemed like I'd flown into a dungeon.

When I floated deep into the foyer, I found that it had been ransacked. There were tapestries sprawling on the floor. Scrollbooks had been thrown down. Ethèrlamps had been broken. The chandelier above was lightless, with most of the lights broken.

Irrevocable sorrow began cloaking me. I flew through the

halls of my home, unable to hold back my tears. Room after room had been thrashed. Couches were torn. Pillars had been cracked. Family portraits had been burned. Scrolls covered the ground.

In the kitchen, there was old food, spices, and treats all over the floor. There were a few marks where the end of a wing had brushed through spilled flour. In the great hall, our family piano had been splintered into two. I roamed the halls going from room to room. Each had been torn apart, as if someone had come looking for something.

"What in all the stars happened here?" I cried to myself. "Where is Papi? Where is Evanae? Gabriel?" I looked around, my vision blurry. "Stars. Who did this?"

I will undo the damage Cassandrel has done.

Holy stars.

This couldn't be Granmanmi's doing. Could it?

A thought occurred to me in my mind. I raced down the halls, flying as if my life depended on it. I weaved through corridor after corridor, flying faster as my hearts began racing.

When I made it to the other end of our villa I flew up the golden ramp that led to our Spirit Filing chambers. Fear choked out my hearts as I rushed for the holy preservation room. When the door came into view, I threw myself through it and stopped short.

"Holy, burning, stars," I whimpered, covering my mouth. Every last spirit case had been broken and destroyed. And all of the spirits were gone.

I screamed into my palms as I looked around the room.

Hundreds of thousands of spirits had been destroyed, their spirit cases irreparable. And most were still in the stage of Mourning.

"Oh Infinite, forgive us. *Forgive us,*" I screamed, as I sobbed.

The sacrilege. The blasphemy!

For an angel to destroy spirits that were in process to begin their journey from this realm into the Ellelights?

The sight was too much to take. Several thousand candles had been burned to nothing. Ash was sporadically spilled across the floors. There was a terrifying quiet in the chamber now that the hum of the spirits were gone.

Profound sorrow filled me. I didn't know what to do. What to think.

"Papi, where are you?" I whispered, my tears a never-ending river.

Quazar was gone. Manmi was gone.

Now Papi. Evanae. My siblings. Our villa keepers.

My home had been ransacked and ruined.

Stars.

"Safah," a voice called.

I whipped around. There was no one there. I was completely alone. Isolated in a home that was once filled with so much life and love, that was left an empty, desolate mirror of its former self.

"Safah," the voice called again. It was coming from the darkened hall. I was apt to ignore it and planned to fly in the

opposite direction. But then a strange peace filled me, in spite of my growing sorrow.

So I flew into the hall and followed the voice.

It kept calling out to me. Each time I paused in another room and took in the damage. Each time I began sobbing as I found heirloom after heirloom destroyed. Each time I was ready to fold myself into a corner and grieve, the voice called out to me. And I followed.

The voice took me floor to floor in the villa. I kept flying higher, checking rooms, and finding none had gone untouched. Then I reached the floor my family mainly slept on. Papi and Manmi also kept their individual offices up here, and growing up, my siblings and I had to complete all our studies on this floor.

Without thinking about it, I flew to the doors of my youngling bedchamber growing up, throwing them wide open. When my vision cleared, I looked around my bedchambers and gasped.

CHAPTER 55

My room was perfectly intact. My bedcloud was perfectly made. The pillows were fluffed and poised just like I'd left them. There was my comfy desk chair tucked in behind my glass desk with gilded embellishments. The washroom door was hanging ajar as I'd left it because I had been rushing. Even my sprawl of scroll papers where I'd been journaling were still splayed out over my desk like I'd gotten up, planning to return.

And then I didn't.

My rugs were in order. My portraits were still hanging. My windows were closed and not shattered.

Someone did this with intention. To send a message.

One that was being clearly received.

Slowly my sorrow began turning into unmitigated rage.

Angels had been sent to do this, the way they'd done it, on purpose.

I pivoted from the chamber, rushing for Manmi's office. Like I'd expected, it was in shambles. Her desk chair had been tipped over. The glass of the desk had been broken. Her scroll shelves were in disarray. But her drawers were still closed.

I floated over, flying past the mess, and positioned myself behind the drawer of her desk. I waved my hand over it, drawing on my starfire so Manmi's ethèrlock would sense the power.

"Wings high, Safah Eloise Anathelle," a small voice spoke out from the mist of the ethèrlock. It was whimsical and otherworldly. I wished Manmi was alive so I could learn how she did this. "You may open."

"Thank you," I whispered, tugging the drawer back.

It was filled to the brim with scrolls, scrollbooks, and ledgers. A gold mine for anyone hunting for information. What could Manmi possibly have been writing?

I righted the fallen desk chair, and sat in it, crossing my legs, tucking them beneath me. I pulled out one of Manmi's journals, thankful it was still open. The last page ended in an unfinished sentence. I thumbed through it, landing on an entry she'd written a few cycles before she'd passed.

Thorndawn, Julial 7th, cycle 197, Sixth Age, 7th Cycle

Safah is inquisitive, sharp, and still curious. I have no doubts she will uncover what's hidden. Evanae follows in her footsteps, even if she doesn't realize it.

Evanae is my wildling. Always a wonderer, never too shy to question. To poke. To prod.

I believe my fifis will be catalysts for the inevitable. I am ashamed to admit it took me too long to see the truth. But I trust them. Their wit. I also trust my bibis. It will be hard on them, but they will do what is right before the Infinite in the end.

Safah doesn't know about the Star. She cannot. Her knowledge will lead to exposure. If she is exposed, she will die a painful death dragged through the Ages. My only prayer is that her true fire remains dormant. That the bibi of Valoryens finds her. That she learns I lied. I was wrong. He is the only safe place. He is true. He is hers.

I pray to the Infinite they find their way to each other, and neither kills the other before they realize the truth. Perhaps Evanae will play a part. Curious little flower she is. She's even found an Archived tome: History of the Fallenspawn: the Truth of How They Came to Be. *I love my wingmate, my bibis, my fifis. It breaks all seven of my hearts that I will probably be taken before I can reveal to them the truth. But where I have failed, may the Infinite finish the way.*

Arèmen.

I leaned back in the chair, wiping fresh tears from my sodden cheeks. My eyes burned from all the endless crying. Manmi had learned something and she'd been killed for it. Stars.

I took the journal, and a few other ledgers, shoved them

all into a torn satchel I found discarded onto the floor, and shoved them inside. She'd written that Evanae had found a tome on the Fallenspawn. I needed that scrollbook. Racing out of Manmi's office and rushing to Evanae's chambers, I scoured through the mess looking for the scrollbook Manmi had mentioned.

Evanae's bedchambers had been thoroughly thrashed, left in utter shambles. Every piece of furniture was broken. Her bedcloud had been shredded. Every scrollbook was on the floor. Half had been set on fire. There were marks of obsidian majik everywhere.

What in the Hèls did Evanae have that her room had been torn apart like this?

I was about to give up when that little voice from earlier pushed me to check her wardrobe. I plucked up the broken piece of the door, pushing hard so it would pop open. Then I dug in. All I found was a pile of junk. But at the bottom, in the corner, was a lever.

My eyebrows rose to my hairline.

I pulled the lever and marveled as another compartment opened. There were several tomes inside. Including *History of the Fallenspawn: the Truth of How They Came to Be*.

"Holy stars," I breathed.

Looking around me, I found I was still alone. My hearts beat wildly as I snatched each tome and shoved them into the bag before someone snuck up on me. I had to get back to the temple with this satchel without getting caught.

A rumbling noise from the backyard spooked me. I

whipped around, adrenaline flooding my bloodstream. I looked around, seeing if I'd been spotted.

"Who is there?" I called out, unable to fully see the hall from where I was.

The rumbling happened again. It sounded like something quaking from the back of the garden.

Throwing the satchel over my shoulder, I raced to Evanae's balcony, climbing over fallen stone and rock that had been cracked from our villas exterior walls. In the distance, I saw the unmistakable shimmering of a star gate.

"No burning way," I breathed. "Who is that?"

I ran across the balcony jumping into the air. Satchel secured, I raced after the star gate. As I neared, I noticed two angels slipped through it. One had the mark of a thorn embedded into his exposed skin.

"What is one of the Marked doing here?"

You must search diligently, and find the dissenters amongst us, and bring them back with you.

I wrinkled my nose. I'd flown closer, scanning the backyard. There were trails of footprints, all leading to where I believed this star gate was perched. I rushed across the landscape, praying the gate wouldn't close. As I neared, it began trembling, getting ready to shut. Without a second thought, I tucked my wings close to my spine, aimed my body, and shot myself straight through the star gate.

The moment I crossed through, the star gate sealed shut.

CHAPTER 56

I stumbled on slick rock as I landed at an awkward angle. The star gate spit me out over a rocky base that crawled up into a mountainside. I tried standing, only to slip and fall, bending my wrists at an odd angle.

"Stars," I hissed.

One of my palms had an open gash from catching onto one of the crumbling stones wrong. Where in the stars was I? I cast about trying to make sense of my environment.

There were clouds everywhere, thick and billowy, obstructing my view. I took a step and slipped again. I grit my teeth, squeezed my thighs, and forced myself to take a few steps. Each one was wobbly and uncertain. As I crept across the rocks, I saw in the distance a breach between the clouds. And through the clouds, I spotted the Goldstone Bridge.

"What in the—"

The sound of shuffling caught my attention. I whipped

my head around and saw the last remnants of a set of wings slipping around the corner of the mountain base. Careful not to slip, I began prowling after the angel. I couldn't tell which rank they were since they'd been moving so quickly.

I shuffled across the rock, still slipping over my feet no matter how hard I tried to keep my balance. I wasn't crossing the bridge any longer, but I didn't doubt for a second I'd find myself without my feathers if I tried flying out here.

I made it to where I'd spotted the angel and rounded the corner. In the distance, embedded in the rock was a gate made of gold, barring entry into an entrance carved into the side of the mountain. The gate was ajar as I saw the silhouette of the angel again. I watched them slip inside. The angel held two swords, one in each hand. And on his arm was the branded thorn of the Marked.

But even from here, I could tell I didn't know who the angel was. They weren't one of Quazar's Talons. I hadn't seen them in Xadari Legion either. I made my way across the rock, shifting the weight of the satchel on my back. The tomes were heavy. I got a good grip on the satchel, using a pair of wings to hold it up as I made my way to the gate the angel had slipped through.

When I reached the golden entry, a putrid odor smacked me in the face. I stumbled back, losing my balance. It was sharp and gross, a mixture of stench, urine, and old blood filtering into the air.

I pulled the neckline of my gown over my nose, took in a final breath of fresh air, and pushed through the gate. The moment I was inside, I found myself on white stairs made of ancient rock. A long, winding staircase leading *down* sprawled out the further I stepped in.

Each slab of stone that made up the stairs were carved out of obsidian. I'd never seen anything like it. Especially when Temple Efysis, which was perched above ground, was nothing but ivory marble and gilded floors and doors.

I took a step and slipped. I caught myself in time, balancing a hand against the rocky wall. Nearly puking, I wrenched my hand away. The wall was sticky and prickly. I pulled my hand back and found it coated in new blood, some gold, some raven black, with a few metallic shards poking out of my palm.

Adjusting my gown, I gingerly began taking step after step. There were no ethèrlamps here. Only torches with a crimson glow that gave the stuffy corridor a chilling feeling. I looked down, finding almost every stone had some measure of blood or something other carved into it. After a while, I began to see trails of torn feathers, broken talons, and angelic bones.

Rotting stars.

Somehow I'd found myself in the dungeons.

I'd heard stories of dissenters being sent here. Kept here. Dissenters and criminals. Which meant the Scourgers were also down here. That also meant Quazar had been down here each time he was in the custody of the Scourgers.

I swallowed hard, noticing the increasing darkness the further I descended. I wouldn't lie to myself. I was terrified. I didn't know what I was doing down here.

Was this part of the trial? Was I supposed to find something down here? We were told to look for traitors. Had we all somehow been directed here to search for who it was that plotted against the temple?

My foot caught on loose rock and I went stumbling. I rolled down several steps before I was able to stick out my wings to brace my fall and keep me from rolling further. I propped onto my wings, surveying the area. I'd ended up in a cavernous chamber of interconnected stones and staircases, all leading to different directions.

"Now where in the stars did he go?" I whispered to myself.

Even though I kept my voice low, my words traveled, bounding off the walls. I bit my bottom lip, jumping into nearby shadows to tuck myself and hide in case anyone surfaced to look for the source of the sound.

I stayed in the shadows for some time, scared I'd drawn unwanted attention to myself. When no angels surfaced, I shook my shoulders. I was about to leave the shadows when—

"That can only be done with the power from the Star of the Age. Without it, every effort would be rendered useless. I don't understand why we don't double our efforts to find the Nebulari."

"Hunting the Nebulari would be a waste of time. Best to wait and see what Anathelle thinks. I hate her presence in the Order, but have to admit, she's never wrong. She swears the power we need is under our nose. Then we can take it and use it against Zemshaza. We won't need to uphold the treaty with the Fallen High King any longer."

Ice froze over in my gut.

Treaty with the *whom*?

My hearts were racing as I craned my neck to hear the two passing Farasees better.

"Oh please, we'll always have to keep a truce with Zemshaza. At least he's backed off with sending more Fallen..."

The Farasee's words cut off as they calmly walked up the stairs to another level. Not wanting to get caught, I decided to take a chance and start taking more steps down. I shuffled across the stony floor, crossing to the other side of the dungeon. Then I began descending the steps into the bowels of the temple that felt too keenly like walking down into the Hèls.

CHAPTER 57

The dungeon smelled absolutely disgusting. No matter how high I pulled my gown over my nose, I could still smell the stench through my clothes. The further I descended, the darker the lights grew.

I made it onto another platform, a level below the one above, that led out to endless, barred chambers. Several females were behind the blackened iron bars, screaming at the top of their lungs, begging for someone to help them.

My chest tightened at the sound. My hands prickled with a fresh wave of fear at their desperate, hopeless pleas. I heard the unmistakable sound of males doing the unthinkable. The females screamed and cried. My neck grew hot. My hands fisted. But there was nothing I could do. Not now. Not yet.

My hearts were pounding as I crept along, staying in the shadows. I kept away from the torches so my own shadow wouldn't show down the alcoves, hinting at my presence.

My ears rang with the screaming of the female angels, only growing louder as I snuck around the circumference of this level, aiming for the stairs on the other end that descended further.

Chain links sounded in my ear. I gasped, whipping my head to the side. Three Scourgers had surfaced.

One of them was Scourger Jeroah.

I pressed my lips tight, backing into the wall. There was nowhere to hide. If they turned my way, they'd find me.

Rot, rot, *rot*.

I held my breath as the three collectively paused, tilting their hooded heads. Jeroah angled his head, sniffing the air.

"Starfire," the Scourger hissed. "Asmotheus, do you smell it, too?"

Rot. The heads of the Scourgers turned to my direction. I reigned in my powers as much as possible, trying to stifle them so there was no trail. No scent. Starfire could smell sweet, making one heady. I had to cloak it, or else I was dead. The Scourgers turned, looking dead at me, but not seeing me.

"Who hides in the shadows?" Asmotheus asked, sliding forward.

Shadows.

Shadows.

Desperate, I raced across the bond. Quazar's end was still wide open. I rushed into his pool of shadows, drowning myself in the well. I prayed to the Infinite that his shadows were enough to overpower my starfire and remove any trace of me from being spotted. I could feel my body growing cold.

My powers getting muted. Could feel myself slipping into the shadows, almost *becoming* shadows.

I stayed pressed against the blood stained stone, perfectly hidden in the dark. Asmotheus sniffed the air again.

"Gone. A trick of the dark."

"Cruel trick. I love the taste of starfire."

"I want the newest Anathelle."

"Can't. The Dark King wants her to himself."

The Scourgers turned away, gliding down the path into a darkened corridor. They opened one of the cell doors which contained a screaming male. The stench of fire and ash wafted from the chamber. The male shrieked, hanging from his ruined wings, begging for mercy as the Scourgers slipped inside. Before the door to the chamber closed all the way, I heard the male scream loud as an audible break *snapped* in the air.

A wave of nausea almost bowled me. I wanted to vomit at all the various forms of torture taking place around me. This was an Infinite-forsaken place and I needed to get out of here. I was about to go back the way I came, when I heard a cold, cruel, and familiar voice.

"Anathelle's have always been breakable, wouldn't you agree, Papi?"

I felt numb.

No way. It couldn't be.

The voice had filtered up from a level below. Keeping to the shadows, a sudden urgency in my gait, I made it around the circular platform. Keeping to the shadows and away from the crimson lit torches, I began rushing down the stairs, careful to make sure the satchel made no noise. Thanks to Quazar's shadows, my own bodily shadow was still muted.

I made it down the level and rushed to the wall, pressing myself against it so I wouldn't be caught. There was a cell directly across, with the door hanging ajar. I couldn't see the entire chamber.

But I could see the female hanging from the chains inside. She was smaller, her hair hanging limp, drenched in her own golden blood. She'd been broken many times over. Her arms hung from the chains at odd angles. Her foot was bent strangely. And her wings.

Stars.

Her wings.

They'd been shredded. Every talon had been broken. She had open wounds all along her stomach, her chest. She was covered in bruises, her brown skin looking nearly purple with how badly she'd been beaten. Her quiet whimpering told me she was still alive. From the looks of it, she'd been tortured for hours. Stars. She'd probably been tortured for dawns on end if she was in this condition.

Close to the open door was a Farasee and Disciple I'd recognize anywhere. Their golden hair shone like the burning sun. Their strong, broad shoulders were wide with their pride. Both had hands covered in gold blood. I had a strong feeling the blood had come from the female.

"Maybe Safah Anathelle will finally take the hint. This temple is no place for her," Tharic was saying. Cruelty lined every inch of his proud face. He was handsome in a dangerously horrifying way. His bright golden eyes glittered with bloodlust as he grinned at Farasee Kaelthos.

I noticed a deep scar across Tharic's neck. And the new lines, like splintered fissures, on his cheek. Wounds a Raephim had somehow not healed. I wondered if he got those from Quazar when he tried to get into my bedchamber while I was recovering from being butchered by the Scourgers as a...*lesson*.

"Don't mind yourself about that brat. We don't have to do anything with her. Give it enough time and Asarah will break the little buckling herself."

Buckling.

My cheeks burned at the hideous insult. I found myself about to take a step forward, when I saw the female in the chamber had shifted her face. She angled her head, spitting up a wad of blood so thick it made me sick. Then she lifted her purple eyes and found mine in the dark. She'd been beaten so badly I almost didn't recognize her.

But when I did, the ground slipped from beneath my feet.

I lost the air I needed to breathe. Everything in reality flipped upside down.

I blinked, sliding to my knees as I looked across the dungeon cavern and stared into the eyes of Evanae.

CHAPTER 58

"NO!" I screamed at the top of my lungs. The Zamariens whipped around and found me pressed into the wall.

"Well, well. Another one to have a little fun with," Tharic said, his eyes gleaming. "Stars only know how long I've waited for the chance to break *you*."

Tharic started floating towards me, rolling up the sleeves of his robe. I was about to *fyuse* when a star gate surfaced, and dragged me through, leaving the Zamariens gaping on the other end.

I was jerked across the starry passage and spat out into my bedchamber. I shot to my feet, running to the door. I yanked on the handle. It was sealed shut.

No.

I slammed myself against the door again and again, eyes blurry from sobbing. The stupid door wouldn't budge. I *fyused* and began raining starfire bolts on the hinges. The door was sealed shut. I threw the satchel across my chamber, screaming at the top of my lungs.

I yelled and yelled, carelessly throwing my body into the door. When it refused to budge, I aimed for the glass walls that led to the balcony and the cloudy exterior of the wingtower.

I rushed the glass, prepared to shatter the entire thing. My shoulder collided with the glass and the bone snapped. The glass didn't have a single crack. My shoulder throbbed as I was thrown back by an unseen force into the bedchamber and smacked into the floor.

My baby sister had been taken. She'd been tortured. She'd been ripped apart like some animal. By the rotting Zamariens.

NO.

Rage consumed me. I was getting out of here, no matter what it took. I charged for the glass again. The glass didn't break, but a part of my shoulder blade did.

I tried again and again and again, until I could visibly watch the seven suns set in the distance. Still, no matter how unfruitful I was, I kept trying to break the glass. Then I'd try the door. Then I'd try the glass again.

Nothing worked.

I screamed, yelling at the top of my lungs as I wailed with anguish for my baby sister. I was isolated. Alone. Broken. My hearts had been shattered and I no longer knew what to do. All I could feel was pain. Sorrow. Hopelessness.

Defeated, I stomped over to my washroom, back in my

Seraphim skin, curled into a ball in the basin, crying my eyes out as the filth of the dungeons washed away. With a wave of my hand, I made sure the satchel was tucked away somewhere it wouldn't be found in one the nooks behind the platform my bedcloud was perched on.

I had to figure out a way to get Evanae out. She was still so young. She wasn't a youngling, but she was still developing into an adult angel. She had so much life ahead of her yet to live. This was never supposed to be something she experienced.

Sobbing, I dressed myself. My body was clean, but my soul was forever tainted. I didn't hear when the knock came at my door. When the voice warned of a summons. Lost in my despair, I was completely taken off guard when a star gate came for me and spat me out in the presence of the Farasee Council.

This time, Seventh Choir wasn't present.

It was just me.

I looked around to see if the monstrous Zamariens had also been summoned, but they weren't here. I cast about, finding the Iris there again, watching me curiously through their unseeing eyes. I wondered how much more they noticed because of their blindness. Farasee Asarah sat in the middle like earlier, surrounded by Farasees I didn't know besides Presbitari Davithius and Farasee Esau.

The two males I knew watched me. Both looked cataclysmically sad. I couldn't imagine the reason for their sorrow, especially Esau, but it sure as Hèls couldn't be worse than mine.

"Disciple Safah," Farasee Asarah said, addressing me without any pleasantries.

I could no longer look at her and see my Granmanmi. That female was long gone. If she ever existed at all.

Did she know the temple was in custody of Evanae? Did she know her own Granfifi was in the dungeons being brutally tortured and tormented?

I said nothing, glaring at Asarah with a feral rage I was struggling to keep leashed. My eyes burned from hours of crying. I was starving. My body ached. And I wanted to claw out the throats of every Farasee in this place. What had Quazar called it? A Hèls-infested temple.

Stars, if only he knew how right he was.

Then again.

He'd been in the custody of the Scourgers in those dungeons, too.

Rot.

I developed a splitting headache as I blinked at the Farasee who carried my blood but was no family to me. She noticed the shift in my expression. My posture.

She flinched. For the first time in my entire life, I saw panic, and something too close to fear, dance across her hardened eyes. She blinked, watching me for a moment, before speaking again.

"Granfifi—"

"You are no Granmanmi of mine, *Farasee* Asarah," I seethed,my chest rising and falling like a rabid animal.

The Farasees snapped back as if they'd all been slapped. All of them except for Davithius and Esau. Why did I have a prickling feeling that those two knew why I was in such a rage? Knew why I wanted to set this temple on fire with all the angels in it outside of Seventh Choir?

"Spit out what you want and I'll be on my way," I snarled.

Asarah's eyes widened. She slid her gaze to a Farasee who was perched at the end. He looked back at her. I didn't understand everything they shared in that quiet exchange, but I understood enough. Something hadn't gone according to plan. Asarah cleared her throat.

"Earlier, you were sent on a final trial. One of testing loyalty. One to find a traitor that was working diligently against the temple. Here you stand before me." A pause. "*Alone*."

"I found no traitor," I said, my voice bland. "Are we done here?"

Her nostrils flared.

"I find that highly unlikely. You're *my* Granfifi. You're as intelligent as they come. I don't believe for a moment you found no one. Reveal the traitor, and this Council will come to an end. You will go back to your daily duties as a Disciple."

"There was no burning traitor," I snapped, my shrill voice bouncing off the walls of the chamber. Suddenly everything was too ivory. Too golden. Too perfect.

Lies. It was a beautiful palace of *lies*.

I wanted to get out of here. I wanted to go to my sister. I wanted to get the Hèls out of this temple. I wanted to go home.

"You will mind your tone—"

"I will rotting mind nothing, *Granmanmi.*" I hissed. "Tell me. Did you know?"

Hers eyes flashed darkly, as she tilted her head. The question had caught her off guard.

"Did I know what, my youngling?"

"I am *not* your youngling. I belong to Quazar Valoryen. To Amaryss and Cassandrel Anathelle. To Incense Order, First Dominion, Seventh Choir. *Never* will I belong to *you*."

The Farasees gasped. All except Esau and Davithius. Esau watched me curiously as he processed my statement. Davithius's lips curled into a small, triumphant smile.

Asarah slammed her hands on the handles of her throne, pushing to a stand.

"That's *enough*."

"Funny," I said, feeling starfire flood my palms. "I'm just getting started."

"You still haven't learned your rotting lesson," she snarled, starlight swirling around her. I knew she was pissed. Never in my life had she ever had a slip of vulgar language. I relished it. If she was going to push me, I was going to push back. And *hard*.

"Where are you?" The baritone voice slid down our bond, tendrils of shadow slipping into my mind, catching me off

guard. Love and life stirred in my hearts as I felt a piece of myself returning at the sound of his voice.

"Can't talk right now. Pretty sure I'm about to have my wings plucked."

"*Where* are *you?*" he snarled.

Something had angered him.

"What's wrong?"

"Where. Are. You? I can't sense where you are. These rotting Farasees...Safah, where in the Hèls are you?"

"What did you find in the villa, Safah?"

My attention snapped to Farasee Asarah. How had she known...

Wait. If she knew about the villa, then she *had* to know about the dungeon.

My eyes narrowed to slits.

"Did you send them?" I asked her instead.

She flinched. "What in the stars are you referring to, child?"

"Did. You. Send. Them?"

"Send *who*?" she snapped, losing the reins on her self-control.

"Our entire villa has been destroyed," I screamed at her.

My rage flared, exploding around the chamber, while also flooding the bond.

"I'm coming to find you."

Good luck.

"Did you send them, Farasee Asarah?" I looked her in the eyes. Dared her to say anything but the truth. "Are you the reason our family home has been destroyed? Every chamber, every portrait, every tapestry, the *entire* villa, in ruins and on fire. Did you send your little demons to rip our home apart, you miserable wench?"

One moment, she was perched in front of her throne. The next she was in front of me. I was already spinning before I registered that she'd slapped me. Hard. I flew across the chamber, my head slamming into the wall.

"I'm going to teach you the lesson Cassandrel failed to."

I coughed up blood.

"Why don't you just pluck my feathers and forfeit my Ascension, *Granmanmi*?"

Before I could roll out of the way, she was on top of me, slapping me over and over with her wings, cutting me twice with her talons. I moaned, reaching for Quazar down the bond without realizing it.

"This temple will burn," he growled. *"What do I always tell you, Starling? Do not yield!"*

His voice wavered, as if he was mid-flight.

Farasee Asarah snatched me by my throat and yanked me up to my feet. She shook me with a ferocity that made my head knock. I grumbled, growing lightheaded as she spun and launched me across the chamber with a strength that shouldn't be possible for a female her age. I collided into the stone pillars, tumbling to the floor.

"Farasee Asarah!" Presbitari Davithius barked. "This is out of order! We don't care about your personal, familial feelings. You will *not* thrash around my Disciple like she's some wild animal. Another hand laid on her, and I will have you tried before the Empràr. I will ruin you myself."

I opened my eyes, my vision crossing. I found Asarah hovering stone still on the other side of the chamber. Her face was colored with fury. She looked at me with disgust. Like she'd disown me. Hèls if I cared. I was never claiming her again. I wondered if Ezekiel, Hosea, or even Jael had ever seen this side of her. And why in the stars they didn't warn me if they had.

"I've had enough," Asarah said, gathering herself.

She straightened her shoulders. And just like that, she was back to the Farasee that was feared across the empyrean. I was beginning to understand why.

She snapped her fingers.

At the center of the chamber, Evanae surfaced, tumbling to the marbled floor on her hands and knees.

"EVANAE!" I screamed.

With lightning speed I rushed for her, wrapping myself around her. My sweet little sister was soaked with blood and smelled of dried urine and something foul. I remembered the joy in the eyes of the Zamariens. My jaw hung as I turned hateful eyes to Asarah.

"You put your own Granfifi in the hands of *Zamariens*?" I whispered, my shock pulsing through my body. "You turned over your youngest Granfifi for bloodied sport?"

I couldn't believe my own words. I couldn't believe the truth I was seeing. The blind rage I was feeling.

"No," she answered simply. "I turned the little brat over

to teach you a lesson. You didn't think your little stunt at Titombwe would go unpunished?"

I froze, my hands coddling Evanae's head, holding her to my slow beating chest.

"The little ashrat has been working with the Fallenspawn to try and undermine this temple. A boldness she picked up from you no doubt. I will never stand for such a thing. And since you won't listen to reason, when I am through with her, I know you will think twice about forcing my hand ever again."

"What in the stars do you mean, 'when you get through with her'?" I asked.

"Simple. The trial was the easiest one given to you so far, and you *still* failed. No matter. You will remain a Disciple. We have need of you. The Anathelle females must remain in the temple. Well, *you* will. This one will never."

Then Farasee Asarah snatched Evanae up by the neck with a tendril of hardened starlight, yanked her across the chamber, and shoved two talons through her spine.

CHAPTER 59

The world spun, tilting on its axis. I was unbalanced and didn't know if I'd ever be right again. I shot to my feet, stumbled and crashed onto my knees. Evanae's body tilted forward, then she fell face first to the floor. I rose to my feet again and stumbled to my knees once more.

The life had been sucked out of me. Unable to stand to my feet, tears streaming down my face, I crawled on my hands knees, making my way across the expansive Council Chamber to my little sister. Her body was a broken, mangled thing. Endless cuts lined her arms. Her legs. Her wings were pitiful displays of what they once were.

I couldn't help but see the young, vibrant angel who loved to sing loud while bathing so the entire villa could hear. The angel who liked to dance when it rained, swim in the ocean for hours, and stuff her face with fried plantain, even when she was full. The angel who ate caramel-filled donuts then licked her fingers while cleverly prying secrets from you.

My sweet Evanae who'd heard I'd been punished by Scourgers and sent me bowls of cookies. Bowls Quazar consumed half of, becoming obsessed with her desserts. My bright-eyed sister who always believed in the happier things of the world.

Not a single Farasee looked on with pity outside of Davithius. He was disgusted and fuming. Crawling on my knees I made my way to Evanae.

"My sweet Vava," I cried, my voice breaking. "My sweet, sweet, Vava."

She lifted her head, her wide eyes still a beautiful mauve under the lights that shone through the glass windows.

"Sazu." She coughed.

Blood spurted out of her mouth. Racking sobs took over my body. I began shaking, uncontrollably as she coughed more and more blood.

"You," she tried again.

"Shh, don't speak Little Seashell."

I made it to her side, pulling her into my lap. I gently took her into my weakened arms and held her close. I lifted her head to me, brushing back her blood-soaked hair. I could hardly see the young female I knew for all the damage that had been done to her face.

"You are..." she continued anyway. "Everything. Suns,

moons, stars." She lifted her dirty hand to my face. Her nails were gone. Only bloody stumps remained. I could see the life fading from her eyes, as more blood pooled out of her dress, soaking my gown with its warmth.

"My Vava."

I couldn't stop my tears. Couldn't stop my trembling shoulders.

"You are everything I hoped to become one dawn," she breathed, her voice barely above a whisper. "Manmi used to... to tell me to follow...follow you. I'm glad I...listened." She struggled to cling to life. I lifted my hand to her cheek, beginning to *fyuse*. If I had to drain every last drop of my starfire to keep her breathing, I would.

"I love you, Sazu."

Evanae's pretty purple eyes fell shut.

"No," I sobbed, gently slapping her cheeks. "No, Vava. No. Wake up," I cried, voice more tears than sound. I was mid-*fyuse*, ready to do what it took to save Evanae, when a tendril of starlight wrapped around Evanae's body, yanking her from my arms.

"*NO!*" I screamed.

Burning stars, why couldn't I stand? Why was my body choosing now to betray me?

"I don't think so," Asarah said.

In quick succession, she shoved her talons into Evanae's spine three more times. Then she threw my little sister's body into the air, blasting her with a vortex of starlight morphed into deadly spears. The volley of spears went up, piercing Evanae so decidedly, there wasn't an inch of her that wasn't stuck by the spears. Then Asarah crushed her hands, yanking out the spears. Evanae's body tumbled back down. She fell to the marble.

Lifeless.

The chamber tipped to the side as I felt all seven of my hearts give out. I couldn't breathe. I couldn't think. I couldn't make any sense of this world.

"Remember this dawn when you choose to rebel against this temple, against me, again," Asarah purred. "Remember that *you* did this."

She blasted Evanae with hardened starlight, then squeezed her fist. Evanae's body began to burn as her spirit was choked out. My ears rang with cymbals. I could hear the sound of screaming in the distance, a voice shrieking at the top of their lungs, but the sound was far. Foreign.

My body moved on its own, leaping into the air to grab hold of Evanae's spirit, tucking it to my chest, as I crumpled to the floor, watching her body burn. My ears felt like they'd been stuffed with cloud balls. I couldn't hear a thing except for that ring. Someone was screaming loudly at the top of their lungs. And I was pretty sure that someone was me.

I snarled savagely when Asarah slipped forward as if she'd pry away my sister's spirit, too. When she saw the gaze in my eyes, she stumbled back. After looking at me with utter disappointment, she turned away.

"Congratulations on completing your first level of Ascension, Disciple Safah. I'm not proud yet. But for now, your succession will suffice." A brittle, vile chuckle. "You're dismissed."

Then she flew out of the chamber without a backwards glance, leaving me behind with Evanae's spirit and her body's ash.

CHAPTER 60

For a long time I couldn't do anything but scream. Anything but wail. Anything but break.

Bend, but do not break. Burn, but never bleed.

What a burning, monstrous lie.

Misery swallowed me whole as I tipped my head back and sobbed. I was inconsolable, my grief drowning me beneath their waves.

A long time passed before I realized I was in the chamber alone, except for Farasees Davithius and Esau. Everywhere Evanae's blood had been spilled, I began wiping with my wings. Until my gown and my wings were dripping with gold. Until I was covered with my sister's essence. Covered in the last moments she held life.

"Please send me back to my wingtower," I begged, my voice broken.

"Of course, Disciple Safah," Davithius whispered.

In a moment, I went from being in the Council chamber, to the great room of the wingtower. As I landed on the floor, Quazar was stomping over. When I lifted my head, he paused mid-stride his eyes widening.

"Safah," he whispered. "What—"

Seventh Choir was instantly on their feet. I noticed some were covered up in new bruises and open wounds, all forgotten at my crumpled form on the floor. Quazar's Talons looked down at me, the same measure of concern wrinkling their faces.

But it was Quazar I looked at as he slowly approached me, taking care not to walk too hard, lest he startle the wounded, broken creature sprawled out before him.

I had no words.

I had no strength left.

My hands were still cupped to my chest.

"They..." I started, my voice hoarse.

Quazar lowered himself in front of me, careful not to touch me. Not yet.

"They...the...*they*," I spat out. "They beat her," I screamed at the top of my lungs. My voice rang out, bouncing off the walls. "They beat her. And...and clipped her wings. And shred...shredded her feathers. And bro...broke her bones. And ripped out her hair. And cut...cut her open. And they touched her...and...and..."

I couldn't breathe. I was hyperventilating. I struggled for air as that thing, that knot of anxiety, that knot of despair began choking me from the inside.

"And she...Granmanmi...she...with her talons through her spine, she..."

I struggled to make coherent sentences. To make sense.

Ellabeth covered her mouth, her eyes already prickling with tears. I stared at the floor in a daze.

Quazar's wings wrapped around me, as he scooted closer, drawing nearer to me on his knees. Gently, with so much care, so much caution, he placed his hands on my shoulders. Let them slide down to my waist. Began pulling me to his chest.

"My Evanae," I sobbed, tilting my head back and wailing. It wasn't long before Ellabeth's tears could also be heard. "My sweet little sister. My Vava. The joy of our home. The bright light that glued us together. My Evanae. My Evanae."

My words trailed off into whispers. Then into silence.

Head still hanging back, I lifted my cupped hands to Quazar, prying them open so he could see her spirit beginning to wink out in my hands. Then something in me broke as shadows wrapped around me.

And I wailed.

I didn't know how long had passed as the sounds of my broken, jagged, screaming filled the halls of the wingtower. Didn't know how long I sat in the arms of the Fallen Prince as he held me, the only thing steady, the only sure thing in my world. Didn't know how long it was before I was completely undone. Angelically unmade.

My world shattered as I thought of Evanae's screams. Saw her blood dripping down her nail-less fingertips. Watched the talon shove into her spine and poke out through her stomach.

This world was supposed to be pure. Hopeful. A stairway to the Infinite. But the truth was the opposite.

This holy temple was a living Hèls.

I regretted the dawn I told Manmi I would Ascend. Regretted every dawn I looked at Granmanmi Asarah with pride. Like she was some hero. I regretted every moment I thought I wanted to be like her.

I brought Evanae's dying spirit to my chest, feeling the warmth slowly leak out as the spirit started growing cold.

When I finally came to, I found myself sitting in Quazar's lap. He'd tucked me into his chest and wrapped me completely with his wings. He was sitting on the floor, simply holding me, and gently patting my hair, brushing through the strands with his fingers.

He didn't say a word. He didn't rush me. With one hand, he held both my hands that were still cupped around Evanae's spirit. The other brushed my hair. And he used a wing to rub my back in soothing strides.

When I'd run out of tears to cry and words to say, my body turned limp, leaning against Quazar's chest. He'd lowered his wings enough for me to look around. All our friends were on the floor, sitting in a half circle, eyes on Quazar and me. Both groups were thrumming with rage. Hungry for blood. Quazar kissed my forehead, still petting my hair.

"What would you like me to do, my Safah?"

I didn't answer for a long time.

Finally, my head began to clear.

"I need to send her off." I looked at the distant wall as if I was no longer in my own body. "The ocean was her favorite place. We would swim for hours."

My throat was raw. It hurt to speak.

"I need to send her home. At least she will be with Manmi."

"Okay. I will bring you to the Ouanaviel Sea." He kept petting my hair. "But you still haven't told me what you want *me* to do."

For the first time since I'd made it back to the wingtower, I looked up at him. And I mean *really* looked up at him. Quazar's eyes were no longer my favorite shade of emerald green. The jade encircled by gold was gone. His shadows had consumed him entirely. Quazar's eyes were raven black.

He was enraged, and ready to start a war.

"After." I closed my eyes, putting my forehead against his chin. My strength was gone.

"After," I said again.

Then.

"It was the Zamariens you know."

"It was the *WHO*?" Ellabeth shrieked.

I snorted. It sounded more like a bark.

"Imagine my surprise when I saw them outside of her cell in the dungeons. She was whimpering. Hanging from shackles..." I took a shuddering breath. "Asarah gave Evanae to them," I said quietly.

I could taste the tension that lined the air. My friends were ready to set this temple on fire.

"The ocean," I whispered. "Bring me to the ocean."

Quazar kissed my cheek. Then my temple. Then my hands, careful not to disturb Evanae's spirit. He pulled me closer. In one moment we were in the wingtower. The next, he snapped his fingers, and we were on the shores of the Ouanaviel Sea.

CHAPTER 61

I stared out at the Ouanaviel Sea, lost in my grief. Quazar lowered me to my feet. He bent down, unlacing my sandals before taking them off, casting them to the side. The sand warmed my feet and settled between my toes. Quazar removed his own boots, then his socks, standing next to me barefoot.

I stood with him watching the rolling waves of the sea. It wasn't long before the rest of our friends joined us, also kicking off their shoes. Someone came to stand at my right, holding onto my arm. I turned, thinking it was Ellabeth.

It was Ivyana.

Her emerald eyes were bright jewels, just like Quazar's. Hers even had the slightest slant to them, just like his.

"What I am to Kazi, she was to you," she whispered, squeezing my arm. "I'm so sorry, Safah."

Out of all the things that could uplift my spirit, even in

the slightest, somehow this was it. I looked at Ivyana and cracked the smallest smile.

"Kazi?" I whispered.

She nodded her head vigorously. She was vibrant just like my Evanae. The two would have been good friends if they had met.

"I couldn't say Quazar as a youngling. Only Kazi. It stuck ever since."

I turned my head, looking up at Quazar. His eyes were still on the ocean waves.

"No."

I snorted, pressing my lips together.

"Besides, I like when you call me Princeling. Love. Oh, and I'm looking forward to what you'll call me when I throw your legs around my neck and feast."

I coughed, choking on nothing but air.

"Safah, are you okay?" Ivyana asked, gently patting my back.

"Yes. Caught a whiff of sand."

My throat burned with my response. My eyes were beginning to swell shut from crying. I tried to ground myself in reality.

Now that a bit of time had passed, I could feel myself reentering my body again. I had no Spirit Sphere. And even if I summoned one, I had no access to a Spirit Filing chamber since Asarah made sure the one we had at home had been completely destroyed. I knew the temple wouldn't let me file Evanae's spirit.

So I would have to let her go here, knowing her spirit would never make it into the Ellelights.

That all-consuming sorrow began suffocating me again. I let my tears flow as I watched wave after wave roll in and out. The beach was empty. Quiet. We were in a secluded patch that kept us out of view from any creeping eyes. Even if I knew Evanae wouldn't be filed, properly mourned, and crossed into the eternal realms, I said the prayer anyway.

"To the Infinite who is, was, and will always be, I commend the spirit of Evanae Eliza Anathelle into your hands. For all things, there is a season, a time for all activities in the realms beyond Pasaille. A time arrives for us to be born, and also a time to die. You, Infinite, have made all things beautiful in their time, and placed the Ellelights in the hearts of your angels."

I choked on the words as sobs broke out of my throat. I wiped at my eyes, trembling. Quazar wrapped an arm around my waist, holding me tightly to his side. His shadows danced along my bare feet and all around my body, as I pushed through the prayer.

"Oh Infinite, let us be wise as the stars, and be taught to number our dawns, to never forget the vapor that is life, and the brevity of our time in the realms. May we remember our dawns are mere sighs, breaths taken in one moment, and the ending gone in the next. All of us angels are shadows, and our coming and goings come to swift endings, though we live for an Age past another Age. Therefore, every wing of hope we contain, lies with you, forever at your feet."

I cleared my dry throat, steeling myself for the final part.

"When we are in our darkest valleys, fear will never move us, because there you are, always beside us. Your scepter and crown protect, comfort, and guide us all. Infinite, we have full confidence your goodness and unfailing love will never stop pursuing us, each and every dawn of our lives, through the Ages. And we will forever be privileged to live in your house, all through the Ellelights, always and forever. Arèmen."

"Arèmen," my friends chorused.

Quazar squeezed my waist as if communicating he was proud of me. Proud that I still pushed through, messy and all.

Now came the hard part.

I took a step forward. Then another. My friends stayed behind as I walked to the water's edge. I walked until my feet were under water. Then my knees.

I bent down, opened my cupped hands, and looked at my sister's spirit for the last time. Then, I brushed my nose against the bubbling spirit, still bouncing with a bit of life left. A life that would soon wink out.

I kissed the edges of the bubbling spirit. Even in death she was as lively as she was in life.

"I love you, Evanae. Forever will find me, and I will still love you. The Ellelights will claim me, and I will still love you. My fiery, life-loving sister. My whole entire heart of hearts. I love you. Always."

Lifting my hands, I leaned forward over the waters, then let my sister's spirit go. My hearts cleaved into two as I watched the silhouette of light, shaped like an angel bursting with evanescence, bounce away. The further Evanae's spirit went, the weaker her light grew.

Quiet tears streamed down my face as I settled into the ocean water, watching her spirit go away, slowly winking out, as the waves crashed over me. The waves began growing higher, soaking me further, until one large wave rushed forward, soaking me entirely.

It felt good to be soaked by the ocean waves. It felt like being cleansed. Being purified. Like a nod from the Infinite that none of this was over. This was just the beginning.

I believe my fifis will be catalysts for the inevitable.

That's what Manmi had written. Had she known this would take place? She'd been so sure we were the ones who would trigger some great affair. But Evanae was now dead, and I was left behind with my grief. My pain.

And my mounting rage.

I would avenge my sister. Farasee Asarah would not be left to rest until I'd made her pay for how she'd shed my sister's blood like she was cattle.

As the ocean water continued soaking me through, my sorrow began morphing into poignant wrath. I glared at the surface of the sea. Until Evanae's light grew dim. Until her light winked out. Until her spirit was no more.

When Evanae was gone—completely, irrevocably—I did not cry. Tears burned my eyes, but I held them. I fisted my hands below the water, grabbing fistfuls of sand. I ground my teeth. My insides shattered, and in the breaking something hard, something dangerous, something feral, forged in its place. I watched the surface of the waters for a long time, sitting there, stewing with my anger.

"Starling, may I join you?"

I turned my head around. My friends were looking at me. Watching. Waiting.

I looked at Quazar, nudging my head for him to come. When he moved, it was like a spell had been broken. All of them moved at once, settling into the water around me. Quazar came to my side, wrapping a wing around my waist out of reflex.

Before he said a word, the moment he was seated, I reached up with my hands, angled his head, and brought his lips to mine. I didn't care if our friends were watching. Didn't care that I was devouring this male that I adored, that I leaned on, as if he was my very foundation in this world.

Quazar didn't either. He kissed me slowly, thoroughly, taking his time. He sucked on my lip as he bit into it, drawing it into his mouth while running a hand into my hair.

My hearts pounded as he groaned into my mouth, kissing me slow, then fast, driving me into a frenzy. I found myself getting short of breath as I leaned into him, lost in the scent of him. The feel of him.

Quazar kissed me like a male who'd been starved and was finally given his favorite meal. He kissed me like he was parched and I was the last remaining goblet of water. He kissed me like I was his very soul. Like I was his wingmate.

I finally pulled back enough to take a breath. To gulp

down air. His lips were red in all the places I'd bitten him. He brushed a thumb over my lip, lost in the features of my face.

"I love you," I whispered, leaning into his embrace. I tucked my head against his chest. His wing tucked me closer.

"I love you, my Starling. My love. So rotting much."

"I mean, not to be *that* angel, but I love you, too," Ellabeth said, eyes on the waves, a small mischievous smile on her face. A twinkling light surfacing in her grief-ridden eyes. Dakairi chuckled, but nodded along in agreement, sitting by her side, one of his wings wrapped low around her waist.

"Okay, I'm glad you said it first, because I, *too*, love you, Sazu," Daelun butted in, chin lifted. His eyes were on Quazar and I, and they were positively dancing. Stars. He was just as bad a gossip as Ellabeth.

I snorted, laughing at my friends. The Talons all looked at me with a fresh kindness, and a certain...protectiveness, in their eyes. They looked at me as their new friend. They looked at me as one to protect, like they did with their Fallen Prince.

I smiled, nuzzling into Quazar's side. Held in his arms, I sat with him, with our friends as we watched the ocean waves roll. As we watched the sun descend and change into a myriad of beautiful colors. The more time passed, the more rage colored my hearts black.

"I will Ascend," I said down my bond to Quazar. *"And when I do, they will beg the Infinite for the payment of blood to be enough. And even then, it will never be."*

"Please tell me I get to join in all the fun."

"I wouldn't want to do this with anyone else."

Quazar let out a sigh down the bond that almost sounded like a growl. *"I rotting adore you, Safah Starling."*

I nuzzled into him deeper, enjoy the crashing waves of warm water rushing over my feet, coating me in the salty film of the sea. A long time passed with all of us sitting in the quiet, in the tension, when Ivyana cleared her throat.

"Kazi, can I tell her now?"

"Yes," Quazar said, squeezing my waist.

I blinked at the sun. "Tell me what, Ivy? Wait." I cleared my throat. "Can I call you Ivy?"

"Only if I get to call you Sazu."

I smiled.

Stars.

"I swear she's just *like Evanae."*

"They would've been great friends."

"I know."

"Of course you can."

"Good. Anyway. So, while we were eating cookies and cake and dancing around with the Scourgers before Timtobwe..." she began.

I snorted at the sarcasm, yawning.

"I may or may not have heard something."

"Something like?" I pressed.

"Well, you would imagine *my* surprise when I learned the Scourgers are greedy little monsters *and* gossips. Turns out, they know more about what's going on than we think. And they like to talk about it."

"Pray tell, Ivy. Just what in the Hèls were they on about

that could have possibly gotten your attention while you were...eating cookies and cake?"

Quazar snorted, chuckling at the dry humor.

"Your Manmi isn't dead."

I shot out of Quazar's embrace, stumbling to my knees. I glared at Ivyana, every bone in my body growing unnaturally still. She blinked her jeweled eyes at me, the emerald blazing with fury.

"Safah, your Manmi is alive and in the custody of High Farasee Manazzra Ahabiah."

AUTHOR'S NOTE

Hello Elledellien,

I'm grateful for you. Thank you for taking the time to read *Wicked Prince of Curses*. I hope you loved reading it as much as I loved writing it. If you enjoyed this story, would you mind:

writing a review on my website, Amazon, and Goodreads?

A few words on how you felt about the story will help me in more ways than you know. Thank you a million!

Until next time, see you in Elledelle.

Keep Reading: StephanieBwaBwa.com

GLOSSARY

ANGELS & BEINGS

Amaryss Anathelle (am-ah-riss—ana-thelle): Farasee in the Farasee Order of Temple Efysis. Wife and Wingmate of Cassandrel Anathelle. Mother of Safah, Ezekiel, Jael, Hosea, Uriah, Gabriel, and Evanae Anathelle. Daughter of Asarah Anathelle.

Amayah Kamron (ah-mai-ya—kam-ron): Disciple of Temple Efysis. Member of Incense Order, First Dominion, Seventh Choir. Friend to Safah Anathelle.

Anida Melin (ah-knee-da—mel-in): Ascendant of Temple Efysis.

Ariella Rozara (air-ree-ella—ro-zara): Legionnaire of Azarath Academy. Member of Xadari Legion, Sixth Host, Talons Unit. Fallenspawn.

Asarah Anathelle (ah-sar-ah—ana-thelle): Farasee in the Farasee Order of Temple Efysis. Mother of Amaryss Anathelle. Grandmother of Safah, Ezekiel, Jael, Hosea, Uriah, Gabriel, and Evanae Anathelle.

Assefah (ah-sef-ah): Apprentice of Farasee Esau Nakumba.

Asmotheus (as-moe-thee-us): Scourger of Temple Efysis.

Caliana (cali-ana): Goddess slave of Temple Efysis.

Cassandrel Anathelle (cass-an-drul—ana-thelle): Husband and Wingmate of Amaryss Anathelle. Father of Safah, Ezekiel, Jael, Hosea, Uriah, Gabriel, and Evanae Anathelle. Daughter of Asarah Anathelle. Son-in-law of Asarah Anathelle. Brother-in-law of Taevia Othru.

Chen Kaxura (shen-kah-zoo-rah): Legionnaire of Azarath Academy. Member of Xadari Legion, Sixth Host, Talons Unit. Fallenspawn.

Dakairi Saurel (dak-eye-ree–sore-el): Childhood best friend of Quazar Valoryen. Legionnaire of Azarath Academy. Member of Xadari Legion, Sixth Host, Talons Unit. Fallenspawn.

Daelun Shenric (die-loon–shen-rick): Disciple of Temple Efysis. Member of Incense Order, First Dominion, Seventh Choir. Friend to Safah Anathelle.

Davithius Solman (dah-vih-thius—sole-man): Farasee and Professor of Temple Efysis. Presbitari of Incense Order.

Ellabeth Riventhelle (ella-beth—riven-thelle): Childhood best friend of Safah Anathelle. Disciple of Temple Efysis. Member of Incense Order, First Dominion, Seventh Choir.

Ellie (elle-ee): Nickname of Ellabeth Riventhelle.

Esau Nakumba (ee-saw—nah-koom-bah): Farasee and Professor of Temple Efysis.

Evanae Eliza Anathelle (eh-vah-nay—e-lie-zah—ana-thelle): Little sister of Safah, Ezekiel, Jael, Hosea, Uriah, Gabriel, and Evanae Anathelle. Daughter of Amaryss and Cassandrel Anathelle. Granddaughter of Asarah Anathelle. Niece of Taevia Othru. Cousin of Katia.

Ezekiel Anathelle (ee-zee-kiel—ana-thelle): Eldest brother of Safah, Ezekiel, Jael, Hosea, Uriah, Gabriel, and Evanae Anathelle. Son of Amaryss and Cassandrel Anathelle. Grandson of Asarah Anathelle. Nephew of Taevia Othru. Cousin of Katia.

Gabriel Anathelle (gay-bree-el—ana-thelle): Little brother of Safah, Ezekiel, Jael, Hosea, Uriah, Gabriel, and older brother of Evanae Anathelle. Son of Amaryss and Cassandrel Anathelle. Grandson of Asarah Anathelle. Nephew of Taevia Othru. Cousin of Katia.

Hosea Anathelle (ho-zay-ah—ana-thelle): Little brother of Ezekiel and Jael Anathelle. Older brother of Safah, Uriah, Gabriel, and Evanae Anathelle. Son of Amaryss and Cassandrel Anathelle. Grandson of Asarah Anathelle. Nephew of Taevia Othru. Cousin of Katia.

Isandra Marisol (is-aun-drah—marie-sol): Disciple of Temple Efysis. Member of Incense Order, First Dominion, Seventh Choir. Friend to Safah Anathelle.

Ivyana Valoryen (ivy-auh-na—vah-lore-ien): Little sister of Quazar Valoryen. Legionnaire of Azarath Academy. Member of Xadari Legion, Sixth Host, Talons Unit. Fallenspawn.

Jael Anathelle (jay-elle—ana-thelle): Younger sister to Ezekiel Anathelle. Eldest sister of Safah, Hosea, Uriah, Gabriel, and Evanae Anathelle. Daughter of Amaryss and Cassandrel Anathelle. Granddaughter of Asarah Anathelle.

Jeroah (juh-row-ah): Scourger of Temple Efysis. Niece of Taevia Othru. Cousin of Katia.

Kaelthos Zamarien (kale-thos—zuh-mare-ien): Farasee and Professor of Temple Efysis. Father of Tharic Zamarien. Presbitari of Scroll Order.

Katia (kah-tea-ah): Cousin of Safah, Ezekiel, Jael, Hosea, Uriah, Gabriel, and Evanae Anathelle. Presbitari of Manna Order.

Kazemir Nhanket (kaz-amir—nan-ket): Disciple of Temple Efysis. Member of Incense Order, First Dominion, Seventh Choir. Friend to Safah Anathelle.

Kazi (kah-zee): Nickname of Quazar Valoryen.

Kyree Forrest (kie-ree–forest: Ascendant of Temple Efysis.

Lilithine (lilith-eye-ne): Scourger of Temple Efysis.

Linora Anathelle (lih-nore-ah—ana-thelle): Great-Grandmother of Safah, Ezekiel, Jael, Hosea, Uriah, Gabriel, and Evanae Anathelle. Grandmother of Amaryss Anathelle. Mother of Asarah Anathelle.

Manazzra Ahabiah (mah-nah-zra—ah-huh-buy-ah): High Farasee of Temple Efysis and the Ouanaviel Empyrean.

Marai Vithoria (muh-rie—vih-thor-ia): Ascendant of Temple Efysis.

Natalie (nah-tuh-lee): Goddess slave of Temple Efysis.

Nathaniel (nuh-than-iel): Farasee of Temple Efysis.

Omarion Wylium (oh-mar-ien—william): Disciple of Temple Efysis. Member of Incense Order, First Dominion, Seventh Choir. Friend to Safah Anathelle.

Quazar Valoryen (kuh-czar–vuh-lore-ien): Temple Mate of Safah Anathelle. Older brother of Ivyana Valoryen. Legionnaire of Azarath Academy. Leader of Xadari Legion, Sixth Host, Talons Unit. Fallenspawn. Fallen Prince and Heir of Fallen High King Zemshaza Beliah. Childhood best friend of Dakairi Saurel.

Refayim (ref-ah-yeem): Scourger of Temple Efysis.

Rhaevion (ray-vee-en): Parilielthai of Quazar Valoryen, his bonded dragon shifter.

Safah Eloise Anathelle (sah-fah—el-oh-wheeze—ana-thelle): Temple Mate of Quazar Valoryen. Little sister of Ezekiel, Jael, and Hosea Anathelle. Big sister to Uriah, Gabriel, and Evanae Anathelle. Daughter of Amaryss and Cassandrel Anathelle. Granddaughter of Asarah Anathelle. Niece of Taevia Othru. Cousin of Katia. Disciple of Temple Efysis. Member of Incense Order, First Dominion, Seventh Choir. Childhood best friend of Ellabeth Riventhelle.

Samaèl (sah-may-el): The High Prophet of the Ouanaviel Empyrean and the most revered angel after the emperor.

Sazu (sah-zoo): Nickname of Safah Anathelle.

Serafina (sarah-fee-na): Goddess slave of Temple Efysis.

Taevia Othru (tay-via—oh-through): Second-born of Asarah Anathelle. Older sister of Amaryss Anathelle (400 years). Aunt of Safah, Ezekiel, Jael, Hosea, Uriah, Gabriel, and Evanae Anathelle. Sister-in-law to Cassandrel Anathelle. Presbitari of Bond Order.

Taraji Hoksa (tuh-rah-ji—hoaks-ah): Ascendant of Temple Efysis.

Tavax Branai (tay-vax—bruh-nigh): Disciple of Temple Efysis. Member of Scroll Order.

Tharic Zamarien (thair-ick—zuh-mare-ien): Disciple of Temple Efysis. Member of Scroll Order. Son of Kaelthos Zamarien.

Uriah Anathelle (you-rie-ah—ana-thelle): Little brother of Ezekiel, Jael, and Hosea Anathelle. Older brother of Safah, Gabriel, and Evanae Anathelle. Son of Amaryss and Cassandrel Anathelle. Grandson of Asarah Anathelle. Nephew of Taevia Othru. Cousin of Katia.

Vashari Mitchyn (vuh-shah-ree—mih-chin): Legionnaire of Azarath Academy. Member of Xadari Legion, Sixth Host, Talons Unit. Fallenspawn.

Zadkias Claudevin (zad-kee-as—claw-da-vin): Emperor of the Ouanaviel Empyrean.

Zara Ondi (zara—on-dee): The designated Raephim for Incense Order.

Zemshaza Beliah (zem-shah-za—buh-lie-ah): Cursed, exiled, and Fallen Angel. High King of the Souls Court and ruler of the six, abominable,

Hèls. Raised Quazar Valoryen and many of the Fallenspawn from a young, impressionable age.

ORDERS & FACTIONS

Cadetti (ka-debt-tea): Cadet.

Bond Order (bond—order): The faction focused on fellowship and building communal safe spaces among the angels, to the Infinite on behalf of the Empire.

Hartari Legion (heart-arie—legion): One of the four Azarath Academy legions made up of six hosts, composed of four units: Talons, Blades, Thorns, Bones. Known for their vicious manipulation and heartlessness.

Incense Order (incense—order): The faction focused on creating incense from collected prayers that is collected and kept for ritual offerings to the Infinite on behalf of the Empire.

Klubari Legion (club-arie—legion): One of the four Azarath Academy legions made up of six hosts, composed of four units: Talons, Blades, Thorns, Bones. Known for their tight bonds and mob mentality.

Legionnaire (legion-air): Warrior, soldier.

Manna Order (man-nah—order): The faction focused on service through food in the Temple and to the Infinite on behalf of the Empire.

Saixari Legion (sigh-za-rie—legion): One of the four Azarath Academy legions made up of six hosts, composed of four units: Talons, Blades, Thorns, Bones. Known for being cut throat, shady, and cunning.

Scroll Order (scroll—order): The faction focused on memorizing the Saccrent and its laws to keep the Empire in right standing with the Infinite and to guide the spiritual morality of the Empire.

Watcher (watch-er): Warrior, soldier.

Xadari Legion (zah-dah-ree—legion): One of the four Azarath Academy legions made up of six hosts, composed of four units: Talons, Blades, Thorns, Bones. Xadari Legion consists entirely of Fallenspawn angels and is led by Quazar Valoryen. They're known for their ruthlessness, ferocity, close bonds, and wickedness. They are always the strongest and deadliest Legion.

REALMS, ISLANDS, & SETTINGS

Azarath Academy (ah-zar-wrath—academy): War college.

Barrenrock (barren-rock): The island formerly known as Namenthys.

Biblarien (bih-blare-ien): Library.

Citadel (sit-ah-dell): An enormous city on the Efysis Islet built for the Farasees and their families to have enjoyment and a sense of living without having to return to the main islands.

Elledelle (ella-dell): The universe in which all realms and worlds are located.

Efysis Islet

Namenthys (nah-men-this): An island that was purged and cleansed after allegedly siding with the Fallen and helping them breach the Seal Gate to access the Ouanaviel Empyrean, giving them the freedom to slaughter millions of innocent Hallowed angels.

Ouanaviel (wah-nah-viel): The main and largest island of the Ouanavial Empyrean. It is home to the Empràr, most of the empyrean's elites, and many prestigious temples and universities.

Port Emprarèl (port-emprah-rel): The capital city of the Ouanaviel Island.

Sorellien (sore-ellie-en): The planetary world containing all twelve islands of the Ouanaviel Empyrean.

Starfelliel (star-fell-liel): Location of the largest waterfall on the Ouanaviel Island, and the setting of where the Starfellien Ascent trial takes place.

Starfelliel Mountains (star-fell-liel–mountain): A large mountain located within Starfelliel.

Temple Efysis (temple-ephesus): The largest, holiest, and most revered temple of worship, studying, and piety in the Ouanaviel Empyrean.

Titombwe (tea-tome-bway): A colossal amphitheater where mass spiritual ceremonies, entertainment ceremonies, sports events, or public punishments are held. Titombwe is the largest amphitheater in the Ouanaviel Empyrean.

Wingyard (wing-yard): Cemetery.

GROUPS & SPECIES

Angelic ranks and Elledelle Species are in status order. All other creatures are alphabetized.

Angels (ain-gels): Divine beings made entirely of ethèr—the raw, original power of creation. They are not born with ethèr; they are born of it. Only angels possess ethèr. They are immortal, winged, and created for specific divine purposes. No other race shares their nature or origin.

Calvaethim (cal-vay-uh-thim): A rank of angel in the Elledelle universe. First-ranking in the angelic hierarchy, function as **enforcers**, serving the Infinite. Their distinctions are their gilded skin, incandescent luminous eyes and twelve feathered wing pairs.

Iris (cal-vay-uh-thim): A rank of angel in the Elledelle universe. Second-ranking in the angelic hierarchy, they function as revelators, serving the Infinite. Their distinctions are their starry skin, unseeing eyes and nine feathered wing pairs.

Seraphim (cal-vay-uh-thim): A rank of angel in the Elledelle universe. Third-ranking in the angelic hierarchy, they function as elementals, serving the Infinite. Their distinctions are their element-shifting skin, elemental eyes and seven feathered wing pairs.

Mortent (cal-vay-uh-thim): A rank of angel in the Elledelle universe. Fourth-ranking in the angelic hierarchy, they function as benders, serving the Infinite. Their distinctions are their smooth, glossy skin, jeweled eyes and six feathered wing pairs.

Lawrent (cal-vay-uh-thim): A rank of angel in the Elledelle universe. Fifth-ranking in the angelic hierarchy, they function as engineers, serving the Infinite. Their distinctions are their galactic skin, multi-colored eyes and five feathered wing pairs.

Goverent (cal-vay-uh-thim): A rank of angel in the Elledelle universe. Sixth-ranking in the angelic hierarchy, they function as governors, serving the Infinite. Their distinctions are their galactic skin, incandescent eyes and five feathered wing pairs.

Chronophim (cal-vay-uh-thim): A rank of angel in the Elledelle universe. Seventh-ranking in the angelic hierarchy, they function as keepers, serving the Infinite. Their distinctions are their galactic skin, starry eyes and five feathered wing pairs.

Nulliphim (cal-vay-uh-thim): A rank of angel in the Elledelle universe. Eighth-ranking in the angelic hierarchy, they function as drainers, serving the Infinite. Their distinctions are their shimmery skin, dark eyes and four feathered wing pairs.

Raephim (cal-vay-uh-thim): A rank of angel in the Elledelle universe. Ninth-ranking in the angelic hierarchy, they function as healers, serving the Infinite. Their distinctions are their shimmery skin, colorful eyes and four feathered wing pairs.

Ampliphim (cal-vay-uh-thim): A rank of angel in the Elledelle universe. Tenth-ranking in the angelic hierarchy, they function as amplifiers, serving the Infinite. Their distinctions are their shimmery skin, multi-colored eyes and two feathered wing pairs.

Cherubim (chair-uh-bim): A rank of angel in the Elledelle universe. Eleventh-ranking in the angelic hierarchy, they function as artists, serving the Infinite. Their distinctions are their multi-color skin, multi-colored eyes and two feathered wing pairs.

Babephim (babe-uh-fim): A rank of angel in the Elledelle universe. Twelfth-ranking in the angelic hierarchy, they function as messengers, serving the Infinite. Their distinctions are their colorful skin, jeweled eyes and one feathered wing pairs.

Shifters (shift-ers): A mutable race with an angelic core form and the innate ability to transform. Their power lies in fluid identity and instinctive adaptation. Unlike other races, Shifters are not bound to a single form—they are creatures of becoming.

Faerèth (fair-eth): Sentient, ageless race shaped by elemental forces and steeped in illusion, beauty, and instinctual power. They are not divine, but they are deeply magical. Glamour, mischief, and unpredictability define them. Faerèth answer to no higher race—and bind only to their own.

Giants (giants): Towering, physically dominant race created from stone and storm. They are long-lived, durable, and structured around strength, tradition, and hierarchy. Giants are not fast, but they are unmatched in raw power and endurance.

Gods (gods): Immortal, born beings with inherent divine power. They are not formed of ethèr like Angels, nor created for service—they are born with the ability to command natural and supernatural forces. Though born, their strength, longevity, and authority set them apart from all other races. They are not based on any known mythology and exist solely within the divine order of Elledelle.

Merriens (mare-iens): Water-aligned race born of the ancient sea. While the ocean is their home, they move freely on land. They are not angelic in form, but possess a more god-like or faerie-like appearance—otherworldly, elegant, and unnerving. Known for their heightened perception, emotional control, and long memory, Merriens are deeply private and resistant to manipulation.

Edennites (ed-uh-nights): Immortal humans—unaltered, unfallen, and original to creation. Though they are physically the weakest of all races, they possess extraordinary curiosity, creativity, and intelligence. Edennites do not have supernatural powers, but their insight and spiritual depth set them apart as the most aware and inventive of all beings.

Bloodhyena (blood-hyena): A kind of hyena.

Dragèth (drag-eth): Dragons.

Serène (sare-en): Sirens.

Stareagles (star-eagles): Eagles.

Unikai (unik-eye): Unicorns.

Winterwood Bear (winter-wood–bear): A kind of bear from the Winterwood.

Ylisks (ill-isks): Basilisks.

ETHÈR, MAJIK & POWER

Ethèr (eth-air): Innate, supernatural, magical powers of Hallowed angels.

Fyuse (fuse): When Seraphim ranked angels morph their bodies from their physical skin to their magical ones, embodying their elemental power entirely.

Majik (mah-jik): Innate, supernatural, magical powers of Fallen angels.

RITUALS & TRIALS

Blood Rites (blood-rights): A ritual of draining the blood out of an angel's body, and collecting that blood to be used for nefarious purposes. Always performed before an audience, whether great or small, and created to make the Fallenspawn suffer.

Empràrs Pass (em-prars-pass): An Azarath Academy graduation exam for fourthlings. It is an endless stretch of rocky terrain in the far northern plains of the Ouanaviel island guarded by ashbats. It's one of several ways to access Barrenrock and reach the Seal Gate.

Spirit Filing (spirit-filing): The ritual of siphoning an angel's spirit out of their body after they have been physically killed. The spirit is siphoned, placed into a Spirit Sphere, and filed in a chamber to enter multiple phases, before the spirit is released to enter eternity by crossing into the timeless realm called: the Ellelights.

Starfellien Ascent (star-fell-ien—ascent): A trial where Ascendants must fly up and through the Starfelliel waterfall, run across the Goldstone Bridge, climb up the side of the Efysien Islet mountain base, and fly through the temple gates, guarded by sunlions, before the descent of the seven suns. Serving allows enthusiasts to become official Temple Efysis Ascendants.

OBJECTS & ARTIFACTS

Bloodletters (blood-letters): Crimson red ethereal cords that pierce into the body to drain it of blood through cylindrical tubes within the cords.

Dragontail Whip (Dragon-tail-whip): A whip akin to a Cat-O-Nine-Tails. A multi-tailed whip covered in spikes, glass, and other objects used for corporal punishement, and also as an instrument of torture by the Scourgers.

Ethèrlamp (eh-thair-lamp): Lamps made with magic.

Ethèrlock (eh-thair-lock): Locks made with magic.

Saccret (say-krent): The Holy Scroll. A sacred, holy compilation of scriptures Hallowed angels live by.

Scrollbook (scroll-book): Book.

Scrollmap (scroll-map): Map.

Spirit Sphere (spirit-sphere): The crystal, jar-like container used to store spirits after they have been siphoned for Spirit Filing after the physical death of an angel.

Star Gate (star-gate): Portal.

TIME & ERAS

Cycle (sigh-cull): Year.

Dawn (dawn): Day.

Ellelights (elle-lights): Eternity. Life beyond angelic death. Transition from the physical angelic plane to an ethereal, transcendent plane their spirits go to for all eternity.

Julial (july-al): July.

Thorndawn (thorn-dawn): Tuesday.

SAYINGS & SWEARS

Asheater (ash-eater): A vulgar term to call someone a piece of...rot.

Blessed Lights (blessed-lights): Oh em gee.

Bloodthorn (blood-thorn): Prostitute or whore.

Burning Stars (burning-stars): Oh em gee.

Hèls (hells): Hell, a devilish location in the Belial Realms and to mean frustrated, confused, annoyed, or vexed.

Rot (rot): Poop, feces, and similar expressions.

Rotpot (rot-pot): Idiot.

Stars (stars): Oh em gee.

MISCELLANEOUS TERMS

Apprenti (app-rent-tea): Apprentice.

Arèmen (ah-rah-men): Amen.

Ascendant (ascend-dant): Angels aspiring to be Disciples in the temples of the Ouanaviel Empyrean.

Bedchamber (bed-chamber): Bedroom. Also interchangeable with differing alcoves within an enlarged bedroom suite.

Bedcloud (bed-cloud): An angelic bed made entirely of clouds and ethereal matter.

Bibi (bee-bee): *Son* in the common language of angels.

Bond (bond): An ethereal, living, golden cord, sometimes ivory, of life and power woven through the center hearts of angels that eternally binds the angels to one another for eternity and allows them functions such as, speaking to one another telepathically and sharing a measure of their *ethèr* with each other.

Bonding (bond-ing): The act of marriage and eternal mating between angels which creates an eternal Bond between angels for their lifetimes.

Buckling (buck-ling): A vulgar insult. A bastard child easily abused and used for vile purposes.

Cloudchair (clowd-chair): A chair. Also interchangeable with a single-seater couch.

Empràr (em-prar): Emperor.

Fallenspawn (fallen-spawn): Angels raised since their youngling cycles by the Fallen High King and his Shadowlords. Marked with a thorn brand from their neck down their shoulder, and the length of their right arm.

Farasee (fair-ah-see): Priest.

Fifi (fee-fee): *Daughter* in the common language of angels.

Firstfast (first-fast): Breakfast or the first meal of the day.

Granmanmi (grun-mum-me): Grandmother.

Infinite (in-fi-nite): God, Supreme ruler, Eternal King.

Kouzi (coo-zee): *Cousin* in the common language of angels.

Manmi (mum-me): *Mother* in the common language of angels.

Papi (pah-pee): *Father* in the common language of angels.

Parenting (parent-lings): *Parents* in the common language of angels.

Parilielthai (pah-reel-liel-thigh): An ethereal, and lifelong bond, enacted by ritual between angels and shifters. Generally, warriors bond to dragons, disciples and farasees bond to pegasi, while nobility bond to ylisks, and so on. On rare occasions, these groups inter-bond, causing seismic shifts across society and the world itself.

Presbitari (pres-bih-tah-ree): Professor.

Profèt (prophet): Prophet.

Spirit Harvester (spirit-harvester): Monstrous creature from the Belial Realm. They are tall, have seven wing pairs, seven eyes, long horns, winged ears, long, bone straight hare, and porcelain white skin while wearing tattered ivory robes.

Stareater (star-eater): Monstrous creature from the Belial Realm. They are tall with porcelain white skin. They have no face. Instead they are creatures whose face, torsos, and stomachs look like an open vortex into the galaxy. They feast on stars, hence why they look like one.

Tati (tah-tea): *Aunt* in the common language of angels.

Wingmate (wing-mate): Mate. Interchangeable with spouse.

Youngling (yung-ling): Young angel. Interchangeable with *child*, *adolescent* or *teenager*.

ABOUT THE AUTHOR

Stephanie BwaBwa is a Best-selling Epic Romantasy author who writes cinematic, immersive, character-driven stories that haunts and heals, where angels rise through darkness and corruption to find freedom, healing, hope, and love.

She's the author behind the Elledelle Universe—the original fantasy universe of angels, captivating readers worldwide.

Also a Christian and Afro-Caribbean, you can usually find her reading with too many snacks. Wings high! May you fly where the angels are.

Connect with Stephanie: stephaniebwabwa.com or @stephaniebwabwa

www.ingramcontent.com/pod-product-compliance
Lightning Source LLC
Chambersburg PA
CBHW020243030826
48979CB00030B/2495/J
9798987212844